PENGUIN BOOKS

THIRTYNOTHING

Praise for *Ralph's Party:*

'A joy . . . a fun, summer read' *Guar*

'Addictive . . . Jilly Cooper for the combat-trou̶ ̶ ̶ration'
Metro

'Deliciously enjoyable . . . although there have been many books
trying to decipher the new rules of engagement, Jewell's is
one of the most refreshing: addictively readable without being
irritating or glib' *The Times*

'A lovely, modern, urban tale of interconnecting relationships,
desires and disasters. Quite the nicest in this vein for some time'
Bookseller

'A shameless flirt of a first novel' *Kirkus Reviews* (US)

'A breath of fresh air' Tom Paulin, *Late Review*

'*Ralph's Party* by Lisa Jewell has the formula perfectly judged:
even the first page of her first novel glows with the kind of
guaranteed readability that Jilly Cooper once made her own'
Times Metro

'A party worth gatecrashing! Lisa Jewell pulls off a rare trick
which even the likes of Helen Fielding and Nick Hornby
couldn't quite manage. She has written a book about
relationships which appeals to men and women . . . It's a spicy
lamb kofta in a sea of bland chicken masala' *Daily Mirror*

Praise for *Thirtynothing*:

'This is a gem' *The Mirror*

'Lisa Jewell's second novel stands out from the mass of chick-fic. like a poppy in a cornfield. It might be a London-based comedy about relationships, but this tale of record-label manager Dig and his photographer chum Nadine glitters with insight' *Nova*

'*Thirtynothing* is not just a diversion for a few train stops on the way to the office, it will keep you up all night in a sweaty, addicted reading frenzy . . . First and foremost, Jewell is a comic writer who makes acute and funny observations about romance. Yet she enjoys life, London and love too much to really make them the butt of the joke. It's a fine balance that should make *Thirtynothing* as popular as its predecessor. Though I would recommend finding out why for yourself' *The Times*

'Bubbly and addictive, it's the best romantic comedy we've read in ages' *Company*

'This is a lovely book – honest fluff. It is informed throughout with a wholesome desire to please and entertain' *The Daily Telegraph*

'Jewell's exceptional skill for story-telling and her insight into the twentysomething psyche makes it easy to relate to her characters as they stumble through adulthood. Very entertaining and very funny' *Heat*

'Do we sneer? We do not. Jewell writes with lashings of what the shrinks might call emotional intelligence – pop fiction at its proudest' *Independent*

PENGUIN BOOKS

Published by the Penguin Group
Penguin Books Ltd, 27 Wrights Lane, London W8 5TZ, England
Penguin Putnam Inc., 375 Hudson Street, New York, New York 10014, USA
Penguin Books Australia Ltd, Ringwood, Victoria, Australia
Penguin Books Canada Ltd, 10 Alcorn Avenue, Toronto, Ontario, Canada M4V 3B2
Penguin Books (NZ) Ltd, Private Bag 102902, NSMC, Auckland, New Zealand

Penguin Books Ltd, Registered Offices: Harmondsworth, Middlesex, England

Published in Penguin Books 2000
14

Copyright © Lisa Jewell, 2000

Set in Monotype 10.5/13.3 Century Schoolbook by Intype London Ltd
Printed in England by Clays Ltd, St Ives plc

for Oliver Cannon Jewell
nephew extraordinaire

———

www.lisa-jewell.co.uk

ACKNOWLEDGEMENTS

Thank you once again to my loyal and lovely readers, Nic, Katy, Sarah and Yasmin. Don't worry – I won't ask you to do it again. Thank you to my agent, Judith, for killing off my excess characters so humanely (so long, Rudy, Rebecca and Tony) and making this almost readable. Thank you, too, to Louise 'Editor of the Year' Moore, for not making me kill off anyone else and making this almost publishable.

Thanks also to all those people I was too shell-shocked to thank last time: Harrie, Sarah and all the fantastic editing types, Peter and his incomparable sales team, Nicky and Katrin, the sanest and calmest PRs I've ever met, John and his hugely imaginative marketeers, to the two Sophies and to Ami for yet another stunning cover.

Thank you to every bookseller who piled the last one high and prominently – I'm eternally grateful. To the panel of the *Late Review* who were so nice about my book on 6 May '99 – I love all of you. To all the readers who have sent me such great e-mails and letters – send me more. And to all the readers who didn't write to me – thanks for buying the book, anyway.

Thank you to Lee for all his advice about A&R and to Seb for never ceasing to inspire me with the vagaries of his love life. And finally, but never leastly, to my top-of-the-range man Jascha, without whose hardworking presence I would spend all day on the Net and this book would never have been written – thank you for being so proud and so supportive. Without you, the days would seem empty and long and I would talk to myself a lot.

CHAPTER ONE

Dig woke with a start.

The first thing he was conscious of was the taste in his mouth, a rancid coating of . . . what was it? Onions? Garlic? Some kind of battery-acid-type thing going on in there as well. He slowly brought a hand from beneath his duvet and cupped it around his mouth. He let out a small puff of coagulated breath and sniffed it back in. Jesus. Grim beyond belief. He clamped his mouth shut again.

The second thing he was conscious of was his head, which appeared to have had a large shipment of ball-bearings dumped in it overnight, while his blood felt as if it had been transfused with silica and come to a grinding, desiccated halt somewhere around his temples.

The third thing was his stomach, a solid, churning area of gas and corrosive fluids, swishing and swirling around together like a kind of miniature primordial soup. He felt a bubbling tube of gas begin to wriggle through his stomach, around his intestine and down towards his bowel. He could tell it was going to be bad when it departed his body in a hot and silent *phut*, and before long his airless room was ripe with the stench of yeast and garlic.

'Oh, Jesus. What the fuck is that smell?'

Which is when Dig became aware of the fourth thing.

The girl in his bed.

He turned his head slowly, and there she was. A girl. A girl with messy blonde hair and black stuff smudged under her eyes and bare bony shoulders and a tattoo of a sea horse on her left arm and one hand covering her mouth and nose while her face wrinkled up in distaste.

'Jesus!' The girl turned over on to her side with a disgusted flounce. She had some sort of accent, and another tattoo on her back, of a butterfly. It was very nicely done. Dig slowly manoeuvred himself up on his elbow and surveyed the girl as if she were some kind of strange sea creature which had been washed up on his bed by the tide. She looked young. Surprise surprise. About twenty, probably. And thin. Very thin indeed. Another surprise. He wondered what she was called.

'Do you have any Nurofen?' Her voice was muffled through her hand but was now recognizably Irish. Northern Irish, to be precise.

'Uh-huh.' Dig's hand found the little tablets on his bedside table, and the glass of water he'd put there last night, a sign that at some point between getting home and going to bed he'd obviously been mentally and physically functioning to some extent. Which also indicated to him that relations had more than likely been had with this small, bony girl in his bed.

He turned to look down at the floor by his bed. Yep. There it was. A shimmery sliver of pearly latex with a neat little knot at the top. Well, that was something, at least.

The level of traffic noise wafting through the half-opened window from Camden Road outside led Dig to believe that it was probably some considerable time after the six in the morning his head was telling him it was.

He turned painfully to look at his radio alarm: 11.48 a.m. It was also hot, stiflingly hot. Strange for the middle of November.

He passed the glass and pills to the bony girl.

'Thanks.' She gulped them down in one. 'What time is it?'

'Ten to twelve.'

'What! Fuck, you're joking!' She sprang out of bed, like a little pink whippet and began jumping into her clothes: a tiny black vest top, no bra, hard little nipples poking through, G-string, no buttocks, combat trousers, pierced belly button, trainers. 'Fuck fuck fuck.' She heaved the curtains apart, sending Dig recoiling across the bed with one elbow over his face. She surveyed the street below.

'Where the fuck am I? Is this Tooting Broadway?'

'What? No – no – Kentish Town – Camden Road.'

'Oh no! Oh fucking no. I have to be in Clapham in ten minutes. Jesus! Can I get a bus from here? Where's the Tube? D'you have a car?'

'No. Five minutes that way. Yes, but it's in for repairs.'

'Oh, Christ – I'll have to get a cab. I only have a fiver. D'you have any cash?'

Dig peeled the last crumpled tenner from his wallet and handed it to her.

She kissed it. 'I'll pay you back.'

'Where are you going?'

'Work.'

'On a Saturday?'

'Yeah – I'm a waitress – shit – it's going to be murderously busy today – look at that sunshine – but it's only a temporary thing, y'know, part time.'

3

'You're a student?' Something had come back to him from the night before.

'Yeah, that's right.' She was scraping her hair back into some kind of knot. The sun was playing on her and she looked quite pretty. She seemed strong and bright.

'Where d'you study?' Dig was suddenly feeling vaguely sociable, as if he might quite like to see her again.

'God, you can't remember a thing we talked about last night, can you?' She smiled. She pulled a pair of yellow sunglasses from her rucksack and sat them on top of her head. 'Well' – she looked pleased with herself, a little embarrassed – 'I'm at sixth-form college right now, but my tutors reckon I'll get a place at Oxford next year – *if* I get my grades.'

Grades? *Grades?* Jesus! 'What – er, what grades?' Dig rubbed at the stubble on his chin.

'A Levels, of course.'

'So – you're – how old?'

'Seventeen.'

Oh dear God!

She was standing at the door now, her rucksack on her back, looking all of a sudden like a child, like a small girl wearing big girl's clothes. She seemed to transmogrify before his eyes, her hips disappearing, her breasts deflating, her waist expanding, her hair morphing as he watched from stylish topknot to perky pigtails. Oh Jesus Christ! Seventeen!

'Hey, look,' she was saying, waving his ten-pound note at him, 'I'll find a way of getting this back to you – I promise. I have your number, I'll ring you.'

I'll ring you. *I'll ring you!* There was a child standing in his bedroom doorway, with a pierced belly button,

4

waving his money at him and telling him she'd ring him. Jesus, what was the world coming to?

'Oh, and by the way – Happy Birthday.' She smiled at him, a nice, warm, intelligent smile, and then she was gone.

Happy Birthday. Oh yes, Happy Birthday indeed. Thirty years old. He was thirty years old. A thirty-year-old pervert. A dirty thirty old man. A heinous, raincoat-wearing, boiled-sweet-carrying, dribbling, drooling old man.

He'd slept with a seventeen-year-old.

OK, so it was the stuff of dreams, the stuff men of his age made lascivious, lustful jokes about over pints in pubs. But to have really done it, to be confronted with the reality of a seventeen-year-old in his bed. His little sister was eighteen and if he'd found out that she'd . . . with a man of thirty . . . he'd have . . . Well, anyway, it just didn't feel right. Dig suddenly felt a little too old to be chasing after much younger women.

The previous evening was starting to come back to him in dribs and drabs. Tequila slammers at Nadine's. Opening presents. Pints at the Lady Somerset with the rest of the crowd. All piling into a cab at midnight. Some club somewhere in town. (A club? They never went to clubs any more.) More tequila. And then dancing – dancing for hours . . . God, he'd probably looked a right arse. And that girl, that child . . . Katie! That was it, that was her name – Katie – except she'd pronounced it 'Kayday'. Dancing with her and telling her, over and over again, 'It's my birthday! It's my birthday!' And then – a curry? Shit, it must have been nearly morning by then . . . where the hell had they managed to find a curry at that time of night?

5

And that girl, Katie, had been there. And . . . yes, that's right, Nadine had started on Maxwell in the restaurant and she'd tipped her raitha into his korma for some reason or, more probably, for no reason whatsoever. Poor Maxwell. It looked like his days were numbered. And then? Well, they must have got a cab or something. He couldn't remember anything after that.

Dig wrapped himself up in his dressing-gown and made his way to his gleaming little Ikea kitchen, where he got himself some coffee. He switched on his ionizer, lit a cigarette and let his hangover wash over him for a while, as he trawled his memory for more detail, but nothing came to him, just blurred images and fuzzy fag-ends of conversation.

The coffee and cigarette, combined with the unimaginable gunk that had already been in his mouth when he woke up, had pushed his breath to crisis point. He absolutely *had* to brush his teeth.

He stared at his reflection in the mirror as he brushed. There's the crunch, he thought, there it is. A couple of years ago I could have had a heavy night and woken up the next morning looking like something that vaguely resembled a human being, instead of this monstrous, clammy-complexioned, open-pored, dark-shadowed, grey-skinned sack of old bones that's staring back at me from my bathroom mirror. But now I'm thirty, and although I still have youth ahead of me, I have left the greatest part of it behind me, and my body is no longer on my side, will no longer collude in my systematic abuse of it. My body is asking for a break, and my punishment for not giving it a break is to make me look this hideous in the mornings.

Still, he thought, he didn't have much to complain

6

about as he entered his fourth decade. He had a great social life and friends he'd known for years. He was liked and respected by nearly everyone he came into contact with. He could pull pretty girls; he owned his own flat – OK, so it was small and noisy and it was up three flights of stairs, but it was his; he had the job of his dreams working as an A&R manager for a small record label in Camden – all right, so it was poor pay for long hours and very little success, but he loved it. Unlike most men he knew of his age, he still had all his hair and a pretty firm stomach. His family lived just round the corner so he got to see his precious mum at least once or twice a week. And now he was thirty.

Thirty wasn't so bad.

Yeah. Thirty was fine.

Actually, it wasn't that different to twenty-nine.

CHAPTER TWO

Nadine rolled sideways towards Maxwell and let his big, bear-like arms wrap her up in a sleepy embrace. His neck smelled sweetly musty, and traces of last night's aftershave lingered on his skin. She could feel the hairs on his chest rubbing against her breasts and his resting heartbeat echoing through her ribcage.

The sun was streaming through the yellow and red sari silk draped over her bedroom windows and the calming sounds of outside activity floated over her bed like a summer breeze: a dog barking, a child discussing his plans for the day with his mother, car engines starting, front doors opening and closing.

'Cup of tea?'

'Ooh, yes please.'

Maxwell pulled his huge frame from the bed, squeezed himself into Nadine's much-too-small red-silk robe and gently padded off towards the kitchen. Nadine stretched herself out in the newly spacious bed and smiled as she heard Maxwell performing his usual clattering pillage of the kitchen drawers and cupboards, unable even after three months to lay his hands on teaspoons, mugs and teabags without first exploring every possible location.

She clicked on the radio and listened to the homely babble of Radio Five Live presenters for a while, and suddenly realized that despite the traces of a headache lingering around her temples, a vaguely nauseous sensation emanating from her stomach and the slightly embarrassing memory of yet another scene with Maxwell in the restaurant last night, she was feeling quite inexplicably, deliriously happy. It was a Saturday morning, the sun was shining, there was a man in the kitchen making her tea, and she had no plans whatsoever for the rest of the day. Maxwell wasn't usually here at the weekend. She'd only seen him last night because it was Dig's birthday and Dig liked Maxwell and had insisted that she invite him. She wasn't used to waking up with a man on a Saturday morning. It was nice. They could do couply things: they could go for a walk, or go out for lunch somewhere and read the papers. Or they could just stay in bed all day, watch the telly, eat bacon sandwiches, chat and have sex.

This, she decided, was one of those moments, one of those utterly perfect moments in life, which you absolutely had to draw into your lungs and hold there and absorb every drop of, because that was what life was all about. If you expected eternal happiness, then you missed the essence of life that was contained in moments like this.

'There you go,' said Maxwell, gently placing steaming mugs of tea on the bedside table – mugs, Nadine noticed, that she never used, her emergency mugs, ugly ones her mother had given her, decorated with insipid roses fading defeatedly after ten years of washing-up and kept at the back of the cupboard, mugs that only someone with no sense of design or aesthetics would have pulled from her cupboard when presented with a selection of at least twenty more attractive mugs. She felt a sudden burst of irritation and her little happiness bubble

9

exploded over her head. Why couldn't he be perfect? Was that too much to ask?

'For God's sake, Maxwell,' she bristled, waspishly, 'why do you always have to choose the ugliest mugs in the kitchen?'

'Eh?' Maxwell looked stumped, and Nadine felt flooded with disdain, at the precise moment she should have felt guilt.

'Haven't you noticed,' she continued, 'that when *I* make the tea I always use those Deco mugs or the Simpsons mugs or the South Park mugs. You know – the nice mugs? Haven't you noticed that I never, ever use these mugs?' She pointed at them in disgust.

Maxwell shrugged and shook his head. 'What's wrong with them?' he asked sadly.

'Huh! Exactly! That's exactly it! If you don't know what's wrong with these mugs then there is no point in having this conversation.' Nadine knew she was being unreasonable but she couldn't help it.

'Do you want me to change them?' he offered.

Nadine jumped out of the bed in exasperation and gesticulated angrily. 'No, Maxwell. I don't want you to change them, I just want you *not* to have chosen them in the first place. I want you to be as unspeakably *repulsed* by these mugs as I am. I want you to look at these mugs and feel a deep sense of pity for the men and women of . . . of' – she picked up a mug and read the inscription on the bottom – 'of Lichfield Pottery, Staffs, who were actually paid to paint these disgusting flowers on to the sides of these disgusting objects and who probably think they're highly talented artists. That's what I want, Maxwell.'

Maxwell's kind face crumpled up with the strain of

comprehension, and Nadine could see that he was trying, he really was trying to understand what she was saying to him and this annoyed her even more. She was being a complete bitch and a real man would have told her to shut the fuck up. But he wasn't a real man, and he had actually picked up one of the mugs and was now turning it around and around in his hand, gazing at it from every possible angle, his face a picture of studious contemplation.

'Mmmm,' he said, 'I suppose it is a bit *plain*. A bit old-fashioned . . .'

'Oh, put it down, for Christ's sake!' she fumed. 'Put the fucking mug down.'

The badly chosen mugs, taken in isolation, were not, evidently, a big deal, but set in the context of their three-month-old relationship they were yet another sign that Maxwell was the Wrong Boyfriend. She'd been trying to convince herself for three months that it could work, that despite the differences between them, despite his penchant for brightly coloured designer menswear, his infatuation with Celine Dion, his unflappable demeanour and his unfeasibly good manners, despite his home being ten miles away from hers, just outside Dagenham in Essex, and despite the fact that he was a courier and she was a photographer who earned five times as much as him, she could make it work. Because Maxwell was as nice a bloke as you could ever hope to meet and Nadine felt that she deserved a nice bloke. But nice blokes aren't necessarily perfect blokes and Nadine was sorry for her pettiness and intolerance, but she couldn't, just couldn't, abide the differences between herself and Maxwell for another moment.

'Nadine,' Maxwell was saying, softly, 'I'm not really

11

sure . . . could you explain to me why you're getting so wound up about a pair of mugs?'

Nadine appreciated that this was a fair question. 'Oh God, Maxwell. It's not just the mugs. It's not the mugs. It's everything. It's us. It's me . . . this just isn't working . . .' Nadine listened to the words echoing in her head and thought how hollow they sounded. She wondered how many times in her life she'd used the same words before. 'It's me,' she always said, 'it's not you, it's me.'

And it was true. It *was* always her. She hadn't been dumped since she was twenty-one. It had been fine when she was younger, going out with unsuitable men, because all her friends were going out with unsuitable men, too. They'd all get together and compare horror stories, revel in the imperfections of each other's ill-advised relationships, bond over mutual disdain for the inferior sex. That's what you do when you're in your twenties. But then, gradually, one by one, all her friends had found decent men, good men, and splintered off. And now, in her thirtieth year, Nadine found herself hanging around, like the Queen of Spades in a game of Old Maid. The game was over, the rest of the pack was in pairs, but she was still playing. And until a few weeks ago, she'd still been enjoying it.

But then she'd turned thirty and had begun to evaluate her situation, and all of a sudden the life of a serial monogamist didn't seem like so much fun and there wasn't the time to waste any more. Her youth was running out, her choices were diminishing, and it had hit Nadine then, the real reason why she went out with so many losers: she only went out with men who didn't threaten her friendship with Dig. The moment a boy-

12

friend started to make claims on her time or her emotions, it was over. The moment a boyfriend began to show any signs of resentment about the amount of time she spent with Dig, it was over. There existed between Dig and Nadine this sort of unwritten law that said that they weren't allowed to spend quality time with anyone but each other. Weekdays were for boyfriends and girlfriends; weekends were for Dig and Nadine.

Dig was Nadine's best friend, her favourite person in the entire world, and as long as they were friends she didn't actually *need* to be in love with anyone else. It would just complicate everything if either of them ever fell in love with another person.

The only problem was that they just didn't fancy each other; each one epitomized the antithesis of the other's 'type'. Dig liked tiny, girl-child-type women (which Nadine most certainly *wasn't*) who made him feel manly, and Nadine liked enormous hairy men (which Dig most certainly *wasn't*) who made her feel delicate. If they'd fancied each other, they would have been married by now. Probably.

Nadine looked at Maxwell, staring warmly but blankly at her, and she suddenly realized that he was going to be the last Wrong Boyfriend. Definitely. Without a doubt. No more Wrong Boyfriends. Only Right Boyfriends from here on in. She would have one last crack at trying to find a suitable man, and if that failed, she'd marry Dig, skinny legs and all.

She took a deep breath. 'Maxwell,' she said, sitting down beside him on the bed and gently removing the mug of tea from between his enormous fingers. 'I think we should talk.'

*
13

Well, thought Nadine, as she closed the front door quietly behind Maxwell's slightly stooped figure, at least he didn't cry. That was the worst thing, the most horrible thing imaginable, to see a grown man cry, especially a man as big as Maxwell. He'd taken it quite well really, almost as if he'd never before considered the concept of being dumped and was going to go home and give it some thought, as if she'd given him some unfathomable lateral-thinking test to consider. Poor Maxwell, she thought. But he'd be fine. He'd be just fine – he was good-looking and funny and caring and generous – he'd find someone else in days. A nice Essex girl who would look up to him and respect him and love every inch of his hairy, chunky body, a kind girl who would appreciate him and make him happy, happier than Nadine had ever made him.

He'd be just fine. Unlike her.

Nadine glanced around her now empty flat, at the dents in her gaudy Bollywood duvet cover left by two bodies, and the hated pair of mugs still sitting accusingly on the bedside table. She absorbed the change in the atmosphere, the stillness of the air, the sudden silence from outside her bedroom window – and then she remembered how she'd felt twenty minutes ago, the thought of the day ahead which had pleased her so greatly and the pure moment of unblemished happiness she'd experienced and embraced.

It occurred to Nadine that maybe those moments weren't meant to be fleeting, that maybe they were like seeds, and you were supposed to plant them and water them, and that if you tended them well, eventually you would grow a Tree of Happiness.

And if that was the case, she wondered, how come every time she was lucky enough to find a Happiness

14

Seed she mashed it up, spat on it, stamped on it and then threw it out of the window? Why did she have to spoil absolutely everything?

Nadine felt her stomach begin to rumble with fake, post-late-night-curry hunger. She contemplated rustling up a quick bacon sarnie but then decided she had to get out of the flat, go for a walk, see someone, talk to someone.

She picked up the phone and called Dig.

CHAPTER THREE

'So,' said Dig, regarding Nadine disbelievingly over a large plate of greasy meat and chips, 'let me get this straight. You dumped Maxwell because he chose the wrong mugs?'

'Well, yes. Among other things. I mean – we both know he wasn't right for me, don't we?'

'I really liked him . . . well, compared to some of the other men you've been out with this decade.'

'Yes. Of course. So did I. Who wouldn't? But he was so annoying, you know? The way he dressed, and the way he was always going on about his mum, and Celine Dion, and the fact that he was allergic to *garlic* of all things – I mean, how can you go through life being allergic to *garlic*? – and he was so pathetic, sometimes, so . . . so . . . so . . .'

'Nice?'

'Very nice. But just so . . .'

'Kind, pleasant, generous?'

'Yes. But, so . . . so . . .'

'In love with you?'

'Look' – Nadine pointed a speared chip at Dig – 'he held his knife and fork like he was going to knit a sweater with them, OK? That's just one of those things I, personally, can't live with.'

'Oh my God, Deen! You complete fucking *snob*!'

'Well, it's the truth. I can't help the way I am, can I?

16

It just used to make my blood boil. And he couldn't spell either, and there is nothing worse than a man who can't spell – it takes all the romance out of cards and love letters and things.'

'You are unreal, Nadine Kite,' said Dig, slowly shaking his head from side to side in wonderment, 'you really are. What planet are you from?'

Nadine looked at him sniffily, sensing that her defence was shaky, to say the least. 'OK,' she conceded, 'I admit it. I am a snob, and I am a fussy cow and I do demand a lot of men but, the bottom line is this: Maxwell wasn't right for me and I didn't want to go out with him any more and I've found a whole load of excuses not to love him back. But, I know, *I know* that when I meet someone who *is* right for me, then I won't care whether or not they can spell, or how they hold their cutlery.'

Dig snorted sceptically.

'Yeah, right. Take the piss. But I know it. OK?'

Dig cut a swathe through the juices on his plate with a chunk of toast and smiled wryly at Nadine. 'Deen,' he said, popping the toast into his mouth, 'you know I love you dearly, you know you're my best girl and I would do anything for you. But you are a nightmare. You are a complete and utter nightmare . . . If you were a bloke, you would be a bastard.'

Nadine dropped her jaw in mock indignation.

' . . . And one day you are going to get your come-uppance. You are going to meet this so-called "perfect guy" and you are going to put up with his appalling table manners and his shocking shirts and he is going to turn around and shit all over you. He is going to turn around to you one day and say, "Nadine, you're a great girl, but I just can't stand those purple trousers you wore

17

last Thursday and the way your ears wiggle when you laugh and, quite frankly, your ginger pubes make me want to puke. So, no hard feelings, eh?'' And Deen – and I say this with all the affection and love in the world – I for one cannot wait for that day to come.'

Nadine took a sharp intake of breath and clutched at her neck. 'You bastard!'

'Since you were twenty-two years old, since the day you left university and realized that you were never going to see Phil again, you have been out with every bloke who was stupid enough to ask you. As if three years with that weirdo wasn't enough. You have never once stopped and asked yourself if you actually *wanted* to go out with them, whether they were suitable, whether you fancied them, or if it stood a chance in hell of working out. You just use men to flatter your ego. You spend a couple of weeks doing everything within your power to ensure that they fall in love with you, and then the minute they do, you spend another two months building up a big enough list of faults and grievances to justify dumping the poor bastard.'

'*I do not!*'

'Yes, you do. Every bloke who asks. Doesn't matter if they're thin, fat, young, old, rich, poor or ugly. All they have to do is ask. Is it any wonder that it always ends in disaster? Is it any wonder that you spend half your life dumping them? Is it any wonder that you haven't met the right guy yet?'

'I do not go out with every guy who asks me.'

'OK then. Name me one guy you've turned down – one guy.'

Nadine thought for a moment and then smiled wickedly. 'Well. Let me think. Oh yes, that's right. There was

18

one bloke – you!' She smiled smugly. 'Got you! I turned *you* down.'

Dig shook his head. 'No no no. That doesn't count. We were kids then. I'm talking about *after* university, after the thing with Phil.'

Nadine went silent for a while as she flicked rapidly through her memory files, her face wrinkled in concentration. 'Well,' she said eventually, 'it's not as if I get asked out every day or anything. You have to take these opportunities when they're offered.'

'Oh, come on! You haven't been single for more than a week in the last ten years and you haven't been out with anyone for longer than a few months. Work it out for yourself.'

'Oh yes,' leered Nadine, triumphantly, 'oh yes, of course! I forgot I was talking to the world's leading relationship expert. I forgot you were the man who had his heart broken when he was eighteen and hasn't let one single woman near it since. I forgot I was talking to the man who hasn't known the surname of the last six girls he's slept with, who thinks commitment is staying the night, who thinks a date is a chewy version of a prune and who *woke up in bed this morning with a seventeen-year-old girl*!'

An old man who had been working his way slowly and disagreeably through a plate of overcooked roast beef and congealed gravy since they arrived threw Dig a look of profound admiration, and a young couple in the corner looked up from their newspapers with raised eyebrows, turning subtly for a glimpse of this apparent paedophile. Dig blushed.

'Yeah, right,' he whispered, 'but at least I don't lead them on, at least they know what they're getting into. I

19

never give them any false hope. And besides, girls that young, they don't actually *want* anything serious, anyway. Not like you lot.'

'You lot, who lot?'

'You,' he said, pointing at her, 'you thirty-something women.'

Nadine raised her eyebrows ceilingwards. 'Oh,' she growled, 'don't start all that business again. I'm far too hungover for that argument. And anyway, I'm not thirty-something, I'm thirty-nothing.'

'What's the difference?'

'Well, thirty is more like a full stop on your twenties, really. I don't think you're actually *in your thirties* until you're thirty-one. Anyway, all I'm saying is, you're in no position to preach to me about how I should be conducting my love life. You're the nicest bloke I know and one day you're going to make somebody a wonderful husband. But right now you should carry a health warning.'

'OK, OK,' sighed Dig, smiling, 'so we're both as bad as each other. You dump perfectly decent men because they choose the wrong mugs, and I'm the Jerry Lee Lewis of Kentish Town . . . Let's face it – we're both crap.'

'Oh God, Dig. Look at us. We're both thirty now – we're *too old* to be crap, we're not supposed to be crap any more. We're supposed to be getting it together. My mum had two kids by the time she was my age and, as far as I can tell, I still *am* a kid. Where's my biological clock, Dig? Where is it? Why haven't I got one? Maybe if I had one then I'd be a bit more selective about who I went out with because I'd be subconsciously looking for a good gene pool, you know, a hunter/gatherer type, a sperm donor rather than a temporary ego boost.'

20

'And I'd be looking for a good, heavy-hipped, child-bearing woman instead of chasing after ectomorphic breastless androgynes with body piercings.'

'What have we been doing for the last ten years, Dig? I mean, I'm under no illusions about everlasting love, but we haven't even come close. We haven't had one long-term relationship between the two of us. Other people spend their twenties learning lessons about love and relationships, and you and I have just been going round and round in circles, learning nothing. We're pathetic. Maybe that's what we should be doing, Dig. Maybe we should at least *pretend* that we're looking for a partner to have children with, even if we're not – that way we might choose a little more wisely.'

'But I don't like heavy-hipped women.'

'Oh, Dig. Don't be ridiculous. Women don't have to have heavy hips to bear children. Look at Pamela Anderson – she's had two and she doesn't look like she could give birth to a clothes-peg. No, it's more a frame of mind, an attitude. I think we should give it a bash, you know. I mean, look around this place. Look at her.' She pointed towards a pretty girl in her late twenties sitting alone with a bacon sandwich. 'She's nice-looking, she's got lovely hair, she's slim and she's most probably single. I bet if you asked her out, she'd say yes.'

'Yeah, but why? Why is she single? If she's so great then why isn't she sharing her bacon sandwich with someone?'

'God, I don't know. Maybe she's just split up with someone, maybe she's just dumped her boyfriend because he put too much sugar in his tea. Maybe she's as bad as us.'

Another girl walked into the café then, and the bacon-sandwich girl's face lit up. The two women greeted each other warmly with a kiss on the lips, and Nadine saw their feet entwine underneath the table.

' . . . Or maybe she's a lesbian. But that's not the point. The point is, we're thirty years old, we're healthy, we've got flats, cars, jobs and security, we're both unbelievably nice people and we're going to wake up one morning and find ourselves all alone. All our friends will have big messy houses full of teenagers and grandchildren and noise and activity, they'll be arranging weddings and going to graduation ceremonies and discussing their children's achievements and sending them off to see the world, and we'll be alone, you in your anally tidy flat, me with fifty years' worth of glossy magazines arranged in piles, with nothing but memories of how it was to be young. That's not right. I don't want that. And the only way we're going to be able to avoid that is by doing something about it *now*.'

Dig had been nodding throughout this and now stuck one hand out towards Nadine. 'I agree,' he said, 'and I think we should make a pact here and now. I'll start looking for a more mature woman and you start looking for a bloke who measures up to your standards.'

'And the first person to start seeing a decent man or woman gets . . . gets . . .' Nadine quickly calculated the chances of Dig recognizing a 'real' woman if she slapped him around the chops with her handbag, smiled and stuck out her hand, 'a hundred quid.'

Dig's eyebrow shot up into his hairline but he grabbed Nadine's hand and shook it hard. 'Yeah,' he said, 'OK. A hundred quid for the first person to start dating a decent person.'

'So that means a woman over the age of twenty-six,

22

for you and a man who I actually *like,* for me. OK?'
  'OK!'
  They shook hands hard and smiled at each other across the table, each one as certain as the other that this was one bet that would never be called in.

starfish and kites

Dig thought Nadine was a bit of a drip when he was allocated the seat next to hers on his first day at the Holy Trinity Convent School for Boys and Girls in Kentish Town.

She had unruly red hair and squidgy white hands with dimples where she should have had knuckles. She was very small and very round, and her grey school skirt stood out starchily from her legs in an angular 'A' shape, ending somewhere near her ankles, which were densely clad in thick-ribbed tights.

Nadine thought Dig was a bit of a nerd when he awkwardly approached the desk next to hers. He was very skinny and very pale, with an overdeveloped head of thick black hair that looked, to her, like a bad wig. His uniform wasn't crisp and brand-new like hers, it looked sad and threadbare and out of sorts. She guessed that he was wearing his big brother's cast-offs and then thought that he probably came from one of those huge Irish Catholic families that her mother had told her all about. He only had one eyebrow and he looked to Nadine like one of the children in *Planet of the Apes*.

Not surprisingly, none of the other children rushed over to get to know Dig and Nadine when the bell for their first break rang at 10.30 a.m., and consequently they had to make do with each other for company while they sat in the playground.

'Dig,' stated Nadine, swinging her plump little legs back and forth, 'that's a really stupid name. Why are you called Dig?'

'It is not a stupid name. It's short for Digby.'

'Well, that's a stupid name, too.'

'No it's not – it's French.'

'Yes it is. "Dig". It's not a name. It's a *verb*.'

'What about you? You can talk. Nadine *Kite*. That's not a name, that's a thing that you fly in the sky.'

'Yes. I *do* know what a kite is, thank you very much.'

'Oh yes – I bet you've never flown one, though, have you? I have. My dad bought it for me. We take it out on Primrose Hill.'

Nadine fell silent for a second and took an extra big slurp of her Banana Nesquik before shrugging. 'Who cares?' she said. 'Kites are for kids. Anyway,' she continued, changing the subject, 'how come you've only got one eyebrow?'

'It's not *one* eyebrow – it's two eyebrows that meet up in the middle, that's all.'

'Looks stupid.'

'Oh,' said Dig, 'thanks a lot.'

'Don't mention it.'

They both stopped talking and began sucking aggressively on their cartons of drink. Dig turned to Nadine and pointed at her hands. 'How come you've got no knuckles, then? How come they're *inside out*?'

'What do you mean?'

'Look,' he said, taking one of her little hands in his own and rubbing his thumb over the dimples in her joints, 'the skin there goes *in*, instead of *out*. They're not normal.'

'Yes they are!' She spread them out like starfish and gazed at them.

'No, they're not. Look at my hands.' He splayed his long white hand open, placed it over her starfish hand and pointed out his sharp knuckles. 'That's what knuckles are supposed to look like.'

'Hmph,' said Nadine.

There was a short silence.

'You can come with us – if you like,' said Dig.

'Where?'

'Kite-flying. Me and my dad.'

'Oh,' said Nadine. 'OK, then.'

They both sat then and stared at their touching hands, and let the warmth seep between their fingers while their cartons of drink sat on either side of them warming up in the September sun and the playground echoed around them with the sounds of a thousand other children.

Nadine looked up at him then, into his kind, brown eyes, and decided at that moment that whatever happened in her life, she was going to marry Digby Ryan.

CHAPTER FOUR

By the time Dig and Nadine had finished breakfast it was early afternoon, and a fairly strong wind had picked up around Primrose Hill, tugging clouds across the sun and throwing dead leaves into the air.

'Fuck it,' said Dig, kicking up a drift of leaves with his trainered foot. 'Should have brought the kites.'

'Should have worn trousers,' said Nadine, clinging on to the fly-away hem of her black chiffon skirt and directing a withering look at a passing pervert admiring her thighs. 'Can we find somewhere to sit? This skirt's pissing me off.'

They sat beneath an oak tree, hands in pockets, legs crossed at the ankles, and stared across the park for a while, in silence.

Nadine turned to Dig and smiled. He looked so sweet. His thick black hair was being furrowed by the wind, flattened into random partings all over his head and sticking up here and there in bizarre little horns. There were tiny rivulets of salt water running downwards from his wind-whipped eyes, and the end of his nose had turned a rather appealing shade of pink. He wasn't so bad looking, she supposed, smiling to herself. Quite cute, really. He was also wearing a somewhat serious, un-Dig-like expression on his face, and a couple of small creases had appeared in the area that should have been the gap between his eyebrows but was in fact just a bridge between the two. Nadine reached out to touch the little furrows with one long-nailed fingertip.

'Oooh, yes,' she said, 'I can see the signs of ageing already.'

'What?' laughed Dig, touching the offending wrinkles.

'Worry lines,' said Nadine, threading her arm through Dig's and resting her head on his shoulder, 'the carefree days of your youth are over, my friend.'

'You jest,' he said, leaning his head against hers and contemplating the brilliant blue and white sky above, 'but I think it might be true.'

'What's up?'

'Oh God. I don't know. It's that girl, last night . . .'

'What girl – Jailbait Girl?'

'Which other?'

'You're not still freaking out about that, are you?'

'Well – yes. I am actually. I just can't get it out of my head. I mean, *seventeen*! You were still a virgin when you were seventeen . . .'

'Well, they grow up faster these days, don't they?'

'I just feel really shitty.'

'I don't suppose *she* does.'

'That's not the point.'

'So what is the point?'

'The point is . . . the point is . . .' He turned to face her and then turned away again. 'I don't know what the point is. I just feel shitty, that's all.'

They stopped talking for a moment. Nadine didn't know what to say. 'Hey,' she changed the subject, 'what time were you born?'

'Eh?'

'What time of the day were you born?'

'Erm, I'm not sure,' replied Dig, 'but it must have been in the evening, because my folks were in the pub when my mum's waters broke.'

'Well. There you go then. You're not thirty yet. Not officially. You've got another four or five hours in your twenties. So . . .'

'What?'

Nadine leaped to her feet, leaned down and scooped up a large armful of russet, auburn and mustard leaves. 'So,' she said, 'you're not too old to have a jolly good leaf fight,' and with that she threw the leaves all over Dig's head like oversized confetti, turned on her heel and ran away laughing.

She ran away, as she would recollect, in an anticlockwise direction, and she would later wonder what uncontrollable forces had led her to that decision. If she'd analysed her thoughts in depth she might have found an answer. But more likely she would have found it to be no more than a random action, plucked from nothing more substantial than pure fancy.

Because what Nadine didn't know when she made that seemingly trivial choice was just *how important* it actually was. Fate had snuck up on her unawares that day on Primrose Hill and as she ran screaming with laughter across the springy grass, Dig in pursuit and closing in on her rapidly with an enormous pile of leaves in his hands and a look of vengeance about him, little did she know that fate was about leap into her path and change the course of her life for ever.

Because, had Nadine *not* taken the anticlockwise route that day, had she set off in the other direction, then they would have exited the park, walked the twenty minutes to Dig's flat, flopped on to his sofa, opened a couple of beers and watched some football, and they would never have bumped into Delilah.

He wasn't sure it was her at first. The hair threw him off a bit. It was a warm golden-brown instead of the five-alarm peroxide white he remembered. And the clothes were different: classic, well cut and definitely expensive. But the moment he saw her face he knew.

It was Delilah. Delilah Lillie! He ignored the scratchiness of the leaves trapped inside his clothing and made his way to the iron railings that separated the park from the pavement. She was walking towards him on Regent's Park Road, her hands full of carrier bags, a pair of sunglasses perched on top of her head. She was staring straight ahead and looked a bit stressed out. His pace quickened as she got closer.

'Where are you going?' Nadine's voice sounded like a whisper in the distance.

She was still very slim, small-waisted, elegant, she still walked with that sway in her hips and she was still quite jaw-droppingly beautiful.

'Di–ig. Where are you going?'

Dig ignored Nadine and carried on walking as if being irresistibly drawn towards a beam of light from an alien spaceship.

'Delilah?' he called. She didn't hear, carried on walking.

'Delilah?' She looked around her, confused.

'Delilah!' He'd reached the iron railings now. Leaves were dropping from his clothing as he walked, falling from beneath his jacket. He didn't notice, didn't care.

He grasped the railings with both hands as Delilah approached, a quizzical, slightly unsure expression on her face. 'It is, isn't it?' he began. 'Delilah. It is you, isn't it?'

Close up, she looked fantastically pretty, fresh-faced, glossy. She'd worn a lot of make-up at school and looked much younger now, bare-faced. She was looking at Dig with a combination of confusion, anticipation, concern and embarrassment. She nodded.

'Dig,' he said, placing a hand on his chest, 'Dig Ryan.'

Her face softened with recognition. 'Oh my God!' she exclaimed. 'Dig Ryan! I don't believe it!'

'God, how are you? How've you been? It's so good to see you.'

'Yeah . . . yeah. I'm great, just great. How're you?' She was smiling widely, looking genuinely pleased to see him.

'Great. I'm great, too. Shit – this is amazing! God, I mean, what've you been up to, what're you doing now, where are you living?'

Delilah indicated the iron railings that divided them.

'Wait,' said Dig, 'wait right there. I'm coming round.'

He skipped back across the grass to where Nadine was waiting for him. 'Quick,' he gestured at her, grinning like an idiot, 'quick! It's Delilah. Come on!'

'Delilah?' muttered Nadine, a shadow falling across her face. 'Delilah Lillie?'

She let the handful of leaves she'd gathered ready for a counter-offensive fall dolefully to the ground and grudgingly followed the bounding figure of Dig across the park and towards the gates.

delilah lillie

Every school had a Delilah Lillie. They were usually blonde, they were always pretty and they were invariably the coolest girl in the school. Delilah Lillie was Debbie Harry, Leslie Ash and Kim Wilde all rolled into one. She had breasts before anyone else and a mop of thick bleached-blonde hair which hung over her eyes like flaxen curtains. She was moody and chewed gum and made her school uniform look sexy. She wore too much black eyeliner, and scuffed stilettos. All the boys wanted to go out with her and all the girls wanted to be her because she was so cool.

She was a woman.

Nadine could remember Delilah's first day at school as if it were yesterday. The corridors and classrooms of the Holy Trinity Convent School for Boys and Girls had been rumbling with the rumours all day. There was a new girl in 4H and she was *really cool*. Her name was Delilah. She'd been expelled from her last school for, among many suggested misdemeanours, getting pregnant, sniffing glue, beating up the headmistress, having sex in the showers, setting fire to the stationery cupboard and stealing the caretaker's car. She lived on the Gospel Oak Estate, the roughest estate in Kentish Town, and her dad was a burglar. She used to go out with Suggs from Madness and she'd slept with everyone in the sixth form of her last school. She sold drugs for a living and if you looked very closely you could see the track marks on her arms. She was a junky, a criminal, a slag and a hard-nut. And she was sexy as hell.

Dig and Nadine sat on the grass outside the science block on their first afternoon back at school. They were fourteen years old. At Dig's feet was his constant companion, a folded and battered copy of the *NME*, and pinned to the lapel of his red blazer was a new badge. It was shaped like a pork-pie hat and it said *Ska For Ever*. He had a big spot on his chin.

Nadine was wearing a baggy red school jumper, her thumbs emerging from tatty holes in the sleeves, and her tie was slung slovenly around her neck. Her frizzy copper hair was held back from her face with a green chiffon scarf and there were traces of mascara clinging to her pale eyelashes, mascara, Dig noticed, which hadn't been there last term.

Nadine had grown nearly four inches in the previous year and she was taller than Dig. Her limbs had stretched into her puppy fat and her knuckles were now the right way round. Dig had filled out a little and grown another inch or two but his eyebrows still joined forces in the middle and his hair still emerged from his scalp like dense black velour.

Dig 'n' Deen, that's what everyone at school called them, because they were inseparable. You never saw one without the other. They occupied a quiet and comfortable position within the school hierarchy – too studious to be cool but too cool to be drips. No one gave them any hassle, but then no one particularly made an effort to befriend them either. Which was fine with them. They lived in a cosy world of study, John Peel, back-combed hair and kite-flying.

33

Nadine hadn't forgotten the pledge she'd made to herself at eleven years old, and if you were to feel around under her mattress you would find her most secret diary, the one she fills with her deepest and darkest thoughts and desires. It is an old school exercise book and it is decorated on the front and the back with doodles – practice signatures, in fact, all loops and hearts and twirls. All of them say the same thing: *Nadine Ryan*. Because even though they're not boyfriend and girl-friend, even though they've never even kissed each other, she *is* going to marry him.

Dig 'n' Deen are going to live on Gloucester Crescent in Camden Town in a big house with shutters and marble floors. Their bed will be a huge pine one with a fluffy white duvet and the sun will shine on to it every morning. They will have parties in their big house every Saturday night, and on Sundays they'll pick up Dig's dad in their powder-blue E-type Jag and take him kite-flying on Prim-rose Hill. They will have four children – Sam, Ben, Emily and Alicia – and they will be incredibly happy.

It's not that Nadine has a crush on Dig or anything, it's just that she can't imagine anyone else marrying him and not being allowed to see him any more. One day they will be man and wife, but for now she is happy just to be his best friend.

'What have you got on Thursday mornings?' Nadine asked Dig, running her finger horizontally across her brand-new timetable.

'Erm . . . erm . . . erm . . .' He trailed off.

'Di–ig.' Nadine tutted and glanced up at Dig from her timetable, following his strange, glassy gaze with her eyes. He was staring across the grass to the netball courts, where a huddle of boys from the fifth form were jostling each other and play-fighting, vying for the attention of a tall girl with white-blonde hair, an awful lot of earrings and a very tight skirt.

'Aaaah,' said Nadine, sucking the end of a pencil, '*that* must be Delilah Lillie.'

Dig remained rigid and speechless, staring at the glamorous figure across the grass, his jaw hanging ever so slightly open.

'She doesn't look like a junky to me,' said Nadine casually, surveying her through her eyelashes, 'she's incredibly pretty.'

Dig gulped and nodded. He opened his mouth to say something but his still-breaking voice cracked and he cleared his throat. 'She . . . she . . . she looks like Leslie Ash in *Quadrophenia*,' he finally managed to squeak.

Quadrophenia was Dig's favourite film of all time and enough people had told Dig that he looked a bit like Phil Daniels for him to have developed a deep affinity with his character in the film. And now there was a girl in the playground, a girl just over there, in fact, a few metres away, who looked just like Leslie Ash, Phil Daniel's, and therefore *Dig's*, dream woman.

Nadine glanced across at her friend and saw the passion glimmering in his eyes, the longing oozing from his pores and the pain already piercing his soul as he looked at something he wanted so much but had already decided he could never have.

'She's beautiful,' he whispered, a blush rising from his frayed shirt-collar to his hairline and his ears. 'She is absolutely beautiful.'

And that was when Nadine knew. That was the moment that Nadine knew that things were never going to be the same again.

All the legends that had accompanied Delilah to the Holy Trinity were proven unfounded within those first six weeks of term. She wasn't a drug addict, she wasn't a dealer, her father wasn't a burglar and she hadn't been expelled from her last school. She had simply moved from south to north London and been put into a new school. She *did*, though, live on the Gospel Oak Estate, and she *had* apparently been out with Suggs's little brother, although only for two weeks. She also proved herself to be a fairly conscientious student who turned up for lessons on time, managed to hand in her homework nine times out of ten and wore her uniform very nearly within the guidelines set down by the school. This lack of sociopathic behaviour did nothing to dent her reputation as the coolest girl in school, however, and she still found herself surrounded wherever she went by swarms of buzzing boys and fussed over by shorter, plainer girls hoping that a little of her magnetism might rub off on them.

Nadine had been right. Things weren't the same between her and Dig after that first day of term. All Dig's priorities changed. Now everything was a constant reference to Delilah. He and Nadine would walk around the school grounds together, apparently aimlessly, but Nadine knew that they were Delilah-hunting, she knew that the moment Dig heard the sound of Delilah's gravelly voice echoing around a corner they would suddenly slow down and Dig would start walking differently and talking to Nadine in a really loud voice about something they hadn't been discussing before, usually something to do with music. He would walk past Delilah and stare resolutely ahead, avoiding her gaze.

36

Dig and Nadine's friendship ended one rainy Tuesday afternoon, just before the end of the first term.

They were sitting together in the canteen, munching on soggy chips and pasty pasta and speed-reading their set pieces from *Animal Farm* for English Lit that afternoon when they became aware of a sallow boy from 3G called Desmond hovering over their table. They looked up questioningly.

'Here,' he said, dragging a grubby finger across his nostrils, 'are you Dig Ryan?'

'Yeah,' he answered. 'Why?'

'Just thought you might want to know that there's a rumour going around' – he looked around shiftily – 'about you.'

'Oh yeah,' said Dig, folding the corner of the page and putting his book down.

'Yeah,' said Desmond, 'about you and Delilah Lillie.'

Dig's eyebrow shot off his forehead and nearly landed on the back of his neck. 'Oh yeah,' he managed, coolly, 'and what's that then?'

'Apparently, she's been going around saying that she thinks you're really cool. She says she wants to talk to you. She says she likes your attitude. She says you've got cha . . . cha . . . char . . . charisma?'

Nadine nodded at Desmond to indicate that he'd found the right word, and he continued. 'Anyway,' he said, 'I just thought you ought to know, you know, what she's been saying and' – he stuck one grimy hand out awkwardly and offered it to Dig to shake – 'I just wanted to say congratulations, like. You must be made up.'

And then he went shuffling back to his table and his mates, who were all eyeing Dig with a new-found respect.

Dig remained quite calm, considering, mindlessly prodding at his flaccid chips with his fork and muttering under his breath, 'Fucking-hell-Deen-fucking-hell-Deen-fucking-hell.' His face was flushed almost purple and his feet were banging together under the table. Suddenly he looked up and straight into Nadine's eyes. 'Fucking hell, Deen,' he almost shouted, 'what am I going to do?'

In the event, he hadn't had to do anything. During the last few days of that term Delilah Lillie became omnipresent. Dig's strategic patrols of the school were no longer necessary, as, wherever he went, Delilah was already there. For a couple of days nothing was said between them, but looks of intense significance were exchanged and the atmosphere between them was so charged that Dig became literally static, every object he touched perforating his skin with little bullets of electricity.

Nadine began to feel more and more superfluous and uncomfortable during these peculiar encounters, but whenever she suggested to Dig that she make herself scarce, find something else to do, he would grab on to her sleeve for dear life and beg her to stay.

Finally, on the last day of term, it happened. Nadine and Dig were sitting together on the stairs outside the language lab when Delilah appeared from nowhere, clutching a pile of books to her chest and apparently in a hurry. But she stopped dead when she rounded the corner and saw Dig on the steps, stopped and stood squarely in front of him. For a second the air tingled with electricity, and silence reverberated around the three of them. Nadine stopped breathing and waited for one of them to say something. Finally, Delilah opened her plump crimson lips, slowly enough, Nadine noticed, for two tiny peaks of skin to form between them and stick together briefly before pinging apart like little rubber bands.

'Hi,' she said.

'Hi,' said Dig, his voice not letting him down by cracking, but emanating resoundingly from beneath his ribcage.

Nadine sat with her hands on her lap and stared at the floor.

'You're Dig, aren't you?' said Delilah.

'Yeah,' he said, still in that deep, clear voice, 'that's right. And *you* are . . .?'

Nadine whistled silently under her breath. You had to hand it to him, she thought to herself, that was pretty fucking cool.

'I'm Delilah,' she said, 'Delilah Lillie. I'm in 4H. You know, Mr Harwood's class.'

'Oh,' said Dig, 'yeah. Right. You're the new girl, aren't you?'

'Yeah,' she said, 'pretty new.' There was a second's silence then, and Delilah bit her lip and threw Nadine a sideways glance, a look which told Nadine everything she needed to know. I'm taking over now, that's what that look said, it's my shift, off you go, you weird-looking, fat-arsed, ginger-haired nobody.

It was time to go, it was time to let Dig get on with this, without her. She pushed her papers together into a pile, swung her bag over her shoulder and got to her feet.

'Right,' she said unnecessarily, as neither of them was paying any attention to her, 'I'm off. See ya.' And then she walked, as fast as she'd ever walked, along corridor after corridor, pushing swing doors open with her shoulder as she went, walked and walked and walked until there was nowhere left to walk. And then she stopped, stopped in her tracks and turned to face the wall as the tears she'd been trying so hard to control spilled over her eyes and cascaded in sheets down her cheeks.

the pub of perpetual darkness

It was a Saturday lunch-time, the week before Nadine was due to start her mock O Levels and four months since her friendship with Dig had ended.

Kentish Town Road was bright with the reflection of a dazzling sun on a slick wet pavement following a thirty-second deluge of rain. People emerged from shops where they'd taken temporary refuge and others shook out umbrellas and folded them up. Nadine was with her mother, looking for a book she needed for her history revision, sulking at the injustice of being in a place she didn't want to be, with a person she didn't want to be with, looking for something she wished she didn't need in the middle of a torrential downpour that had pissed on her quiff and left her drowning in a sea of melting Elnett.

'Take these, will you, Nadine?' her mother asked, handing her a soggy umbrella and a shopping bag full of cabbages. 'I've got to find a lavatory. It's this weather – all this rain,' she said, before disappearing into a nearby pub.

Nadine had never been inside a pub before. She wasn't allowed, which was hardly surprising as she wasn't allowed to do anything. She'd been in 'family' pubs on holiday, consigned to 'family' rooms full of fruit machines and bored children, but never inside an actual pub, a proper London sort of a pub. Curiosity inspired her to hover inside the entrance while she waited for her mother, a little closer to the innards of the pub than her mother would have liked.

The smell got to her first, stale, smoky and stagnant. Slivers of sunlight sneaked in through scratches in the black paint on the tall windows, picking out glittering mites of dust and ribbons of cigarette smoke curling across the top of the room, as if caught in the light of a cinema projector. A juke-box blared out the 'Ace of Spades', an artillery of fruit machines whizzed, crashed and banged and above all of this, from a table in the farthest corner, rose a loud and somewhat frightening cacophony of obscenities and profanities.

Nadine edged a bit further into the cavernous, unlit pub to view the source of this noise. Cloaked in shadow sat a small woman, with dyed black stringy hair, wearing a heavy gold crucifix. She was at least eight months pregnant, her bump accentuated by a too-small white T-shirt emblazoned with the faded legend 'I DON'T GIVE A **** WHAT FRANKIE SAYS.' She was smoking a roll-up and drinking a pint and screaming at the huge man sitting next to her in between drags and sips. He was staring straight ahead with a tightness in his face that threatened to turn from tolerance to violence at any moment.

In front of the table sat a buggy, into which were strapped two rather sullen-looking but attractive children, and to her right sat a beautiful blond-haired boy of about four years old, wearing an Arsenal football strip. He was talking to himself and scribbling in a colouring book with a red crayon. He looked like an angel.

'Mum,' he said, turning to look at the pregnant woman, 'Mum. I need the toilet, Mum.'

'Shut up, Kane,' she spat, stubbing out the spit-soft-ened end of her roll-up and readying herself for the next stage of her verbal assault on the fat man. 'Can't you see I'm talking?'

'But, Mum, I need to go.' One hand had disappeared under the table to hold the end of his willy.

'Will you shut up! You'll just have to hold on! I'm talking!'

'But, Mum . . .'

The woman turned around and fixed the child with a terrifying expression, squeezed the tops of his arms with her bony hands and brought him upwards towards her face. 'If you don't shut up, Kane, I'm going to fucking belt you,' she said, and then, just to make sure he knew she was serious, she slapped him hard across his bare legs, a sharp crack resonating around the pub.

Nadine winced as the child dissolved into tears and watched in horror as a small trickle of pale yellow liquid began to dribble slowly from under the table, across the grubby linoleum. The woman rose up in her seat to view it better and then turned to the boy.

'You fucking little bastard!' She yanked him up by one puny arm. 'You disgusting little fucker!' A large damp patch adorned the front of his football shorts. She carried him by his arm to the men's toilets, pushed open the door with her shoulder and flung him through the door on to the grimy toilet floor. 'Clean yourself up, you filthy bastard.' The boy crouched on the tiled floor on all fours, tears coursing down his cheeks. Nadine gulped as the door came to a close between them, leaving just the muted sound of the boy's distress.

The girl sitting on the other side of the table, with her back to Nadine, stood up then and put out a cigarette.

43

She was wearing skin-tight drainpipe jeans with a pink-and-white-striped vest top. She fixed the woman with a look, blew out her last lungful of smoke and then marched towards the toilet door. She walked in and began to gather the boy into her arms, whispering soothing words into his ear and smoothing down his hair. The door closed, and the two of them emerged a few seconds later, the boy now shortless, his shirt hanging down to his thighs, and clinging on to the girl's leg with both arms. It was only at that moment that Nadine realized who the girl was.

It was Delilah.

Nadine turned then, turned away very quickly and walked out of the pub and into the sunny safety of the street outside. Her heart was beating frighteningly fast and she took in large mouthfuls of air. That was Delilah! And that was Delilah's mum. Oh my God. Poor Delilah. Poor, poor Delilah. Nadine had never witnessed anything quite so hellish before in her life.

That . . . woman, that horrible woman, drinking and smoking with a baby inside her and hitting that beautiful little boy. And how many children did she have? Nadine knew that Delilah had older brothers, too. She must have had millions. Making all her beautiful children sit indoors on a day like today, in that dark, dank, dismal place with all that noise and smoke, while she screamed foul language at some hideous fat man with stained clothes and greasy hair.

All of a sudden, what previously would have seemed to Nadine like the epitome of cool – a mother who actually let her fourteen-year-old daughter smoke in front of her, *with her* – now seemed to her to be a travesty. It was sick. Delilah's mum was sick.

Nadine suddenly realized why Delilah was allowed to do so much, why the rules and regulations which she felt strangled her own development didn't seem to apply to Delilah. It wasn't because Delilah was the lucky winner of the Parent Lottery, proud recipient of a wondrous mother who understood that girls *needed* to stay out later than eleven o'clock and *needed* to go out with boys, and *needed* more than one earring in each lobe and *needed* to do whatever they wanted with their hair. Delilah, she realized, wasn't lucky. She was unlucky. Because her mother didn't care, really didn't care about her or, it seemed, any of her other, numerous children. She didn't care about Delilah's hair or her ear lobes or the state of her health. It was unlikely that she cared about her education or her future or the status of her hymen. It no longer seemed cool to Nadine that Mrs Lillie (if that was her name) didn't turn up to parent-teacher meetings or check Delilah's homework.

Nadine's mother finally emerged from the pub, wiping the palms of her hands distractedly against the sides of her cotton dirndl skirt.

'Those,' she began, a distasteful expression hanging around her mouth, 'are the most terrible lavatories I have ever visited. Except for that hole-in-the-ground affair in Calais. No soap, no towels, no *seats*! I had to sort of squat over the bowl.' She shuddered and began to unburden Nadine of her bags. 'And there are *children* in that place. Can you believe it? Children! I mean who – *who* – would take children into a place like that? It's shocking, it really is . . .'

As they continued on their way that afternoon, stopping for a cup of tea and a Swiss Finger in the baker's shop, browsing through the Education section in

45

W. H. Smiths, searching through the bargain bin in the wool shop for a length of peacock blue angora to finish off a sweater her mother was knitting for her, Nadine began to regain a sense of normality, of humanity, of *cleanliness*. And, for the first time since she'd begun her journey through adolescence towards adulthood, she felt lucky.

Her mother was traditional and overbearing and her father was distant and predictable. Her little brother was a precocious pain in the arse who could do no wrong and she was treated like a wayward child who could do no right. Their flat was small and old-fashioned, furnished with her dead grandparents' dark and sombre pre-war furniture, and everyone in her family took this whole Catholicism thing just a bit too seriously.

But, she concluded, after the shock of seeing a fragment of Delilah's existence outside school, at least I have love. At least I have affection. At least my family cares about me, even if they care too much, sometimes. At least, she thought, I am not forced to be a grown-up when I am not ready. She would rather *want* to be an adult and not be allowed than be made to be one.

Delilah might have been the most beautiful girl at the Holy T but her life away from school was ugly and sordid; she might have been the queen of cool but she had a witch for a mother and a pig for a stepfather and she might have taken Nadine's best friend away from her, but she had to spend sunny afternoons in places like that.

Poor Delilah. Poor old Delilah.

Nadine vowed then that despite Delilah's sneering indifference to her initial attempts at friendship she would make one final attempt to befriend her.

*
46

The first thing she saw when she walked towards the doors of Holy T on Monday morning was Delilah, one leg bent up behind her against a wall, a fag in one hand and a crappy photo-strip magazine in the other, giving Nadine the evil eye. Nadine swallowed her feelings and walked towards her.

'Hi,' she said, forcing a smile, 'nice weekend?'

Delilah looked momentarily surprised by this unexpected encounter but quickly regained her composure and self-consciously flicked the long ash off the end of her cigarette. 'Yeah,' she said, 'it was all right.' She was unable to meet Nadine's gaze and began looking over her shoulder and then distractedly around the street, almost like she was panicking, hoping to be rescued. She spotted Dig walking up the road and beckoned to him with a trace of desperation. He came bounding towards them, and Delilah's face softened as she drew him to her and sunk into his embrace. She took a deep drag on her cigarette and smiled at Nadine. She had Dig. She was strong again.

Nadine didn't bother making an effort with Delilah after that day. She felt sorry for Delilah's unfortunate circumstances, but trying to be friends really wasn't worth it.

She had never liked Delilah, and Delilah had never liked her, and on that morning Nadine finally decided that it would be easier all round just to leave the two of them alone and get on with her life.

the king and queen of the holy t

At around 4.15 p.m. on 17 July 1985 a loud bell from within the school walls pierced the silence, and the playground erupted.

It was the last day of school.

Folders and textbooks and feint-ruled pads with margins flew into the air, red-and-grey-striped nylon ties were unknotted from worn shirt-collars and spun like lassos around heads, previously muted transistors were turned up full blast and 120 red-blazered sixteen-year-olds moved as one out of the school gates for the last time, a mass of pent-up energy and hormones released from the confines of five years of study and discipline, erupting like a stream of red-hot molten larva on to the oven-baked summer streets of Kentish Town.

Nadine found her friends and they joined the crowds rushing towards Caledonian Park for an afternoon of fighting and drinking and pelting kids from other schools with flour and eggs. They drank flat cider from big plastic litre bottles that went floppy in their hands as the sun warmed the liquid inside. They watched the boys showing off. They talked about their plans for the summer and their plans for the rest of their lives. It was all ahead of them, but Nadine couldn't shake the feeling that the most important part was already behind her.

It was all over. Not just school, not just five years of

48

rules and regulations, homework and assembly, mass on Fridays and cross-country runs in the rain, wearing a tie and eating school dinners, but what remained of her friendship with Dig. It wasn't going to survive this, she knew that. He was going to do his A Levels at a college in Holloway; she was doing hers at a grammar school in Archway.

He was still firmly ensconced in his partnership with Delilah. They were the king and queen of the Holy T, together to the exclusion of everyone else, particularly Nadine. It looked horribly and sadly to Nadine as if it was all over between her and Dig, what had been and what could have been.

There were going to be no sunny mornings together on a big pine bed, no hosting of raucous Saturday-night parties and cosy shopping trips together. There would never again be any such thing as 'Dig 'n' Deen', only 'Dig and Delilah'. Delilah had him wrapped up like a fly in a web and he was happy to be there. There was nothing left over for Nadine, no bit of the Dig that Nadine had loved so much for so long, and the thought left her with a lump in her throat and an awful sense of incompleteness in her heart.

As if to add poignancy to her thoughts, a cloud moved across the sun, a small chill breeze wafted over her, and Nadine looked up just in time to see Dig and Delilah a few feet away exchanging a kiss. The sun was just starting to set across the tops of the council blocks that lined the horizon, they'd run out of cider and two of her friends had fallen asleep on the grass. It was nearly ten and Nadine decided it was time to go home. She gathered her belongings together, her transistor, her cardigan, the bits and pieces of stationery and equipment that

49

symbolized the last five years of her life, got up and began walking.

Dig caught up with her at the park gates. He was breathless from running. 'Deen,' he squeaked incredulously, 'where are you going?'

Nadine could see Delilah across the park, sitting up stiffly, her back poker-straight, her eyes slanted closed against the low light, watching the exchange closely.

'Home,' said Nadine, pulling the sleeves of her cardigan tighter around her waist. 'It's getting late.'

Dig's face wrinkled in confusion. 'Oh,' he said, scratching his head, 'right.'

'So,' she said, 'goodbye and good luck, yeah?'

'What? I mean . . . yeah. But we'll still be meeting up, won't we? You know – the kites and everything?' He looked anxious.

Nadine shrugged. 'Oh,' she said, 'I don't know. I think we'll probably be too busy, what with schoolwork and being at different colleges, you know?'

Dig's eyes clouded over with sadness. 'Right. Yeah. I suppose you're right.'

Nadine squeezed a small smile through tight lips. 'So have a nice life . . .'

'Oh. Right. I see. You too. Yeah,' he said, looking like he had now given the matter some thought and was beginning to get used to the idea. 'Yeah. You have a good life, too, Nadine.'

And then they ran out of things to say, a few moments before they lost the desire to talk, standing together awkwardly, shuffling a little, smiling, making and losing eye contact. The screaming, shouting and swearing of the other kids faded into the background and slivers of light from the ebbing sun perforated through the branches of a large elm and painted the two of them with salmon-pink stripes. Nadine leaned down to pull up her socks. Dig picked up a folder that had slid from the top of her pile and handed it back to her. The furthest tips of their fingers touched and then retracted instantly.

In the background Delilah still sat and watched, a piece of grass between her lips, her long legs folded up beneath her, an expression of disquiet hewn into her features. Dig turned to look at her and then turned back to Nadine. He opened his mouth to say something but then realized that he didn't need to. He shrugged instead and began to back away. Nadine shot him one last smile and then turned to leave the park.

Outside the park, a Ford Cortina parked sideways across North Road billowed flames from an overheated engine while three firemen attacked the fire with wild hoses of water, watched by a small audience of people. A river of blackened water snaked along the pavement and Nadine skipped over it before walking blindly towards York Way, her feet leading her homewards while her heart urged her to turn around, tear through the park towards Dig, her best friend, her soulmate, to make amends and reseal their bond, before it was too late.

But she didn't – her pride wouldn't let her – and she carried on walking through the darkening streets of Kentish Town, walking and walking and feeling it all slowly slip away from her grasp. She let herself into her parents' tiny flat on Bartholomew Road, sat with them while they watched *Dynasty* and answered their questions about her last day at school. At eleven o'clock she yawned and padded upstairs to her bedroom. She stared around her dreary room for a while and let her mind fill up with memories and images of her and Dig. Her kite was pinned to one wall, little lines of dust forming in the creases, the bright colours starting to fade to shadows. The tail drooped sadly, looking like it had lost the will to live, ever to fly again.

It was to be two years before Nadine would unpin her kite from the wall, blow off the dust and watch it skitting once more across the London skyline.

CHAPTER FIVE

Anticlockwise! Anticlockwise! Why had she gone anticlockwise? It was a fifty-fifty thing. She could have
gone clockwise. She could have been back at Dig's by
now, safe and cosy, watching the football, instead of
sitting in some hoity-toity tea-shop in Primrose Hill
drinking overpriced cappuccino and watching her best
friend regress within seconds to the fourteen-year-old
schoolboy he'd always been.

And oh my God, look at her. Just look at her, will you?
It's sickening. How can she look younger now than she
did then? How can she be more beautiful, more poised,
more *everything*? She has acquired polish and gloss. Her
accent is now neutral. She has a dazzling smile and even
a certain amount of charm. That's definitely something
with a designer label in it that she's wearing so *effort-
lessly*. And look at the size of that rock on her ring finger
– Gibraltar has nothing on it.

She has expensive hair – what is it that hairdressers
in expensive salons actually *do* to hair to make it look
expensive like that? She's wearing the sort of make-up
that looks like you're wearing none at all, and she has
that smell about her, not quite perfume, but something
more intrinsic, like cleanliness, like dew. She smells like
she bathes in the morning dew. It probably costs about
eighty quid a bottle.

Nadine looks at Dig. She hasn't seen him this excited

for years. Every angle of his body is directed towards Delilah, his elbows, his knees, his head. Nadine may as well not be here, may as well not exist. She's a big ginger gooseberry again.

They're talking about Delilah's marriage, about the life she's been living for the past twelve years. She's not called Delilah Lillie any more, she's called, somewhat unfortunately and much to Nadine's delight, Delilah *Biggins*. Her husband is called Alex. He owns a small chain of brasserie-style restaurants in the north-west and they live together in neo-Georgian splendour in Chester. When he's not overseeing his empire, he's to be found on the golf course, squash court and cricket pitch. They have three horses and a swimming pool. Every couple of months Alex pays for Delilah to fly to New York first class and slips her his platinum credit card. She shops till she drops and is the envy of every other woman in Chester.

It all sounds pretty dull to Nadine, but Dig's riveted by every word, like it was ten years' worth of *Brookside* storylines. But then, just as Nadine is about to nod off, the conversation suddenly changes direction in a most dramatic manner. All is not as it seems. Delilah admits, falteringly and nervously, her eyes glazing over with tears, that she's left Alex. She's taken off and left him in bed, with just a note to wake up to, which Nadine thinks is pretty cruel. But then, any man stupid enough to marry a heart-hazard like Delilah gets what he deserves, quite frankly. I mean, you can tell just by *looking* at her that she's going to leave you one day.

She doesn't expand on the subject and Dig doesn't ask her any of the *right* questions, about why she's left her husband and come back to London, but then he's a boy.

She'd ask them herself but she's in too much of a mood to give her voice that inquisitive, interested edge it needs to form questions.

And that's another thing. You'd have thought, wouldn't you, that Dig would be demanding some sort of explanation right now, demanding to know why exactly Delilah disappeared and left him all those years ago, why she broke his heart into so many pieces that he'd never found them all to glue back together again? You'd have thought he'd be a bit *frosty* with her about the way she behaved back then, but he's not. He's acting like none of that ever happened, like everything is all right.

Nadine makes little peaks in the froth on her coffee with a fingertip and looks around her. The place is packed full with people wearing expensive clothes, pink-cheeked after a bracing walk on Primrose Hill with their labs and retrievers, mud caked on to the soles of their Russell & Bromley walking boots, people who have so much money that they don't so much as *blanch* at the outrageous £4.50 they're charging for a rather slim slice of chocolate truffle cake in this place. Nadine decides that she doesn't like anyone in this tea-shop, that she doesn't, in fact, like Primrose Hill with its faux-village atmosphere, and its pretend pubs and its overpriced everything. Primrose Hill, concludes Nadine, does not belong in Inner London – it is too small and too twee and too genteel, and it should be disassembled piece by piece and taken to Esher, where it would make a charming side-street.

'So,' Dig is asking Delilah, 'how long have you been back?'

'I just arrived this morning, believe it or not. Got the first train down.'

'Really?' smiles Dig, the look of a man blessed with fantastic serendipity spreading across his face. 'And where are you staying? At your mum's?'

Delilah takes a slurp of her filter coffee – black, no sugar – and puts the cup down, shaking her head. 'Oh God no,' she says. 'I haven't spoken to her since I was eighteen. I moved out and went to stay with my cousin. Remember? Marina. That's where I'm staying now. Just around the corner, up there.' She indicates the road opposite. 'Elsworthy Road,' she says.

Why? Nadine wants to scream. Why did you move out when you were eighteen? Why did you move in with your cousin? Why didn't you tell Dig you were going? And why the fuck isn't Dig asking you these questions?

'Very nice,' says Dig, nodding respectfully in appreciation of the fact that Delilah's cousin is obviously rolling in it and probably itching to ask her how another member of her Gospel Oak estate family found their way into the bourgeoisie. 'Very nice.' He controls himself. 'And what are your plans? What are you going to do with yourself here?'

Delilah shrugs and looks anxious. This is obviously a tricky question for her to answer. Please, thinks Nadine, please say you're just here for a couple of days, you're very busy, people to see, places to go. Please say that you probably won't be seeing us again because you're *going to New York tomorrow*.

But Nadine already has this very strange, uncomfortable feeling that this isn't to be the last time they see Delilah, that Delilah is, in fact, going to be around one hell of a lot, a portent that is borne out seconds later when Delilah smiles, tucks her Pantene-girl-eat-your-heart-out hair behind her ears with two beautifully manicured sets of fingertips and says, 'Well, I was just going to hang out, really, you know, catch up with old friends, that sort of thing.'

Dig's face performs a theatre of ecstatic emotions. 'Excellent,' he smiles, 'that's fantastic.' The two of them stop for a second then and beam, positively *beam*, at each other. Nadine wants to be sick.

Dig offers Delilah a cigarette. She waves it away. 'Not smoking any more?' he asks, surprised. In both of their minds, Delilah Lillie *invented* smoking.

She grimaces. 'Given up,' she says. 'Only twelve days. Don't want to talk about it.' Dig sucks in his breath in appreciation of the enormity of her sacrifice and withdraws the offered packet. 'It's just *so* great to see you,' he grins.

'I'm so glad I bumped into you, too,' smiles Delilah. 'I felt a bit lost and lonely when I arrived and then I ran into you two and now I feel much better.'

Nadine grits her teeth, hates Delilah for a moment, hates her and wants her dead, which makes her feel like a total bitch, the biggest bitch that ever lived. Which makes her feel ugly, makes her feel like a wicked, wart-faced witch, which in turn makes her feel like Delilah is some flaxen-haired, *flawless*, fucking fairy-princess type, which makes her hate her even more. Nadine smiles grimly and traces a happy face into the froth on top of her coffee, the coffee she hasn't actually drunk yet, the coffee she is feeling far too discomfited even to contemplate drinking.

'You two,' Delilah is saying, 'you two have changed so much. I would never have recognized you. Especially you, Deen. You're a . . . you're a babe, you really are. You're absolutely gorgeous. I love all these little clips in

57

your hair. And I love your fingernails' – she takes Nadine's turquoise talons in her hands and examines them – 'how do you get them to grow so long? Mine always split down here.' She indicates the pink of her perfect nails.

'Jelly cubes,' says Nadine, 'I eat jelly cubes every day. Rowntrees, lemon and lime flavour.' And she's thinking, Oh no, don't do this, Delilah. Don't do this whole trying-to-make-me-like-you thing. I don't want to like you. I can't like you. I've never liked you. However many conversations we have about nails and cellulite and facial hair and cabbage-soup diets, I am not going to like you. I am never going to like you because no matter how much you might have changed, I will never be able to forget the way you treated me at school, the way you disregarded me and belittled me and broke my heart.

I know what women like you can do to normal, sane men. Women like you have ultimate power. Women like you just have to walk into a room for all hell to let loose and for all men to become retarded. Women like you can take the heart of a warm, trusting and gentle man like Dig and make mincemeat out of it. And I am always going to resent you, Delilah, because you're beautiful, and because the beauty you possess is something that no woman can ever buy, from a beauty counter, from a plastic surgeon or from South Molton Street. I can't compete with you on any level. I am deeply threatened by you and I don't want you in my life. I don't want you in my nice, safe, happy world, where I am secure and where I know my place. It has taken me a decade and a half to emerge from your shadow, to become desirable in my own right. Call me selfish, thinks Nadine, call me an egocentric bitch, call me insecure and call me paranoid,

I don't care. I just want you out of London, out of my life and out of Dig's life.

'So, you're a photographer, are you?'

'Uh-huh,' replies Nadine, 'that's me. I take pictures.' She tells Delilah briefly about the exotic locations and the financial rewards.

'Wow,' says Delilah, genuinely impressed, 'that must be amazing. I remember talking once about what we all wanted to be when we grew up and you said that you wanted to be married and writing cookbooks, or something, wasn't it? And look at you now. So glamorous and gorgeous and successful, with an exciting job and your own place. God, Deen' – she reaches out and squeezes Nadine's hand – 'I'm so jealous of you, I really am.'

Oh stop it, thinks Nadine. Just stop it. You're not jealous at all, you're just trying to make me feel better about not being as beautiful as you. You've got tons of money and satin hair and flawless skin – how could you possibly be jealous of me?

Nadine forces a saccharine smile and pats Delilah's hand back. 'Oh, don't be silly,' she says, wishing she could rise above all the small-minded, mean-spirited jealousy she's feeling. She looks across the table at Dig, trying to remind herself how to be nice – he always brings out the best in her – but he's lost in Delilahland. The Dig Ryan she knows and loves is nowhere to be seen.

'Well' – Delilah is knocking back the dregs of her coffee and making moves towards her handbag – 'I'd better get back. I've left my dog alone with a hundred starving cats. They've probably eaten *him* by now.' She smiles and drops a pile of coins on to the bill. She fixes them both with a deeply sincere gaze, brimming with warmth and good feeling, and says, 'I hope I'll see you both again soon. It would *so nice* if we could get together some time.'

'Yeah – definitely,' oozes Dig, 'definitely,' and Nadine can tell he's mentally reorganizing his entire diary to make sure there's no question that they'll be able to 'get together some time'.

'Actually,' he says, reaching into the pocket of his black leather coat and pulling out a scrappy piece of paper and a Biro, 'let me take your number at your cousin's. I'm not up to much this week. Maybe we could go out one night. You know. Catch up on old times.'

No, thinks Nadine. No. Please. Not again. This can't be happening again.

'That would be great, Dig. Thanks.'

Nadine's heart sinks.

They all exchange phone numbers, they schmooze all over each other and act delighted (which Nadine is, because Delilah's finally leaving) and then go their separate ways.

Nadine watches Delilah struggling across the road with her excess of carrier bags, trying to keep the curtain of hair out of her eyes with the back of one hand, and feels a brief flickering second of sympathy for her. The hairs on her arms stand up on end and a painful little lump forms in the back of her throat. Poor Delilah, she thinks, poor old Delilah.

Delilah gets to the other side of the road, whereupon a very handsome man who's just climbed out of a shiny red Lotus Elise approaches her and begins charmingly to unburden her of her shopping. 'Oh thank you, thank you so much,' she can just make out Delilah cooing to the gorgeous stranger. 'Really, you shouldn't have, you're too kind.'

The hairs on Nadine's arms fall flat, the lump in her throat deflates and her hands ball themselves up into tight little knots of hatred.

CHAPTER SIX

On Monday morning, Dig gets to work at half past ten.

Late, by anybody else's standards, but perfectly acceptable by his, especially considering that he had to pick his car up from those thieving shysters in Tufnell Park on his way in.

Johnny-Boy Records is housed in a dinky little pink, stucco-fronted cottage in a Camden Town mews; it used to be Toby's home, when he started the label back in 1989, but now Toby lives in a five-bedroom house in Primrose Hill with his ex-model wife, their three strangely named children and a South African nanny, and the cottage is used as an office.

The inside hasn't changed much since Toby lived here; it's very cosy and homely. The floors are all distressed reclaim boards and threadbare kilims. There are table lamps and pictures and plants and flowers all over the place. In reception there is a widescreen Nicam TV and a big squidgy jacquard sofa where they all sit and watch *Neighbours* every day with their feet up on the Balinese coffee table. A wrought-iron spiral staircase leads to a galleried area overhead and from there another leads on to a tiny roof terrace where everyone eats their lunch in summer.

Dig loves the fact that his workplace is nicer than his flat. It's just one of many reasons why he's stayed here so long. Seven years, in fact. He's been here since he was twenty-three. He started off as an A&R assistant and was promoted to A&R manager the following year when his boss left to form a band of his own. Not that he actually manages anyone. He has the odd work-experience student in for a few weeks here and there, but on the whole, he's a one-man department and he likes it that way.

The other reasons why he's stayed here so long are:

1) It's a five-minute drive from home and he has a dedicated parking space

2) Nobody bats an eyelid when he gets in late

3) He gets on extraordinarily well with Toby, who is less like a boss and more like a second dad – well, one he can get stoned with, anyway

4) He's allowed to smoke at his desk, whenever and whatever he likes

5) He can spend an entire day making personal phone calls and no one even notices

6) He hardly has to do any work.

Dig didn't use to be this slack. He used to be a workaholic. He'd be in at nine, work through lunch, stay till seven and then hit the trail, going to two or three gigs every night, because in those days Dig was on a mission – a mission to find the 'next big thing'. A label the size of Johnny-Boy Records could easily support itself with a few reasonably successful acts, the occasional Top Fifty album. But Dig wanted more. And in 1995 he found more: Fruit. The biggest sensation of the year. He found them playing in a pub in Cheltenham, of all places, back in the days when he could be bothered to go outside the M25 to see bands playing in pubs. They were eighteen years old, good-looking and brilliant. Their first single went to number one and became the summer anthem, booming out of Oxford Street jeans shops and fairground rides all over the country for weeks on end. The first album went straight in at number one and stayed in the Top Fifty for nearly a year. They were on the front cover of all the music papers and appeared on every pop show on the telly.

It had been a mad year for Dig. He was headhunted by every A&R department in London and consequently given a payrise by a somewhat scared Toby, big enough for him to finally leave home and buy a flat at the ripe old age of twenty-seven. His reputation was made. Everyone knew who he was and what he'd achieved. So he sat back and relaxed for a while, safe in the knowledge that no one could touch him because he was the guy who discovered Fruit.

Dig can't ever imagine leaving Johnny-Boy Records. It's easy. It's cosy. It's *family*. He knows everyone, from the tiny elderly cleaner who turns up every evening in a vast Rolls-Royce Silver Shadow which was left to her by her ex-employer and which she refuses to sell even though she's paid only £6 an hour, to the guy who turns up once every three months sporting a ridiculously smart suit and over-gelled hair to service the photocopier. Dig knows where everything goes, where everything comes from and where everything belongs. Johnny-Boy Records is his second home.

'You're looking a bit pleased with yourself this morning,' says Charlie, their pneumatically blonde but strangely droll receptionist, shoving bits of paper into internal envelopes, which always makes Dig laugh because there's only seven of them. Charlie used to work for EMI and still does all her admin on a grand scale.

Dig considers his expression and realizes that he does

indeed have a smug smile hovering around his lips. He decides this is highly inappropriate for a Monday morning and removes it.

'You recovered from Friday night yet?' inquires Charlie, in a tone of voice laden with the suggestion that he'd been drunker than he thought.

'Just about,' he says, picking his mail out of the pile on her desk.

'You know that girl was only seventeen, don't you?'

Dig blushes and rips open an envelope.

'You shagged her, didn't you?'

Dig blushes even more and pretends to be very interested in the contents of a Viking Direct catalogue.

'You dirty old bastard,' she says, eyeing Dig with evident delight and tying the string on an internal envelope into a little bow, before handing it to him.

Dig climbs the spiral staircase and ignores Charlie's calls of 'Lock up your daughters – paed on the loose!'

'What are you looking so happy about?' says Toby, loitering around the coffee machine.

Dig again realizes he has that inappropriate smile on his face and quickly disassembles it.

'*Cradle-snatcher!*' Charlie bellows up the stairs.

'Aaah,' smiles Toby. 'Yes. That girl. Friday night. I take it you . . . er . . .'

Dig nods stiffly. 'She was totally up for it, you know.'

Toby nods, too. 'Of course,' he says, 'of course she was. You'd better get used to this now.'

'What?'

'Well, you're thirty now. You've got the *allure* of an older man. You'll have them throwing themselves at you. You want to get yourself one of these, too.' He points at his wedding band and winks. 'Fanny magnet,' he says and then turns away, laughing hoarsely.

Dig laughs, too, because he knows that as much as he moans about them and makes jokes about his supposed pulling power, Toby is tied completely to his wife and family and wouldn't have the energy even if he *did* have the opportunities. He's worked too hard and too long for everything he's got and he's far too clever to risk it all on a shag.

Dig pulls off his leather coat and hangs it up. He reaches into the inside pocket and feels around a bit until he locates what he's looking for. A small, manky shred of paper. He gently smooths it out, running his finger lingeringly across the creases, and places it on his desk, next to his phone. He looks at it for a while and feels that smile forming on his lips again.

He won't call her now. He'll call her later. He'll have a cup of coffee first, open his mail, check his e-mails.

And then he'll phone Delilah Lillie.

Nadine always feels a little shiver of excitement going to work. First of all there's the unadulterated *thrill* of driving around in her gleaming white Alfa Spider, which is beautiful beyond words and which she paid for herself. Even in the depths of winter she takes the roof down and cranks up the heating and drives around with the wind in her hair. Nadine can't see any point in owning a convertible if you only go topless for six weeks of the year.

And then there's the sign outside her studio, nailed

to the wall: NADINE KITE PHOTOGRAPHY. It gets her every time.

Her very own studio. She worked long and hard for it. Five years of underpaid and overworked assisting, first of all for a temperamental interiors photographer who called her *Nay*-deen even after three years, no matter how many times she told him it was *Nadd*-een and then for a wonderful, old page-three photographer called Sandy, who'd been her inspiration.

Nadine never expected to make a living from photographing half-naked women. She aspired, as most photography graduates do, to a much higher plane. Fashion, maybe, or portraiture. But she started doing freelance photography at around the same time that 'lads' magazines became big business and an ex-boyfriend who was a journalist on *Him* magazine at the time had recommended her for some still-life work. She'd built on that initial contact over the years and was now the magazine's most popular photographer, doing their main features and their cover shots. She'd found a niche for herself, a place where the rewards were high and the work enjoyable, a place she loved being. She got to meet Australian soap stars and TV presenters and DJs, and even the occasional Hollywood film star. She'd photographed everyone from Jeri Ryan to Danii Minogue to Denise van Outen, and she'd yet to work with a girl she hadn't liked.

Her subjects were always completely disarmed to meet Nadine. 'God,' they'd say, 'you don't look like a photographer.' And she doesn't suppose she does.

Nadine is in a particularly good mood for a Monday morning. She's already been to the gym for one of her thrice-weekly work-outs and it's left her feeling uncharacteristically energized and chirpy. The sun is shining and she's wearing a beautiful pink sequinned cardigan she picked up from a car-boot sale yesterday for a mere pound. One quid to make her feel like a million dollars. There's little in life as exhilarating and satisfying as a true bargain.

The scales at the gym this morning informed her that she'd finally got down to nine and a half stone, having hovered annoyingly around the ten stone mark since a gluttonous holiday in Disneyland six months earlier.

The bank statement that arrived in the morning's post informed her that her business has finally started to pay out after what had been a slow start.

And she's single again! She loves being single, she really does. And this time she's going to stay single for as long as it takes to find a decent bloke, not just give in at the first moment of insecurity or urge for a shag. This time she's going to do it properly, and this time she has a rather attractive financial carrot to make sure she does.

In the car park behind her studio Nadine clips up her soft top and attaches her Krooklok. She whistles under her breath as she approaches the front door and the big pink plastic sign with her name on it.

Nadine flicks on the kettle in the tiny kitchen and stretches out on her pink leather sofa to read her mail. It's going to be a quiet day today. For once. A meeting at the *Him* office in Shaftesbury Avenue to pick the shot for the February cover and lunch afterwards with the commissioning editor. She'll use the rest of the day to catch up on paperwork and have a bit of a tidy-up. And maybe start phoning around her girlfriends to see if anyone has a male friend she could borrow to win this bet with Dig.

She smiles to herself. She *is* going to win, there's no doubt about that. Nadine has a fierce competitive streak, especially when it comes to Dig. Maybe it has something to do with working in a man's world. Maybe it's the way her parents always compared her unfavourably to her little brother. Maybe it was spending two years at an all-boys school to do her A Levels. Who knows? But it's there, and it's got her where she is today. It's got her her flat and her car and a healthy bank balance. It's got her respect and status and a constant stream of high-quality commissions from some of the top magazines in the country.

And although she doesn't know it yet, it's just about to get her the prestigious Ruckham's Motor Oil calendar, a commission that will send her earning potential on a quite unbelievable trajectory, straight to the stars.

Mitchell Tuft, Ruckham's Brand Manager, asked her to bike over her portfolio last week. It was returned the same day with a blank compliment slip, and Nadine had assumed that was that.

But the phone has just rung and Mitchell Tuft is talking to her now, gushing forth about how much he loves her work, how fresh her style is and how he would like to offer her a month in the Polynesian Islands with some of the most beautiful women in the world and a pay-cheque big enough to mean that she could comfortably take the rest of the year off.

No nipples, states Nadine – that's her only rule, no nipples, says Mitchell Tuft.

It's time for an injection of new blood into the glamour-calendar scene. The same old photographers, he complains, year after year. It's a new millennium. It's time for a change. We'll give you a free hand, he says, we want

2001 to be as different and exciting as you can make it.

If she was interested, of course.

'Well, yes, Mitchell. Yes. I'd be honoured. Of course. Yes. I look forward to it very much. Thank you.' Nadine puts down the phone and takes a deep breath to calm her racing heart. '£40,000,' she whispers to herself, '£40,000. For four weeks' work. Jesus Christ.'

She silently congratulates herself, not for the first time, on deciding to work without an agent. And then she gets to her feet and starts screaming. 'Oh my God! Oh my God – I'm going to be *rich*!' She runs around her studio in circles. 'Rich! Rich! Rich! Totally bloody rolling in it!'

This is it. Her professional destiny. She's worked for so long without any real sense of where she's heading, just taking jobs as and when they're offered to her, but this is different – this feels right, somehow. Editorial work pays quite well, but calendars, that's where the real money is, and Ruckham's isn't any old calendar. It isn't like the tacky ones covered in tea-stains in mechanics' workshops. It's artistic and innovative. Some of the models even wear clothes.

Ruckham's. Jesus.

She has to tell Dig. Dig is always so impressed by Nadine's professional achievements and Nadine loves to impress him. She picks up the phone.

'Dig! Dig! Guess what?'

'Urm, Jenny McCarthy's breast implants have just exploded all over your Leica?'

'No no no.'

'You saw Gail Porter naked and she's got a knob?'

'Oh, don't be silly. Listen. I've got the Ruckham's calendar commission.'

70

'*Ruckham's!* Jesus! You're joking!'

'No. I'm serious. I'm going to be rich!'

'Sod rich,' says Dig, 'who cares about money? You're going to be sent off to some exotic paradise with twelve fantastic, incredible, stunning women. Oh man – can I come? I'll be the bikini valet. I'll be the baby-oil applicator. I'll do anything. Please, please, *please*, can I come?'

'Sounds like you already have.'

'When are you going?'

'Middle of January. Isn't that perfect? Could there be a better time to get out of England and go to Bora-Bora?'

'You're going to Bora-Bora! That's Polynesia, isn't it?'

'Uh-huh.'

'Shit, Deen. You're going to paradise. Do you realize that? And they're bound to put you up somewhere really swank, somewhere five star. I am so jealous.'

'I'll bring you back a stick of rock.'

'Thanks. A lot. Anyway. Look. We'll celebrate at the weekend, yeah? I'm just on my way out so I can't chat. I need your advice.'

'Fire ahead.'

'Restaurants. I need you to recommend me a restaurant.'

'What for?' Nadine wrinkles her nose in confusion. Dig doesn't go to restaurants.

Dig's voice is almost trembling with excitement. 'I asked her out.'

'Who?'

'Delilah, of course. I just phoned her and I asked her out.'

'What do you mean, asked her out?' Nadine's mouth has gone dry.

71

'I mean, I said, would you like to come out for dinner with me? And she said yes.'

'You're joking, right?' Nadine can feel bile rising unpleasantly at the back of her throat.

Dig appears not to have picked up on the sudden change of tone in Nadine's voice.

' . . . It's all just coming together, Deen, y'know? That girl on my birthday night, Katie, she was like my wake-up call. If I hadn't woken up in bed with her, I wouldn't have felt so shit. If I hadn't felt so shit, I wouldn't have suggested going for a walk in the park with you. And if I hadn't gone for a walk in the park with you, I'd never have bumped into Delilah and I wouldn't have asked her out and I wouldn't be feeling as fucking . . . *good* as I'm feeling right now. I mean, God – she's just *gorgeous*. Isn't she? Don't you think that she's actually *more* beautiful than she was when we were at school? . . . And nicer, too?'

Nadine feels her stomach constrict and her heart shrivel and is glad they're talking on the phone, otherwise Dig would be able to see the look in her eyes.

Delilah? How can he possibly fancy Delilah? She's stunningly beautiful, of course, but she's just not his type. She weighs more than five pounds for a start. She has breasts. She wears a bra. She's *taller* than him. She's nine months older than him. She has creases in the corners of her eyes. And she's *married*, for fuck's sake. What in God's name does he think he's playing at?

'Dig,' she hisses, petulantly, 'what are you expecting to actually *happen* with Delilah? She *is* still married, y'know.'

'Yes. I do realize that,' sniffs Dig, having finally picked up on Nadine's attitude. 'And I'm not expecting anything to *happen*. Well, not immediately. I just want to see her, that's all. You know, just be with her.'

'Well, in that case, might I suggest taking some *conversation cards* with you?'

'Eh?'

'You know. Delilah. She's not exactly the brightest girl in the world, is she? You might need some help.' She can almost feel her throat blistering with the acidity of the venom that is spewing forth from it, but she just can't help herself.

'That's a bit uncalled for, Deen.'

'I'm just saying, *Digby*, that Delilah was all well and good when you were teenagers, but she's not particularly your kind of girl nowadays, is she? I mean, she was fine for a first romance, you know, first love. But ultimately there's not much more to her than a pretty face, is there?' Oh dear God. She really hadn't meant to be like this – men found this sort of behaviour so *unbecoming* – but she's started now and she already knows there's no way she's going to be able to stop. ' . . . And if you think that this *date* qualifies for our bet you've got another think coming. This is not what I would call an attempt at a mature relationship. This is what I would call chasing around after an unattainable, unstable married woman who will never, ever make you happy in a million years, who is pre-programmed to fuck men over, who will break your heart into a thousand pieces and hand-feed them to her sodding dog!'

'Jesus, Deen. What the fuck's the matter with you? Getting your period, or something?'

'No, Digby. I'm not getting my period, I'm just . . . I just don't want to see you get hurt . . . I know how you feel about Delilah, how you *felt* about her, and I think

73

you've probably lost any sense of objectivity – I'm just trying to give you a *little objectivity*. That's all.'

'Well, thanks all the same, Nadine, but I don't need your *objectivity*. OK? Delilah's back in town. She's just left her husband and she doesn't know anyone . . .'

'Oh yes! And have you actually asked her yet, what she's doing here, why she's in London, why she's *abandoned* her husband? Have you? Don't you think there might be a bit more to it than just wanting to "catch up with old friends"? Has it occurred to you that she might just want some space right now, she might want some room, to sort her head out? The woman's just left her husband, for Christ's sake. She's been here for five minutes and you're already plaguing her with phone calls and asking her out on dates!'

'Jesus, Nadine! I just want to spend the evening with her. That's all. And she wants to spend the evening with me, too.'

'OK. Fine. But I think you'll find that it's a disappointment. Being with Delilah. After all these years. You won't have anything in common, you know. She's been living in the sticks for ten years, living a completely different life to us.'

'*That* might not be such a bad thing . . .'

' . . . She's not the same girl you knew at school, she's not the same cool chick. I'll bet she listens to Phil Collins, these days. And did you notice, the other day, she was wearing *pearl* earrings. I mean . . . that's positively middle-aged . . . she's probably got a *Barbour* hidden away somewhere, as well.'

'My God! What's the matter with you? You're basing your entire opinion of her on a pair of *earrings*? How shallow is that, Deen? Delilah's got class. She dresses

74

beautifully – that classic look really suits her. And by the way – I did not ask her out just to win this bet, but I have to say that I think it counts.'

'Forget it,' snaps Nadine. 'No way. Married women don't count.'

'Who said? Who said married women don't count? That wasn't in the rules.'

'Oh Jesus, Dig. Whatever. I really don't care any more. You go out on your stupid date with stupid Delilah and you have fun.'

'OK,' Dig says tersely, 'but what about restaurants? Where shall I take her?'

'What's wrong with the Bengal Lancer?'

'I can't take her there.'

'Why not?'

'Because – because she's Delilah, that's why. I want to take her somewhere special.'

'I'm sorry, Dig, I can't think of anywhere.'

'Fine,' Dig says angrily, 'just fine. I'll sort it out myself.' And then he hangs up, suddenly, leaving Nadine standing there in her studio, the barren receiver hanging limply from her hand and a film of tears forming rapidly over her eyes.

CHAPTER SEVEN

People come to London from all over the world to dip into its enormous wealth of diverse cuisines. There are Korean, Vietnamese, Turkish, Brazilian, Burmese and Havanese restaurants everywhere you look. There are restaurants with Michelin stars and infamous chefs, restaurants with views over the Thames and the whole of London, restaurants with live music and conveyor-belted sushi. You can sip minted Algerian tea from tiny coloured glasses or chew on the ribs of a large cow with a bib around your neck. You can eat ostrich in Chiswick and octopus in Shepherds Bush. You can, in fact, eat anything you want, wherever you want, whenever you want.

So why was the only restaurant that Dig could think of in the whole extraordinary culinary melting-pot of London the Bengal Lancer on Kentish Town Road?

The Bengal Lancer was his favourite restaurant, without a doubt. The proprietor, Archad, was friendly and welcoming, the naan bread was the fluffiest in all of London and, most importantly, they served until midnight. But come on – he couldn't take *Delilah Lillie* there for dinner, could he?

He'd finally called her at midday. Her phone number had sat next to his phone, burning a hole into his consciousness all morning, and he had hardly been able to contain himself. They'd had a nice little chat and he'd suggested Tuesday night, for dinner, and she'd said yes, just like that. She'd actually said, 'Yes, that would be lovely,' and then commented at least three more times during the conversation, how much she was looking forward to it.

And then something vaguely surreal had happened. He'd been half-way through a sentence when Delilah had suddenly interjected with, 'Oh my God, I have to go – the cats are holding Digby hostage in the corner – I think one of them's got a gun.'

Eh? 'Digby?'

'Yeah, my dog, Digby. I named him after you. Ha. Look. Phone me tomorrow. Let me know where to meet you, or whatever. OK?'

'Er, yeah,' Dig had said, losing his composure, 'OK.'

And then she'd gone. Hung up. Left him feeling . . . all . . . all . . . Digby? *Digby?* She'd named her dog *Digby?* Jesus. I mean, in one way, he supposed, it was flattering. She'd obviously remembered him, thought about him over the years. But . . . a dog? He felt emasculated. God, he hoped it was a big dog, a Rotty or a Ridgeback. He'd die, just die, if it was something small and yappy. He was discomfited by the image of this dog, *Digby*, being held hostage by a few cats. He was obviously some kind of a wimp, a poofter dog.

It had taken Dig a while to get over the fact that Delilah had named her dog after him, before he started feeling his usual chirpy self again. It's a compliment, he'd persuaded himself, I'll bet she loves her dog more than anything, take it as a compliment.

And then he'd started feeling excited, incredibly excited. This was all just amazing, the timing, the coincidence. Within minutes of his conversation with Nadine

77

in the café on Saturday, within minutes of making that bet with her, a bet which, in reality, neither of them had any intention of or capacity for honouring, who should stumble so fortuitously into his path but the only thirty-year-old woman on the face of the earth who he could ever seriously contemplate being with. Delilah Lillie. The Love of His Life. The One Who Got Away. It was like a . . . sign, like a message from God. Not only did he get to spend an evening with a woman who wouldn't look out of place on the cover of *Marie-Claire*, but he also got a hundred quid. Result.

Delilah could have let him down, been a disappointment after all these years. She could have been fat, or old-looking, or happily married with loads of children. She could've been rude or stand offish. But she wasn't – she was even better looking than he remembered, she was obviously unhappily married, had no children and was actually much nicer than she'd ever been when they were together – brighter, breezier, friendlier and easier to get on with.

'You choose,' she'd said, when Dig asked her where she fancied eating, 'you know London better than me. I haven't got a clue where's good these days.' Which was funny really, because neither had Dig.

And then Nadine had phoned with her incredible news about the Ruckham's calendar – jammy cow, she *always* landed on her feet – and he'd tried asking her for a recommendation for a good restaurant: she was a walking *Time Out Food Guide*. And now he really wished he hadn't. She'd been *awful*. Really bitchy and unpleasant, not like her usual self, at all. God knows what was the matter with her. She'd just been given the best news of her career – *£40,000*! What Dig could do with £40,000 – and she seemed just miserable. It seemed like she had something against Delilah, for some strange reason. It made no sense to Dig, no sense at all.

So he was now desperately scanning the food pages of the *Evening Standard* hoping that good old Fay Maschler would provide him with some little gem of inspiration, some wonderful Moroccan place just up the road from him that he'd never realized existed, twinkling with stained glass and brass filigree, scented with cumin and rose-water and only about fifteen pounds a head.

But no. Not today. Today she was reviewing some stark Modern European place, in *Victoria* of all places, that looked cold and echoey and was, anyway, horribly expensive, and a new restaurant in Mayfair that was the latest offering from one of those infamous Michelin-starred very *loud* chef-types. So that was out of the question – outrageously overpriced and you'd probably have had to have booked it back in January or something to secure a table.

Just as he was losing hope of ever finding somewhere to take Delilah, Nick Jeffries, PR Superstar and general wanker, wandered into Dig's office. Not that you could really call it 'his office', as such – Johnny-Boy Records was very lateral and non-hierarchical and flat-structured and all those other things that it was so fashionable for offices to be these days – it was more of an alcove, really.

Nick knew Meg Mathews. He knew everyone. He was always hanging out in hotel bars in the centre of town where models drank things with cranberry juice and where Madonna had been seen. (Was there anywhere left in London, apart from Dig's flat, where Madonna *hadn't* been seen?) He knew other people, too, like trendy novelists and conceptual artists and DJs and stylists. He would know about things like restaurants. He was bound to know a cool place that Dig could take Delilah.

'Where can I take a girl, tomorrow night, dinner, not too expensive, not too spicy, not too far away?'

'What sort of girl?'

'Sort of girl I've been in love with since I was fourteen who looks like a goddess.' Nick had a low boredom threshold so any attempts at conversation had to be succinct and to the point.

'Hmmmm' – Nick scratched at his bumfluff and perched his skinny, combats-clad butt on the edge of Dig's table – 'she in love with you?'

'She was. Not any more. Least, I don't think she is.'

'You still in love with her?'

'Don't know. Might be.'

'Hmmmm.'

'I was thinking Moroccan.'

'Yeah . . . Momo. Heddon Street. Not what it was, but you could probably get a table.'

'Expensive?'

'Yeah. Right. Got ya. What about sushi?'

'Nah. She's been living in the country. She won't want raw fish.'

'Got it.' Nick clicked his fingers, reached across Dig, grabbed his phone and began punching in numbers.

PR people always did this, Dig had noticed, brought third parties into conversations via the phone. They always had someone else's phone number on the tips of their fingers and they always used it.

'Freddie,' Nick was saying to him, 'mate of mine. Just opened a place in . . . oh, yeah, hi, Freddie. Nick. Listen. You got a table free tomorrow night? Two people? Great.

Dig. Thanks, mate. Take care. You too. Tomorrow. All sorted.' Dig started as he realized that Nick had put the phone down and was now talking to him again. 'Eight o'clock. Exmouth Market. It's called *ex*. He'll give you a good table. He'll give you a good night. Don't worry. She'll *love* it,' he said with a wink and a minimal grin.

'Yeah, but what sort of food is it?' asked Dig nervously. Nick didn't like too many questions.

'God, I dunno. Meat. Or something. It's a meat place.'

And then he was gone. Leaving Dig with a hundred unanswered questions, like, where in Exmouth Market? What sort of meat? How much? What sort of atmosphere? *ex* sounded a bit poncey, not much like his kind of place. But . . . oh well . . . it was more than he'd been able to come up with, wasn't it? And it was bound to be trendy, and at least Delilah would be able to tell people that she'd been to some new place in Clerkenwell, before anyone else, while it was still hot. Yeah. He'd go. He'd take Delilah to *ex*.

It couldn't be that bad, could it?

CHAPTER EIGHT

It is.

That bad.

Jesus. Look at this place. Dig isn't actually sure whether they've even finished building it yet. Or is it supposed to look like this?

A pale Spanish girl with red lipstick has just led them to their table. It's an incredibly big table, stretching almost the entire length and width of the small concrete room. It's fashioned from one seamless piece of oak, limewashed and varnished to a glassy finish and must have cost a small fortune. It is laid with immense white china plates and chunky tumblers. It is also the only table in the room. There is a large chandelier overhanging the table constructed from what look like – sun-bleached bones? Extremely *long* sun-bleached bones. The shades covering the unpleasantly high-voltage bulbs appear to be pterodactyl eggshells, fissured all over with small cracks. Very *Jurassic Park*. Very bright. Very weird.

They are seated next to each other (thankfully – Dig had imagined for one worrying moment that they were going to be seated at opposite ends of this huge table, smiling regretfully at each other all night) somewhere near the middle of the table.

'So,' says Dig to the translucent Spanish girl as she helps him slide his pony-skin-clad chair towards the table, 'expecting a busy night tonight?'

'This is only our first week, you know?' she replies somewhat defensively, having obviously read sarcasm into Dig's innocent question. 'First week is always quiet.'

'Yeah. Of course.' Dig smiles nervously. 'Of course it is.'

She disappears then and Dig turns towards Delilah who is examining her cutlery with fascination. The fork is designed to look like a bird's leg, all gnarled and knobbly with talons for tines. The knife looks like some kind of feather thing, with vicious serrations, and the spoon is an egg, on the end of a twig. Delilah grimaces at Dig and puts them back down on the table. 'Weird,' she mouths, silently. Dig couldn't agree more.

There is no atmosphere in the place. Not one drop of it. Nothing even vaguely resembling an atmosphere is present here, in any form. Dig is suddenly blinded by the extent of his own stupidity to ever have taken a recommendation from Nick. I mean, *honestly*. He should have known Nick wouldn't have been thinking about what was best for him, for Dig, he'd just have been thinking how cool it was that he had one mate who needed customers for his new restaurant and another mate who needed somewhere to eat and how cool it was that he'd managed to put the two of them together. It would have given him a great sense of satisfaction. What the hell would Nick heart-of-an-anaconda Jeffries know about romance, about an atmosphere conducive to *conversation*, for God's sake? Nick didn't have conversations; he had public relations . . .

Still, thinks Dig, may as well make the most of it, the most of being alone in a room with Delilah Lillie. He turns to her and grins. 'So,' he says, looking around at their strangely unsettling surroundings, 'here's a bit of hip and happening London for you.'

'Looks more like Jeffrey Dahmer's basement to me,' whispers Delilah, and Dig sniggers, thinking that he's never heard Delilah crack a joke before.

He would love to launch into a conversation now – there's so much to talk about, so many questions to ask – but he can't because this place has an echo, and that Spanish girl is just standing there staring into space, and how the hell can you start having a deeply personal and intimate conversation when there's a bunch of old bones looming over your head and thirty empty places at your table and no music, anyway?

Dig has already explained to Delilah that he has no idea what the food is like at this place but that he has been told it has a meat 'bias'. Luckily for him, Delilah hasn't turned vegetarian in the years since school and sounded very pleased at the prospect. 'Great,' she said, 'I love meat.'

The way she said the word 'meat' raised a sweat on Dig's neck. 'Good,' he'd managed to squeak, 'that's good.'

Dig wishes they had a menu or a wine list or something that he could look at, something to do. He smiles hopefully at the waitress, who immediately snaps out of her reverie and almost runs towards them. 'Yes?' she demands, defensively again, obviously preparing for a complaint of some kind.

'Er – I wondered if we could maybe have a look at a wine list, maybe? And a menu? If possible. Thank you.' He grins, apprehensively, hoping she won't take his request the wrong way.

She positively *beams* at them then. Her mouth splits open from ear to ear, revealing a large set of intensely white teeth adorned with a small smudge of her lipstick. And then she shakes her head. Still smiling, she says, 'No.'

Dig decides he must have misheard her. 'Sorry,' he says, returning her wide smile.

'No menus. You are *at home* tonight. You understand?'

Dig and Delilah shake their heads slowly.

'*ex* is *our home*. You,' she points at them, 'are *our guests*. Chef is *your host*. This . . .' – she indicates the table – 'is *our dinner table*. This is like dinner party. You see?'

Dig and Delilah nod slowly.

'So. Chef has prepared one meal, four courses, for *his guests* and our *sommelier* will give you wine which will complement the food of the chef. And you will eat and you will drink and then, you will pay!' She has brightened considerably by this point. 'It is *brilliant* new concept!' she trills. 'So. You are comfortable?'

They nod again, and she smiles again. '*Sommelier* will be with you soon,' she says, before walking to the counter and going back into a trance.

Dig and Delilah exchange looks and shrug. Dig is imagining how pissed off she must be about him bringing her here and is just about to embark upon a nervous apology, try and explain about Nick and how this wasn't really his idea, and how they could leave if she wanted and how dreadful he is to have dragged her all the way out here to this awful *communist*-style place where their basic right to freedom of choice is being withheld, when he suddenly realizes that she's smiling.

'Damn,' she says, theatrically, 'I feel so rude. I should have brought our *host* a box of Black Magic.' Delilah begins giggling like a naughty kid.

85

Dig is confused for a second and then realizes with wonder that Delilah has cracked another joke. He sniggers and joins in. 'Wonder where they've taken our coats? D'you reckon they've put them on a *bed* upstairs?'

Delilah giggles even more and then pulls a serious face and pretends to get up from her seat. 'Just going to see if he needs a hand in the kitchen,' she says, before laughing uncontrollably and collapsing back into her chair.

'Here,' says Dig, leaning in to Delilah's ear, 'I hope we're getting Viennetta for pudding.'

They both dissolve into helpless laughter then, and the ice, it seems, is well and truly broken. Delilah Lillie, *circa* 1999, has a sense of humour! The Spanish girl finally has the sense to put some music on, lifting the atmosphere an iota above 'morgue', and Dig turns to Delilah, breathes in a lungful of her beauty and holds it inside, next to his heart, which is close to bursting with joy.

CHAPTER NINE

Nadine slouches on her cracked-brown-leather Deco sofa in her marabou-trimmed fifties-starlet negligé and her Bart Simpson slippers, sipping Cadbury's Highlights from one of her *South Park* mugs and trying desperately *not* to think about what might be happening with Dig and Delilah tonight. She's failing miserably.

She looks at the time display on her video: 12.20. Which means that it's actually 9.45 p.m. Because that display's been wrong since 1994.

9.45 p.m. They're probably eating pudding by now. Nadine's mind fills up with images of Dig spoon-feeding strawberries into Delilah's soft, red welcoming mouth and laughing as a pink trickle of juice dribbles seductively down her chin. She imagines him in his new Jigsaw Menswear jumper, the camel cashmere one with the V-neck which she helped him choose and which he looks so cuddly in, and his big leather coat which makes him look chunkier than he is. It's his best outfit of the moment, his special-occasion outfit, and he's bound to be wearing it tonight. He'd have made an extra-special effort tonight, polished his teeth, perfumed his neck, deodorized his trainers, combed his eyebrow, shined his hair. She knows what he's like.

Nadine feels awful. She still can't get over the way she behaved yesterday on the phone to Dig. She still can't believe that she's fallen out with him, that he hung up on her, that they argued. It's all so out of character. What must Dig be thinking? she wonders. What must he be thinking of me? Nadine has always been his equal, someone he credits with a good, orderly, *male* rationale, someone he holds in high esteem in terms of her lack of what he sees as overtly female traits such as bitchiness, gossip-mongering, excessive vanity and general cloying girliness. He's always told her that she has just the right balance of oestrogen and testosterone, but for a few awful, poisonous moments she'd let her oestrogen wear the trousers and she'd been bitchy and catty and out of control.

Nadine wishes that life was like a word processor, complete with Undo and Delete buttons. She wishes that the entire phone call could be erased from both their memories.

As it is, the whole scenario is now festering away in her sub-and-not-so-subconscious like a sweaty sardine. Dig, she hopes, has by now put the episode down to some momentary hormonal aberration and forgotten all about it in his excitement about seeing Delilah – men don't tend to dwell too much on things of this nature. But the more she thinks about it, the more her general sense of gloom and despair deepens and the more she hates herself.

She is also hurt by what she, neurotically maybe, sees as the implicit assertion in Dig's comments that he doesn't like the way she dresses. 'Delilah's got class,' he'd said. 'She dresses beautifully.' What is that supposed to mean? Is that what Dig really wants? A classy woman? Someone who buys tailored suits from Escada? Who wears navy pumps and gold jewellery? Who has expensive highlights and pearl earrings? Nadine has always seen him with someone more interesting than that, someone with a bit more character, a bit more *style*. Someone a bit more like herself, quite frankly.

Nadine realizes that her own sense of style is maybe a bit . . . challenging, for some people's tastes. She's used to comments from cabbies and bus drivers and even from boyfriends, some of whom have been embarrassed by her appearance.

As far as men are concerned, women's clothes are a form of language, and they fall into two categories: clothes that they *can* understand and clothes they *can't*. These categories have nothing to do with fashionability. Women's clothes are meant either tantalizingly to camouflage their sexuality or brashly celebrate it. Anything else may as well be a foreign language.

Nadine knows that most men find her wardrobe as easy to understand as an ancient Flemish dialect. For a start, they don't understand why anyone who earns as much as she does would want to wear second-hand clothes or sew things herself.

Women, on the other hand, tend to appreciate the innate sense of style with which she puts the disparate elements of her wardrobe together so that they form one definitive and pleasing look. They appreciate the charm and craftsmanship of some of her unusual pieces of vintage clothing and they love the old-fashioned femininity of the fact that Nadine gets dressed up every day of her life, providing the glamour that's missing from their own lives. They like the fact that she does things with her hair when they can't find the time or the inclination to bother with their own. 'You're so brave,' they say. 'I'd love to have the nerve to wear things like that.'

Nadine has always assumed that Dig approves of her

dress sense, maybe even *admires* it. She's always assumed that he isn't like other men – that he *understands* the language of her dress. But now it seems that he finds it as alien as every other man.

And then there's her flat. It's the flat of a mad woman. Look at it. Miffy the Rabbit wallpaper and princess telephone. Flashing-neon Elvis mirror and flamenco-dancing lampstand. Leopardskin and zebra-print fake-fur cushions. Cocktail cabinet. Clarice Cliffe tea-set. Cactus fairy lights. Stuffed toys. Tack, memorabilia and other people's junk. It's mayhem in here, but somehow it works. They did a feature on her flat once in the *Observer* magazine. It's a great flat – everyone who sees it loves it – but if she lives alone for much longer it will go *too far* and she will probably start collecting newspapers and dead pigeons and carrier bags full of old men's shoes. They will have to break down her door when someone finally notices that she hasn't been seen for a few months, and they'll find her buried beneath an avalanche of back issues of *OK* magazine and weird second-hand clothes and empty fag packets. 'Poor old thing,' they'll say, 'she had a lonely life. But at least she had her junk to keep her company.'

Oh God. Nadine is about to have a crisis.

She puts on her negligé tonight with a sense of self-loathing. She is a hateful, gruesome, badly dressed, batty old bitch and she wants to look the part. She is tempted to rub some black eyeliner under her eyes and smudge her lipstick, drink a whole bottle of gin and start shouting at herself. She wants to be Bette Davis in *Whatever Happened to Baby Jane?* Faye Dunaway in *Mommie Dearest* and Elizabeth Taylor in *Who's Afraid of Virginia Woolf?* all rolled into one.

She wishes she had some curly-haired little lap-dog with a ribbon in its hair, and a Southern drawl to complete the picture. She wants to sit here all night, wallowing in her own misery and hatefulness and imagining Delilah in her 'classy' clothes and her expensive earrings and her huge solitaire diamond engagement ring, looking elegant and refined in some posh restaurant with lovely Dig, *her Dig*, wearing all his best clothes and being on his best behaviour, and making him fall in love with her all over again.

He can't. He *can't* fall in love with someone else. He just can't.

Where would that leave her?

Hot tears begin cascading down Nadine's cheeks. She's spiralling into a frenzied hysteria. A few days ago she was sane and normal. A few days ago she had a handsome boyfriend and a great life. A few days ago she was a free-living, happy girl with a brilliant job and a wonderful flat and a best mate who meant the world to her. Now she is a miserable, bitter and twisted old spinster with poison in her bloodstream and bad taste in clothes. She has fallen out with her best friend and fallen out with herself and she is once again the awkward, shy and frizzy-haired girl of her dim and distant youth.

And all because of Delilah-fucking-bloody-Lillie.

Nadine tips a cigarette from the pack on the coffee-table with the baby-blue-painted toenails of one foot and transfers it to her mouth. The cigarette falls to one side of her lips and hangs there, sluttishly.

She lets it.

CHAPTER TEN

Half an hour after their arrival at the painful *ex* Dig and Delilah have relocated to an Indian restaurant a few doors down the road. The mausoleum atmosphere they could just about handle, the lack of choice they could have lived with, the empty table was not too much of a problem and the strange waitress was almost endearing.

But when she'd approached them bearing two steaming bowls of slightly grey soup, all afloat with what looked like bits of brain tissue, and told them that it was *menudo*, a very famous Spanish soup made with tripe, and then hastened to assure them after registering their apprehension that it was made using only the best tripe, the honeycomb tripe from the animal's second stomach chamber, and that chef was the most renowned offal chef currently working in London – didn't they know? Isn't that why they'd come? – they'd decided to cut their losses and run.

She'd tried to persuade them to stay and then the chef had emerged from the kitchen looking horribly anxious and tried to tempt them with descriptions of the high-quality baby-calf sweetbreads he employed in his famous Veal Soufflé, the glutinous succulence of his Twice-Cooked Smoked Pig-Foot Stew, and the wonderfully coarse texture of his signature Corned Tongue Hash. He knew, he pleaded with them, that most people were scared of offal, but that if they were only to try these things once in their lives, then it should be here, tonight, now. Please . . .

Dig liked to think of himself as an adventurous eater, but he was happy to be a coward on this occasion. So the two of them had collected their coats, apologized profusely to the waitress and the chef and spilled gratefully on to the pavement outside the restaurant, grimacing and laughing at each other as they contemplated their lucky escape.

In the Indian they chatted away over a pile of poppadams and a particularly good selection of chutneys. Dig was thoroughly enjoying himself. It was so long since he'd done this – taken a woman out to dinner, *conversed* with someone he didn't see every week of his life. He was so used to the young girls he met and slept with and went to parties and bars with, talking crap and messing about and playing the big man. This was different. This was serious. This was special.

'God . . . you know, Alex would have *loved* that place,' Delilah was saying, in her strange new voice, all Benson & Hedges and Bombay Sapphire, polo matches and shopping trips to New York. 'He loves offal – all those horrid bits – kidneys and livers and brains and things. Thank God he can get all that sort of stuff cooked for him at his restaurants, otherwise I'd be expected to do it.'

It was strange for Dig to hear Delilah talking like this, using words like 'horrid'. Delilah had customized her Kentish Town accent with new bits and pieces of pronunciation and intonation, accent and inflection picked up from her time mixing in another society, far removed from her own. Her voice had retained its gravelly hoarseness and some of its lost ends of words but had also acquired a polished sparkle and a soft northern lilt. She sounded unbelievably sexy.

'Thanks for tonight,' she said. 'I really appreciate it.'

'Oh – God – it's nothing. Sorry it's all been such a disaster.'

'Not at all – it's been great. And so good to see you. It's hard to know what to expect when you haven't seen people for so long – whether you'll still have anything in common or not. I've thought about you so often over the years, wondered what you were up to, where you were.'

'Oh yeah?' began Dig in trepidation. 'I thought about you, too. Wondered about you.'

'Really!' smiled Delilah. 'And what exactly did you wonder?'

'Well,' he said, seriously, 'I suppose, really, I worried, more than wondered. I was worried about you.'

The smile fell from Delilah's face. She fiddled awkwardly with her napkin and deftly changed the subject. 'You know,' she said, 'I think I could probably have guessed that this is what your life would be like now. Music biz. Still living in the area, not too far from your mum, eh?' She smiled wickedly. 'And I think I could have guessed that you wouldn't have settled down yet. You always used to say that you didn't want kids till you were forty, till you owned your own record label – d'you remember?'

Dig smiled wryly. 'Yeah, I did say that, didn't I? I was going to be a millionaire and we were going to go off and live on a tropical island somewhere. I was going to be the next Richard Branson.'

'Oh yes,' she laughed, 'you were, weren't you? I was going to sit on the beach all day drinking cocktails and

94

waiting for you to return from your yachting trip. How hysterical!' Her laughter turned into a nostalgic smile and she looked into Dig's eyes, suddenly serious. 'God, we were great together, weren't we? Invincible. Dig and Delilah! We thought we could do anything. We thought we'd change the world one day. It's funny, when I first started at the Holy T, there were all these good-looking boys hanging around me all the time, Rob Dennis, Mark Barr, Tony whatsisname, all the fifth-formers, but I used to see you and Nadine wandering about together, always studying and looking so serious and so full of secrets. You had all that weird hair and knew so much about music, and Nadine had her big ginger quiff and holey jumpers and the two of you looked *so cool*. I was so jealous of you two. I wanted to be like you. I worshipped the ground you walked on . . .'

Dig choked on a fragment of poppadam. How had his life changed so dramatically? How come when he was a spotty fourteen-year-old geek he'd had women like Delilah 'worshipping the ground he walked on', and now he was reduced to chasing around after teenage girls like some pathetic middle-aged man?

'I remember our first date. I was so nervous, but you were so nice to me. You listened to me. I wasn't used to that in those days. You gave me so much confidence in myself . . . you shaped my life in a funny kind of way. I wouldn't be the person I am today if it wasn't for you. Isn't that weird?'

Dig nodded. It *was* weird. It was very weird. He'd never really thought about it before, but it was true. Parents expended so much energy worrying about the effect that their own actions and decisions would have on the development of their offspring when it seemed that your

95

character was determined, on the whole, by your peers. It was friends who formed you: your first mate, your first girlfriend, your first party, your first day at school, your experiences away from home. Personalities, on the whole, were formed in the playground.

Delilah, Dig suddenly realized, was an enormous part of him.

Getting the most beautiful girl in the school, the girl everyone wanted, and feeling the jealousy and respect of every boy around him had filled him with an unshakeable confidence in his ability to attract women, despite not being conventionally attractive. If it hadn't been for Delilah, he would have probably left school with his virginity intact and ended up marrying the first girl who'd let him sleep with her just in case no one else ever let him again. He still had that confidence all these years later, and he owed it to Delilah.

'So,' he said, nervously, 'tell me about Alex.'

Delilah looked slightly surprised. 'What do you mean?'

'Well, I don't know. What's he like? How did you meet him? What went wrong? That kind of thing. Unless . . . you don't want to . . .'

Delilah shook her head affirmatively. 'No,' she said, 'it's OK. It's fine.' She took a deep breath, and a warm smile spread across her face. 'I met him on Primrose Hill. He was a business studies student. I was . . . I fell over. He picked me up and took me to Casualty.'

'Were you hurt?'

'No – well, not really – just a cut, some stitches. It was nothing.'

'When was this?'

'Not long after you and I split up. I was eighteen. He

96

was twenty-two. And so tall and so handsome. Here – look.' She grinned and began poking around in her handbag. She pulled out her purse and took a photo from it. 'This is Alex.'

Dig took the photo from her fingers and studied it. A black-haired man wearing a DJ and bow-tie. He looked like Pierce Brosnan. God. Dig gulped and handed it back.

Delilah slid it back into her purse and continued. 'Even though we were so different and came from such completely different backgrounds, we connected immediately. He was so strong and so together. Exactly what I needed.'

Dig felt the expression of interest freeze on to his features.

'Things were really tough for me around that time, and he became my best friend. There was no romance. But then he graduated and his father offered to set him up in business back in Cheshire, gave him the premises for his first restaurant.'

'So you went to live with him?'

'Not immediately. I had things to sort out down here. But we kept in touch and when his restaurant opened he offered me a job and a room above.'

'And what was that like?'

Delilah shrugged. 'Weird,' she said, 'I'd never been out of London before that, and I'd never really worked. I was incredibly lonely and it was really hard work. I nearly came home, but there was nothing to come back to and I couldn't let Alex down. So I stuck it out. And besides, I think I'd already fallen in love with him by then.'

'So, what er . . . what was the *arrangement* then, with you and Alex?'

'What? You mean sleeping-wise?'

Dig nodded. A rude question, he knew, but he just couldn't help it.

'Well, there wasn't one. We were just friends and colleagues. He was my boss. Until my twentieth birthday, that is.' She smiled warmly at what was obviously a treasured memory. 'It was so unexpected. I'd started to worry that I was just a pet project to Alex, a little urchin he'd picked up off the streets of London who'd scrubbed up nicely and kept him company. You know, some sort of *Pygmalion* scenario. There was never any indication that he had any sort of *amorous* feelings towards me. But on that night, my birthday, Alex had arranged a big dinner for me at the restaurant, all my favourite foods, candles, music, presents. He made a real fuss. And then he started saying things like how much he loved having me around, how I'd improved the quality of his life, how just knowing that I was there in my little room above the restaurant made him sleep easier. He said I was his "missing half", that he couldn't imagine his life without me.

'And then he got down on one knee and pulled out a little box with this' – she pointed at the rock on her finger – 'in it. And he asked me to marry him!'

'And you said yes?'

'On the spot. There and then. The minute he said it – "Will you marry me?" – I just knew that it was the right thing to do. It was perfect.'

'So. When did you, er . . . you know? You and Alex. When did you first . . .?'

'Sleep together? Oh, our wedding night. Not until our wedding night, believe it or not!'

Dig tried to look unfazed. 'And . . . how was that?'

'What – you mean – ?'

'No . . . no. I mean. Not in detail. Just generally. Waiting until your wedding night. Was it a mistake? Was it OK?'

Delilah smiled tightly and screwed up her napkin between her hands. 'Well, you know,' she said, 'the first time's never anything to write letters home about really, is it? And I, well, let's put it this way, sex isn't really a priority for me these days.' She laughed. Dig felt slightly shocked. 'You look shocked,' she smiled. 'Don't be. I'm just not a very sexual person any more. I am working on it, mind you, but right now – well . . . it's just something that has to be done.'

'Do you . . . well, do you still sleep together?' Dig was embarrassed asking Delilah about her personal life, but the picture she was painting of herself as an asexual loner just didn't fit in with his memories of her.

Delilah laughed, ironically. 'High days and holidays,' she said.

'Eh?'

'Special occasions. We sleep together on special occasions. Anniversaries, birthdays, that kind of thing.'

'And that's enough for you?!'

Delilah raised her eyebrows. '*More* than enough!'

'And Alex?'

'Oh. Alex doesn't mind. He'd much rather be working, or playing golf.'

They fell silent again. Dig didn't know what to say. What a waste. What an absolutely shocking waste of a beautiful woman in the prime of her sexuality. How could any man possibly share a bed with Delilah Lillie and not want to shag her senseless every night? This Alex character must be a raving shirt-lifter. It was the only explanation. Either that or he was shagging one of his waitresses on the sly.

'And you left him?'

'Hmm,' Delilah said, her face falling, 'I suppose I did.'

Dig composed himself to ask her the burning question. 'Why?'

For the first time in the conversation Delilah's body language closed in on itself and she became awkward. 'I'd rather not say,' she squirmed. 'It's er . . . it's rather personal.'

'OK. OK. No problem. But can I ask you just one more question?'

Delilah nodded cautiously.

'Are you back for good? This thing with Alex, is it over? Or what?' He looked straight into Delilah's eyes, hoping his gaze didn't betray the urgency inside, and then looked away again. 'I mean, are you staying?' Oh God, Delilah, he thought, please say you're staying, *please say you're staying.*

Delilah stiffened slightly and cleared her throat. 'Haven't quite decided about that yet,' she said, 'not quite sure.'

'Oh,' sighed Dig, 'right.'

'I've, er . . . I've got some stuff to deal with in London, stuff I need to do to sort my head out. It all depends, really, on how that all works out, you know.'

'Oh yeah,' said Dig, 'what sort of stuff?'

Delilah looked awkward again and was silent for a moment. Eventually she looked at him. 'Oh, you know. Emotional stuff.' Her eyes opened wide as she said the word 'emotional' and she smiled wryly.

She was being very cagey and Dig didn't know how to handle the conversation. It was obviously making her

100

feel very uncomfortable and the last thing he wanted to do was make her uncomfortable. He would let it go – for now, anyway.

'So,' she said brightly, unselfconsciously changing the subject, 'what about you? How's *your* love life?'

'Well,' he smiled, 'existent. Active. But far from perfect.'

'Girlfriend?'

'Oh no,' he interjected briskly, 'I haven't got one of *those*,' as if she'd just said 'Mouldy toothbrush?' or 'Incontinent guinea-pig?' or something.

'Anyone special since . . . since . . . well, you know?'

'What – you mean since we split up?'

'Yeah.'

'No,' he answered. 'No. No one.' And then he laughed ironically as the sadness of this fact hit him.

'You're joking! No one special in ten years? How come?'

He shrugged, blew out a lungful of breath. 'I dunno,' he said, 'I just really haven't wanted anything like that from anyone, haven't needed it.'

'I find that surprising,' she said, 'I always thought you were the one-woman-man type.'

'Well, I guess I used to be' – he smiled, stubbed out his cigarette – 'when there was . . . just the one woman, if you see what I mean. But these days – I dunno – there just doesn't seem to be anyone else special out there and life's too short to mess around with people who aren't special. It's like, take Nadine. She drives me insane. Beautiful girl and everything – bright, funny, intelligent, talented and just all-round lovely person, but she keeps on getting involved with men who are – I don't know – just, unworthy of her. Underdogs. She always goes for

Learning Zone
City of Westminster College
North Wharf Road
London   W2 1LF

the underdogs. She feels sorry for them and she gets involved with them, you know, gives them the key to her life – oh, do come in, make yourself at home, put your feet up, these are my parents, this is my social life, these are my closest friends, stay the night, stay for breakfast, here's a spare door key for you. And then two, three months later it's all over because she's finally realized that she doesn't want to spend any more time with a loser, she wants her life back, and then it all gets really messy and unpleasant. That's why I think it's safer just to stay uninvolved, so I go for the, er, younger woman, mainly, these days . . .'

Dig trailed off as he realized that Delilah probably wouldn't be too impressed by this admission, but she didn't seem to notice, as she leaned in towards him then and said, 'D'you mind if I ask you something, something personal?'

Dig bristled pleasantly and nodded. 'Please,' he said, 'be my guest.'

Delilah spooned a little yoghurt and mint on to her poppadam, popped it into her mouth and began crunching. She was flapping the spoon up and down in rhythm with her chewing, indicating her intention to start talking the moment she'd swallowed. Dig sat transfixed, watching her succulent lips in motion. Finally, she swallowed, took a slurp of water and looked Dig straight in the eye.

'What's the deal with you and Nadine?'

'Eh?'

'I mean, what's going on between you two? Are you sleeping together?'

Dig choked. 'I'm sorry,' he spluttered, 'me and Nadine? What on earth made you suggest that?'

'Oh,' she replied, picking bits of coriander-flecked tomato out of the relish and chewing on them, 'just a vibe I picked up on, that's all.'

'What do you mean?'

'Well. When I bumped into you. In the park. At first I just . . . assumed that you were together, you know, a couple. You looked like a couple. And then when we were in the coffee-shop and you and I were chatting. I'd worked out by then that you weren't together, that you were just mates, but Nadine seemed . . . she was very *prickly*, almost like she was sulking. And I got the feeling that I was treading on her toes – that she didn't want me around? And I couldn't work out why. I mean, we were never exactly great friends at school or anything, but that was so long ago, it couldn't be that, so all I could think of was that something had happened between you two, some other time, that she saw me as some kind of *threat*. For whatever reason. I mean, tell me if you think I'm being ridiculous or nosy or anything.'

'Well. No. Nothing. Nothing's ever happened between me and Deen. Well, not really.' Dig was rubbing his chin and beginning to feel very uncomfortable. 'It's always been just a friendship, pretty much.'

'Look. I'm sorry. I shouldn't have said anything. It's none of my business.'

'No. But you're right. Sort of. Nadine *has* been behaving very strangely lately.' He told Delilah how aggressive Nadine had been that morning on the phone.

'And she's never behaved like this before now?'

'Never. That's the great thing about Nadine. I've always known what makes her tick, I've always *understood* her.'

'Anything happened in her private life? Man troubles? Family troubles?'

'Well, she's just finished with *yet another* unsuitable underdog boyfriend. But I don't think it's that. I think she's happy about that. And she's just been offered the most fantastic job imaginable – loads of money and a month in paradise. She should be really happy.'

'Well,' said Delilah, moving out of the way to make room for their waiter to unload his trolley of steaming food, 'she doesn't seem happy. She doesn't seem *at all* happy. And she's got a real problem with me. That's why I left the coffee-shop in such a hurry – I was getting such bad vibes off Nadine. She was making me feel really uncomfortable.' She dipped her spoon into a dish of emerald-green spinach, flecked with creamy cubes of paneer cheese, and then flashed Dig an intense gaze. She took a deep breath.

'Have you ever considered the possibility that she might be in love with you?'

Dig's eyebrow shot off the top of his forehead. He snorted derisively. 'Nadine? Don't be daft! She wouldn't be in love with me if I was the last bloke on earth! She's my mate, that's all.'

'I wouldn't be quite so sure about that.'

'You don't know Nadine. There's no way, just no way, that she would *ever* feel that way about me. It's *unthinkable*. It's ridiculous! It's – it's – '

'True?' offered Delilah, raising an eyebrow at him.

'No! No! You've got it all wrong. You don't know Nadine the way I do. Nadine doesn't *do* love. All Nadine wants is a huge man with a small ego who she can boss around and then dump when she gets bored with him. She's the most independent person I've ever known. I don't think Nadine's *capable* of being in love, with anyone. Let alone with me.'

'Women know about these things, you know?'

'Yeah. I know. Female intuition. But I know Nadine and I know that what you're saying is laughable. I mean, I'm sorry, but it is.'

'Right. Well. Whatever, Dig. But I've been right about these things before. And *I* think that girl is in love with you. I can see it in her eyes.' She laughed wryly. 'And I can see in her eyes that she wishes I'd never come back on the scene.'

'No – that's not true.'

'Oh it is. She sees me as competition.'

Dig had to bite his lip to stop himself blurting out that in his opinion Nadine *did* see Delilah as competition but only in terms of losing this stupid bet. Nadine just couldn't bear to lose. At anything.

'And tell me this,' Delilah continued, leaning forward towards Dig with her elbows on the table, 'can you put your hand on your heart and swear to me that you've never, in all the years you've known Nadine, in all the years you've been friends, close friends, never felt more than just friendship? You've never been tempted to take things a step further? Never had a drunken night when things could have *happened*, you know? Never *fancied* her, even just a little bit?'

'No! God! No. Never. I mean, there might have been a time, you know, *years* ago, when we were younger, just before university, just after you and I . . . But then she met some photographer guy at college and I sort of grew up and – no. No. Nothing ever happened. And now – it's been so long and we're such good mates. It just wouldn't happen.'

105

'Really? I can't think why not, you know. She's very sexy, very attractive.'

'Oh I know. Of course she is. But she's . . . well, she's just Nadine, to me. Always has been. Always will be. And besides, she wouldn't want me even if I *did* fancy her.'

'So,' smiled Delilah, 'it's not true then. What they say. About how men can never be truly platonic friends, that there'll always be some sort of sexual tension, bubbling away, beneath the surface. You know, that *When Harry Met Sally* kind of thing.'

'Well. Obviously not.' Dig was hating every second of this conversation. He'd rather be discussing the fruits of Posh Spice's latest shopping spree, or the contents of Dale Winton's knicker drawer. This was all nonsense. Him? And Nadine? The concept was making his brain hurt. He didn't want to think about it. And he certainly didn't want to talk about it with Delilah.

' . . . Well, for what it's worth,' she was saying, 'I think you'd make a great couple. I think you'd be really good together. You've always had this bond. You've always been so similar.'

Similar? He and Nadine? Well, of course they were. That's why they were such good friends. That's why they spent so much time together. But that didn't mean to say that they should *fancy* each other, did it? That didn't mean they should be a couple? And anyway, why was Delilah saying all this? What did all this have to do with tonight – with *them*?

'But, anyway. It's none of my business so I'll shut up now.'

Thank God, thought Dig, thank God.

CHAPTER ELEVEN

Nadine was feeling more and more insane by the second. More and more unhinged, churned up, inside out, upside-down and all over the place.

She hadn't known what else to do with herself, so she'd phoned Dig. She'd known he was going to be out, of course she had. But there was always a slight chance, wasn't there, that something might have gone wrong, he might have come home early? So she'd phoned him, listened to his answerphone message, the one with the James Bond theme playing in the background. And then she'd called him again. Five minutes later. Just in case, you know, he'd just that second walked into the flat. And then again, five minutes later. And again. And again. And again. Twenty-six times in all.

Pathetic. Absolutely pathetic. She didn't even have anything she particularly wanted to say to him. She just wanted to hear him say 'hello' so that she'd know he was home, that his night with Delilah was over, that *he wasn't with her any more*. That's all.

She could have called him on his mobile, but the bastard always had it switched off. Which was just as well, really. What would she have said? 'Are you having a good time with your dream-girl?' He'd have said, 'Yes, great, brilliant, you owe me a hundred quid.' The line would have been alive with the atmosphere of some groovy place, a place where she *wasn't*, and she'd have ended up feeling a hundred times worse. If that was possible.

It was now eleven thirty and possibly the sort of time they'd be leaving the restaurant. They could be back in about half an hour, depending on where they were coming from and how quickly they could get a cab. But it was also the sort of time when they would be deciding whether they wanted the evening to end or not, that standing-on-the-pavement, stamping-their-feet-to-keep-warm-and-discussing-the-options sort of time. If they decided to go on somewhere, then there was no knowing what time Dig would be home. Nadine didn't think she could stand it. She'd worked herself into such a frenzy by now that there was no way she'd be able to sleep. Her heart was pumping violently and adrenalin coursed dizzyingly through her body.

Suddenly she knew what to do. She stood up, marched towards the coat stand, pulled down her ankle-length fake fur, threw it on, picked up her car keys and headed for her Spider, the front door slamming heavily behind her and her Bart Simpson slippers making barely a sound as she ran along the cold pavement.

CHAPTER TWELVE

After their meal Delilah seemed exhilarated, grinning widely and looping her arm through Dig's. Dig felt himself grow five inches taller. She asked him if he would take her to a gig – it had been so many years since she'd been to see a band. She didn't care who they saw – anyone, anyone at all, she said. Well, it was Dig's job to know exactly who was playing where, and he was on the guest list for at least a dozen different gigs around town every night of the week.

'Sure,' he said. 'What do you fancy? A bit of Britpop at a pub in Tufnell Park? Girl guitar band in Clapham South? Northern Soul revival band in Peckham?'

They decided to see a band called Paranoid who'd just been signed by Johnny-Boy Records' Camden Town rivals and were playing at a new venue in King's Cross, right on the canal. They'd been hyped up to a colossal extent and this was their first live outing since they'd signed their contract. It was going to be a big night, full of celebrities. He didn't know why he hadn't thought about this before. He'd been so overwhelmed by the prospect of spending an entire evening with Delilah that he'd had an imagination bypass. The only thing he could think of to do with a girl as beautiful as Delilah was to take her out for dinner. That's what you did with beautiful girls. Going to gigs was what he did with his colleagues every night of the week; it was work, it was standing at the bar with a load of cynical blokes coolly ignoring some poor kids playing their hearts out for them on the stage, and drinking freebie beers. It had been a long time since he'd been to a gig for pleasure. But judging by the expression of pure excitement on Delilah's face as she hailed a taxi on Rosebery Avenue and clambered into the back seat, it was going to be very pleasurable indeed.

Delilah switched on the cab heater, pulled down the window and began smiling into the cool autumn wind that blew into her face. 'You know,' she said, turning towards Dig suddenly, 'I've spent ten years in the countryside, ten years breathing in some of the cleanest air in the country, but nothing compares to the smell of London in winter. It smells so . . . so . . . full of possibility, doesn't it? Country air smells reassuring, safe, dependable. But this,' she said, taking in another deep breath of the chill air, 'this smells of life.'

Dig had certainly never thought about London's polluted oxygen in those terms before but, watching Delilah's exquisite face aglow with happiness, excitement exuding from her like an intoxicating perfume, he was prepared to believe anything.

'Oh my God! I just saw Robbie Williams!!' screamed Delilah, as they made their way down the steep basement steps leading to the main club area. 'Did you see? Robbie Williams!'

Dig smiled happily. This evening was going so well.

'I always liked him best, you know, when he was in Take That. I was *far* too old, of course, to be into Take That – it was a bit of a secret, really. Alex would have been horrified. But it's all right to like him now, isn't it?

It's quite cool to like Robbie these days. And I know loads of women my age who like him, too – he's the older woman's crumpet, isn't he? And I love all of his songs, I know the lyrics off by heart. Oh my God, Dig, being here with you, after all these years, being in London, going to gigs – it's like going back in time. I feel like a teenage girl again!'

Dig glanced quizzically at Delilah. Take That? Was this really the same girl who'd body-surfed through the crowds at a New Model Army gig at the Town & Country back in '84, wearing a shredded black T-shirt and stiletto-heeled pixie boots?

She grinned widely at him and he decided to forgive her – it was probably some kind of post-modern, ironic thing.

Downstairs was dark and dingy. The ceiling was low and the décor was all grubby red velveteen, scuffed mahogany, peeling gold and muted candle-light. It had obviously been styled to look like one of those night-clubs in old films where raunchy young women in spangles danced for penguin-suited gangsters and their glamorous lady friends to the crazy sounds of syncopated jazz.

They headed towards the bar at the back and Dig said 'All right' to a few people he recognized. He could see it in their eyes when they clocked Delilah following behind him: Fucking hell, they were thinking, Dig's done well for himself, didn't think he had it in him.

'Are you sure you don't want a proper drink?' he said, when Delilah asked if she could have an orange juice and lemonade.

'No. Really,' she said, 'I won't.'

'It's all right, you know. I'm not trying to get you

drunk. I'm not going to try and take advantage of you, or anything,' he said, smiling, feeling quite giddy at the thought.

'Don't be silly,' she said, disconcertingly quickly, 'I know you're not. It's not that.'

'Don't tell me you've given up drinking, too.' He laughed. 'I don't know – Delilah Lillie, given up the fags, given up the booze – what *have* they been doing to you up there in yokel-land?'

'Course I haven't given up,' she laughed, 'course I haven't. I'm just trying to cut back, that's all. You know, turning thirty and everything. Besides,' she said, patting his arm, 'who needs drink when you're having such a great time stone-cold sober, hmm?'

'I suppose so.' He smiled, ordering himself a double scotch on the rocks.

They took a table very close to the stage and spent half an hour celebrity-spotting.

'That's another great thing about London – you get to see famous people just sort of wandering about, don't you? Just shopping and eating and stuff. Not very common in Chester, although that fat girl from *Emmerdale* did come into Alex's Oldham branch for dinner once.'

Dig could listen to Delilah all night. He was so used to being with cynical people, people who'd lived and worked in London for so long, spent so many years struggling with the Tube every morning, trying to negotiate the tourists jamming up Oxford Street, dealing with truly dreadful, pretentious *arseholes* on a daily basis, that he'd forgotten how exciting and magical it could seem when seen through the eyes of someone less jaded.

Delilah's face was tinted pink from candle-light glowing through a red glass dome on the table, and her glossy hair swung backwards and forwards as she talked and laughed and looked around her. Her teeth were extraordinarily white and straight and she seemed to have an awful lot of them. As the support band left the stage, and the lights dimmed, the excitement mounted and Delilah turned towards him, smiled the most beautiful smile he'd ever seen and squeezed his hand on top of the table.

She turned back to watch the stage, but Dig's eyes remained glued to her, glued to her kneecap, where the sharp dome of bone pushed into the black twill of her tailored trousers, accentuating the length of thigh and calf, to the line of her nose in profile, the tiny fold in her stomach where she was bent at the waist and the indentations made by her breasts into the charcoal grey cashmere of her tight sweater.

She was perfect. In every way. Perfect.

Dig finally took his eyes from her and turned to watch the band.

CHAPTER THIRTEEN

The heater in Nadine's Spider had packed up, and she was freezing, even in her furry coat and slippers. She'd been parked opposite Dig's flat for more than two hours now, and there was still no sign of him. She was listening to the Supernaturals on her Discman and smoking many, many cigarettes, her deep-violet fingernails tapping up and down on the synthetic wood of her steering-wheel. Where the hell was he? It was nearly two in the morning. She'd counted twelve cabs pull up in the vicinity since she'd arrived, twelve pairs of headlights, twelve sets of rumbling baritone diesel engines and twelve complete strangers disembarking. She'd crouched down in her seat every time she'd heard the familiar sound of a black cab applying its brakes and then sat up straight again when it wasn't Dig.

Her breath was leaving her lips in big icy clouds and she slipped her hands under her bottom to keep them warm. She knew she was being ridiculous. She knew that if anyone else had been doing what she was doing she would have felt terribly sorry for them, imagined them to be emotionally and psychologically deficient. But she wasn't someone else, she was herself, and it was *her* sitting in a freezing-cold car in a starlet negligé, fake-fur coat and Bart Simpson slippers at two in the morning, waiting for her best friend to get home from a date so that she could stand even the slightest chance of getting any sleep tonight at all. She knew she wasn't emotionally or psychologically deficient – she was just concerned for Dig's welfare. And besides, if she let herself admit that she was here because she was rancidly jealous, then she would never be able to look herself in the eye again.

Another rumble broke the silence of the traffic-free road. Nadine checked in her rear-view mirror: another cab. She slunk down in her seat as the cab passed her and took a deep breath when she heard the engine slowing down. It pulled up a few metres ahead and Nadine craned her neck to catch sight of the two sil-houetted heads in the back seat.

'Are you sure you'll be all right?' Dig asked, as the cab pulled up outside his flat, 'I really don't mind walking back from yours.'

'Don't be silly, Dig. Of course I'll be all right.'

'Here,' he said, forcing a ten-pound note into her hand, 'I want to get this.'

'Why? Honestly, Dig. After everything you've done tonight, organized for me, I'm not going to let you pay for the cab, too.' She pushed his hand away from hers. 'Keep it. I don't want it.'

Dig finally gave up and tucked the note back into his pocket.

'So,' he said, pulling his leather coat around him and getting ready to get out of the cab, 'erm. Maybe see you at the weekend, or something?' He gulped.

'Yeah,' smiled Delilah, 'maybe.'

Dig nodded happily. 'Cool,' he said, 'that's great.' He leaned towards the door handle, took hold of it and then turned abruptly to Delilah. 'I've had a really, really good time tonight, you know. Really. Best night, in a long time. Thank you.'

'Me too,' she said warmly. 'Thank you for the restaurants! And for the gig and for reintroducing me to London. I haven't had so much fun in years. And you've been fantastic company. Isn't it funny – I thought I knew you so well when we were together, thought I knew everything about you, but in just one night, I feel like I know you a hundred times better than I ever did before. It's been a real pleasure getting to know you again, Digby Ryan!' She laughed then and leaned in towards him.

When Dig looked back on this moment afterwards, it took on a strange stretched-out quality, as if it had happened over a period of a few minutes rather than the second and a half it had actually lasted. He could remember every last detail, the rhythmic ticking of the cab's engine, the sound of a Heart FM DJ announcing the two o'clock news, the orange streetlight shining through Delilah's golden hair as she moved towards him, the little creases that formed in her lips as they puckered together, the shiver that ran down his spine as her hair whipped gently across his cheek and the spasm that rocked his body as he felt his lips being dampened by hers.

She pulled away slowly but left her arms where they were, loosely draped around his neck. She was staring deeply into his eyes and smiling. 'Mmm,' she drawled, touching her lips with the tip of her tongue, 'that was nice.'

Dig nodded and smiled and leaned in towards her again, his eyes slanting closed and his lips softening up for a repeat, but his descent towards her lips was impeded by her hands on his shoulders, gently pushing him away. 'That was nice,' she said, using a more measured inton- ation and raising her eyebrows, 'thank you.' She smiled. 'Thank you,' she said again.

Dig took his cue. He knew what she was saying. She was a married woman. She'd come to London to sort out her problems, not to get involved in any more. There'd be time. He lifted her hand and kissed the back of it. 'It's good to have you back,' he said as he stepped out of the cab and on to the freezing pavement, 'really good.'

Delilah slid across the seat and leaned through the open window. She grabbed his hand. 'Sleep tight, lovely Digby Ryan,' she said. And then the cab pulled off, executed a perfect turning circle and bore Delilah away towards Primrose Hill.

Dig stood where he'd been dropped, on the side of Camden Road, and watched the receding cab, his hands in his pockets, his heart in his mouth and a smile on his face.

As the cab pulled away from the traffic lights at the next junction and disappeared from view, Dig slowly pulled his hands from his pockets, bunched them up into triumphant fists and brought them down from the air above his head towards his chest. '*Yes!*' he said under his breath, '*YES!*'

Oh my God, thought Nadine, watching him from the shadows across the road, her face in her hands, her jaw slack, oh my God.

It's happening again.

Dig's in love.

lime-green teeth

One morning, when Nadine was eighteen years old, an invitation dropped on to the doormat of her family home. Little did she know when she opened it that it was going to lead to one of the most unexpected nights of her life.

It was an invitation to a Holy T reunion. It had been organized by Anna O'Riordan, one of the perky, popular, button-nosed girls in their year, and was to be held at a wine bar in Camden Town. According to the invite it was meant as an 'opportunity to catch up with old friends and renew contact before we spread our wings to all four corners of the globe in the pursuit of a Higher Education'.

Anna O'Riordan always had been a pretentious cow.

The party was taking place on 12 September, Nadine's last weekend in London. She was all packed up, had passed her driving test, chucked in her summer job and cleared out her bedroom, which now stood empty and sad, nothing left of her eighteen years but her Enid Blyton books and her etiolated kite.

It had been a scorching-hot summer and Nadine's usually chalky-white complexion had been toasted to a shimmery golden-brown festooned with freckles, and her auburn hair had picked up strands of honey-coloured highlights. She didn't know it at the time – what eighteen-year-old girl does? – but she was at her peak. Her skin was as fresh as it would ever be, her hair as thick and shiny, her thighs as firm and her energy as boundless. Her life was free of worries, commitments and entanglements, her sights set firmly on the future. She was a vision to behold, a picture of youth, strength and vitality. When Nadine walked down the street men would stop and stare because she was more than just a good-looking girl – she was special, she was sexy, and energy oozed from her. She was the sort of girl who made middle-aged women want to weep for their lost youth and middle-aged men want to start afresh.

Nadine was, of course, blissfully unaware of her all-round gorgeousness and the power of her youth, and as she got ready for the party she felt incredibly nervous. Who was going to be there? What would they think of her? Would they even remember her? Would she have anything to say to anyone?

But, most importantly, would Dig and Delilah be there? The thought unleashed a mob of epileptic butter-flies in her stomach. How was she going to handle that possibility? She envisaged herself walking into the wine bar and clapping eyes on them for the first time in two years. What should she be expecting? Delilah possibly full-term pregnant with three inches of black roots and a fag hanging out of her mouth? Dig looking like a man whose dreams have withered and died? That was a pleasing thought. Or maybe they just wouldn't turn up at all ... Nadine began hoping nervously for this last option.

But as she walked from Bartholomew Road towards Camden that evening, the air still warm, the sun just starting to sink and a gentle breeze ruffling the crinkle cotton of her Indian skirt, she began to feel brave and strong. Why was she still bothered about Dig and Delilah

119

after all this time? Who cared if they were there or not, happy or unhappy, together or apart? She'd just spent two of the best years of her life at St Julian's, one of only twelve girls in a sixth form of ninety boys. Her confidence had grown beyond belief while she was there. She was a different person now and she had more important things to worry about than Dig and bloody Delilah. She had a future, a degree, a career to think about. She didn't need anyone else's approval and she refused to be intimidated ever again by Delilah or her allegiance with her former best friend.

She was a kid then; she was an adult now.

She walked into the wine bar with her shoulders back and her head held high. She would show them, she would show everyone just how far mousy little Nadine Kite had come.

Dig was the first person she saw when she walked in.

He was standing on his own, wearing ripped jeans, moccasins and an old check flannel shirt. His thick hair had grown untidily long, flopping on to his forehead and covering his ears and he was sporting a sleeper in his right earlobe. He was holding a bottle of Sol and examining the slice of lime in the neck with some confusion, unsure what it was there for or what he was supposed to do with it. Nadine watched him with gentle amusement as he attempted to push the segment down the neck and into the bottle and, when this didn't work, pull it out again and try daintily to squeeze its juice into the beer. The slice released one drop of liquid and refused to yield any more, so Dig transferred it from his fingers to his mouth and began sucking on it.

And so it was that when Dig looked up and noticed Nadine staring at him, when their eyes locked for the first time in two years and their faces broke open into wide smiles of recognition, Dig Ryan was wearing a dazzling set of lime-green teeth.

'It's just meant to be for decoration, you daft bugger!'

'Deen!' he exclaimed, the lime segment falling from his lips and on to the floor. 'Didn't recognize you for a moment there. You look really . . . totally . . . shit. I didn't think you were going to come.'

'Of course I was going to come!' she laughed, hugging him to her. 'Why on earth wouldn't I?'

'I dunno,' he shrugged, smiling, 'I thought a St Julian's girl like you would be too posh for a do like this, it might be a bit beneath you.'

Nadine rolled her eyes at him. 'You shouldn't believe everything you hear.' Her gaze wandered up and down his face and she realized that Dig looked different. Not just older, but intrinsically *different*. Was it the hair? Or the increased facial shadow? No. Neither of those. Was it his manner – nervous, uncomfortable, slightly arrogant? No. So what was it? Her eyes traversed his face and then she saw it.

'Dig Ryan,' she laughed, staring at him intently and making him squirm, 'what the fuck happened to your eyebrow?!'

'What?' he demanded, affronted, putting a finger up to it.

'It's . . . it's *separated*!'

'What are you talking about?'

'Your eyebrow. It's two eyebrows. What have you done to the middle bit?!'

Dig blushed, looked away. 'Phphphphph,' he mumbled.

'What?'

121

'*I shaved it off, all right! – I shaved it off.*' He brought his beer bottle to his lips and took a large mouthful, his eyes swivelling self-consciously around the room.

Nadine was doubled over with mirth. 'Oh Dig,' she cried, 'that's *hysterical*! You look so *weird* with two eyebrows. I just can't take it in! Oh come on,' she laughed, nudging him in the ribs, 'loosen up.'

A smile began to twitch at the corners of Dig's lips, and before long they were both laughing. 'It was Delilah's idea,' he wheezed through his laughter, 'she thought ... she thought ...' He fought to control himself. 'She thought it would make me look ... *more intelligent.*' He dissolved again, and Nadine slapped her thighs and screamed with laughter. 'Oh don't,' she breathed, 'don't. I'm going to wet myself! You look so funny! Oh grow it back, Dig, please. For the love of God, grow it back! You just don't look like *you* any more!'

'Maybe,' laughed Dig, slowly regaining his composure, 'maybe. Anyway,' he said, indicating her empty hands, 'what about a drink? Do you want to go to the bar?'

Nadine shrugged, wiping a tear from under her eyes. 'Yeah,' she said, 'I guess so.'

They turned to survey the rest of the party then, and Nadine felt her spirits drop as she looked around her. 'Oh God,' she complained.

'Yeah, I know,' said Dig. 'Depressing, isn't it?'

'God. Just look at them all. They're all so *boring.*'

'I know. I know. I was going to leave after this drink. I tried to make an effort when I got here, but I got trapped in the corner with Anna O'Riordan for quarter of an hour, telling me all about her summer in the States and her American boyfriend in this pathetic pretend American accent. She must have told me how "neat" he

122

was and how "cute" about a hundred times.' Dig put two fingers into his mouth and mock-gagged.

Nadine sneered in sympathy. 'So,' she said, looking around her, trying to appear unbothered, 'Delilah not here?'

Dig shook his head, took another slurp of beer. 'Nah.'

'Couldn't face it, eh?' she smiled. 'Don't really blame her.'

Dig shrugged. 'Don't even know if she was invited. I haven't seen her since March.'

Nadine quelled the wave of excitement in her belly and tried to look unfazed. 'Oh,' she said, 'why not?'

'You tell me,' he said bluntly. 'One minute everything was fine between us. Then she started behaving really oddly.'

'Oddly?'

'Yeah. After her eighteenth birthday. She just ... Here' – he stopped suddenly – 'look. How d'you fancy making an escape. I'll tell you all about it over a decent pint. No one's noticed you're here yet. We could just go somewhere?'

Nadine nodded. There was nothing she would like more.

They wandered down Chalk Farm Road, past pine-furniture shops and window displays of black leather and studded belts, fluorescent wigs and enormous silver rings in the shapes of skulls. They stopped for a moment on the hump-backed bridge over the canal and watched the black water below shimmering with reflections of the purple streaks that the setting sun had left in the sky.

Someone was having a party on one of the roof terraces overhead and music blared out loudly as they passed by.

In a canalside pub, they bought pints at the bar and took them outside to a table overlooking the water. 'Pooh,' said Nadine, waving her hand in front of her nose, 'it *stinks* out here. It smells like rotten eggs.'

'We can go inside if you'd like.'

'No,' she said, 'don't worry. I'll get used to it.' She started ferreting around inside her duffel bag as she talked and brought out a packet of Silk Cut and a box of matches. Dig pretended to collapse. 'No!' he exclaimed, 'surely not. Not you! Not Nadine Kite! You can't *smoke*. It's not natural!'

She offered the packet to him, and lit them both up.

'Shit, Deen. You are the last person in the whole world I would ever have expected to smoke. How long . . . I mean . . . when did all this start?' He pointed at her mouth.

'About a week after I started at St Julian's,' she said, exhaling. 'You were treated like a freak there if you *didn't* smoke. It was actively encouraged, in fact.'

'But I thought that St Julian's was supposed to be really old-fashioned and tough?'

'Myth,' she said, 'complete myth. That's what they *want* people to think, otherwise they'd only get people applying who wanted to doss around for two years.'

'So it was good?'

'It was the best. I've just had the best two years of my life.' She told him all about the smoky common-room and the flexible timetables, the 'Call-me-Tony' teachers and the non-existent dress codes.

They discussed Holloway Tech, where Dig had taken his A Levels and which sounded like quite a laugh. He'd got fairly good grades but he'd already decided that he didn't want to go to university. He'd spent the summer

124

doing unpaid work experience for a record company in Soho and now they'd offered him a permanent job as office assistant, starting on Monday.

They talked about their families – his parents were fine and so was his little sister, who'd just started at primary school; her parents were fine, too, and her little brother had just got ten 'A' grades in his O Levels and was currently held on a par with Jesus Christ in the Kite household.

'So,' said Nadine, finally, 'you were going to tell me about Delilah? About what happened with you and Delilah?'

'Yeah. Right.' Dig dropped the end of his cigarette on to the ground and crushed it with the heel of his moccasin. 'I dunno, it was really weird. Things probably *had* got a bit stuck in a rut towards the end – neither of us had any money so we just used to stay in at mine most of the time. It all got a bit routine after we left school. She started doing this secretarial course, but she dropped out after the first couple of weeks because she didn't like the teacher, or something, then she started on some YOP scheme, working in a florist's and she hated that, too. So in the end she just got some shitty weekend job in a chemist, cash in hand, and that created a bit of friction because I had all this college work to worry about and I was making all these new friends, and she was just stuck at home all day with her old hag of a mother.'

'Oh!' exclaimed Nadine, remembering her one unpleasant encounter with Delilah's mother years earlier. 'You met her mother?'

'Yeah,' Dig grimaced. 'Once or twice.'

'What was she like?'

'The devil's daughter.' He shuddered. 'I think she was a bit unbalanced, a bit schizo. Delilah never wanted me to go to her house – she hated it there, spent more time at mine. So yeah, things were a bit tense, but I thought once I'd finished my A Levels I'd get a job, work hard, get promoted and then I'd be able to afford a flat, somewhere for us to live together. You know, I wanted Delilah to be a lady of leisure, I wanted to look after her. I really thought we were going to be together for ever. I didn't think there was anything we couldn't work out.

'We even planned to get engaged on her eighteenth, we talked about where we'd live.

'But the night after her birthday I came home from college and Delilah didn't turn up. I phoned her at her mum's and one of her brothers answered the phone and said she wasn't there, he hadn't seen her since that morning, but that she'd left with a big bag and there'd been a lot of shouting and his mum was really angry with her.

'So all night, and the next and the next, I waited for her and I phoned her and nobody knew where she was and nobody seemed to give a shit . . . I mean, her family, they were just all so . . . *fucked*. I nearly went to the police. But then I thought of something. Wherever she was, she'd need money. And she was eighteen now, she could sign on, and I knew she would – she'd been talking about it for two years – so I bunked off college for a week and I hid behind a tree outside the DHSS, every day. She turned up on the Friday morning. She looked awful. Really awful. I almost didn't recognize her. I ran up to her and I grabbed her, and d'you know what? She couldn't even look me in the eye. It was like she was ashamed or something.

'Anyway. In the end, she came back to my house. She stayed for a couple of weeks but she was so miserable – she didn't want to go out, she didn't want to watch telly, she didn't want to have sex. I tried getting her to talk but she just kept saying that she was fine, nothing was wrong.

'Then one day I got back from college and she wasn't there. I asked my mum where she'd gone and she told me she'd popped out to get a paper. I knew instantly that something was wrong – Delilah would *never* pop out to get a paper. So I ran up to my room and all her stuff had gone. She'd left a note.'

'What did it say?' asked Nadine.

'Oh, exactly what I'd been expecting really. Sorry to hurt you but I can't be with you any more. It's not that I don't love you, I will always love you. But I have to go. It's over. Please don't try to contact me. Please forget about me.'

'I went round to her mum's place, demanded to know where Delilah was. But she just said, "I don't know no one called Delilah. I ain't got no daughter." And then she slammed the door in my face. Scary bitch.'

'Then what?'

Dig shrugged. 'Then just sort of trying to get over her, I suppose. Just getting on with things. Concentrating on my college work, revising, going to gigs.'

'You haven't seen her since?'

Dig shook his head glumly.

'Oh Dig,' said Nadine, putting on her best sympathetic voice, while thinking *'Good, I'm glad, I hated that girl.'* 'You poor, poor thing. How are you?'

'Oh,' he said, brightening, 'I'm fine, I'm cool. I really am. It was bad for a while – very bad. But this work experience, it's turned my life around. I know what I want now. I've got a direction in my life and that really helps.'

'So . . . have you started seeing anyone else, you know . . . since?'

Dig shook his head. 'Nah,' he said, 'I've been too busy, what with my A Levels and work experience and everything. Nah.' He breathed in, looked up at Nadine. 'What about you? You . . . seeing anyone?'

'Uh-uh.' She shook her head. 'No.'

A smile tickled Dig's lips.

'What?' smirked Nadine.

'Oh. Nothing,' he grinned.

'What!'

'Nothing!' he repeated, light-heartedly. 'Just wondering if you'd – you know – have you . . . lost it, yet?'

'It?'

'Yes. It. You know!'

Nadine blushed crimson. She'd never talked about sex with Dig before. 'Oh,' she muttered, 'right. That. No. Not yet.'

Dig nodded knowingly and took a swig of his beer, a smile still lingering on his face.

'What!'

'Nothing!'

'I'm only eighteen you know,' she smarted.

'Good,' smiled Dig infuriatingly, 'fine. That's just great.'

'I'm waiting,' she said, getting more indignant by the minute. 'It's just not something I want to rush into, that's all. I want to wait until *I'm* ready, and if I have to wait another ten years, then I will.'

'Deen. Calm down, will you! I think you're right. I think you're absolutely right.'

'Good,' said Nadine firmly, squirming slightly.

They fell silent for a second and sipped from their pints. Nadine looked up and found Dig staring at her intently. She looked away, embarrassed.

'That place suited you,' he commented, obscurely, scrutinizing her face as he spoke.

'What place?'

'That St Julian's.'

'What do you mean?' Nadine replied coyly.

'You just seem so . . . different. You look so . . . so . . .' A blush spread across Dig's face as he searched for a word. 'You look so . . .'

'Ye–es?' joked Nadine, tapping her fingernails up and down against the table-top.

'Jesus Christ, Deen, you look . . . *so fucking gorgeous.*' Dig's eyes seemed to bulge slightly as he said this and his blush went up a few gears from pale pink to throbbing purple.

Nadine snorted and burst into giggles, holding her cheeks in her hands. 'Oh,' she said finally, 'thank you!' Her blush matched his now, and the two of them sat side by side like a pair of matchsticks, giggling awkwardly. They stopped laughing every now and then and looked up at each other's crimson faces and started giggling afresh.

'Oh God – I am so embarrassed,' said Dig, putting his head in his hands. 'I can't believe I just said that to you! To you! Nadine. My old mate, Deen!'

'Neither can I!' laughed Nadine. 'In fact, I'm so embarrassed that I'm going to have to go to the toilet!'

Nadine was still smiling by the time she'd walked from

129

the beer garden, through the bar and to the toilets. She was still smiling as she peed and she was still smiling when she regarded herself in the mirror while she washed her hands. This was so weird. Seeing Dig again after so long, sitting in a pub with him like a grown-up, drinking and smoking and chatting like adults. And that, just now, that compliment. That was *bizarre*. Dig thought she was gorgeous. And the way he'd said it – it reminded her of something. It reminded her a day years ago at the Holy T, a summer's day when Dig had first set eyes on Delilah Lillie and he'd said that she looked just like Leslie Ash in *Quadrophenia*. And then he'd said, 'Oh my God, she is absolutely beautiful,' and she'd known then that she'd lost him. He'd used exactly the same tone of voice just then, when he told her that *she* was gorgeous – definitely – exactly the same.

A shudder ran down her spine.

They stayed in the pub until closing time, until a chill breeze had started blowing across their table and Dig had put one arm around Nadine's shoulders to stop her shivering.

His arm stayed there, on her shoulder, as they walked home, and Nadine wondered whether or not she liked it being there. What did it mean? Was she supposed to collude by placing her arm around his waist? Was it just a casual gesture, an act of affection? Or was it a prelude to something altogether unthinkable? After all those years of indifference and disregard, was Dig Ryan suddenly and unexpectedly going to do what she'd wanted for so long? Was he going to *want* her?

Nadine tried to put these exciting but unsettling thoughts to the back of her mind as they wandered slowly through the Saturday-night mayhem of Camden Town. The streets were overrun with litter and people and pungent with the aroma of falafel and spicy sausages being fried up for the closing-time crowds. Dig and Nadine picked their way over old food containers and empty Coke cans and ignored the urgent whisperings of the dealers outside Camden Town Tube station as they passed.

But what if something were to happen? What then? It would be the worst timing imaginable. Tomorrow was her last day in London. On Monday she was going to Manchester, to start a new life, to become a new person. Did she really want to start something here that would tie her to the past, tie her to London? Instead of spending her weekends getting to know Manchester, making friends, concentrating on her photography, she would be on trains, constantly whizzing up and down between Manchester Piccadilly and Euston, living out of a holdall, missing someone, wanting to be somewhere else.

That wasn't what she wanted.

But then, wasn't *this* – Dig, her, together, no Delilah, just the two of them – wasn't *this* what she had always, always wanted?

She looked up towards Dig. He was animated, chatting away about his plans for world domination in the music business, how he was going to give himself a year to eighteen months, tops, as an office assistant at Electro-gram Records before he would start pushing his way forwards into the A&R department. A year or two there and then he would move sideways to a smaller label where he could be a big fish in a small pond, make an impact. It would be another year or so before he would discover the greatest guitar band in the world, make his name, make a packet and then – his master plan: Dig-It Records, his own label, a millionaire by the time he was twenty-five. Sorted. In the bag. No problem.

He genuinely believed every word he was saying: it *was* going to happen, there was no doubt in his mind about that – his career progression, Dig-It Records, early retirement. All of it.

He was, Nadine realized, as full of ambition and plans for the future as she was. He had no room in his life for a long-distance love affair, that much was obvious.

They turned off Kentish Town Road and began the walk down Bartholomew Road towards her parents' flat. She'd already decided she wouldn't invite him in. Her parents would make a real fuss and say things like 'Well, howdy, stranger' and 'Long time no see' and 'Here's a blast from the past,' and he'd have to make small talk with them for ages about what he'd been up to for the past two years and how his parents were, and it was late, too late in the night, for all that, so when they arrived outside her house she stopped at the bottom of the steps to the front door and turned towards him.

'Well,' she said, shyly, 'thank you for rescuing me from the horrors of the Holy T reunion. I've had a really nice night. It's been ... er ...' She searched for the right words to bring the night to a close without spoiling it but Dig wasn't really listening. He was anxiously staring into her eyes, his lips open and poised to say something, his body stiff, his fists tightly furled.

'I have to see you again,' he stated firmly, his mouth hard, his eyes nervous.

Nadine shot him a look. 'Well,' she began, 'of course ... I mean ... of course we will ... it's ... er ...'

132

'No,' he growled, 'I mean *I have to see you again*. Soon. Tomorrow. What are you doing tomorrow?' His voice was desperate, he was holding her hands in his, tightly, too tightly.

Nadine was confused. She didn't know what to say. She squeezed his hands back and decided. She wanted to see him tomorrow, romance or no romance. She *wanted* to spend her last day in London with Dig.

'Nothing,' she said, finally, shrugging and smiling goofily, 'I'm not doing anything tomorrow.'

Dig smiled. 'Let's do something. We'll do something tomorrow. You and me. Yeah?'

'Yeah,' smiled Nadine, relief at deferring the tearful farewells lighting up her face and widening her smile, 'we'll do something tomorrow.' Her heart was racing, and a light sweat had broken out on the palms of her hands.

And then, before she knew what was happening, before she had a chance to decide whether it was what she wanted or not, Dig had wrapped his arms tightly around her shoulders, brought his face down towards hers and kissed her squarely on the lips.

Nadine was unresponsive for a second or two, her lips firmly glued together, her body tensed. But then the smell of Dig's flesh under her nose joined forces with the quite spectacular effect his lips were having on her groin and suddenly she relaxed completely into the kiss. Dig's mouth was soft and gentle, his breath tasted like hers, of beer and cigarettes. His tongue, which was now snaking its way around her teeth and into the crevices of her mouth, was sensual and alive. It was happening – it was finally happening – Dig Ryan was kissing her! She was being kissed by Dig Ryan! She and Dig Ryan were kissing!

A Golf GTI with a loud engine and acid house music blaring from four open windows passed by and slowed down. 'Oi – give her one for me!' shouted a man in a baseball cap, laughing lecherously before screeching off again.

Dig and Nadine smiled and slowly pulled apart, staring with wonder into each other's eyes.

'Well,' said Nadine, eventually, 'I'd better get in.'

'Yeah,' said Dig, 'right. OK. Give us a ring when you wake up, yeah? If it's a nice day we could go for a picnic or something.'

'Yeah,' Nadine nodded enthusiastically. 'Yeah. That would be really lovely.'

They exchanged another kiss and another look of wonderment and then Dig turned to leave. Nadine watched him for a while as he sauntered down Bartholomew Road towards Kentish Town Road. He had his hands in his pockets and an awkward, slightly loping walk, as if he wasn't quite used to having legs yet. A warm feeling flooded Nadine's heart, a feeling of familiarity and cosiness seasoned with excitement and freshness. That's Dig Ryan, she thought to herself happily, that's Dig Ryan walking down my road, having just kissed me so firmly and passionately on the lips and turned all my insides to semolina, that's him, my soul mate, my dream man, the person I want to wake up with on Saturday mornings on a big pine bed. There he goes . . .

She smiled warmly to herself and was just about to turn and go indoors when she saw Dig, at the head of her road and thinking no one was watching him, suddenly break into a hop, skip and a jump, leap on to a garden wall, punch the air with his fist and whoop at the top of his voice before turning the corner and disappearing from view.

see-through dress

The following morning Nadine knew exactly what she was going to do. She'd been thinking about it all night. What she was going to do was this: enjoy herself. She would go with the flow and let whatever unfolded unfold. She would act as if tomorrow was just any other Monday and not the end of her London life. And then, at the end of the day, when she and Dig came to say goodbye, she would walk away and say nothing about another meeting or discuss what happened next. She would walk away, go home, and forget that any of it had ever happened, forget that she had ever kissed Dig Ryan, forget that he had any feelings for her. And then the following day she and her mother would pack up her car and drive to Manchester and her new life would start, and her September Sunday with Dig Ryan would fade into a distant memory.

It was a golden late-summer morning when she awoke at ten o'clock. Her mother was at church – she'd long since stopped trying to drag Nadine along, faced with her daughter's protestations of atheism and paganism and, lately, just to prove her point, Satanism – and her father and brother had gone fishing together. She ran around the flat in her bra and knickers as she got ready, the windows open, the radio blaring, singing along at the top of her voice. At eleven o'clock she phoned Dig and arranged to meet him on Primrose Hill at half past twelve.

'Bring your kite,' he said. 'Apparently the wind's going to pick up later.'

Dig had two Cullens' carrier bags with him when they met on the brow of the hill. He was draped all over a bench and smoking a cigarette. He had on the same jeans as the night before and a Happy Mondays T-shirt. He sat up straight when he saw Nadine approaching and his face broke open into a lecherous grin.

'You know that dress is see-through, don't you?' he commented lasciviously when she sat down next to him.

Nadine pretended to be embarrassed, but she knew full well the diaphanous qualities of her ankle-length Indian voile dress. She was wearing black-leather monkey-boots with pink laces and her hair was tied on top of her head into a cascading pony-tail. It was what her mother disparagingly referred to as her 'hippy-dippy' look.

Dig peeled the Cullens' carrier bags apart to reveal warm baguettes and tubs of taramasalata, bags of Kettle Chips and twelve bottles of beer. Nadine had brought a blanket, and they wandered around together until they found a spot that would afford them a little privacy.

And then, for the rest of the day, from lunch-time, through the afternoon and as evening approached, they lay on Nadine's blanket and kissed. They kissed for five hours. They kissed so much and so hard that Nadine's lips felt like blisters, and a stubble rash broke out on her chin. Every now and then they would break apart to eat a little something or to take a swig of beer, quickly finding each other's mouths again seconds later. They barely talked all day; when they weren't kissing they would stare dreamily into the distance, smiling at the frisky dogs that scampered by every few minutes and at the overexcited children dashing around in circles. They watched the sun beginning to set in silence, silly smiles glued to their faces and their hands entwined.

And then, just as they were about to leave, their litter disposed of in a plastic bin, their blanket folded and their beer drunk, a breeze blew Dig's fringe off his forehead.

'Did you see that?' he said.

'What?'

Another breeze picked up the hem of Nadine's skirt and tossed it sideways.

'That,' he said, pointing at her skirt, '*that*,' he said, pointing at the furrows in the grass, '*THAT*,' he said, pointing at a candy-striped carrier bag filled with wind and bouncing across the footpath. 'Come on. *Quick*. Get your kite out!'

He grabbed her hand and they ran as fast as they could up towards the peak of Primrose Hill.

It didn't take long for Dig and Nadine's kites to become animated in the powerful wind that seemed to come from nowhere that evening. It was a warm wind, gentle but alive, tangling up their hair and clothes like the hands of an overenthusiastic lover. The sun sank down slowly in the sky as the last hour of daylight ebbed away, and their kites danced in front of a golden backdrop. Finally the sun dropped beneath the horizon and at the very moment that darkness descended upon Primrose Hill, the wind died away as suddenly as it had arrived and it was still and dark. Dig and Nadine looked around the hill. They were all alone, the last people there. They collected their kites from where they lay, spent, on the summer-dry grass, and arm-in-arm they began the walk back to Kentish Town.

'I've worked it out,' said Dig, as they walked down Prince of Wales Road. 'Even if I give my mum £20 a week rent *and* start payments on a car, say £20 a week, plus a Travelcard at £5 a week, I'll *still* be able to afford to come up and see you at least once a fortnight – I mean, it's not going to be much more than fifteen quid, is it, with a Young Person's Railcard?'

He turned to Nadine and smiled, squeezing her shoulders with his arm. She smiled tightly.

'And then, of course,' he continued, 'there'll be holidays as well, won't there? You'll come home for holidays, won't you? Do you have half-terms on degree courses?'

Nadine shrugged and smiled nervously.

'Yeah, anyway. So what with holidays and weekends we should get to see quite a bit of each other. The three years should go in a flash and you'll be back in London before you know it and . . .'

Oh God. Oh Jesus, thought Nadine, this is exactly what I *didn't* want to happen.

Hang on just a minute, buddy-boy, she wanted to shout out, hold your horses. If I was some girl you'd just met in a wine bar last night, you'd be taking it slowly right now, feeling your way. You wouldn't be making these enormous assumptions about what happens next, but because you knew me when I had scabs on my knees and buckle-up shoes, you think you know the score.

But you don't, actually, you don't know anything about what's going on in my head, about what I want or who I want. And I'm a strong woman, I have dreams and a

139

direction and I have things I want to do, things that *don't involve you*, believe it or not. Just because Delilah-bitch-of-the-century-Lillie fell for your charms, it doesn't make you irresistible, it doesn't mean that I am going to drop my hopes and dreams for my future. *I* am the priority in my life, Digby Ryan, not you, not any more, never again. I am stronger than you. Yes! It's true! I *am* stronger than you and I don't need you.

Nadine felt a flush of excitement as these thoughts buzzed around her head. After all those miserable years at Holy T, watching Delilah Lillie slowly steal away her best friend and take apart her dreams, after so many years of wanting what she couldn't have and feeling like a third wheel, she was now firmly installed in the driver's seat and totally in control. She had Dig Ryan exactly where she'd always wanted him and now she was going to show him that she didn't need him.

'Dig,' she said, coming to a halt outside a record shop on Kentish Town Road and turning to face him, 'actually, I don't think this is a very good idea . . .'

'What?' Dig's face clouded over in confusion.

'This,' she said. 'You and me. I don't think it's going to work out.'

'What do you mean?'

Nadine sighed. 'Maybe we should just take things a bit slower, you know.' She explained her feelings to him, about her new life at Manchester, wanting a clean break from London, needing to be unfettered by the past. Dig blinked a lot and nodded stiffly.

'D'you understand, Dig?' she asked. 'It's just not the right time. It wouldn't be fair on either of us.'

Dig nodded again and attempted a smile.

'So you understand?'

Once again, Dig nodded, but the nod slowly became a shake.

'No!' he shouted, shrugging Nadine's hand from his arm and backing away from her. 'No, actually, I don't fucking understand. I don't fucking understand *at all.* I think it's all bollocks. Jesus, Deen. Since the minute I set eyes on you last night I have been . . . I have been . . . oh God, I don't even know *what* I've been, but it's been great. Feeling the way you've made me feel has been great and I want to carry on feeling like this. I want to look forward to the weekends. I want to queue up at Euston station on a Friday evening with a change of clothing in a bag and ask for a return ticket to Manchester Piccadilly. I want to sit on a train for three hours and imagine you waiting for me on the concourse wearing a see-through dress with your hair all over the place and dream about the weekend ahead. I want a chance to get to know you properly, not just as Nadine Kite, my old mate, but as this new wonderful person I only met last night, this amazing, *amazing* person who I've only known for forty-eight hours.'

'You've known me for years, Dig.'

'No! No I haven't! You were different before. You're a new person now and I can't just let you go without getting to know you properly, without giving us a chance. Jesus, Deen – I can't believe this is happening!'

Nadine stared at the ground. She couldn't believe this was happening either. She couldn't look into Dig's eyes. She was too scared of what she might find there. 'Sorry,' she mumbled, 'I'm sorry. But that's just the way things are. It's called bad timing and it's been the story of you and me, all through the years.'

'What do you mean?'

141

Nadine took a deep breath, opened her mouth and then closed it again. There was no point, no point whatsoever, in raking up the past. She shook her head. 'Nothing,' she sighed, 'nothing.'

'Look. Deen. Can't we even give it a try? Can't we at least see if things would work out, you know, instead of just writing it off from the outset? I know what you're saying, I really do, about new lives and fresh starts and all that, but, Deen, I have never felt like this before and I don't think I could cope if we didn't at least try.'

'Oh Dig! You don't understand, do you! Of course it will work! That's the whole fucking point. It will work. You and I would be perfect together and that's exactly why I don't want to get involved with you. Not now. Not the day before I leave London. It's not what I want!'

'But you want me?' asked Dig, his hand on his chest. 'You *do* want me?'

Nadine shrugged. Of course she wanted him. More than anything. But she'd made up her mind. If she said yes now, then she would lose control once again. 'No' – she shook her head firmly – 'no, Dig. I don't want you. I know you might find that hard to believe, but I don't want you. OK? I hate to dent your big macho ego, but that's just the way it is.' She spun around and began walking brusquely down Kentish Town Road. There were tears tickling at the back of her throat and she refused to let Dig see her crying.

Dig chased after her and grabbed her arm, forcing her to face him. 'So that's it, is it? Hmm? That's . . . it?'

Nadine nodded.

'And you're happy just to walk away tonight, are you? Just walk away and get on with your life without ever finding out what it could have been like?'

She nodded again. Dig sucked in his breath and eyed her with scepticism. 'I don't believe you, Nadine Kite' – he shook his head slowly from side to side – 'I really don't believe you.'

'That's your prerogative,' she replied sniffily, avoiding his gaze.

'Yeah,' he said, 'yeah. I suppose it is. And it's my prerogative to let you know that this isn't finished yet. I've never felt like this about anyone, ever. You are so beautiful and so special and so fucking *amazing*, Nadine, and this' – he indicated the two of them – '*us*, this isn't finished yet. Just remember I said that, OK? You're wrong, tonight, you're in the wrong. You're making a mistake, Nadine.'

'I'm sorry,' she said, as they turned to face each other outside her parents' house. 'I should have been more honest with you – I just didn't think things were going to work out like this. I had no idea – I'm really sorry.'

'Look – Deen.' Dig took her hands and looked deep into her eyes. 'I hear everything you're saying about not wanting to get involved but can't we at least be friends? I have to know that you'll still be in my life. Can I write to you? Maybe just see you to hang out with when you're home for the holidays? Please?'

Nadine nodded. 'Sure,' she said, desperate now to finish what she'd started, to get indoors and away from Dig. 'Sure. Why not?' And then she turned away abruptly as tears started rising again in her throat and her eyes began shimmering. 'See ya,' she managed to squeak before sliding her key in the lock and stumbling through the door, letting it slam loudly behind her.

'*Is that you, love?*' She heard her mother's concerned

voice drifting across the hallway from the living room, where her family were watching television.

'Yeah,' she said, brittlely, holding back a choke. 'I'll be in in a minute.' She ran then, two steps at a time, towards her bedroom and collapsed sobbing on to her bed. As she lay there she heard a strange scuffling noise coming from outside. She peered between her curtains and saw Dig slowly backing away from the front door with his hands in his pockets and then she watched him walking down Bartholomew Road, dragging his feet awkwardly and heavily along the pavement.

'*Nadine. Nadine, what is this on the carpet?*' Her mother was hollering up the stairs. '*I really do wish you'd learn to pick up after yourself – you won't have me to do it for you after tomorrow, you know.*'

Nadine waited until she heard her mother's slippers shuffling back into the living room before slipping down the stairs.

Sitting at the bottom of the stairs was something that looked like a very brightly coloured cat, with an extra long tail. As she approached it she saw that it wasn't a cat at all, but Dig's kite, the one with the red, white and yellow chequers, the one he'd brought with him to the park today.

She sat down heavily on the bottom stair and gently picked up the grubby old kite. She brought it to her nose and sniffed it. It smelled of fresh air and plastic. It smelled of today, her day with Dig. It smelled of their picnic and Dig's breath and the woollen blanket and the dried-out grass of Primrose Hill. It smelled of Kettle Chips and warm baguettes. It smelled of sunshine and hope and happiness. It smelled of her childhood, Dig's father. It smelled of the past.

She turned it over in her hands and noticed something written on the other side, in black Biro. Some of the letters hadn't come out properly, the Biro ink not taking to the plastic, so she held it up to the light and was eventually able to make out the words:

Dig 'n' Deen
13 September 1987
For ever ♥

She sadly folded the string around the kite, got to her feet and went back to her bedroom.

CHAPTER FOURTEEN

Nadine had been expecting the inevitable gushing phone call from Dig all morning, the phone call that would crushingly confirm what she already knew: that he'd had a fantastic time with Delilah last night, that they'd had a laugh, stayed out late and kissed in the back of a black cab, that he'd never been happier, that Delilah was the most amazing woman he'd ever met, *that he was in love.*

She was working on an advertorial feature for *Him* magazine and had been casting models all day with the magazine's art director and some tedious little marketing person from the Korean car company whose brief it was. The client wanted an Emma Peel-type who'd look good in black PVC while brandishing a derringer on the bonnet of one of their nasty little cars. The normal procedure was to call in some girls who would arrive minimally made up and casually dressed, have a two-minute chat with them, look politely at their portfolios and tell them you'd be in touch.

However, the small and rather sweaty marketing person from Poowoo cars, or whatever they were called, had insisted that each girl in turn, all fifteen of them, squeeze themselves into the catsuit, pout, brandish a can of Spray-Mount in lieu of the derringer and pose for a Polaroid, which he deftly pocketed at the end of the casting, claiming that he had to take them to a 'top level' marketing meeting that afternoon.

Top-level bedside drawer, more like, Nadine had thought distastefully.

She hated advertorial work. Horrid businessmen. Had no idea about art, no idea about creativity. Thought that *Him* magazine was just a lower-shelf, more credible version of *Penthouse* or *Playboy*. Thought it was just a load of tits and arses. Which it was, to a certain extent. But there was more to it than that – articles on how to be a better boyfriend, how to be a better cook, dozens of pages of beautiful fashion photography, travel articles, sports, hobbies, health, music and film.

It was a quality magazine written by quality journalists and this was how Nadine justified her dependence on the magazine for her living.

So when nasty little businessmen turned up, all hot and sweaty under the collar at the prospect of leering over a parade of nubile women young enough to be their daughters, rustling the metaphorical rolls of banknotes in their trouser pockets and treating Nadine like she was some kind of pornmonger, it made her feel very angry.

They'd left her after lunch amid a sea of leftover Prêt sandwiches and empty sushi containers and she'd finally been able to give in to her feelings of total and utter abject misery by throwing herself on to her pink couch and having a tantrum.

'Men!' she shouted at Pia, her tiny, hyperactive assistant. 'Bloody fucking men. All they want is perfection, all they want is tits like this and arses like that

147

and legs this long and thighs that firm and youth and sex and lots of it.'

Pia, twenty-two, with tits like this and an arse like that, nodded wholeheartedly in agreement.

'They don't want reality, they don't want longevity, they don't want character or personality or anything even vaguely three-dimensional. They want fantasy and unattainability and when will they all finally grow up and realize that they can't have it!

'Even Dig!' she continued. 'Even lovely, sane, together Dig. I thought he was different, but he's not. He's just the same. Show him a pair of long legs and a pair of 34Cs, show him perfect bone structure and long blonde hair and he's away – whoosh – just watch him go.'

Pia nodded sympathetically and handed Nadine half a satsuma she'd just unpeeled.

'So shallow' – Nadine shook her head slowly in disappointment – 'so very shallow. And he thinks he can win the bet – ha! Thinks that this counts! Well, it doesn't. When I said "over twenty-six" I meant a *nice* girl who was over twenty-six, not some blonde bimbo with a husband and a "To Let" sign where her personality should be. Delilah *does not count.*'

Pia shook her head sagely and plopped another segment of satsuma into her uncharacteristically silent mouth.

'That girl,' continued Nadine, 'that girl made me miserable at school, miserable. And I know I'm a grown woman and I should have got over it by now, but I haven't. From the second I set eyes on her on Saturday it all came flooding back. I hate her. I really, really hate her – aaargh!' She let out a frustrated cry and flopped about petulantly on the sofa for a while.

'Fuckin' hell, Deen,' said Pia, eyeing Nadine with concern, 'd'you fancy him, or something?'

'Eh?'

'Dig – have you got a thing about him?'

'Oh, don't be ridiculous.'

'Then why are you getting so worked up about him and this Delilah bird?'

'*I'm not getting worked up . . .*'

Pia shot her a hard, 'don't-give-me-that-bullshit' stare.

'I'm not getting worked up,' she said again, less aggressively, 'I just . . . it's just. Oh God – I dunno. I just don't want Dig to go out with Delilah, because I know what she's like, and Dig's my best mate and I don't want anything bad to happen to him. Because I love him. That's all.'

'But how come you've never been bothered in the past? About Dig's girlfriends?'

'Because . . .' Nadine paused and sat up straight. 'Because . . . they weren't real. Because they were pretend girlfriends.'

'Because they didn't threaten your friendship with Dig?'

'*Exactly!* That's exactly it!'

'You have really got to sort yourself out,' said Pia. 'You're a bloody disaster.'

'I know,' sniffed Nadine, 'I know. Oh God – d'you know what I did last night?' She groaned and told Pia about the humiliating stalking episode outside Dig's flat.

'Fucking hell, we have really got to sort this out. You are losing it – totally. There's only one thing for it, you've got to win the bet. Take your mind off this Delilah tart. What was your part of the deal?'

'Oh, I had to go out with someone I genuinely liked instead of someone I *wanted* to like.'

'OK. So, who do you like?'

'No one. That's the whole problem. I don't like anyone.'

'Oh, come on. You must like someone. Everyone likes someone. What about that stylist from *Him*. The blond guy? He's cute.'

'David? No way. Too trendy, too vain, too pretty.'

'OK – what about that guy you shot for *Cosmo*'s 50 Most Eligible last year, that merchant banker with the unpronounceable name. He really fancied you.'

Nadine shook her head firmly. 'Absolutely no way. He had a stupid accent and a horrible bottom.'

'All right. How about Danny, that courier bloke who's always flirting with you? He's quite sexy.'

'Uh-uh. No more couriers, thank you. And besides, he has that spit-build-up thing in the corners of his mouth – yuck.'

'Jesus, Deen. You're a fussy cow, aren't you?'

'Well, apparently not. Apparently that's the problem – not fussy enough. I can't just go on looks or the fact that they fancy me. It has to be someone I can honestly imagine having a proper relationship with.'

'And have you ever managed that before?'

'What do you mean?'

'Well – in the past. Have you ever been in love with someone who was right for you?'

Good question. Nadine squinted and thought back, through rows and rows of unsuitable men, wimps and weirdos and holes that needed filling. She thought back through Maxwell and Tony and John, through Simon and Raffy and Tom, and she didn't stop until she got to

150

her first and only serious boyfriend, to the love of her life, the man who broke her heart.

'Phil,' she said, finally. 'Phil was right for me.'

Philip Rich had been everything that Dig wasn't. He was ten years older for a start, at twenty-eight, which had seemed enormously old to Nadine at the time and had been, without a doubt, the most handsome man at Manchester Polytechnic, with intense indigo eyes and a perfect Roman nose.

He drove a black MG Midget, he wore black-leather trousers and he had black shiny hair which was cut into a dramatic jaw-length bob. He was divorced. He arrived at college every morning carrying an aluminium brief-case and another metal-clad box full of state-of-the-art photography equipment. He was unfeasibly cool and completely unattainable and from the minute Nadine set eyes on him on her first day at poly, she knew she wanted him.

She'd lived with him for three years. He failed his degree and then broke off their relationship two weeks before the end of university, took the last £50 out of their supposed 'summer travel' piggy bank and just disappeared one Tuesday afternoon. She'd been devastated.

'So, what went wrong?' asked Pia.

Nadine shrugged. 'I've got absolutely no idea,' she said, 'it's a mystery. He just took off.'

'Why don't you ring him?'

'What!'

'Ring him. Arrange to see him.'

'Don't be ridiculous! I haven't seen him for ten years! He's probably married by now.'

'Yes, but he might not be. He might be single and

151

lonely.' Pia was an eternal optimist and a hopeless romantic.

'No,' said Nadine firmly, 'I can't phone him. He'll think I'm weird.'

'Of course he won't. He'll be made up. Have you still got his number?'

'Well, I've got his parents' number – somewhere – I think.'

'OK then – no excuses. Find it and phone them. Get his number. Meet up with him. You'll feel *so* much better about this Dig and Delilah thing.'

'D'you think?'

'I don't think,' said Pia sternly, '*I know.*'

CHAPTER FIFTEEN

'You did *what*?!' Dig exclaimed loudly down the phone a few minutes later. 'You phoned *Phil*? What the fuck did you phone Phil for?'

'Well,' Nadine replied sniffily, 'why not?'

'Why not! How can you say "why not?" Because he was the most self-centred, arrogant, pretentious twat I have ever met, because he belittled you and controlled you and put you down, because he used you for money and sex and everything he could get out of you.'

'That is not true! He loved me! He did not use me!'

'So who paid the rent for the last two years you were there? Who went out to work in a bar every night to pay the rent while he sat around on his arse moaning about how nobody understood his "art"? Who paid for his clothes and his haircuts and his poncey fucking Australian shampoo? Eh?'

'He paid me back!'

'He gave you a hundred quid! That's about 5 per cent of what he owed you!'

'Look, it wasn't his fault his marriage didn't work out, it wasn't his fault he had to pay the woman all that alimony.'

'Students? Paying alimony? Didn't that strike you as wrong, Nadine? He was ripping you off and you were too blind and too gullible to see it! Jesus! I can't believe you! It took you months to get over what that bastard did to you. You were like a little mouse when you got back from Manchester.'

'I was not!'

'Yes you were! Don't you remember how you stopped wearing make-up, and the way you dressed, in all that baggy black stuff, and how you had no confidence whatsoever.'

'God, Dig! You're talking about nine years ago! People change, you know? Phil had a bad time at Manchester. He sounded completely different when I spoke to him on the phone, he sounded really relaxed and laid back.'

'Nadine. What are you doing? Why are you doing this? Why, after nine years of getting on with your life perfectly well, are you suddenly phoning up some fucked-up old wanker you used to go out with when you were nineteen?'

'*Exactly!* That's exactly it. I am *not* getting on with my life perfectly well. That's the whole problem. As you yourself have pointed out, I'm getting on with my life perfectly *unwell.*'

'I don't understand.'

Nadine sighed. 'Phil is the only bloke I've ever loved, ever cared about, and I want to see him. That's all there is to understand.'

'Oh! *I* get it! This is for the bet, isn't it?'

'Oh, don't be ridiculous!'

'Of course it is! Why else would you suddenly decide that you just have to see some bloke you went out with ten years ago?'

'Oh,' exclaimed Nadine, sarcastically, 'oh, I see! It's perfectly all right for you to go off on dates with disastrous women from your past, it's perfectly all right for you to go off with Delilah Lillie after what she did to you.

It's perfectly all right for you, but when *I* want to see someone who I used to be in love with, someone who hurt *me*, then there's something wrong with it! You fucking hypocrite!!'

'I haven't *gone off* with Delilah! What are you talking about? We had dinner, that's all. We had dinner and we went to see a band!'

'And that is all I intend to do when I see Phil tonight. We're going to have a drink together and see how it goes.'

'Well, that's fine. You go and you have a good time. But don't expect to come crying to me when he starts pulling you apart again and you're handing out cash left, right and centre and your self-esteem is in tatters.'

'I can assure you, I won't!'

'Good!'

'Fine!'

Oh dear. The conversation was unravelling at an alarming rate of knots. For the second time in less than a week, Dig and Nadine were having an argument that they couldn't joke their way out of.

'I'm going now,' said Dig, brusquely, after a short, tense silence, 'I'm really busy.'

'That's fine,' sniffed Nadine, '*I* happen to be rather busy, too.'

'See you?' he ventured, unenthusiastically.

'Yeah. See you,' she returned with a corresponding lack of enthusiasm. She took the receiver from her ear and was about to replace it when she decided she had one last thing to say. 'Oh,' she began, 'by the way. I'm not *stupid*, you know? You don't need to lie to me, about you and Delilah. I know *everything* about you and Delilah. So don't give me all that "just good friends" bullshit, OK, because it won't wash.'

155

And with that she forcefully and noisily dropped the receiver back on to its cradle, threw herself down on to her studio sofa and started crying again.

Dig forcefully and noisily dropped the receiver back on to its cradle, lit a cigarette and sighed deeply. Jesus, he thought to himself, what the fuck is going on here? I mean, will someone please tell me what the fuck is happening?

He'd phoned Nadine to make things up with her, to patch over their argument of Monday, and instead things had ended up a hundred times worse.

Phil?

Philip Rich?

How could it be possible that this awful character was re-entering his life after so many years?

Dig hadn't liked many of Nadine's boyfriends over the years but there'd been none he'd disliked as heartily as Philip Rich. Philip Rich with his ridiculous shiny bob and effeminate leather trousers. Philip Rich with his long words and condescending manner. Philip Rich with all his supposed good taste and maturity and sophistication. Philip Rich who'd morphed into Philip Poor so suspiciously quickly.

Philip Rich who'd picked up his tender, teenage heart with hairless, careless hands and snapped it clean in two.

the worst weekend . . . ever

Nadine had been in Manchester nearly two months and Dig was in a bad way, still reeling from the emotional punch in the stomach she'd dealt him after their day in the park.

He wrote to her nearly every day. He sent her letters and comical postcards; he sent her promo copies of new singles, and posters and stickers and T-shirts, all freebies from his new job. He tried to keep things light-hearted, pretend that he was only interested in the so-called friendship he'd conjured up so desperately on Nadine's doorstep that night, pretend that he was too busy being successful and indispensable in his exciting job to have time to think about what had happened between the two of them on that September weekend.

Which was, of course, completely and utterly not true.

The truth was, that Dig Ryan had fallen madly, passionately and devotedly in love with Nadine Kite.

He dreamed of her at night. He wrote songs for her by day. He pinned up the Holy T class photo by his bed and kissed Nadine's fuzzy-haired image good-night before he went to sleep. He kept dried blades of grass from their day on Primrose Hill in a paper bag in his drawer.

Nadine wrote back occasionally, not as often as he, and after seven weeks, three days and fourteen hours of this façade, Dig felt that strong enough foundations had been laid for him to suggest a weekend visit to Manchester, without scaring her away. She put him off at first, but eventually they organized a date, and it was all he could think about for the week before he went.

So, here he was, as he'd imagined himself so many times, clutching his weekend bag, striding purposefully up the concourse at Euston station towards the train that was to bear him Nadine-wards, to the land of see-through dresses and radiant skin, spring-water laughs and silken mouths. She'd moved out of digs and into a flat now, and he presumed that he'd be bunged on to some kind of sofa and treated like a kid brother, but he didn't care. Just to be there would be enough, actually to be in Nadine's flat.

Nadine's flat. It sounded like poetry to Dig. He had images of it in his mind, images of voiley, floaty things and joss sticks, coloured muslins, embroidered throws and dried flowers, Water Lilies posters on the walls and loads of green-packaged Body Shop stuff in the bathroom.

It seemed she had a flatmate of some sort, who she referred to in her letters as 'Phil' – he was probably gay – but hopefully he'd be out a lot and he and Nadine could hang out together in her jasmine-scented living room, listening to all the records he'd brought up with him from Electrogram and smoking the hash he'd gone to so much trouble acquiring from a bloke with gold teeth in Ealing Broadway.

Dig was prepared to accept that there was unlikely to be any kissing this weekend. Nadine was more than likely still going to be in her 'independent woman' phase and he didn't want to rush things. All he could do for now was develop the intimacy between them. The rest, despite everything his surging, raging hormones were trying so hard to tell him, could wait till later.

He resisted the urge to buy Nadine a bunch of flowers as he dismounted his train at Piccadilly and instead bought her a bag of Cola Bottles and a stupid lighter with 'Welcome to Manchester – Britain's Second City' on it and thought to himself how glad he was to have had the good fortune to have been born in Britain's *first* city. He'd made an arrangement to meet Nadine outside, by the taxi rank, and as he emerged from the train station he looked around him for a fountain of auburn hair flecked with gold and an elusive shimmer of translucent cotton.

He was therefore more than a little surprised when he turned around to see Nadine, her beautiful hair chopped off into a severe bob at her chin, dressed entirely in black and wearing a vicious slash of red lipstick across her mouth. She looked very pale and very thin and very trendy.

She was nervous with him as they sat in the back of the taxi on the way to her flat. She kept talking about this Phil character and how much she hoped Dig would like him and how he shouldn't be put off by his manner – he could be a bit abrupt with people sometimes – and how he was very interested to meet Dig as he hadn't met any of her London friends yet and Dig was thinking, all right, all right, what's the big deal, it's you I've come to see, not your bender flatmate. But instead he smiled reassuringly and said that he was looking forward to meeting him, too, and he was sure they'd get on fine, and Nadine had looked disproportionately relieved to hear him say so.

Dig should have twigged when she started saying

159

things like 'I don't know how much we'll be able to do this weekend, *we* haven't got much money at the moment' and 'there's a vegetarian café around the corner from *us* where *we* go for breakfast sometimes' but he didn't. He certainly should have twigged when she referred to '*our* bedroom', but he didn't. When he looked back on the whole episode the following day, he would wonder at his own stupidity and never again would he snort sceptically at those 'cross wires' comedy sketches on the telly when two people manage to discuss entirely different topics together without either of them realizing it.

Dig's first sense that something was afoot came as he crossed the threshold into Nadine's flat. It was horrible. Not that this fact aroused any suspicion in itself. But it was absolutely horrible. It was on the second floor of a discoloured thirties block, built above a parade of shops, with bucket-shaped concrete balconies attached to the front and paint peeling off the walls in enormous flaps. The flat itself had no central heating and was wretchedly furnished with the sort of furniture more usually associated with skips outside buildings and house-clearance sales. Many of the aluminium-framed windows were cracked or missing entirely and patched over with gungy layers of mud-coloured parcel tape.

Far from the feminine bouquet of jasmine and white musk and Body Shop peppermint foot lotion that Dig had expected to encounter, the flat smelled overpoweringly and depressingly of damp and mildew. No attempt had been made to personalize it or to camouflage its ugliness, other than the rows of rather pretentious and badly composed black and white photographs in Clip-frames which hung on nearly every wall in the flat.

160

'We're going to decorate it next term, when we've both got a bit more money,' said Nadine, hanging her black nylon bomber jacket from a hook in the hallway and leading Dig towards a door at the bottom of the corridor.

This time the 'we' reference resonated a little more unambiguously and Dig began to feel vaguely uncomfortable. He tucked his hair behind his ears self-consciously as Nadine pushed open the door, and attempted to flatten his fringe on to his forehead.

The door creaked open slowly and somewhat dramatically and there, sitting cross-legged on the floor, smoking a stinking Gauloise and reading the *Guardian* was the most enormous arsehole Dig had ever set eyes on. On a bleak November morning, in a dank and overcast flat, this man was wearing sunglasses.

Really and truly, without a word of a lie.

RayBans.

Tortoiseshell ones.

Unbelievable.

He was barefoot and wearing pristine white jeans with a big black linen shirt, the sleeves held up to his elbows by stretchy metal suspenders. His hair was ludicrous, a soigné wedge of over-polished black, tied back from his face into a stumpy pony-tail. He was in possession of a proud and well-constructed nose of which, Dig could tell, he was inordinately enamoured and when he looked up slowly, calcu*late*dly slowly, from his paper to acknowledge Dig's presence in the room, his expression arranged itself into a strange and unnatural contortion of his facial features which didn't suit him in the slightest. Dig suspected he was trying to smile.

'All right,' he said, lifting his glasses an inch or two from the bridge of his nose and leaving them resting on his forehead while he regarded Dig through squinted eyes. After a second or two, he tapped the glasses nonchalantly, letting them fall back on to his nose, before going back to his newspaper and his smouldering Gauloise.

It was antipathy at first sight. Dig had never before in his life felt so much dislike towards another person within such a short space of time. This bloke, whoever he was, was a complete wanker. He was a wanker of the highest order and of the greatest magnitude. He was the beginning and the end of the wanker universe, the original wanker, the top wanker, the wanker to end all other wankers. You had to hand it to him: this bloke was at the cutting edge of wankerdom.

Dig hated him.

As Dig stood awkwardly at the edge of the room, absorbing this unexpected surge of negative feelings and the fact that the lovely and ravishing Nadine was living in near-squalor with the Antichrist, the most terrible thing happened.

Nadine, who, he now noticed, was wearing a worryingly similar black linen shirt, the sleeves hoisted up with the same metal suspenders, suddenly dropped her bag on to the sofa, kicked off her DM shoes, walked up to Phil, crouched down behind him and wrapped her lovely arms around his shoulders, squeezed him gently and planted a great big kiss on the back of his neck.

Dig's jaw dropped and his eyelids sprung apart. All of a sudden, everything fell into place; all of a sudden, everything made blindingly obvious, disgusting, foul and rancid sense. This *person*, this ridiculous, affected and contrived assortment of mannerisms, pretensions and

162

vanities was Nadine's lover. This person who represented in one full set of human organs and limbs everything that Dig could possibly find to hate in another person, was sharing his bed with Nadine Kite – the same Nadine Kite who had by her own admission been a lush and lovely virgin as little as eight short weeks ago, waiting sensibly for the right time with the right person, prepared to hold out till her thirtieth year if necessary. And now here she was giving it out, every night and with bountiful generosity, he presumed, to the foulest man he'd ever met.

Dig couldn't really remember much about the rest of the weekend. He didn't let his surprise show and he didn't ask Nadine about her relationship with Phil. He acted like he'd been expecting to find her in this cohabitation. He played it cool, he played the role of the scruffy, innocuous schoolfriend from years gone by, up to see his old pal for the weekend, exchanging nostalgic tales from the past around the breakfast table with Phil and Nadine, messing around, making adolescent jokes and talking with overblown enthusiasm about his new job and his new car. In fact, cars were the only thing that he and Phil found in common that weekend, and Phil even took him for a drive around the block in his little MG Midget – the high spot in an otherwise wretched weekend.

Dig had no time alone with Nadine and he didn't get to play her any of his records. Phil seemed to think that the hunk of hash Dig had brought with him was some sort of *gift*, hijacked it entirely and smoked the whole lot, constructing painstakingly complicated little spliffs as if performing origami, the Rizlas all folded on the diagonal and the tip folded into some kind of triangle, which took fifteen minutes each to make and smoked like shit.

By the time Dig had decided that the whole weekend had sunk as low as it possibly could, and that all he had to do now was get through the night and then he could go home, things got even worse.

After an excruciating evening in a miserable pub watching Phil become more and more morose and distant as the night and the conversation ground on, Dig was installed, as he'd predicted, on the sofa in the living room. The sofa was spectacularly uncomfortable, the room Arctically cold and the quilt they'd given him to sleep under was thin and smelled of old people.

And then, just as he was starting to drift off, to forget where he was, something woke him up. A squeak. Followed by another squeak. Followed by yet another. Rhythmic squeaks, one after the other. And then a soft banging, in time with the squeaks. Bangsqueak, bangsqueak, bangsqueak . . .

Dig's heart fell into his toes as it dawned on him what he was listening to – the sounds of Nadine, *his* Nadine, being soundly and roundly porked by Philip Rich. He felt instantly nauseous and pulled a cushion over his head. The cushion, however, proved insufficient in the face of what was to come. After about fifteen minutes of a progressively louder and more insistent bangsqueak, Nadine started to wail – a whimpery sort of moan to start with, developing into a blood-curdling howl later. This continued for another five minutes or so and was then augmented by the voice of Philip Rich, whose loins were quite obviously fit to explode, judging by the rawness of his groaning.

The banging reached pneumatic-drill proportions, the

shouting began to crescendo and Dig stuck fingers in both his ears and started humming gently to himself in an attempt to drown out the noise. By the time he pulled his fingers from his ears and emerged from under the quilt, all was quiet again, except for the sound of the tap running in the bathroom and the toilet being flushed.

He heard Phil and Nadine's bedroom door close and turned sadly on to his side.

He really, really, hadn't wanted to hear that. That was, in fact, the last thing in the entire world he had ever wanted to hear. He felt sick. He felt dirty. He felt disgusting. He felt contaminated.

He felt as jealous as fucking hell.

He left fairly early the following morning, politely turning down Phil's offer of a lift and claiming that he'd rather get a cab, not put him to any trouble. He refused Nadine's offer to accompany him to the station also, as he really couldn't think of one thing that he would have to say to her if she did. He would either break down uncontrollably and start sobbing, 'Why? Why? Why? For the love of God, tell me why?' or he'd be sarcastic and unpleasant and scathing and make Nadine hate him. So he shook hands with Phil and thanked him for his hospitality, and Nadine saw him off from outside the flat.

'God, Dig,' she said, looking inexplicably happy, 'thanks so much for coming – it's been really, really nice having you here. I wasn't sure how things were going to work out, you know, with Phil being around but – he really liked you!' She was bursting over with excitement about this. 'He told me last night, when we were in bed . . .'

Dig shuddered at the thought.

165

' . . . He says you can come and stay any time, he thinks you're a really sweet bloke . . .'

Oh God – she was so thrilled and he was quite obviously expected to be thrilled, too. He smiled grimly and said something inconsequential and filthily dishonest along the lines of 'Yeah, he's a nice bloke,' before a well-timed taxi appeared at the head of the road and he stuck his arm out for it. There was just enough time for a quick peck on the cheek and a couple of niceties before the cab took him away and deposited him, like a half-demented hostage being thrown from a moving car after twenty-four hours of interrogation, at Manchester Piccadilly.

Dig never returned to Manchester, despite Nadine's numerous and regular invitations.

He did, however, meet up with the dreaded Phil on a few more occasions, when the happy couple returned to London for holidays and the odd weekend. Phil did appear to have a genuine fondness for Dig, a patronizing, big-brotherly sort of fondness which consisted of poking fun at him whenever possible and using him to magnify his own rather small reserves of humour and intelligence. Dig took this in his stride for Nadine's sake but after a while began making excuses and turning down invitations.

Nadine became a different person during those three years with Philip Rich. She appeared to have no opinions or ideas of her own, and it broke Dig's heart to think of that strong, determined, stubborn girl who'd turned him down all those years ago because there was more she wanted from life than the constraints of a relationship would allow, so easily surrendering herself and her independence to a waste of space like Phil.

Very infrequently Nadine would be in London on her own and on these occasions, Dig would always try his hardest to make her see sense, to convince her that it was *him*, not Phil, who should be the object of her fragrant affections. But she was in love – completely. Nadine would shrug his arm from her shoulder, slap his fingers from her bottom, push his lips from her mouth, but always with a sense of humour. There was never again any *serious* reference to the weekend of 12 September 1987 – it got used in moments of piss-take and teasing, it was treated as a rather amusing incident from their past, as a joke. And even when Nadine returned to London for good, her heart in tatters and her relationship with Phil categorically over, there was no looking back. He still tried his luck with the occasional affectionate gesture but something had grown between them in the time she was in Manchester that left such gestures impotent.

Gradually Nadine found herself again. Her career was a success story from the start, her wardrobe and disposition accumulated layers of colour day by day, and as the years went by she developed into one of the most extraordinary, incredible people Dig knew. Dig loved Nadine more than anyone – he loved her as much as he loved his mum, and that was saying something. The love he'd felt for her that weekend in 1987 when she'd broken his heart and hurt him more than he'd ever thought possible was just the building block for a lifetime of love.

Occasionally, even now, he would look at Nadine and something deep inside him would stir, something beyond platonic love, something *carnal*. But that was only occasional and he was a horny bastard, so it was inevitable really. He held her in the highest esteem and had the greatest respect for her. He loved her, cherished her and cared for her.

He would go so far as to say that he *adored* her.

But right now, at this precise moment in time, Dig Ryan thought that Nadine Kite was the stupidest, most ridiculous, idiotic, irrational, absurd and preposterous *fool* of a woman he had ever had the misfortune to know and love.

Phil?

Philip Rich?

Jesus Christ.

CHAPTER SIXTEEN

As the day drew to a close, and Dig's frustration had matured nicely into a full-blown bad mood, he became overcome by a desperate desire to get steaming drunk. Images of ice-cold lagers and chunky tumblers of iced whiskey danced in front of his eyes and the scent of a good old-fashioned boozer tickled his nostrils. Anything to take his mind off Nadine and her ridiculous 'date'.

Nobody in the office had been interested in the suggestion of a post-work drink so Dig had attempted to track down Delilah to suggest that maybe they do something together. He was intending to tempt her with the offer of another gig, or maybe even two. But there'd been no answer at the Primrose Hill number all day, and by the time he got home at eight o'clock he'd given up on the idea.

As ever, there were any number of gigs and general music-biz schmoozathons he could have attended but, glancing out of his window at a wet and chilly Wednesday evening, he decided on reflection that his fridgeful of big Buds, two packets of Marlboro Lights and something on video that he'd taped earlier on in the week would make for a mighty pleasant night in, so he plumped up his cushions, stretched out his legs and settled down for a night of vegetating.

At about nine o'clock his stomach started growling and he leafed through his ever-expanding library of takeaway menus, deciding on a meat vindaloo and a prawn dopiaza from the Indian down the road.

Half an hour later his doorbell rang and he padded down his hall towards the entry phone clutching a twenty-pound note. 'Top floor,' he said into the mouthpiece, without waiting to be addressed. He opened his front door and listened to the sound of footsteps against the cold linoleum, resentful footsteps that grew slower and slower as they neared the dizzying heights of the top floor. Restaurant-delivery drivers hated him for making them take the stairs and always arrived at his door in very poor spirits indeed. Consequently Dig had prearranged his features into his usual disarming toothy smile, ready to be charming and placatory.

The smile fell off his face like a badly hung painting from a wall, however, when a dishevelled, small and extremely ugly Yorkshire Terrier suddenly bounded up the top flight of stairs and came careering round the corner and straight into his flat, leaving a trail of tiny grubby footprints all over his oatmeal seagrass.

'Digby!' echoed a female voice around the stairwell. 'You bad boy! Come back here this instant!' The female voice was followed a couple of seconds later by the form of Delilah, equally as dishevelled as the deliriously damp Digby and shaking out a half-furled and very soggy umbrella. 'Hi,' she said, stopping in her tracks when she saw Dig's shocked expression.

'Hi,' replied Dig, mindlessly folding his twenty-pound note into a square and tucking it into his pocket.

They stood like that for a moment or two, Delilah slowly dripping all over the floor, Digby running around Dig's flat in frenetic circles, while he himself stared in wonderment at Delilah.

'I was . . . er . . . expecting a curry,' said Dig, eventually, in the absence of anything more relevant to say.

'Oh,' said Delilah, 'and you got me instead!'

'Yeah,' laughed Dig, wondering whether Delilah was ever going to offer an explanation for her presence.

'So,' said Delilah, running her fingers through her damp hair and peering around the doorway, 'are you going to invite me in?'

Dig started and moved out of the way. 'Oh God,' he said, 'of course. Yeah. Come in. Come in.'

He held open the door for Delilah and caught his breath as her sheepskin coat flapped open briefly to reveal a thoroughly waterlogged cotton blouse sticking like clingfilm to her breasts. The collar was slightly askew, revealing just a hint of damp cleavage and the smell emanating from Delilah's dripping personage was quite overpoweringly delicious.

He had no idea what she was doing here, but she was a lot more welcome than a dopiaza.

CHAPTER SEVENTEEN

That same evening, a quarter of a mile away to the east, Nadine finds herself sitting in a low-level seventies red-brick monstrosity loudly advertising 'sizzlin' steaks for £2.99' and going under the name of the Brecknock Arms.

She's only been here a few minutes but she's already sensing, very strongly, that she's made a mistake. This is all Dig's fault, she thinks to herself. *He* drove me to it.

She is sitting on a torn red vinyl barstool, wearing – inappropriately, she now feels – an emerald-green angora cardigan over a fuchsia crocheted dress, a silk poppy in her hair, staring at a beer- and ash-stained *swirl* of tan and orange carpeting, drinking a watered-down pint of Theakstones and wondering what has happened to the mysterious and debonair Phil of her memories, the Phil with the shiny black bob and the slick leather trousers and the elegant Roman nose.

The man now sitting in front of her is *so old*. His face has the crumpled-newspaper look of an over-the-hill rock star. His cheekbones, once such a feature, now give his face a desolate geography, and his teeth are in the sort of condition that would give a Californian nightmares. The once glossy black hair now hangs limply and finely over his ears and forehead in a style better suited to a man half his age, and his beautiful nose has acquired sharp lines and large open pores, overpowering his hollow face.

172

He has dark circles around his eyes and an earring with a crucifix hanging off it and he is wearing an old lambswool jumper, black jeans and a pair of football boots. There's an indistinguishable black-ink tattoo on his very white forearm that wasn't there before, and he smells faintly of fags and booze.

Looking back, Nadine supposes that Phil always had the kind of face that would age cruelly, but it still shocks her to see someone she last remembered as a young man so drained of his youth.

This is what Keith Richards would have looked like if he'd left the Stones twenty years ago and become a bus driver, she thinks to herself.

All Nadine's foolish, pathetic little fantasies about some over-the-top romantic reunion with her first love, her idiotic visions of their eyes meeting and twelve years disappearing, her naïve dreams of a charming, atmospheric pub, dazzling conversation and reignited passion, all crumpled and died within seconds of walking into the Brecknock Arms. Phil was supposed to look the same as she remembered, with maybe just a touch of distinguished grey at the temples. He wasn't supposed to look like this. The pub wasn't supposed to be like this.

This is a huge mistake. She is a fool.

Phil, on the other hand, had been speechless with joy to see Nadine walk in.

'Nadine Kite,' he'd drawled, grasping her hands, 'Nadine Kite. You fucking came, man. You're here! Look at you. You look great. I love your outfit, it's wild!' And then he looked like he was about to hug her, so Nadine deftly extricated herself from his grip and balanced herself on her barstool. He introduced her to the man behind the bar, a large, white-haired Scotsman wearing a nylon shirt and slightly too tight trousers. 'Murdo, this is Nadine Kite,' he said, beaming, 'we used to live together, at university. Murdo served me my first legal pint when I was eighteen.'

Murdo smiled grimly, gave Nadine's hand a good hard shake and turned round to remove a rather half-hearted ploughman's from the dumb waiter behind him, obviously as unsure as Nadine as to why they'd been introduced.

Phil insisted on paying for the first round, despite Nadine's best efforts to swing the balance of the evening towards a *Dutch* sort of thing by paying for them herself, and he then, worse still, insisted on carrying her drink to their table, thereby potentially setting the tone for a night of false expectations and crossed wires.

'So,' she says, keeping her body language neutral and taking a measured sip from her Theakstones, 'Phil. How've you been?'

'Oh, you know. Not bad.' He takes a noisy slurp of his beer and wipes his mouth with the back of one hand. 'You?' He looks nervous, as if he's scared of her.

'Fine,' she smiles, 'great, in fact.'

'So,' he says, 'what *inspired* you to get in touch again, after all this time – do I owe you money?' He laughs, extra loud to ensure that Nadine knows he's only joking, but it occurs to her that this is what he's really thinking.

'Well,' she replies, 'there was that fifty quid you took out of the piggy-bank! But seriously – I just wanted to find out how you were. What you've been up to. I just felt ... I dunno ... you spend so many years with someone, you're so close to someone and then suddenly, overnight, they're not in your life any more. They just get on a train

174

and disappear for ten years. I wanted to hear your story, I suppose, the "Story of Philip Rich"!'

Phil exhales through tight lips and eyes her sceptically. 'You got all night?' he asks.

Nadine nods, enthusiastically. She senses a story here, something behind that look, and suddenly decides that the only way she is going to be able to get through this evening is by pretending that Phil isn't really a part of her history, isn't a bloke she lived with and loved ten years ago, but is in fact someone she's interviewing for a magazine or researching for a novel, that sort of thing. 'Start at the beginning,' she says. 'Start at the end of us . . .'

Nadine was disappointed to learn that Phil had gone back to London when they split up, gone back home and not to the remote Yorkshire village she'd been fondly imagining for some strange reason. He had come back, moved in with his parents, sold all his camera equipment, extended his bank loan and, with a shocking lack of business judgement, at the height of an international recession bought back the photographic lighting company he'd sold to fund his degree. For a song, he said, laughing wryly at his own stupidity.

He was made bankrupt six months later and had a nervous breakdown.

His life then, it seemed, took a series of very unexpected and out-of-character turns, and Phil spent most of the nineties trying to 'find himself' through one alternative route after another – crystals, meditation, Chinese herbs, Buddhism and Taoism. He moved from town to town and from woman to woman in search of happiness and fulfilment until his failure to find either led him to a drink problem and yet another broken relationship on a travellers' site in Warwickshire.

On the day he left the site, he walked three miles to Nuneaton in the rain clutching a bottle of Taunton Dry, walked into a launderette, pissed in a tumble-drier, swore at an old man and nicked the money he'd left out for his next wash. He stole £1.50 and for that he got a three-month prison sentence.

'Best thing that ever happened to me,' he said, 'cut through all my bullshit.'

'What do you mean?' said Nadine, who was as gripped by his story as any *Cutting Edge* documentary.

'Being inside – I dunno, I'd spent so much of my life convinced that there was some big reason for me being here. First I thought it was to be rich, to be the consummate businessman with the mobile phone and the sharp suit and the keen mind. That didn't work out. Then I thought I was supposed to be creative and stylish, on the cutting edge, you know, some really cool photographer-type with dark glasses and a sexy girlfriend.' He glanced at Nadine and raised his eyebrows at her. She laughed. 'And that, as you know, didn't work out *at all*. So I got into all that alternative stuff, thought maybe I was meant to be a great healer or something. And when that didn't make me happy I moved towards the whole lifestyle thing, thought that if I could immerse myself in another world, then that would make me special.

'It was like . . . it was like I was trying on personas for fit, d'you know what I mean? Seeing what suited me. And then discarding them when I realized that they made me look like a twat.' He laughed hoarsely.

'It took a stretch inside to make me understand that some people aren't here for any big reason – they're just

176

here. And I realized then that I'm one of those people and that there's nothing actually wrong with that – d'you know what I mean? It's all right just to be a normal bloke, do a normal job and have normal friends. It was like a huge weight off my shoulders working that one out. And the pressure just sort of disappeared – it had been like this great big ugly parrot sitting on my shoulder all my life, and while I was inside it flew away.' Phil shrugged and lit a Rothman.

Nadine breathed out deeply. 'Fuck, Phil,' she said, 'I mean – I always knew that you wouldn't have had a boring life, but I can't believe how much has happened to you, how many changes you've made. It makes me feel so boring and ... predictable. God – I haven't done *anything* with my life.'

'What about the photography? Still taking pictures?'

She nodded.

'Making a living from it?'

'Yeah,' she said, 'a very good living, actually.'

'Oh yeah?' His body language suddenly became very focused on Nadine. 'Got a nice flat and all that?'

'Yes,' nodded Nadine, proudly.

'That's great. I'm really pleased for you. What sort of work have you been doing?'

'Oh' – she shrugged, suddenly remembering what Phil's attitude towards commercial photography had been at university, and expecting him to judge her – 'editorial, mainly. *Him* magazine. Do you know it?'

'Yeah. Tits and arses, isn't it?'

'Well, there's a lot more to it than that. But I have been known to take the odd picture of an arse, yes.' She smiled, nervously, waiting for Phil to chastise her for selling out. But he didn't. He smiled, too, and then he almost laughed. Nadine breathed a sigh of relief. 'I thought you'd be horrified,' she said. 'I thought I was about to get a lecture about the evils of commerce!'

'Nah,' said Phil, 'I think it's great. Really great. Christ, I was a right wanker at Manchester, wasn't I? So pretentious. Who the fuck did I think I was?' He laughed then, properly and, as the conversation progressed, it became more and more obvious that Phil wasn't the same person she'd known all those years ago, at all. He was ten years older, at least a stone thinner, and seemed to have a completely different set of priorities.

'So,' she said, 'when did you move back to London again?'

'Straight from the nick. March 1997.'

'Back to your parents?'

'Yeah.'

'And you're still there?'

Phil shook his head. 'Nah,' he said, 'nah. I've got a place in Finsbury Park now. A Peabody flat. My . . . er . . . grandparents sublet it to me.'

Nadine was confused. 'But you were at your parents' when I phoned their number?'

Phil shook his head, again. 'Nah. I was at mine, in Finsbury Park. I took the number with me when I went.'

'But . . . but . . . didn't your parents want to keep their number?'

Phil put down his pint and took a deep breath. He stared deep into Nadine's eyes, hardened his mouth and clenched his jaw.

'No. They don't need their number any more. They're dead.'

The bluntness of his response took Nadine somewhat by surprise. 'I see,' she said, having managed to train

178

herself out of the knee-jerk response of apologizing for the bereaved's misfortune. 'How long? How long have they been dead?'

Phil shrugged and took a slug of his beer. 'A year,' he said, 'a year and a bit.'

'What? Both of them?'

'Uh-huh.'

'They died together?'

'Yeah.'

'Oh God – how awful. What happened?'

'You don't want to know.'

'Yes I do.'

'It's not nice.'

'Tell me,' said Nadine, her curiosity now stimulated beyond her control. 'I can take it.'

Phil sighed and fell into a thoughtful silence, staring into the depths of his pint. Nadine thought he wasn't going to tell her, but eventually he looked up and opened his mouth, gazing into the distance while he waited, like a sluggish standpipe, for the words to come.

'My mum had lung cancer,' he began, 'she'd fought it for three years. They thought she was dead at one time, performed last rites and everything. But my mum wasn't having any of that. You remember my mum? She was a right old battleaxe and she fought it. And the tumour just kind of *dissolved*. They X-rayed her lungs one day and the tumour had gone. Everyone said it was a miracle. She said it was the evil thoughts she'd sent it – she called it Beelzebub, that lump. She hated it.' He smiled wryly. 'She reckoned that's what killed it – none of this positive-thinking malarkey, none of all that alternative stuff that I was into. Anyway, she makes a full recovery, and then two months later my dad's diagnosed with breast cancer.

179

Nah,' he said, 'I didn't know men could get it either, but they can. Here.' He indicated his pectorals. 'So, he's in hospital, having tests, operations, treatments, just like my mum, and it's looking bad for a while – the lump's quite big and they have to remove most of the flesh from around his chest, they've taken away his nipple and everything – it was a fucking mess' – he winced – 'but a year later and he's got the all-clear from the hospital and he's told he can get on with his life.

'So, after, you know, everything the pair of them have been through, they decide that they deserve a bit of a break, a bit of time away in the sunshine. So they cash in some Premium Bonds and book themselves a two-week cruise around the Mediterranean – it was off-season, so it wasn't too pricey. And I wave them off at Portsmouth and away they go. I'll never forget their faces on that deck – they looked so happy and, you know, excited.

'Anyway. And this is all according to witnesses, you know, obviously I wasn't there, but this is what happened, apparently. Mum had had a bad sardine, or something – she wasn't used to that sort of food – and she had a dodgy gut, you know, puking up, the squits, the works. So she's hanging off the side of the boat one night, puking her guts up while my dad's stroking her back and all that. Suddenly the ship lurches to one side, quite violently, and Mum's thrown to the other side of the boat, puking up as she goes, and there's puke absolutely everywhere. She's landed by some steep steps down to the next deck, metal steps, you know, like you get on boats, and knocked her head off one of those pipe things, and when Dad sees the blood starting to drip down her face he comes legging it across the deck towards her, not noticing that the floor's all slick with vomit.

'So' – Phil took a deep breath and slurp of beer before continuing – 'he's legging it across all this vomit, and he slips, and as he slips the boat lurches again and he's gone, according to someone who saw it all, he's gone *gliding* like a fucking ice-skater over the floor and then sort of tipped over, head first, through the door-way leading to the staircase and straight down those metal steps, head over heel over head, over heel, bang bang bang bang bang bang . . .'

He stopped again for a second to compose himself. Nadine held her breath. 'He copped it immediately, according to the ship's doctor. The fall snapped his spine. He didn't suffer . . .'

'Oh God. That's awful,' gasped Nadine, 'and what about your mother? What happened to your mother?'

Phil exhaled loudly. 'Well, she was in a bit of a state, obviously, what with my dad being dead and everything, and she was still puking up. The doctor sticks a plaster on her head where it's cut and gives her a sedative and something for her stomach, and she's sent back to her cabin. When the doctor knocked on her door early the next morning there was no answer so he got the steward bloke to let him in, and there she was, lying in bed' – he took another swig of his drink and looked at Nadine – 'dead.'

'What! But how?!'

'It was the knock on the head. It was worse than they'd thought. A blood clot, apparently. She would've died in her sleep. She wouldn't have suffered, either. At least neither of them suffered.'

'Oh, Phil. You poor thing. That's one of the worst stories I've ever heard.'

'I told you, didn't I? Told you it was bad. My dad died from slipping over in my mum's puke. Nice, isn't it?'

'Oh, Phil' – Nadine instinctively grabbed his hand across the table – 'you poor, poor thing.'

'Yeah,' he muttered, 'well.'

'So. You couldn't bear to live in the house any more after they went?'

'Eh?'

'You know. Your parents' house . . .?'

'Oh. Right. No. It . . . er . . . I did live there for a while after they died. It was mine, legally. They left it to me.'

'What. And you sold it?'

'Erm . . . no. Not exactly. I . . . I . . . Oh God. This is another bad thing, you know. The house. Another bad thing.'

'Go on,' soothed Nadine.

'You sure you want to hear this?'

Nadine nodded. 'If you're sure you want to tell me.'

'I haven't really talked about all this before, properly, you know.'

'Well, maybe you should.'

Phil sighed and took a deep breath. 'Yeah,' he said, 'you're right. I might as well tell you everything then, eh? Since you're listening.' He stopped and stared at her then, intently. 'You know something,' he said, 'you're still as beautiful as you ever were. Even more beautiful, if anything.'

Nadine blushed and looked away, embarrassed by the unexpected compliment and Phil's piercing gaze.

'Sorry,' he smiled, 'sorry. I shouldn't have said that. Anyway. The house. I met this girl, Mandy, when I was

182

inside. She was a visitor. Came to see me every day. We were both in our late thirties, both single, both a bit lost and lonely. She was such a great girl, a real laugh, game for anything, you know what I mean? She kind of brought me out of myself, gave me self-confidence, that sort of thing. It was different this time – she was a real person and I wasn't looking for anything from her, I wasn't looking for this mystical life any more. I just wanted to settle down with her, maybe a kid or two, an ordinary life. Anyway, when I got out we got engaged. I wanted to do it properly – the traditional way. My parents were made up, her parents were made up, everyone was over the moon. She was working for a computer company, technical stuff, and I'd just started working for this company, erecting marquees, earning a fair bit, and we opened a joint bank account, started putting away a couple of hundred quid a month. Saving up for the wedding. She wanted a big wedding. That was her dream. Big white dress and flower arrangements and string quartets – she wanted the lot, not just what our parents could afford. I wasn't bothered, myself, but I went along with it. Anything Mandy wanted was fine by me. So we're both working all the hours, saving every month, staying in, watching this money growing slowly, day by day.

'After a year, we had five grand in that bank account. Then Mandy gets a promotion – becomes a programmer – and suddenly she's earning, three, four, five times as much as me, and she's putting that much more in the account. A few months later and there's twelve grand in it. We'd reached our goal, we can afford the silver-service dinner and the master of ceremonies and the real champagne and the honeymoon in Antigua. Mandy's really excited. We set a date, we send out the invites, we book the honeymoon, the reception. It's all systems go.

'Then Mandy phones me at work one day – she's going off to pick up her wedding dress after work. It was costing two grand, this thing, it's all she could talk about – the dress this, the dress that, the dress the other. This dress was the most important thing in the world to her. Anyway. I'm on my way home that night, and I happen to be driving past this dress shop, you know, where she's picking her dress up from, and I decide to pop in, give her a lift. So, I walk into this shop and the assistant tells me, "Oh no, Miss Taylor, she's already left. She left about ten minutes ago. Are you the groom?" "Yes, I say, I'm the groom." "Well," she says, "maybe you should make sure she's all right, she seemed a bit" – what was it she said? – she seemed a bit *agitated*, yeah, agitated when she left." "Agitated?" I say. "Yeah," she says, "a bit upset."

'So, I suddenly get this really bad feeling. You know how they say – someone walking over your grave? Well, that's what it was like. So I goes legging it from this shop, and it was summer so it was still light, and I'm running towards the river as fast as I can – I don't know why, I've just got this feeling. And then, as I get towards Putney Bridge, dodging the traffic, running between the cars, I see her, half-way up the bridge. And I'm shouting her name, over and over – "Mandy! Mandy!" She's got her dress on, this huge wedding dress, and a big veil and tiara and everything. And she's just standing there, staring into the river. I'm calling her name but she doesn't turn around, and I'm running towards her, towards the bridge. And as I'm running I'm watching her, like it's in slow motion, watching her lift up this big

184

petticoat skirt of her dress and climbing on to the bridge, on to the actual stone-wall thing. She's standing there on the wall and staring into the water, just staring.' Phil stopped talking for a while and Nadine didn't try to fill the silence.

'I'm nearly on the bridge by now and I'm still calling out her name, and then, just as I set foot on the bridge, she turns towards me and I can see that she's smiling. She's smiling straight at me, a strange sort of smile. She slowly lifts up her veil and throws it back over her head, and then she turns back towards the water, and I'm running and running, and even though it feels like she's doing all this really slowly, she can't be because I don't get there in time, and as I'm running towards her I see her reach up on to her tiptoes, and then she puts her arms out, like this, out by her sides, and then . . . then she just lets herself fall, she doesn't jump, just lets herself fall, face first into the water, and all the fabric in her dress makes her sort of float down, like a para-chute. And I stop, just for a second, I stop running and I turn to look in the water, because, and this sounds really bad, but because it looks so extraordinary, *she* looks so extraordinary, floating there, in the black water, in her big white dress. She looks like a swan or some-thing, you know? It was *surreal* . . .

'So – obviously I'm straight in there, straight in the water, but I'm not a very good swimmer, as you might remember, I'm a doggy-paddler, and it's taking me ages to get to her, and the tide's quite strong, and I'm flailing around, calling her name, swallowing loads of this rancid disgusting water, and she just seems to be floating away from me – the closer I get, the further she gets – and I'm choking by now, I've got so much water in my

185

pipes and I'm getting really tired. But I keep on swimming towards her, I can still see this white blob, and it's not moving, and I feel like I've been in the water for hours now. Then suddenly this boat appears, it's a speedboat and there's some posh people on it, sunning themselves and drinking champagne, and I can hear the engine being turned off and the boat slowing down, and then someone's dragging me out of the water and I'm saying "Mandy. Get Mandy." "There's no one there," they're saying. "She's wearing a white dress," I tell them. But we went round and round in circles looking for her, all round that part of the river, for about an hour, and she wasn't there. She was gone.' Phil fell silent again.

'Her body washed up in Rotherhithe, three days later.'
Nadine gasped.

'We still don't know why she did it. Nobody knows why she did it. Everyone who knew her said she was happy, everyone said she really loved me, that she was so excited about the wedding, about the future. It doesn't make any sense. You know, that was nearly a year ago, and every day that goes by I want to talk to her, even if it's only for a minute, just so I can ask her why. It's the worst thing in the world not to know why. I know how, I know where and I know when – I just need to know why. That's all.'

'Oh God. Phil. I couldn't imagine . . . how can you . . . it must have been just awful . . . I mean . . .'

'It's all right,' he smiled, 'you're not supposed to know what to say. Don't worry. No one knows what to say. There's nothing anyone can say . . . That was a year ago. Then, like I told you, a couple of months later, my parents died. I was a bit of a mess for a while, as you can probably imagine, didn't really have much faith in anything,

186

nearly lost my job, messed up a lot of friendships, a lot of drinking, drugs, self-pitying, you know. I was wallowing in it, really.

'And then one morning, earlier this year, I woke up and the sun was shining and I could hear kids playing outside in the street, and I thought, Phil, you're nearly forty years old and what have you got? Nothing, I thought, nothing except this house and this body. That's all you've got. So I decided to take more care of them, and I started doing up my parents' house and looking after my body. No drugs, booze only at the weekends, a healthy diet. I bought myself a recipe book and I learned to cook – you know, Indian veg stuff, pasta, stir-fries – healthy stuff. I bet you can't believe that, eh! And I spent a fortune on my folks' house, every penny I earned went into that house. I put central heating in, a new bathroom, I knocked through from the front room to the back room and put these big adjoining doors in between. I chucked out all their old furniture and bought all new, stripped off all the wallpaper, painted the whole house, every room, every door. I replaced the door-handles with these really expensive brass ones, pulled up the carpets and polished the floorboards. It took me six months but it was the most rewarding thing I'd ever done. And it took my mind off the . . . bad stuff. When it was finished I put on my best clothes and I just sort of walked around it for ages, you know, imagining that it was somebody else's house, trying to imagine it through somebody else's eyes. And it looked fantastic! You should have seen it, Nadine. It was immaculate.

'So. I start feeling better about myself, you know, I'm getting back some self-respect, and there's this girl at work, a secretary at the office, called Fiona. I've always thought she was really nice but I'd never have done anything about it before, would have been too scared she'd turn me down, humiliate me. But one day I'm in the office, talking to Payroll about something that's gone wrong with my overtime, and on my way out I bump into Fiona, and I suddenly find myself asking her out and she's saying yes! Just like that. So we arrange to have a drink on the Friday night. It's the first time I've been out for six months, and I'm in a bit of a state getting ready, you know, not being able to decide what to wear, that sort of thing. So I'm running around, I'm scared I'm going to be late, and I just kind of run out the front door and slam it behind me.

'So anyway. Me and Fiona, we're drinking and chatting, and I'm not doing what I'm doing here with you, I'm not telling her about everything that's happened, I'm keeping it light-hearted, keeping it lively, making her laugh, asking her all about herself. You know, being the *other* Phil. And it's going really well. We go off and have dinner and I order some champagne, and she's really impressed, and for the first time in months I'm feeling like a human being again. This girl, this Fiona, she really likes me, and I start feeling like I like myself, too. Before we know it, it's one in the morning and we're both a bit pissed, so I suggest that she comes back to mine to order a cab. I really want her to see my house, I want her to be the first person to see how beautiful it looks, how hard I've worked. So she says, yeah, that would be lovely and then she says maybe she could stay the night, and I'm thinking, Christ, what a result, and I'm so excited I'm almost running home. We're laughing and we're chatting and we're holding hands, and as we get towards the house, there's this smell in the air, it's acrid, it catches in the back of the throat. And then' – he stopped and pointed at Nadine's empty glass – 'd'you want another drink, by the way?'

Nadine shook her head vigorously. 'No,' she said, 'no thanks. I'm fine. Carry on.'

He nodded. 'OK,' he said. 'Yeah. So. There's this smell in the air, and as we get closer to home there's smoke, too. Thick, thick clouds of black smoke. We turn the corner into my road and the street's wall-to-wall fire engines – dozens of them – and I start walking faster now, really fast, and Fiona's running behind me in these high heels, saying, "It's not your house, is it, Phil, it's not your house?" And you know what? It *was* my house. It was *my* fucking house, man. Gutted, from top to bottom. All the windows gone, all the furniture, fixtures, fittings, everything. Gone. It was a shell.'

'Oh my God,' cried Nadine. 'How? What happened?'

'Huh.' He shrugged. 'It was my fault. I left a fag burning, didn't I? Can you believe it? One fag, one measly little fag.' He took one out of the packet in front of him and held it under Nadine's gaze. 'Something that small, that *puny*, it's hard to believe. If you'd seen what it did to my house – to three storeys and four bedrooms, and the way it just ate up all those months of hard work. It's frightening,' he said.

'What did you do?'

'Well, that's the thing, right. I don't know what happened after that. Not really. Only what other people have told me. I think I must have gone into some sort of shock. Fiona took me to the hospital, and they treated the shock, and then she took me home with her and got in touch with my grandparents, who came and picked me up and took me back with them to Bournemouth. I don't really remember any of this. I was there for three weeks apparently – it was summer, I can remember vague things like the beach and the seagulls, the fat people with sunburn, the smell of frying onions, the sound of fruit machines, but I can't remember any *events*, I can't remember what I was actually doing there. I reckon I had some kind of breakdown because I became quite unmanageable apparently, talking to myself, disappearing for hours on end, not washing, not eating. I was a bit of a nutter by all accounts and eventually my grandparents couldn't take it any more, so they sent me to a hospital.

'I was there for three months and they gave me pills and they gave me psychotherapy and they gave me counselling, all that bollocks, and then they sent me home. My grandparents kicked another tenant out of their old Peabody flat and got it ready for me. I've been there for a couple of months, you know, trying to live a normal life, getting to know people.'

'What about Fiona?' asked Nadine. 'What happened to Fiona?'

Phil shrugged. 'Never heard from her again. I got my job back at the marquee company, but she wasn't working there any more. Got a job in the City or something.'

'So, you're all alone?'

'Well,' he said, 'I met this girl called Jo a couple of weeks ago, down the pub with all her mates, and we got talking. Turns out she was a student, and her and all her student mates ended up coming back to mine because most of that lot live with their parents or in tiny rented flats with no living rooms. They come round most nights now – all of them, just for a drink and a smoke and somewhere to hang out. It's nice for them to have somewhere to come and I like having them around. It makes me feel like I'm not all alone, even though none of them really talk to me or anything. I think they think I'm a bit boring, you know?' he smiled. 'A bit of a weird old fart. But I don't mind, really. The company's nice. I feel safe. I don't feel safe when I'm on my own. Not really. Not any more. When I'm on my own I feel like if I look out the window the streets could be deserted and everyone could have disappeared and I'd be the only person left in the whole world, d'you know what I mean? The only person left . . .

'Everything feels so – so – ephemeral sometimes. I don't know what's real and what's not. It's like, I wasn't expecting you to come tonight, not really. I thought maybe I'd imagined your phone call, imagined *you*. But you came! You're here, man. And it's so great. D'you know something?' he continued happily. 'I don't care what we do tonight. I don't care what we talk about, and I don't care where we talk about it. Just so long as you're actually here, in front of me, where I can see you. That's all. That's all I want.'

Phil fell into another silence then and Nadine fished her purse out of her bag. 'Let me get you a drink,' she said, resting her hand on his shoulder, her heart close to bursting with sympathy and pity. Poor, poor Phil.

'Great,' he said, 'thanks.'

At the bar, Murdo leaned towards Nadine. 'Everything all right?' he asked in his Highland growl.

'Yes,' said Nadine lightly, 'of course.'

'You better be careful with that lad,' he said, swivelling his eyes in the direction of Phil's slouched figure, 'he's had a hard life, you know?'

'Yes. I know. He's just been telling me.'

'He's trouble, that one, so you better look out for him. He dis'nae need any more trouble in his life than he's already had. Anyway, what'll it be?'

Nadine took the drinks back to their table and Phil looked up at her gratefully. 'Thanks,' he said, 'thank you, Nadine Kite.'

And Nadine smiled back at him nervously and thought to herself that she was not just walking but positively *sprinting* up a path in her life that she was never, ever supposed to take, and then she thought to herself how even if she tried to turn around now, this very minute, and get off the path, it was already too late, far too late to ever find her way back.

CHAPTER EIGHTEEN

Delilah hadn't arrived at Dig's empty handed. As well as her tiny and unattractive dog, she had produced from somewhere, God knows where, a pair of enormous and ominously bulging suitcases.

'You going somewhere?' Dig asked, eyeing the cases with deep suspicion.

Delilah smiled and shrugged. 'Well,' she said, 'that's the thing. It's not really working out for us at Marina's. I've . . . er . . . I've just had a huge row with her.'

'With Marina? What about?'

'Oh God. Nothing. Nothing, really. She's just such a pious, sanctimonious old cow. I don't know why I ever thought it would be a good idea to stay with her. I'd have stayed in a hotel, you know, but I can't because of the dog. And *then* she threatened to tell my mum I was back in town, so I just told her to fuck off, packed a bag and walked.

'You should have seen her face. It was as if she'd never heard the word "fuck" before. I tell you, there's little in life worse than a frustrated nun, there really isn't . . .'

There was a brief silence as Dig absorbed this information, waiting tensely for the inevitable.

'So, anyway, I – er – was sort of hoping that me and Digby could maybe crash here for a while. We won't be any trouble, I promise you and we'll be gone as soon as we can find somewhere else to go. It's just that there's no one else for me to turn to right now, what with me not talking to my mum and my brothers all with houses full of children and everything, and it would only be for a few days. And Digby's fully house-trained and very quiet.'

The tiny creature suddenly threw himself on to Dig's corduroy sofa and began yapping incredibly loudly.

' . . . Well, usually he's quiet. He's just excited to be somewhere new. I'll cook for you and keep the place tidy. Not,' she said, peering around the door-way into Dig's spotless flat, 'that it actually needs it. So. What do you think?' She beamed at him.

Dig was speechless for a second, his head telling him that there wasn't enough room in his flat for a girl and a dog and two suitcases full of their belongings, while his heart told him that there was a devastatingly beautiful woman who he might well be in love with on his doorstep begging most appealingly for a place to stay and of course he should invite her in. As he grappled with his dilemma, the awkward silence was broken by the buzz of the doorbell.

'*Takeaway*,' said a muffled Indian voice.

'Top floor,' said Dig, suddenly flustered by the preponderance of issues bearing down on him all at once and the thought of so many people, animals and large objects jostling for space on his tiny landing. Something would have to give.

'Right,' he said, turning back to Delilah, 'I'd better give you a hand with these cases.'

'Oh,' squeaked Delilah, 'really? I can stay? Oh thank you! Thank you so much.' And then she threw her arms around Dig's neck and hugged him hard.

Dig's arms crept slowly around her waist and through

the dampness of her coat he could feel the shape of her backbone, the softness of the flesh that covered her hips, the squashiness of her breasts against his chest and the heat of her body emanating through her clothes and as her lips found his cheek and pressed themselves against his flushed skin, Dig decided that this arrangement could actually work out after all.

CHAPTER NINETEEN

Nadine is on *at least* her fifth large tumbler of vodka.

And they've been *extremely* large. Equivalent to two or three pub measures. She started off drinking them with some lime cordial she found in the kitchen but gave up on the mixer after the first couple. Since then, she's been drinking them neat – without ice. She can't actually taste the vodka any more.

She'd said no, at first, when Phil had invited her back to his flat after the pub closed. Despite the fact that they'd ended up having a fairly pleasant evening together, helped along considerably by the four pints of Theakstones she'd consumed, the weight of the dreadful unfolding of events in Phil's life had started to make itself felt around her temples and she wanted to get away before things got any heavier.

But he'd looked so deflated by her refusal, almost like he was going to cry, and all of a sudden she'd thought, 'Oh my God, he's an orphan, he's got no one.' And before she knew what was happening she was agreeing to come back for a smoke, just to assuage her conscience.

Phil's flat was in the Peabody estate off the Holloway Road, up three flights of echoing concrete stairs, and very strangely decorated, like an old people's home. 'I haven't done anything with it since I moved in. You can probably guess why.' He smiled ironically.

There were about half a dozen people already in his

draughty living room when they walked in, listening to Gomez and sitting under a thick fleece of smoke. None of them looked up when Phil walked in, except for one tall, skinny girl with waist-length hair and enormous breasts straining beneath a child's T-shirt who unfolded herself from a cushion on the floor to greet him.

'Nadine, this is Jo. Jo, this is Nadine. Me and Nadine used to live together at university.'

'Oh yeah,' said Jo, handing Phil the bum end of a spliff and lowering herself back on to her cushion, 'didn't know you went to university.'

Nadine looked around her. Everyone in this room was so young and so distant, she felt almost as if she didn't exist in their eyes, as if she was of no consequence – which was ridiculous considering the fact that they were a bunch of students and she was a successful photographer with a sports car, a flat and a £40,000 commission. But if she was going to stand even the slightest chance of enjoying herself with these people, then she was going to have to get a lot more drunk than she was right now.

Phil led her to the kitchen and fixed her what would be the first of many vodkas.

An hour and five large vodkas later and Nadine is suddenly feeling very brave and self-confident, and all the incredibly strong spliff she's smoked has given her surroundings a slightly surreal edge. She feels like she's in some kind of lovely floaty dream, and now Phil feels like one of those strange characters who wander in and out of your dreams sometimes, pretend-people who you don't know in real life – made-up people.

She's been using Phil as a sounding-board for the last half an hour, chewing his ear off about Dig and Delilah

197

and what a mistake Dig's making and how he won't pay any attention to what Nadine has been trying to tell him *for his own good*, and how he's going to end up getting his heart broken all over again, and Phil, despite having so many problems of his own, real problems, big problems, has turned out to be a great, great listener, agreeing wholeheartedly with everything Nadine says and endearing himself to her more than he could possibly imagine in the process. He met Dig a few times in London during holidays, so Nadine respects his opinion. He also has a large personal supply of grass and is being very generous with it, letting Nadine roll spliff after spliff while they chat.

And now he's smiling at her and ferreting around his jeans pockets looking for something. He reaches into his pocket and brings out a tiny Indian pillbox encrusted with multicoloured stones. 'You sound like you could do with a little something to *lift* your spirits,' he says, pulling the lid off the tiny box.

'What's that?' Nadine asks.

'Little miracles,' he smiles. 'One of these, and the whole world will seem like a better place.'

Nadine's eyes open wide. 'Eeeeeeeeee?' she asks, thinking that even though that's what it looks like, it can't be, because Phil was always so anti-anything connected with rave culture.

Phil nods and hands her a pill. 'You might just want half,' he says, 'if it's your first.'

'Oh no,' she says 'let me have a whole one.' Despite having lived what she considers to be a fairly colourful life, Nadine's never done an E before and she swallows it, gleefully and quickly and waits for it to take effect.

Half an hour later and she doesn't really feel any

different. She's much more stoned, that's for certain, and much more pissed, and maybe that's why she's suddenly feeling so strangely drawn to Phil, suddenly feeling like she'd like to touch him, hug him, maybe even kiss him.

'So, you must be very muscly now, I suppose, under that baggy top, *erecting* all those big, heavy marquee things.' She pulls at the fabric of his lambswool sleeve. She's feeling very brazen, very forward, very *physical*.

He laughs. 'Nah,' he says, 'not really. Still as puny as ever.'

'Are you sure you're not really a *drug-dealer*?' she asks, jokingly, even though she's secretly started to think that maybe he is. It would explain all these students in his flat and the abundance of strong weed and the pill she's just swallowed.

'Nah,' he smiles. And then, suddenly and most unexpectedly, he turns and stares into her eyes and says, 'God, Nadine, you're so fucking beautiful.'

Nadine chokes on her vodka. 'Oh,' she says, 'don't be daft.'

Phil shakes his head very slowly and stares at her. 'I'm not being daft,' he says. 'You're fucking gorgeous.' He leans in towards her as he says this, so that his face is only a couple of millimetres from hers. He locks his eyes on to hers, and she starts to feel vaguely uncomfortable but strangely excited. He pulls his face away from hers unhurriedly, gently takes the spliff from between her stiff fingers, puts it to his lips, inhales deeply, inhales again and disposes of it in an empty beer can. 'And you've really kept your body in good nick.' His gaze slowly pans up and down her, eating her up.

Nadine feels a shudder run up and down her spine in

time with the rhythm of his eyes. She feels exposed and titillated at the same time. She blushes.

'You've still got those great tits,' he says, staring at them like they were a pair of juicy rare fillet steaks, 'those perfect, perfect tits. Just the right size, right shape. They haven't drooped at all. Some women's tits start *drooping*, you know.'

Any feminist leanings that Nadine may once have had desert her. She knows that she should, in all decency, slap him round the face and storm off with some rant or other about how she will not be spoken to like that by a sexist pig like him. But her ego is suffering from malnutrition and she laps up his graceless compliment like it was vintage wine. She is grateful to him for thinking that she has great tits and actually says *thank you*.

'Thank you,' she says, smiling coyly.

Nadine's head is spinning; a combination of booze, spliff and too many knee-trembling compliments. Not to mention the Class A chemical currently swishing around her brain cells.

Inside Nadine's drug-and-alcohol-addled head, Phil is now larger than life – he is a legend. Phil has lived a big life, full of change and adversity. He has battled with depression. He has been to prison. He has lost his parents and the love of his life killed herself. His house burned down. He's had two nervous breakdowns. He has been accepted into the homes and worlds of so many different people. He has taken risks and lived life according to his heart. He has reinvented himself and pulled himself out of the quagmire time after time. He is strong and resilient. He is brave and unpredictable.

He is everything that Nadine is not.

He is better than Nadine.

And all of a sudden, through the blur of her thoughts, Nadine realizes that this is what's been wrong with every man she's been out with since she and Phil split up. None of them have been better than her. They've all been inferior – at least in her mind – and she has been unable to respect them. Weak, weak men, they seemed to follow her around. It was like she was giving out some ultrasound, audible only to men with gaps in their lives and low self-esteem.

She's had enough of weak men. She wants a strong man, a man like Phil. Phil isn't perfect – he is far from perfect – he is as flawed as it is possible for a man to be. But he is strong. He is special. He's different. He's exciting.

If Nadine was sober and straight and happier, if Nadine hadn't just taken an E, she would be thinking exactly the opposite; she would probably call it a night now, start making her excuses, get her coat, order a cab, go home, because it is becoming increasingly obvious what sort of turn this evening is about to take, and there is a sensible, wise part of Nadine deep down somewhere beneath all the narcotics which knows that she shouldn't be following this path, knows that Phil has always managed to manipulate her and control her and that if she stays now she is more or less bound to let him do it again.

But she is not sober and she is not straight and she is not happy, so she smiles at Phil instead and thinks how much she's enjoying herself and how she still loves him in a funny kind of way, and how, if he was to try to kiss her, she probably wouldn't fight him off.

As if reading her thoughts, Phil puts one hand on her

201

shoulder and the other over her hand, and his fingers are moving over her flesh. Nadine would like to touch him, too, feel his flesh, his bones, his heartbeat through his jumper. She grabs hold of his hand and traces her fingertips over the smooth, hairless skin, skin she hasn't touched for twelve years, skin she used to love so much – and it's beautiful, so beautiful to be with this man, this man who she's missed so much, who's changed so much, who's *lived* so much and who's turned out to be so *beautiful* and full of kindness and warmth, and just to be able to touch him, touch him and feel the blood running through his veins, and he's been through so much these last years, and now she wants to hold him in her arms and look after him and protect him and be even closer to him and share herself with him and have *sensations* with him and just to *love him* like she used to . . .

'I think,' says Phil, stroking the side of Nadine's neck, 'we should – go somewhere else – a bit quieter, y'know? Let's go somewhere?' Phil reaches out to touch her hair again. He strokes it and then brings the back of his hand down softly against her cheek. It is such a tender gesture that Nadine immediately turns to blancmange inside and knows that she has to do this, that this is what life is all about, after all, people and being with people and loving people, and that it's not wrong, it's all right, it's all right, because Phil is good and Phil is beautiful and it will be beautiful and it's the right thing to do, the most perfect thing to do, just to love someone . . .

'I want to get to know you all over again, Nadine Kite. I want to be alone with you. Come with me.' He holds out his hand for her.

'Where are we going?'

'Just come with me.'

There is something so surreal about all this, about Phil, this flat, this evening, that Nadine is starting to feel like she's in a film or something, that none of this is really happening to her.

She takes his hand and follows him.

CHAPTER TWENTY

Dig was trying to be chilled out but was finding it very hard. Delilah had just committed the greatest domestic crime known to man. There were many domestic crimes – not replacing the toilet roll when it was finished, not rinsing things before putting them in the dishwasher, not putting lids back on things, not rewinding videos and not plumping up cushions – but that one, just now – leaving CDs out of their boxes – was the worst, by far. He'd tried so hard not to say anything. It had been his suggestion, after all, that she choose some music to put on. But he'd just meant for her to select one CD and put it on. Instead, she'd been completely overwhelmed by his shelves and shelves of alphabetically organized CDs and was now playing DJ, excitedly pulling one plastic case after another off the shelves. Dig lost the battle to control his neurosis.

'Erm – you couldn't put those back in their boxes, could you?'

'Sure,' replied Delilah, distractedly, pulling some shit by Vengaboys off the shelf and sticking it in the machine. She slid the Shania Twain album she'd just listened to back into its case and seemed satisfied that this act constituted a reasonable response to Dig's request.

Dig sat back and sighed. His CD shelves were full of music that he didn't like. He got it all free. Every day he came home with a handful of new CDs that he was never going to listen to. He used to consider these free CDs to be a perk of the job, but over the last couple of years British pop music had slipped tragically and dramatically into a cesspool of bland Euro-bollocks music-by-numbers, and Dig was now starting to feel that these freebies were more of an encumbrance. Steps, for Christ's sake. B*witched. Billie. Britney Spears. How had this happened? What sort of children were we breeding?

He winced as he heard the opening bars to 'Boom Boom Boom Boom' and then stared in horror at Delilah, who was jauntily bouncing up and down and humming under her breath. She couldn't really like this sort of thing, could she?

'This is great,' she beamed at him.

Oh dear God, thought Dig.

'I've really lost touch with music over the years. I've only bought one CD this year: Robbie Williams, *I've Been Expecting You*. Which is brilliant, of course! But Alex likes jazz, on the whole. So that's what we listen to. But this new stuff is *great*, isn't it? So simple and such good tunes. Good old-fashioned pop music!' She grinned and turned away and began rifling through Dig's shelves to find something else dreadful to put on.

Dig dropped his head into his hands. Nadine had been right. Delilah *wasn't* the same girl he remembered from years ago. Phil Collins would have been a *relief* right now. The old Delilah had thrown empty beer cans at Bucks Fizz on the telly and used a selection of well-chosen swearwords to express her disgust at such blandness and unoriginality. The old Delilah had stalked around the Holy T raining disdain upon screaming Duranies, pulling posters off notice-boards and peeling stickers off desks. The old Delilah had sat on his shoulders waving a pint of snakebite in the air while they watched the Cure and Echo and the Bunnymen and the Smiths at lager-soaked venues all over London.

The new Delilah had the musical taste of a twelve-year-old girl.

The passage of time could do cruel things to people.

Anyway. He would give them to her. All of them. Tomorrow he would get a big cardboard box, pick every technicolored, vacuous and sterile CD off his shelves, put them in the box and give them to her. With pleasure.

Digby was sitting at his feet staring up at him with watery eyes. He vibrated briefly and then emitted a strange little high-pitched whimper.

God he was an ugly dog. Not cute-ugly. Not bred to be ugly, like a pug or a bulldog. Just ugly.

'What do you want?' he said quietly.

Digby whimpered again.

'Delilah. I think there's something wrong with your dog. He keeps shivering and moaning.'

'Oh no,' said Delilah, 'he just needs to go to the toilet, that's all. D'you mind taking him?'

'Taking him? Where?' Dig had an image in his mind of some plastic contraption in Delilah's luggage with a seat and a lid – a little doggy-toilet.

'The nearest tree would be good,' she replied, a little sarcastically, Dig thought.

'Oh. Right. OK.' He glanced from his window and noticed that it was still raining. Great. He pulled on his leather coat and picked up an umbrella, attached Digby to his Louis Vuitton lead – pausing for a second to register the fact that the dog had a Louis Vuitton lead: good grief – and then dragged him down the stairs to the chestnut tree outside his house.

Digby cocked his leg and then released the smallest squirt of urine that Dig had ever seen in his life.

'Is that it?' he barked at the dog. 'Is that it? Are you telling me that you dragged me out here in the pissing rain in the middle of the night just for that? That . . . that dribble? I've seen more liquid come out of a fucking teat! Jesus.' He sighed and began dragging the dog back towards the house, but the dog seemed to have decided that he quite liked it out there in the rain and wanted to go out walking, explore the neighbourhood.

'No,' shouted Dig, 'we're going in. You've had your lot.'

The dog ignored him and stood his ground, looking pleadingly into Dig's eyes.

'That's it,' sighed Dig, 'if you can't behave like a grown-up, then I'm going to have to treat you like a puppy. Come here.' He leaned down to pick Digby up and the dog scampered backwards. He bent down again and the dog moved back even further. This continued for a few seconds until they were nearly in the road, and just as Dig managed to get his hands on the animal and pick him up, a large lorry drove past and threw the entire contents of an enormous puddle all over him.

Dig stood for a second, in shock, water rolling down his face from his hair, and his trousers sticking heavily to his legs.

'Oh,' he muttered, 'for fuck's sake.'

When he returned to the flat Delilah had moved away from the CD player, having left every single CD out of its case and strewn around the place, and was now busily unpacking, chucking items of clothing and undergarments randomly around the room. She spun round when she heard the front door go.

'Oh,' she said, 'you're back. Did he go all right?'

'Yes,' murmured Dig, dripping on to the floor and waiting for some sort of sympathetic comment from her about his dramatic state of wetness.

Instead, Delilah turned her attention immediately to Digby and began petting him furiously. 'Good boy,' she squeaked in some kind of strange, other-worldly voice, ''oos a good boy then? Did 'oo do a wee-wee for your uncle Dig, did you? Good boy!' And then she went back to her haphazard unpacking.

Dig watched her fiddling around in a small black-suede pouch. She emptied four glistening crystals into the palm of her hand and rubbed them gently with a thumb. They were attached to lengths of thread. She got to her feet and began placing them carefully in the four corners of the room.

Dig watched her with bemusement.

'Crystals,' she said, illuminatingly. 'Room Pattern Crystals. They create an energy field which projects positive vibrations, removes all negativity and strengthens your energies every day.'

'Aaaah,' said Dig, nodding and feeling that sense of nervous anxiety he always experienced whenever anyone started talking about 'alternative' stuff. It was the same sense of tension that seized him when people started talking about God as if he was more than just a vague notion or a mild swearword.

'White jade,' she said, pointing out a stone. 'Said to help direct energies to their most advantageous outlet, help filter out distraction and aid in solution-oriented thinking. Which is just what I need.

'Peridot' – she indicated another – 'helps connect us to our destinies and attain spiritual truth. Emerald –

208

said to give wisdom so that the possessor is motivated to give love and wisdom to others. Aquamarine – a great healer. It helps you to understand difficult situations from a love-filled viewpoint.

'And this one,' she said, sombrely, reaching enticingly into her still-damp blouse and pulling out a shard of something prismatic and luminescent, 'this one I wear next to my heart. Mother-of-pearl. This stone is a great protector. It's meant to represent a mother's love.' She stared meaningfully at the stone and caressed it between her fingertips.

Dig didn't know what to say, and the room fell silent. He watched her tuck the stone sadly back inside her bra and gulped.

Delilah sighed and pulled her hair back from her face. 'I wouldn't mind turning in now, Dig, if that's all right with you? It's been kind of a long day.'

Dig looked at his watch. It was ten past ten. He didn't usually go to bed until at least midnight. He didn't have a television in his room. He hadn't even *begun* to digest his curry yet. He wasn't quite sure what he was going to do. 'Er – yeah – sure. I'll get the sofabed up for you.'

Shit, he thought as he made up the bed for her – without even a glimmer of an offer of help – I'm going to have to read a book. What a nightmare. He'd been reading *The Beach* for the last six months and was still only on page 85. He used it as a coaster for his morning cup of coffee, mainly. Dig wasn't one of life's great readers.

'Right,' he said, scratching his head, 'I'll see you in the morning. You know where everything is, don't you? Do you need me to wake you up tomorrow morning or anything?'

209

'No,' said Delilah, smiling, 'no. I'll just get up when you get up.' She walked towards him and placed her hands on his arms. 'Thank you, Dig. Thank you so much. This is so kind of you. I just . . . I . . . er – oh, just thank you! You're lovely, you really are.'

She grabbed him then, and squeezed him to her in a bear-hug, and Dig thought, *excellent*, and lifted himself on to his tiptoes to match her height. He squeezed her back and buried his face into her cool, silky hair and breathed in that smell, that morning-dew fragrance. Oh Jesus, he thought, oh Delilah. You have *no idea* what you do to me. You are so fucking beautiful and so fucking sexy and I just want to drag you into my bedroom right now and lick every inch of you and fuck you senseless.

Dig could feel Delilah caressing his back through his wet clothes and – *boing* – right on cue, there he was, Mr Happy, in his trousers.

'Oh Delilah,' he murmured into her hair, bringing his nose up towards her face, 'oh Delilah.' He closed his eyes and puckered up, almost exploding with the intensity of the desire he was experiencing, and then, suddenly, she was gone. Slithered from his embrace like a Vaselined cat.

She was half-way to the hallway. 'Sleep tight,' she said, and threw him a little wave before disappearing into the bathroom.

Dig shook his head in confusion.

Fuck.

What happened? One minute she was . . . and the next she was . . . And now he had a huge hard-on. And . . . and . . .

He sighed, turned off the central light, looked briefly around at the four crystals hanging ominously in the corners of his living room and went to bed.

CHAPTER TWENTY-ONE

Nadine wasn't sure how she and Phil had got here.

They had walked in and out of a few of the rooms in his flat at first, all of which had been occupied by small groups of people in shadow who looked up guiltily from whatever they were doing as the door opened. Then they left by the front door of the flat and walked along a corridor, under an archway, through a door, through another door, and Nadine had lost track of where they were by the time they emerged in a small lock-up garage with a low ceiling.

The floor was concrete and the atmosphere was scorching hot and dry, heat emanating from three wall-mounted gas fires on full power. The air was rank with the smell of used cat litter and Whiskas Supermeat and a dozen or more cats of varying shapes and sizes were dozing, eating and playing in the room.

Before Nadine had a chance to ask about the garage or to wonder why all these cats were locked up in it, Phil had his tongue half-way down her throat and was running his hands up and down her back like he was playing a zither. Within seconds they were tearing at each other's clothing: they were unbuttoning, unzipping, unpopping, pulling off, pulling down and pulling over.

Her clothes were in a heap on the floor at her feet, Phil's jeans and lambswool jumper were draped over a trestle-table, their underwear was in varying stages of removal and a coffee-and-cream Persian with a face like Les Dawson had begun sharpening his claws on Phil's abandoned trainers.

He picked her up; she wrapped her legs around his back. He carried her and deposited her gently upon the edge of the trestle-table. A large marmalade with odd-coloured eyes mewed loudly and leaped out of their way. Phil deftly removed her knickers, even more deftly removed his own (yellow cotton briefs, Nadine observed for one fleeting, worrying second). He bent down and fiddled around inside the socks that he was still wearing, and bizarrely, and Nadine thought miraculously, came up bearing a condom.

'Gosh,' she said breathlessly, 'that was a bit of luck!'

Phil smiled and tore open the glossy purple packet with his teeth. He unfurled it expertly and then, effort-lessly, without Nadine even really noticing, he was inside her.

For a few moments they stayed like that, barely moved, staring into each other's eyes, breathing in rhythm. Nadine surrendered all conscious thought to wave after wave of pure physical sensation. Nadine had never before felt so in tune with the rhythm of her own body, with the rhythm of someone else's body. It was like making music, like playing the most sublime duet on the piano, singing together in perfect harmony, two pairs of hands caressing the same harp. It was beautiful . . .

An elderly black cat with white whiskers snaked ner-vously around Phil's bare ankles, sniffed at them deli-cately, turned slowly, raised his tail elegantly and then silently released a squirt of bright yellow urine all over the backs of his legs.

'Shit,' hissed Phil, kicking backwards at the cat, who scampered off nimbly, avoiding the blow.

They were moving faster now, but still together, still as one, and Nadine found herself lost in mesmeric synchronicity. And then she started to think about the beautiful, *beautiful* differences between them, the way she was soft and he was hard, and how she was smooth and he was hairy, and he was strong and she was weak, but that when they were together like this it all made perfect sense, it was like a key in a lock, and how come she'd never noticed any of this before, how come she'd never realized before how beautiful sex really was and how this must be what God meant it to be like . . .

A skinny blue cross-eyed Burmese stared meaningfully at her from a tartan bed, looked away, abruptly cocked one back leg stiffly into the air and proceeded to lick his anus, meticulously and enthusiastically.

Nadine closed her eyes, dug her fingers into Phil's hair and was amazed by the feel of his scalp underneath her fingertips, by the fact that you could see it but you could never touch it because there was hair on it, and then she wondered what it would feel like if Phil was to shave it all off, but then there'd be stubble, so you'd have to wax it off, *wax it off*, to be able to really feel what that scalp skin felt like. She began to imagine spreading hot wax on to Phil's scalp, hot, red, wet wax, and peeling it off with big bits of white paper . . .

A fat-faced English Blue who'd been sniffing the end of her nose jumped through the air with a blood-curdling howl and landed on Phil's back.

Phil screamed.

Nadine opened her eyes to find Phil staring into them. 'Oh my God, are you all right?' she exclaimed.

213

Phil nodded and kept thrusting.

Nadine found herself lost again in the natural rhythm of their movements, in the way their bodies produced sweat where they touched, in the whiteness of the skin on Phil's shoulders, in the feel of him moving up and down inside her, so smooth, so slick, so in and out and in and out, and just perfect, perfectly designed pieces of machinery, working in perfect hydraulic harmony. In and out and in and out and in and out . . . like a well-oiled piston. Imagery flooded her head: huge shining, gleaming chrome apparatus and engines moving constantly and smoothly . . .

The machinery pumped away, and Nadine was oblivious to everything. She didn't notice the passage of time, she didn't notice that her arms had gone numb, she didn't notice the cats, didn't notice how sore she was getting or how fast Phil was now going. She didn't notice his eyes suddenly screw close, and she didn't hear him saying, 'oh thank Christ oh thank Christ I'm coming I'm coming I'm coming.'

They dropped to the floor, kissing, sweating, sighing. Phil wrapped his legs around Nadine and held her tight, very tight. He kissed the top of her sweaty head and stroked her face. The English Blue approached stealthily and began sniffing Phil's bottom.

They lay together silently for a while and Nadine let her eyes close. She was suddenly very, very tired and wanted to sleep. It was hot in here, like a jungle, and Nadine felt miles away from anywhere, detached from reality. Her head was full of lovely, meandering thoughts.

'That was very special, Nadine Kite,' Phil whispered in her ear, ignoring the cat now licking the soles of his feet, 'you'll never, ever know how much that meant to me.' He kissed her eyelids and brought her head back into his embrace.

Nadine smiled and let herself drift away.

'Saffron! Amber! Dill! Jethro! Here babies! Come to Mummy!'

Nadine awoke.

'Murphy! Mack! Topaz! Where are you, my angels?'

Nadine sat bolt upright, covering her naked breasts with her hands.

'Sienna! Mummy's here.'

Phil sat up, too. They looked at each other.

'Shit,' whispered Phil, looping his frighteningly yellow briefs around his ankles and working them up his legs. 'Shit. It's Freda. Hide!' He lifted the plastic cloth from the trestle-table next to them and indicated that she should scoot underneath. She grabbed her clothes and slid under. A pair of alabaster-white Siamese shot out from under the table.

'Who's Freda?' hissed Nadine.

'Shhhhh.'

'Philip?' She could hear the woman's voice, maybe a couple of feet away from her. She could see her feet. She was wearing enormous silver platform shoes, and her fat ankles were covered in broken blood vessels and flea-bites. Nadine scratched an imaginary itch.

'Philip? What*ever* are you doing in here with my babies?' The woman had a bizarre telephone-voice accent.

'Sorry, Freda,' said Phil, sheepishly, 'just ... er ... just wanted to come and say hello to the cats ... make sure they were all right ... hello, boy, hello.' He put on

215

a rather silly voice and waggled his fingers at a passing Persian with an imperious face who sniffed haughtily at his fingers, regarded him with disdain and immediately began curling himself around the woman's legs.

'At two o'clock a.m. in the bally morning? With half of your apparels removed?' she said, sounding unconvinced.

'Oh – yeah – right. Well. It's pretty hot in here. You know.'

Nadine could see his feet nervously stepping from side to side.

'Hmmmm,' said the woman. 'Well. I must say that I think the hour for visiting my babies has passed. And by the by,' she began in rather a loud, deliberate voice, almost like she wasn't talking to Phil any more, was talking to somebody else, '*by the by*. There's been an almighty commotion in the vicinity of your so-called flat this evening, Philip. A rather elderly and distressed gentleman claiming to be your *father* and wailing about a portable television set. He was taken away by the caretaker but he voiced his intention to return *most* vociferously and to keep on returning until he and his portable television set are reunited. So I suggest that you return to your "flat" and to your so-called "flatmates", forthwith, Philip.'

Nadine saw her lean down to stroke a few of the cats, who were knitting themselves around her legs. She was about seventy, with an extraordinary meringue of yellow spun-sugar hair and a dazzling spectrum of apricot and baby-blue cosmetics trowelled all over her features without, it appeared, benefit of a mirror. Nadine watched her lavishly mascaraed eyes sweep along the floor of the

216

room like searchlights, sweep under the cat hammocks and behind the scratching posts and then under the trestle-table. Nadine flinched and brought her feet closer into her body, made herself into a smaller ball.

'So, Philip,' continued Freda, straightening herself briskly, 'might I suggest that you *move upstairs, immediately*, and maybe you and your young friends could contemplate the prospect of *bed*. Tonight. Soon. You understand, of course, that no one appreciates the party *esprit* like Freda appreciates the party *esprit*. But it is no longer the hour for festivity and jolly-making and it is, in fact, the hour for sleeping. Please. Philip. Thank you.'

And then she went. Nadine watched her platformed feet clomping across the concrete floor. She heard the door at the other end of the garage slide open and closed and heard the footsteps recede to a distant echo.

She began to breathe again. She scrambled out from under the table and Phil pulled her into his open arms.

'Who the hell was that?' she said, gently extricating herself from his embrace, which suddenly felt constricting and overpowering.

'Freda,' he said, nuzzling her ear.

'Who's Freda?'

'Mad old coot. Lives next door. This is her garage. Used to be an erotic dancer or something in the fifties – thinks she's a famous film star.'

'These hers?' asked Nadine surveying their feline company.

'Yeah,' he said, 'she keeps them in here because she doesn't like all the hair and smell in her flat.'

'Bit cruel, isn't it?'

He shrugged and kissed her shoulders.

'And what was all that about old men and televisions?'

'Fuck knows,' he sighed, 'this building's full of deranged old pensioners who think their mother's still alive and the country's still at war. He probably thought I was someone else. Probably never even *owned* a TV. Anyway,' he drawled, 'anyway – who cares about senile old men, come over 'ere, you gorgeous sex-goddess.' He grinned and pulled her firmly towards him, leaving her little choice in the matter. 'You are incredible,' he whispered into her ear. 'I could fuck you for ever.'

Oooh, she thought to herself, I wish you hadn't said that. I feel all *weird* now. In fact, Nadine was starting to feel all weird about this whole situation. What the hell was she doing in here? What was she doing disappearing into some stinking, cat-pissy hole in the middle of the night to have sex with a deeply damaged man, on a cocktail of drugs and alcohol. It might have been rock 'n' roll but it certainly wasn't her style.

She knew that he'd tugged her heart-strings nearly to oblivion in the pub earlier on and then, in his living room he'd been a really good listener, he'd been sympathetic and attentive and kind, and then she knew that he'd hit her with some pretty powerful compliments and that she'd agreed quite willingly to come down here with him, and she particularly remembered how much she'd enjoyed the sex – it was *mind-blowing* – but now . . . well, what the hell was she doing down here?

Despite her lingering feelings of love and affection for him, Phil *really* wasn't her type, at all. Too thin, too pale and all that *very black* body hair that stood out in such stark contrast to his lime-washed flesh that you could see each individual follicle. And those long, shapely legs that looked like women's legs. She'd forgotten about

218

those. His hair, which she had been so enthusiastically grabbing hold of a couple of hours ago, looked like it could do with a good wash, and his hands didn't have any hair on them, were all smooth and fleshy like he didn't have any bones, like he was wearing surgeon's gloves. But worst of all were those *underpants* – Nadine had never slept with a man who wore *underpants* before, particularly not bright-lemon underpants.

She was just starting to notice his eyes, too. Those denim-blue eyes she'd loved so much at poly. There was something strange about them now. They stared too much, ate through what they observed like blowtorches through a metal door. He was like a manta ray. Nadine shuddered a little.

'We could just stay here – no one will find us in here,' he was saying, 'no one knows about this room except me.'

And he had bad teeth! Really bad teeth.

'Just another half an hour. Give me another half an hour and I'll see if I can make it *even better* this time.'

Oh what! Oh no. No no no no no. Nadine dragged her knickers up her legs and over her hips as quickly as she could, using them as some kind of symbolic chastity belt.

She stood up and pulled on her crocheted dress. 'Sorry, Phil,' she said, 'but I've got to go home now. Really.' She looked at her watch. 'Shit! It's nearly two! We've been in here for ages.'

'Yeah,' smiled Phil proudly, 'I know.'

'Better get back then, eh?' she said brightly, starting to pull her cardigan sleeves up her arms.

She looked at Phil. He was sitting in his lemon briefs, cross-legged, strangling a strand of his grubby-looking hair into a knot. His stomach had folded itself into a small pale flap of skin over the waistband of his briefs and an aged Siamese cat with only one eye was gingerly settling himself into his lap.

Nadine shuddered.

She wanted to go home.

The girl called Jo was waiting anxiously in the hallway when they finally walked back into the flat, picking at the skin around her nails and holding a smouldering cigarette.

'Where the fuck have you been?' she demanded rudely of Phil. 'It's been a fucking nightmare here.' She threw Nadine a contemptuous look and blew a cloud of cigarette smoke into the air around her head. 'Your old man turned up and had a screaming fucking fit about some fucking TV, and then that old hag from next door started snooping around and moaning about the noise, and then . . .'

'Chill, girl,' said Phil, putting a hand firmly on her shoulder and turning to smile at Nadine. 'Just chill. I've been showing Nadine Freda's cats, that's all. I'm here now.'

'Yeah, but what about your old man? He said he's going to come back every night until . . .'

'*Just. Chill.* He's just a senile old man. OK?' he said firmly, putting a finger to Jo's lips and turning her around. And then he turned and winked at Nadine before placing his hand firmly on Jo's back and disappearing with her into one of the many rooms leading off his hallway.

Nadine stood blinking for a moment or two, feeling slightly foolish. Was he coming back? Was she supposed to be waiting for him? Was she supposed to have followed him? And what the hell was all that about his 'old man'? He didn't have an 'old man'. His father was dead.

After a couple of minutes she decided that he wasn't coming back and that she was presently making a giant fool of herself, so she located a mini-cab card on the telephone table and started to dial.

She didn't want to be here any more.

She arranged to meet the cab on the street outside the flats and paced up and down agitatedly while she waited. A few minutes later a dark-blue Granada Ghia pulled up and she gratefully fell into the back seat and explained to the Turkish driver where she wanted to be taken.

The entire area between her legs felt raw and used and her thigh muscles had begun to ache tenderly. The skin around her mouth was taut and sore and her head felt thick and woolly and dense with confusing images and blurred thoughts. The streetlights and window displays danced in front of her eyes and made pinhead patterns of light on her retinas.

Nadine didn't know what had happened tonight. She didn't know who she was or where she'd been or where she was going.

She was all alone.

She wanted a bath.

She wanted to go home.

CHAPTER TWENTY-TWO

Dig woke with a start at seven o'clock, emerging from a very peculiar but pleasant dream involving ice-cream cones and Kylie Minogue to find a greasy-snouted, curry-breathed Digby frantically snuffling at his ear.

Imagining that this urgent awakening might have something to do with the fullness of Digby's bladder and the severity of his need to empty it, not to mention any unexpected effect that his snaffling of last night's vindaloo might have had on his doubtless delicate stomach, Dig hopped briskly out of bed, jumped into a pair of boxers and encouraged the creature into the living room with a slap to the back of his bare thighs, hoping that he would then leap up on to the recumbent figure of Delilah nestled into Dig's sofabed, and begin snuffling into *her* ear the news of his full bladder.

This plan didn't work. Instead of waking his mistress, Digby sat stiffly on the floor at the foot of her bed, staring imploringly at Dig and whimpering very quietly, a grain of yellow rice hanging resolutely from his oily whiskers. Dig patted gently at the duvet covering the apparently dead Delilah in an attempt to lure Digby towards her ear but the dog just looked at him as if he was slightly retarded and whimpered again, and Dig realized that he had only three choices:

a) wake up the angelically, beautifully slumbering Delilah and insist that she take the dog outside

222

b) take responsibility himself for the emptying of Digby's bladder, or

c) let him piss on the carpet.

Option a) seemed a bit cruel, and option c) was a complete no-no, which left him only one feasible alternative. However, it was seven o'clock in the morning, it was still raining and Dig would have to get properly dressed and take the dog outside, as he had no access to a garden. These were all truly horrible considerations and it was the prospect of these that led to Dig gingerly gripping the beast around his bony undercarriage, picking his way over the scavenged foil curry containers strewn around the kitchen floor, and holding him firmly aloft out of the kitchen window, over the early rush-hour noises of Camden Road, while making 'whooshing' noises under his breath in an attempt to charm open Digby's urethra.

The dog reacted badly to the situation he found himself in, flailing around wildly in Dig's hands and staring at him with madly bulging eyes as if to ask, 'Why are you trying to kill me? What have I ever done to you?'

Dig realigned his fingers beneath Digby's belly and began to push his fingertips into the point where he imagined his bladder sat, attempting to *squeeze* the business out of him as if emptying a hot-water bottle. Digby liked this even less and started kicking his tiny legs around ever more frantically, but finally Dig felt the animal begin to relax in his hands and breathed a sigh of relief as a jet of dog pee streamed elegantly from between the creature's legs like the squirt of water from a cherubic statue in a water fountain, arcing gently and cascading down towards the lower branches of the chestnut tree outside Dig's window. 'Good boy,' said Dig, 'that's a good boy . . .'

'Oh my God!! Oh Jesus!! What are you *doing*?'

Dig jumped in his skin as a shrill female voice reverberated around the kitchen, and he felt a pair of hands dragging him away from the window.

'Put him down – let go of him, for God's sake!!'

He spun around without thinking and certainly without first verifying with the dog that his bladder was fully empty and watched in horror as Digby's still-active spray sprinkled in a generous crescent all over the kitchen surfaces, across the hob, into the sink and, finally, all down the front of Delilah's bra and knickers and into a foil container at her feet.

Dig barely had time to register the disaster before he was overcome by the breathtakingly erotic realization that Delilah was standing in front of him in her bra and knickers looking like some kind of Greek goddess, despite the rivulets of lemon-coloured dog-pee trickling down her fantastically flat stomach and into the waistband of her knickers. He gulped. The stream of pee stopped as suddenly as it had started, and the shell-shocked trio found themselves rooted silently to the spot in horror, the only sound that of the last few droplets of Digby's pee hitting the tiled floor ... *splish* ... *splish* ... *splish*.

Delilah opened her mouth and looked down with disgust at her dampened body, her face contorting as the full horror of her situation hit her. 'Eeeeeegh!!' she squeaked, ineffectually flapping her arms up and down. 'Eeeegh!!'

Dig dropped the dog to the floor, where he began slipping and sliding around in the puddles he'd made there. 'Oh Jesus! Oh Delilah! I'm so sorry ... oh God ... here' – he grabbed a brand-new J-cloth from the side of the sink – 'here – let me help you.' He started sponging at Delilah's rigid body, desperately trying to avoid the rude bits, which was tricky as that's where most of the pee was.

'Eeeeegh!' said Delilah.

'Here,' said Dig, handing her the damp cloth, 'you do the other ... bits. I'll ... er ... put the shower on for you.'

'Eeeeegh!' said Delilah again, picking the cloth gingerly from his hands and rubbing it stiffly along her inside legs. Dig tried not to stare at the soft golden down poking from her knickers as he made his way past her towards the bathroom.

. He had to negotiate piles of Delilah's belongings in the overcast gloom of what had been his living room and was now effectively Delilah's bedroom. Her two suitcases had been left on the floor and opened wide, their entrails spilt all over the floor and piled up in small heaps here and there. There were *three* glasses of water balanced on the table by the bed and stacks of paperwork spread out all over the place. Dig had to resist the urge to start tidying things as he made his way across the room, and he clenched his fists into balls as he walked, repeating silently to himself, 'Don't be anal, don't be anal, don't be anal.'

The bathroom, too, was unrecognizable, sporting a sophisticated array of white-packaged bottles and jars containing all manner of fluids for the removal, cleansing and general facilitation of the contact lenses that Dig hadn't realized Delilah wore, plus a variety of beauty products housed in mint-green packaging that promised to perform what sounded to Dig like the stuff of miracles, and a simply *enormous* bag of cotton-wool balls on top of the cistern. She had also used one of *his* towels, which threw his weekly towel rota into complete disarray, and had left the bathmat *on the floor*, instead of leaving it on the side of the bath, so that it was still damp this morning even though she'd used it the night before and – oh God – she'd finished a toilet roll at some point and had left the new one just sitting balanced on top of the empty one – just sitting there – balanced – when all she had to do – it was *so simple* – was to take the old roll off, throw it in the bin and slip the new one on. I mean – for God's sake – how could anyone be so *lazy*.

Don't be anal. Don't be anal. Don't be anal.

He flicked the switch for the shower and tested the temperature, straightened the towels, replaced the toilet roll and put all of Delilah's bottles into nice straight, satisfying lines before heading back towards the kitchen, where Digby was still where Dig had left him, curled up on the floor in a puddle of his own pee, wondering where he was and why strange men were trying to throw him out of windows, and where Delilah was still scrubbing at herself with the new-five-minutes-ago-but-soon-to-be-thrown-in-the-bin J-cloth.

Dig stopped at the threshold of the kitchen, stopped and just stared for a moment at the sight before him – not the mess, not the dog pee all over everything and the bits of turmeric-tinted sauce staining his porous white floor tiles and the grains of oily rice slowly solidifying and sticking to the floor – but the glorious sight of Delilah, standing with her back to him, her long legs splayed out at strange angles to allow for cleaning, her golden hair swinging back and forth in the slowly pervading sunlight from the window, her stretch-jersey underwear dazzlingly white. She looked like the models in the photographs on the underwear packets he'd seen in M&S. She was magnificent. How could he have ever let her get away, all those years ago? He should have followed her to the ends of the earth and back, he should have been there at the church ten years ago to stop her marrying this Alex person, he should have fought for her. Girls like Delilah only came along once in a lifetime . . . or did they?

His fantastic reverie was disturbed at that moment when Delilah suddenly spun around violently on the spot, regarded him with bulging, tearful eyes, brought one hand up to her mouth and charged past him, pushing him out of the way with her other hand and running noisily towards the bathroom.

'Are you OK?' he called after her, following.

He caught up with her just in time to see her grip the wash-basin firmly with one hand, pull her hair back from her face with the other and throw up rambunctiously into the sink.

'Oh God,' he thought to himself, 'not the sink! Please – not the sink! That's what toilets are for.' But instead he said, 'Oh Delilah! You poor thing. Are you OK?', and patted her back and brought her a glass of water. She assured him that she was fine while she sat shivering and shaking on the edge of the bath, her creamy skin looking clammy and damp, gripping the glass to death between her hands.

He shuffled out when she said she wanted to take a shower and wandered blindly through his messy living room, deliberately ignored the rancid mayhem and disoriented dog in his kitchen and made his way towards the blessed sanctuary of his bedroom. He flopped wearily on to his bed and turned his head to view the time.

7.15 a.m. Had so many disgusting things really occurred in such a short amount of time? Could so much have gone so disastrously wrong in the space of just fifteen minutes? He turned the other way, brought his knees into chest and closed his eyes. His mind soon filled with images of Delilah in her underwear, but this time without the dog and the pee and the curry and the mess and the vomit – this time, just Delilah, her underwear and him . . .

By the time Dig's alarm went off at 8.15, he'd had a couple of gorgeous day-dreams and a long and, he thought, extremely well-deserved wank and he was feeling ready to start the day again, putting his previous attempt at day-starting well behind him.

The rain had stopped and the sun was positively bursting through his curtains. Delilah was wearing a pair of faded jeans, black crocodile-skin boots with high heels and a black polo neck when he walked into the now-uncurtained brightness of the living room. She was one of the few women who Dig considered suited to wearing jeans. She was crouching on the floor and leafing frantically through her paperwork, spreading the piles ever further and slurping on a mug of coffee as she went. She turned around when she sensed Dig behind her.

'Hi!' she beamed happily, rocking on her heels, 'you recovered from earlier on yet?'

'I think so,' he said, scratching his head and balancing himself on the arm of the sofabed, which had not, he noted, been put away.

'Sorry about all that. And sorry about shouting at you about the dog – I should have known that you weren't trying to harm him – I'm probably a bit over-protective sometimes.'

'Oh,' said Dig, dismissively, 'don't worry about that. How are *you*, anyway? You know . . .' He rubbed his tummy.

'Oh God. Sorry about that, too! I've had a bit of a dodgy gut lately. I'll try to do it in the toilet next time!' She laughed, getting to her feet and rubbing at the knees of her jeans.

'Oh don't be silly! It's fine. I mean – when you've gotta puke, you've gotta puke really, haven't you?' He giggled foolishly and then cleared his throat.

'So, Dig,' she asked, 'heard anything from Nadine yet?'

Dig jumped a little – for such a closed book, Delilah had a disarming ability to ask awkward questions at very unexpected junctures. 'Yeah,' he said, tersely, 'I spoke to her yesterday afternoon, actually. We had another row.'

'About me?'

Dig shook his head. 'Nah. About her. She's an idiot. She's getting back in touch with this wanker she went out with at university. She saw him last night. I don't understand her.'

'Well,' said Delilah, decisively, 'I do. She's trying to get back at you.'

'What are you talking about?'

'It's obvious. She's pissed off with you for spending time with me, so she's phoned up her ex to try and make you jealous.'

'Oh, don't be ridiculous.'

'I'm not. I'm right. I know I am. She wants you to know what she feels like. Why else would she choose now, of all times, to get back in touch with this bloke?'

Dig shrugged petulantly.

'You gonna call her?'

'No.' Dig was aware that he sounded like a child but he didn't care. If Nadine could play it like a brat, then he could play it like an even bigger brat.

'Jesus,' sighed Delilah, 'you two are behaving like a pair of kids. It's just like when we were at school, remember? When you and me first started going out together and Nadine wouldn't talk to you any more? Twelve years later and nothing's changed – it's pathetic.' She scooped together a pile of papers and beat them off the floor to straighten the edges.

'She started it,' said Dig, continuing his brat theme.

'So. Why can't you finish it? Just pick up the phone and say, "All right, Deen, fancy a drink?" You'll go out, you'll chat, within an hour everything will be back to normal – I guarantee you. Honestly. You two should be married to each other and instead you're not even *talking* to each other – it's infuriating!'

Dig winced at this new reference to him and Nadine.

'D'you want another coffee?' he asked, gesturing at her mug with his eyes.

'Er . . . no thanks,' she said, 'I'm actually really late for something.'

'Oh yeah? What's that then?'

'Oh – nothing really. I've just got be somewhere in twenty minutes, somewhere in Surrey.'

She suddenly became deeply distracted, flapping the papers about ever more wantonly, and Dig thought better of probing her with more questions and made his way to the kitchen to get himself a coffee. He was alarmed to note that Delilah had apparently managed to manoeuvre herself around the kitchen to make herself a cup of coffee *and* a bowl of porridge, with hot milk (the slimy-looking pan had been left unwashed and *unrinsed* in the sink), without feeling the need to clean up any of Digby's piss or at the very least pick the curry containers off the fucking floor. Dig was rendered speechless for a moment, well aware that even though he was cleaner and had higher standards than most, there could be very few people in this world who would feel happy about preparing food in amongst congealed curry and dog pee.

Delilah wandered into the kitchen, busily rearranging things in her handbag and clutching the spare set of door keys he'd given her the night before, a black sheepskin jacket slung crookedly over her shoulders. 'Erm,' she began, biting at her lower lip, 'Dig. I . . . er . . . need to ask you a favour.'

'Oh God,' thought Dig, 'what now?'

'Sure!' he smiled. 'No problem!'

'I was sort of hoping, if it wasn't too much trouble, that you could maybe have Digby today?' She smiled at him apprehensively.

'Eh?' said Dig.

'Well, I wouldn't normally ask, but I'll be on trains and God knows what today, and I don't know when I'll be home, and it would just make everything so much easier if he wasn't with me . . .'

'But I've . . . um . . . I've got to go to work, Delilah. I can't look after him. Can't you just leave him here?'

Delilah shook her head sadly. 'He's awful when he's left alone – he makes this terrible noise, like goats being tortured or something – painful. And he deliberately pees on beds. And he eats things. Toilet paper and stuff. It's a spite thing. Can't you take him with you? He's ever so small and incredibly well-behaved – just stick him under your desk, I'm sure no one will mind.' She opened up her face pleadingly.

'Well . . . it's not really up to me, you see – it's my boss – we get all sorts of important people coming to the office, and he might not like it very much if Digby here was around.'

'Oh I'm sure he won't mind little Digby – he'll probably love him! Please Dig – please. I'm begging of you. I'll make it up to you tonight – I'll cook you my famous lamb casserole – it's Alex's favourite! Please!'

Dig stared into Delilah's huge blue eyes and felt his minuscule reserves of resolve diminish rapidly to nothing. Toby wouldn't mind about the dog – he would probably think it was quite cool having a dog around the place – and he was sure that Digby could behave himself for at least a day, and poor old Delilah really, *really* needed him to help her – she would be so grateful, and grateful women were, generally speaking, a *very good thing*.

So he nodded and he smiled and he said, 'Yeah, sure, why not?', and Delilah hugged him yet again, and Dig thought to himself that he really was building up a good, big stock of brownie-points here and that at some stage all this Good Samaritan stuff was going to start paying dividends, surely, and he hugged her back and imagined the lovely luminous *white* stuff she had on underneath all those clothes.

Delilah didn't get back to Dig's flat until half past ten that night. She didn't tell him where she'd been all day and Dig didn't ask, and there was certainly no mention whatsoever of the promised lamb casserole.

CHAPTER TWENTY-THREE

Nadine was experiencing what could fairly be described as the worst hangover of her life. Without a doubt. Her head was throbbing, her heart was racing, her blood was fizzing, her stomach was churning and she was feeling as miserable as sin. She was having rather severe difficulty piecing together the fragmented bits of last night's events. She could just about remember having sex with Phil (bleugh), but she had absolutely no idea how such a terrible thing could have happened.

She'd managed to crawl out of bed forty-five minutes ago and had been dragging her pained body around the flat ever since, trying to make it do the things it normally did in the mornings, like wash its hair and make its toast and brush its teeth. It had been extremely difficult and extremely unpleasant, but she'd managed it somehow, and had been about to leave for work when she'd heard the phone ringing.

'Hello,' she sighed, painfully, perching on the arm of the sofa, expecting to hear her mother's voice on the end of the line, telling her something bizarre, like that she'd been clearing out the loft and found Nadine's old retainer brace and would she like her to bring it over that weekend or should she throw it away?

'Is that the sexiest woman in Kentish Town?' said a strange male voice.

'I'm sorry?'

'Hello, darlin'. It's me, Phil.'

Nadine experienced a sudden knot of tension in her stomach.

'Hello . . . hello . . . are you there?'

'Oh . . . yeah . . . sorry.' Nadine let her weary body flop sideways on to the sofa. 'So . . . how are you?'

'Yeah. Great. Great. You?'

'Not so great, actually.'

'Feeling bad?'

'Yeah – you could say that.'

'Can't say I'm surprised, really. All that vodka you were drinking and then – you know – what I gave you, later?'

'What?'

'That pill.'

'What pill?'

'You know – I gave you a pill – when you were getting upset about things.'

Oh yes. That E! Oh my God – she had, hadn't she? She'd taken an E. Jesus – she was thirty years old and she'd just taken her first E. That would explain *a lot* of things about last night.

'You might feel a bit low, today, a bit blue. Just drink a lot of coffee. Keep yourself busy.'

God – she was so stupid. She could have killed herself. She could imagine the headlines: PHOTOGRAPHER FOUND DEAD AFTER LETHAL COCKTAIL OF ALCOHOL AND DRUGS – *Police Say 'She Was Very Stupid.'*

'Yeah. Right. I will . . . Thanks.' She buried her face into the cushions on the sofa and closed her eyes. She was aware that the line had gone silent but was feeling too dreadful to be able to think of anything to say.

'Hey, Nadine' – Phil's voice broke the silence – 'you

234

know something? I haven't slept since you left. I've been up all night. Just thinking about you, about *us* . . . about how great we still are together.'

Oh no, thought Nadine, oh God.

'I've been wanting to phone you since you left. And I just wanted to say thanks, for getting in touch, for last night, for listening, for being you.'

Nadine wanted to reciprocate his enthusiasm, to say something nice – she felt *so sorry* for him – but all she could manage was a weak laugh.

'I meant everything I said last night, you know. I meant it.'

What did he say? What had he said? Nadine couldn't remember.

' . . . You are . . . special. Totally.'

Ooooh, thought Nadine, stop it.

'So I . . . er . . . just wondered. What are you up to later? Thought we could, like, meet up. Or something. Yeah?'

Nadine sat up straight. This was all a bit much, all a bit full-on for 8.30 on a Thursday morning with a raging hangover. 'Oh well,' she stalled, 'later? Erm, well – the thing is, I'm off to Barcelona at the weekend so . . .'

'Oh right, yeah. Fair enough. You'll want an early night, I suppose.'

'Yeah. That sort of thing.'

'Well, when are you back? Maybe we could get together then?'

'Back on Tuesday evening, actually.'

'So – maybe late next week?'

'Yeah. Maybe.'

'Great. Cool,' he said, and the line went quiet again. 'Erm, Nadine?' he said, eventually.

'Yeah.'

'I just wanted to say to you, I'm so glad you're back in my life. It feels like a miracle, you know, a fucking miracle.'

Nadine managed another weak laugh.

' . . . And next week, when I see you, I'm going to prove it to you, prove how much I care.'

Nadine felt a sickly little butterfly start fluttering its wings inside her tummy.

'I should never, ever have let you go, before. I should never have let my ego come between us the way it did. I'm older now and I've learned so much in life, and one thing I realize now, the most important thing I've learned, is that true love is what life is all about and nothing should ever, *ever* get in its way. And you were my true love, Nadine. I knew it then and I sure as hell know it now.'

Nadine's cheeks pinkened with horror.

'I can't believe I'm lucky enough to be given a second chance with you. I wanna make it work this time, I wanna make it perfect. Yeah? So I'll give you a ring on Tuesday, OK? And we'll meet up?'

'Yeah,' said Nadine, not knowing what else to say and wondering, not for the first time in her life, why it was so hard to use the word 'no'. 'Yes, sure.' It wasn't until she put the phone down that she realized her voice had gone up by about twelve octaves during the course of the conversation so that by the time she'd made her parting comments she'd sounded like Sandra Dickinson on helium.

She wondered for a moment why this should be and then decided that it really didn't matter.

CHAPTER TWENTY-FOUR

The next morning Dig waited until he heard the door slam behind Delilah and her footsteps bouncing down the front steps before crawling out of bed and into the living room.

Bloody hell – it was a nightmare in here. She hadn't even opened the curtains this time. There was half a bowl of porridge encrusting on the coffee-table, half her wardrobe strewn across her bed, and Digby was shivering furiously under the radiator.

'Great,' Dig muttered under his breath.

He strode towards the television and switched it off. Quarter to eight in the morning was no time for Johnny Vaughan, as far as he was concerned. He dragged the curtains apart and peered through the window. Delilah was standing on the other side of the road pacing back and forth and looking at her watch. Christ, she looked gorgeous. She was wearing leggings, which accentuated the shape of her fantastic legs, pristine white trainers and a huge knee-length puffa jacket. She'd put her hair up into a sort of fluffy, tufty thing on the back of her head, which bounced up and down as she walked around, giving her the look of a dressage pony. A very beautiful dressage pony.

A cab screeched to a halt next to her, and a couple of seconds later she was gone.

Dig scratched his chin, yawned and turned towards

the kitchen, the smell of Delilah's freshly brewed coffee luring him away from the window. He took one
step forward and then recoiled in agony, clasping his
knee to him and rubbing furiously at the sole of his
foot.

'Aaargh! Fucking shitting bollocking FUCK!' he
yelled, hopping around. He looked down and saw one
of Delilah's high-heeled shoes lying on its side. He'd
trodden on the heel and it fucking hurt.

What the *fuck* was Delilah's shoe doing over here
anyway? Where was the other one? Why couldn't she
keep them together? In a pair? Like a normal human
being?

Dig felt anger percolating in his chest. He picked the
shoe up and hurled it across the room with a roar, and
then he sat down heavily on the arm of the sofa and took
a lot of deep breaths, to calm his inner rage.

He couldn't stand this, he really, really couldn't bear
it. He knew he was being anal, he knew other people
would be able to ignore all this . . . this *shit*, all this stuff
everywhere, clothes and mess and paper and dogs and
fucking *crystals*. Other people would just think, Well,
it's not perfect, but it's only temporary, and she's a friend
and it's only a bit of mess. But Dig just couldn't. It fucked
his head up. He couldn't concentrate. He couldn't relax.
He couldn't *breathe*, for God's sake.

He hobbled towards his stereo and traced his finger
across the 'B' section of his CD collection. There was
only one thing for it, only one person who could help
him now.

He reverently laid the disc in its tray, slid shut the
door and pressed play. There was different music for
different moments. Music to work to (Radiohead, Travis,

238

the Manics), music to bathe to (Paul Westerberg, Paul Weller), music to cook and wash up to (Blondie, Abba, 70s compilations), music to have sex to (Portishead, Chris Isaaks, Dean Martin), music to dance to (*Saturday Night Fever* soundtrack and any Northern soul) and then there was music to tidy up to, and when it came to a mess of this magnitude, there was only one man for the job.

The One and Only.

The Godfather.

James.

Brown.

Get down.

Dig swivelled the volume as loud as it would go without bouncing ornaments off his shelves and set to it.

Dig loved to tidy, he really did. It was one of his favourite occupations. But this was a bit trickier than usual because it wasn't his stuff. It was weird, alien bits and pieces from somebody else's life, stuff that belonged on the shelves and in the cupboards of a house he'd never visited, in a part of the country he'd never been to. And a lot of it was underwear.

Digby still sat quaking under the radiator and watched Dig as he picked up tailored trousers, sweatshirts, jeans and cashmere jumpers and folded them painstakingly into perfect little cubes. Episode. Phase Eight. Donna Karan. Marks and Spencer. Tommy Hilfiger. He feigned disinterest in her bits of white-jersey underwear, lumping them together nonchalantly, like old rugby socks, almost as if someone might be watching him for signs of sad-old-gitness. He collected her mugs and bowls and glasses of water and put them in the kitchen sink. He rolled up the duvet and shoved it in the hall cupboard, along with the pillows. He heaved the sofabed back into its cavity, retrieved his cushions from where they lay scattered around the room, plumped them up voraciously and arranged them into a nice overlapping pattern across the sofa back.

He stepped back to appraise his cushions, screwing up his face as he joined James to hit a high note. Now – where to put all these beautifully folded bits of designer clothing? He spotted one of her vast suitcases in the corner, dragged it into the middle of the room and threw it open. And then he stopped in his tracks. Paper. Loads of it. Loose-leaf papers in clear plastic folders. Notebooks. Folders. Letters.

Clues.

Again, acting as if there might be a CCTV in operation in his flat, he pretended not to notice. Oh no, he thought to himself, I most certainly am *not* the sort of fellow who would snoop in other people's possessions, thank you very much. Not me. Oh no.

He hoped that the imaginary people watching him on their imaginary monitor were impressed by his restraint.

He shuffled the papers around a bit to make room in the case for her clothes, and let his eyes wander across the letter that lay on the top as he put her clothing, piece by piece, into the case. It was an official-looking letter on crisp white laid.

Dig scanned it quickly.

Rosemary Bentall
Clinical Psychologist
The Old School Buildings
Liverpool Road
Chester
CH2 1UL

Phone: 01244 555000
Fax: 01244 555129

10th November 1999

Mrs Delilah Biggins
Dorrington Lodge
Chester
CH8 7LN

Dear Delilah,

I have been trying to phone you since you walked out of
our session yesterday afternoon but your housekeeper
was unable to tell me where you were.

I am very concerned about you, Delilah, and can only
hope that you haven't carried out your threat to return
to London. I understand your need to uncover the past,
especially in the light of what you told me yesterday,
but I really feel that this trip will not be in your best
interests and could in fact be detrimental to your
progress at this stage in our work together. We have both
worked so hard to get to this point and leaving now will
put your recovery in jeopardy.

241

However, if you do insist on going ahead with your plans, then I beseech you to talk to Alex about it. He has supported you in everything over the years and shutting him out now would be unfair on both of you.

I don't think there is anything else I can say, except to urge you once more to heed my advice and postpone this visit until you're stronger.

Warm wishes,

Rosie

Dr Rosemary Bentall

Dig closed his mouth, cleared his throat and quickly piled the rest of the clothes on top of the paperwork.

His heart raced in rhythm to the music as he tried to go about his business, but he found it impossible to feel normal. 'Uncover the past'? What did that mean? And what the hell was Delilah doing seeing a shrink? Delilah wasn't mad. O K – so she was into crystals and feng shui and stuff. She was messy and disorganized and talked too much. But she wasn't *mad*.

This threw a new complexion on everything. When Delilah had told Dig that she was in London to 'sort her head out', he'd interpreted it as meaning that she wanted to get away from Alex. He'd thought she was here to contemplate her marriage, which was why he'd kept out of her face. But it was nothing to do with her marriage.

242

It was to do with the past. Of which he was a part. It was his business, now. He had a right to know.

He was about to zip up Delilah's suitcase when he had a sudden thought. He grabbed a pen and scribbled down Dr Rosemary Bentall's phone number. Just in case. He probably wouldn't need it.

But if a woman in Chester with letters after her name was worried about Delilah, then so was he.

CHAPTER TWENTY-FIVE

Nadine had received a most unexpected phone call the previous day.

From Delilah.

It had thrown her completely, suffering, as she was, so terribly with a hangover, not to mention the guilt and anxiety and spine-chilling remorse her reckless actions of Wednesday evening were punishing her with.

'Hi,' she'd said, jauntily, 'it's me. Delilah' – as if they were old mates.

'Oh,' Nadine had said, 'hi.'

'Look – I was talking to Dig last night,' she'd continued.

Oh yes, thought Nadine, I bet you were.

'And he mentioned that you go to the gym regularly.'

'Ye–es.'

Delilah wondered whether Nadine would mind if she came to the gym with her, because, in her own highly amusing words, she was starting to feel really fat. Apparently she used to go running every day in the countryside and she was missing the exercise – oh, and the reason she didn't want to go jogging in London was because she felt self-conscious about her 'wobbly bottom'.

If there was one thing more annoying than a naturally thin girl, it was a naturally thin girl who went on about being fat all the time.

So Nadine had had approximately one and a half

seconds to form a reply and because she was incapable of using the word 'no', the only alternative had been to say, 'Of course, great, no problem – that would be lovely.'

She had no one to blame but herself.

Delilah arrived at Nadine's flat on Friday morning on the dot of eight o'clock. Nadine had managed to forget about this arrangement until half past seven and had consequently spent the last half an hour frantically running around her flat trying to clear up, defumigate and make herself look beautiful all at the same time.

When the doorbell rang at eight o'clock she'd achieved none of the above. She had been unable to find any of her sexy, expensive, *shiny* Lycra gym things, those tight purple, black and red things that skimmed gleamingly over her body, sucking her in and making her look like a Gladiator, and instead had had to throw on her baggy old *grey* things with the holes in them that made her look like a dumpy housewife with low self-esteem who doesn't know that her husband is shagging his secretary.

She'd attempted to put her hair up in some sort of jaunty, sporty-looking pony-tail thing and had ended up with this strange *cottage-loaf*-type structure on her head that looked like it might be housing a pair of chaffinches. And, in an attempt to rid her flat of the stench of three weeks' worth of Marlboro Light emissions (the last time she'd opened a window), she'd actually managed to *smash* the kitchen window. Actually broken the fucking thing. No idea how. And there was now a force-ten icy gale wailing through the angry-looking hole. She'd taped a carrier bag over it, to no great effect, and given that she didn't have time to phone a glazier, was just hoping and praying that the burglars in her area weren't quick-

245

witted enough to break in in the hour or so she'd be out of the house.

She opened the door breathlessly and was greeted, unsurprisingly, by a vision of female perfection. There she was, her golden hair scraped back immaculately into a sleek pony-tail, her body encased in a simple pair of black cotton leggings, black vest top and an enormous, all-enveloping black puffa jacket which made her look like a fragile little doll. Pah! Her skin was glowing like she'd already been for a two-mile jog, and she was grinning from ear to ear.

'Hi! I'm not late, am I?' she oozed.

'No . . . no' – Nadine suddenly realized she had left her fag hanging out of her mouth and quickly transferred it to her fingers – 'no . . . not at all. Come in.'

Nadine wasn't a flake. Not usually. She wasn't one of those girls who couldn't get out of the front door without laddering her tights or who couldn't cook a lasagne without setting the house on fire. She was usually pretty cool and poised. So why was she now falling apart at the seams just because of the mere presence, the sheer *existence* of a girl called Delilah Lillie? It was pathetic. If this was any other girl, literally any other girl, she would have just said, 'Come in, excuse the mess, sorry about the fag smell, and don't I look dreadful.' So why did she feel this overwhelming need to be perfect for Delilah?

'Wow,' said Delilah, as she moved through Nadine's cluttered hallway, 'what an incredible place. I love what you've done to the walls.' She was running her fingers across the rose-pink foil. 'Where did you get this stuff from?'

'It's sweet wrapping. I found a big box of it in one of

246

the studios upstairs from mine when they moved out. It was a fucking nightmare to put up.'

'Amazing,' sighed Delilah, 'you've got such an imagination. I would *never* have thought of something like that. So original.'

Oh God. She was doing that thing again, that self-effacing,   you're-so-much-better-than-crappy-little-old-me bollocks.

'Oh my God! That's so cute!' said Delilah, eyeing up the tiny motifs on Nadine's wallpaper in the living room. 'It's Miffy the Rabbit, isn't it?' She put her index fingers to her upper lip and crossed them over each other, into an X, and then giggled. 'I used to love Miffy the Rabbit. Where did you get it?'

'Oh' – Nadine gritted her teeth at Delilah's cloying attempt at cuteness – 'it was from a children's shop in Crouch End that was closing down. It wasn't a top-selling line, apparently – couldn't compete with Thomas the Tank Engine and Postman Pat.'

'Incredible. Absolutely incredible . . . So clever the way it looks like little flowers from a distance and you can't see it till you get close up. Magnolia's about my limit on the home-décor front.'

Delilah loved her car, too – of course. 'Wow. Sex on wheels. What is it?'

'It's an Alpha. Spider.'

'It's beautiful. God, you're so lucky. Only car I've ever driven is my Renault Clio. It's nice but not exactly sexy, though.'

Yeah right, thought Nadine, yawn yawn. If you got much more self-deprecating you'd cease to exist, you'd end up vanishing vaporously into the ether. Either this girl was suffering from a severe case of low self-esteem or this really was the only way she could communicate with women who weren't as beautiful as her. Either way, it was beginning to grate on her nerves. She'd almost preferred the old-style cocky, arrogant Delilah.

Nadine was aware that she was being rather unfair on Delilah. She knew that Delilah was just trying to be friendly, trying to be a girl's girl. But that was the problem. She just *wasn't* a girl's girl and she sounded insincere and fake. She wasn't the cool Delilah that Nadine had known and hated at school. She was just plain irritating.

Unpeeled and bobbing up and down on the step machine, Delilah looked extraordinary – she made it look so effortless. Not a drop of sweat on her, not a hair out of place.

'Ever used one of these before?' puffed Nadine.

'Nah,' replied Delilah, sounding frighteningly *un*breathless.

'What setting are you on?' Nadine asked her.

Delilah moved her towel away from the dot-matrix screen. 'Erm . . . thirteen, I think. No – fourteen.'

Fourteen! *Fourteen!* Nadine had almost thrown a party when, after weeks and weeks, she'd finally gone up to level *ten* on the step machine. 'Uh-huh,' she squeaked, breathlessly, 'really.'

Nadine was desperately trying to control her urge to ask after Dig. The question was sitting, quivering, on the tip of her tongue, like a diver's toes gripping the edge of the diving-board.

She could hear herself asking the question in her head, it echoed over and over, varying in intonation and construction, but try as she might, she just couldn't

248

launch the words from her mouth. She was scared her voice would suddenly crack and that tears would appear from nowhere and that right here, in the middle of this gym, in front of *Delilah Lillie*, of all people, she would lose control.

She couldn't bear to ask Delilah the question because she didn't think she'd be able to handle even the smallest hint of intimacy in her reply. It made her feel bad enough as it was to imagine that Delilah had been talking to Dig last night, having normal conversations with him, being a part of his life, while she herself – *his best friend* – was not even on talking terms with him. Nadine couldn't believe how much things had changed over the last few days.

On the treadmill, Delilah ran as if being swept along by the wind through an endless, sunlit field of corn-flowers and poppies, her feet not making a sound against the rubber tread, her pony-tail flying out behind her as if on a gust of summer breeze. Nadine had tried the treadmill only once and had felt so paranoid that she was going to lose her footing and go shooting off the back end and into the lap of someone doing sit-ups behind her that she'd not tried it again since.

They stood side by side on the machines that Nadine had never found a name for and so referred to as the 'swish' machines. Nadine always felt a little insecure on this contraption, too, gripping on to the handlebars for dear life while her legs 'swished' away beneath her. Delilah, she noticed, was fearlessly unattached to the machine, positively *marching* back and forth, her arms swinging freely at her sides. And she was on the highest ramp setting.

Delilah turned and hit Nadine with a wide, adrenalin-

249

fuelled grin that seemed to suggest that she was actually enjoying herself, and then turned away again.

It had taken Nadine a long time to feel comfortable at the gym. She'd first joined after realizing with an overpowering sense of desolation that only a few years after finally shedding her puppy-fat she was about to experience the ill-effects of a rapidly slowing metabolism. The carefree life of one who could eat Mars Bars and burgers and cream cakes with impunity was not to be hers.

It had been anathema to her at first, lining up at these soulless machines to walk up and down or cycle on the spot for forty-five minutes or so feeling utterly ridiculous and thinking, Is this what God intended? Is this what two hundred million years of evolution have boiled down to? Me – paying a hundred quid a month to run on the spot in a stupid outfit?

But she'd got used to it eventually, it had become just another part of her routine, and she no longer thought about it. Felt almost at home in this peculiar place, in fact. She knew the form, could programme any of these machines in two or three deft button configurations, no longer felt embarrassed doing her stretches in front of other people, looked positively *cool* at the water fountains, had it all down pat.

But now, accompanied by Delilah, she was feeling like a graceless, lumpen novice again.

'God – I enjoyed that,' said Delilah, joyfully, after effortlessly executing 150 sit-ups in the manner of a US marine in training, and leaping down the stairs towards the changing rooms. Nadine followed behind, her legs wobbling slightly as a result of her efforts to keep pace with Delilah's work-out.

250

'Yeah. Me too,' said Nadine, her leaden, exhausted voice suggesting anything *but*.

In the changing room Delilah began to remove her barely damp clothes with the confidence of one who has nothing to hide: no bumps, no lumps, no ripples, no hairs.

Yup, thought Nadine, as she glanced at a startlingly naked Delilah, she was that sort of clotted-cream colour all over, and she was definitely a natural blonde, and she did have the body of a finely tuned race horse and her bottom did stand up all by itself.

She hoped sincerely that Delilah got down on her hands and knees every morning when she woke up and thanked God for what he'd chosen to give her.

Over a cup of coffee in the gym's café, Delilah seemed less nervous and eager to please than she'd been earlier, and Nadine was surprised by how easy-going and pleasant she was – she'd always been so sullen and moody at school. Nadine couldn't recall ever seeing her smiling in those days. But now she was almost enjoying the conversation. They'd been talking generally about keeping fit, healthy eating, giving up smoking – which Delilah was having trouble with and which Nadine had been meaning to get around to for the last ten years – and the shock of turning thirty.

'And of course,' said Nadine, 'the scariest thing about turning thirty is that you're running out of time to defer the *baby* issue, aren't you? You know, for years and years you've said that you'll have kids before you're thirty – that seems reasonable enough – and then you turn twenty-eight, twenty-nine, and suddenly you're thinking, hold on a sec, not sure if I'm ready quite yet, maybe when I'm thirty-two. Then you turn thirty and realize that you're no more ready for it than you were ten years ago – *less* ready, if anything, and you start wondering if you'll ever actually be ready.' She stopped stirring her sugar lump into her coffee and looked up at Delilah. 'Do you know what I mean?'

Delilah smiled and shrugged. 'Haven't really given it that much thought,' she said, which struck Nadine as very odd. Thirty-year-old women who hadn't given the baby issue much thought simply didn't exist as far as she was concerned.

'Oh, come on, Delilah,' she snorted, 'you've been married for ten years. You must have at least *talked* about it?'

'Well,' she said, 'Alex – his business is his life. I don't think there's any room for a child.'

'Yeah, but what about you? Don't you want kids?'

Delilah was turning Nadine's lighter over and over between her fingers and staring at the top of the table. 'Oh God,' she said, 'I don't know. I suppose so. One day. I just feel too ... *selfish* right now. I feel I've got too much to sacrifice. Do you know what I mean?'

Nadine nodded enthusiastically. She knew *exactly* what she meant. 'I sometimes wish that I'd done it when I was younger. Got it out of the way when I was eighteen. My kid would have been in school by the time I was twenty-four and I could have caught up with my life then, without being deafened by the sound of my biological clock nagging at me.' She laughed. 'Don't you ever wish you'd done it when you were younger?'

Delilah laughed, too. 'Not really,' she shrugged. And then she glanced at her watch. 'Oh God,' she said, 'it's nearly ten! Look, Deen. I'm sorry, but I've really got to dash.' She was collecting her belongings to her, her puffa, her bag, her scarf.

'Here,' said Nadine, picking up her car keys and getting to her feet, 'let me give you a lift home – your cousin's place isn't far from the studio.'

'Oh. No. Really, thanks. I'll be fine walking. I'd like to walk,' she smiled tightly and threw her bag over her shoulder. 'Really.'

'If you're sure?'

She nodded effusively. 'Yeah – there's some things I need to do, you know, on the way home. But thanks. And thanks for this' – she indicated the gym – 'maybe we could do this again?'

Nadine nodded and smiled and thought, 'Yeah – *maybe.*'

'Actually, Nadine,' said Delilah, sliding her hold-all off her shoulder and putting her hands on the table, 'I haven't been entirely honest with you. I'm not . . . um . . . I'm not here just for the sake of my bottom, actually.' Nadine saw her take a deep breath. She was nervous.

'Oh yeah,' said Nadine, apprehensively.

'No,' she said, 'I wanted to talk to you, really. There was something I wanted to say to you.'

Nadine sat down and put her car keys back on the table.

'I know you don't really like me, Nadine and I know that you see me as some sort of threat to your friendship with Dig. But that's not why I'm here – honestly. There's nothing going on between Dig and me and there never will be. I've always liked you, Nadine. I was a bit in awe of you at school and maybe that sometimes came across as rudeness, but I suppose I was just jealous of you. You were so clever and so cool and you had everything going for you. I used to want to *be* you, you know, and if I was ever mean to you it was only because I was scared of you. I never meant to come between you and Dig then, and I really, *really* don't want to come between you again now. I hate it that you're not speaking.

'Dig's so stubborn,' continued Delilah, 'and he's not going to call you even though I can tell he's desperate to. And I know you're just as stubborn as him. But please. Call him,' she pleaded. 'Don't waste any more time, Nadine. Life's too short. Make up. Be friends. You two need each other, you two were made for each other. You two,' she said pointedly, 'should be *together*.'

And with that highly overdramatic and perfectly ludicrous closing comment, she disappeared, leaving behind her a cloud of her unidentifiable morning-dew perfume and an atmosphere of sadness and confusion.

CHAPTER TWENTY-SIX

The arsehole driver of the Porsche 911 in front of him finally ran out of water. Dig felt like he'd been here for ever, parked behind him, watching him circle round and round his precious extra inch of manhood, squirting at it mincily with the water jet-spray like he was the only man in the history of the world who'd ever owned a Porsche.

Dig watched him drying his hands distastefully on a piece of paper towel pulled from a barrel attached to the wall, and just when Dig thought he was finally going to get into his car and drive away, he began circling it again, eagle-eyed, with a soft cloth in his hand, rubbing meticulously at various points on the paintwork.

He was taking his time. He could see Dig waiting behind him, but he wasn't going to let that unsettle him. Because he was a Porsche driver and in the evolutionary scale of car ownership he was the boss, Dig, in his silver G-reg Honda Civic was just Monkey-Boy to him, a lower form of life.

Finally, the man in the Porsche lowered himself into his car, fiddled around with his stereo a bit, adjusted his wing mirrors electronically and drove away, apparently quite pleased with himself. Dig sighed and moved his car forward towards the jet-spray.

Dig had been driving home from work tonight, Digby vibrating nervously in the passenger seat next to him, when he'd stopped to fill up at the petrol station on Oval Road and had had a sudden and unprecedented urge to wash his car. This had never happened to him before – especially not at one of those manual jet-spray jobs where you actually had to *get out* of your car.

Despite his domestic fastidiousness, Dig operated a complete set of double standards when it came to his car. The inside of his car resembled Notting Hill the morning after the carnival, strewn with fast-food packaging and empty cans, the outside festooned with monochromatic bird-shits and tear-drops of sticky red sap.

The reason he kept his flat so clean and his car so dirty was simple. He loved his flat and he hated his car. Hated it. He'd had to fork out another £150 on Monday morning to get it fixed – the fifth time in six years he'd had major problems with it. He'd already paid for the car twice over in maintenance alone. And it wasn't even a car he'd ever actually wanted. It was a car he'd somehow ended up with. But tonight, strangely, he felt warmly disposed towards his car. Tonight he decided that maybe if he treated his car a little more nicely then his car might treat him a little more fairly.

He aimed the spray at the side panels and watched with satisfaction as layers of grime and goo began to fall away and a fresh new skin of shiny silver revealed itself. It symbolized, he realized in an uncharacteristic moment of philosophical reflection, the way he himself was feeling today.

He'd had a revelation today, at work – in fact, he'd had a series of revelations, and washing his car was just the start. A new Dig was going to be born tonight.

After the disastrous start to his unplanned cohabitation with Delilah, after the dreadful scene with Digby the other morning, and the puking up and the mess everywhere and disorganized towel rotas, Dig wanted to bring some *class* to the situation.

Delilah, in her Chester palace, was probably accustomed to eating her evening meal at a dining table. She was used to large rooms and open spaces, fresh air and privacy. She probably had her own en-suite bathroom. She *wasn't* accustomed to living in cramped quarters, eating off her lap and tidying up after herself. She had a *housekeeper*, for God's sake.

Despite Delilah's ignominious start in life, she had always exuded a kind of star quality and it was easier for Dig to imagine her living in neo-Georgian splendour than living as she had done on the Gospel Oak estate, among dirty nappies, empty beer cans, bawling, snot-nosed infants and overflowing ashtrays. Delilah *belonged* in her huge six-bedroomed, feng-shui-ed house with its ruffles and valances, its conservatory and water feature in the garden, she was born to be pampered and spoiled. She didn't belong on his sofabed. It was all wrong.

So tonight he was going to do everything he could to make his lifestyle compare favourably with Delilah's life in Chester. Why? Because, as inconvenient and uncomfortable as it was sharing his tiny flat with Delilah, as much as he hated her mess and her mood swings, her crystals and her dog, he wanted her to stay.

Not necessarily in his flat, but in London.

He didn't want her to turn around to him and say, 'This sucks, London sucks, your flat sucks, I'm going home.' Because it felt very suspiciously to Dig like he was falling in love with Delilah.

Yes, he knew: he knew exactly what Nadine would

think of that, he knew that he shouldn't, he knew it was probably a huge mistake, but he couldn't help it. She was just so . . . so unutterably delicious. The smell of her, like fresh laundry and damp grass, the feel of her, like marshmallows and satin, and the sight of her, that extraordinary hair which you could almost see your reflection in, those lips, those legs, those duck-egg-blue eyes . . .

But it was more than all that. It was her *vulnerability* more than anything that made Dig love her – or want to love her. She was like a lost little girl, all alone in the world, full of secrets and pain. He wanted to help her, protect her, look after her. Reading that letter from her shrink had unleashed a whole new set of emotions within him. He'd looked up 'clinical psychologist' on the Internet at work this morning, trying to find out more about what they did, and it sounded like they were pretty serious shit. It was more than just 'my father never hugged me' kind of stuff. Clinical psychologists, it seemed, tried to mend broken people.

Dig's water allocation ran out and he replaced the jet-spray in its holder. He got back into his car, gave the increasingly quivering Digby a reassuring chuck under the chin and drove towards the vacuum machine.

Far from putting Dig off Delilah, finding out that she was a fruitloop had intensified his feelings for her. It made her more real, more attainable in a way, like finding out that she was more than just the coolest girl in school, finding the soft spots that she'd let only him see, was what had made him fall in love with her all those years ago. People with weaknesses made Dig feel strong in the same way that small women made him feel big.

Since reading that letter, Dig had been consumed by

an overwhelming desire for intimacy. He missed the way he'd been in his youth, he missed the time in his life when he'd been carefree and careless with his heart, when he'd been capable of falling helplessly and hopelessly in love. He'd been such a soft-hearted romantic when he was young, his heart on his sleeve and his emotions on a plate. And since he'd first set eyes on Delilah, last Saturday, he had begun to experience similar sensations again. It was incredibly exciting to discover that he was still capable of feeling this way.

For the first time since he was a teenager, since that hideous weekend in Manchester, Dig could imagine, without a hint of queasiness or panic, a future life which involved somebody else. He could imagine seeing the same face on the pillow next to him every single morning, and he could imagine saying 'we' a lot instead of 'I'. He could imagine being a provider and taking care of someone. He could envisage the golden world that Nadine had conjured up in the café the other day, the world full of teenage children and mess and noise and joyful rites of passage.

Dig was ready to open up again. He was ready for anything, including getting hurt.

He slid into the back seat of his car, thinking briefly what an alien place the back seat of one's own car was to be, and began stuffing handfuls of rubbish into a carrier bag.

Him and Delilah.

Delilah and him.

It was a distinct possibility.

He just had to persuade her to stay. He had to convince her that whatever it was she had going on with Alex in Chester was not that special. And let's face it, this Alex couldn't be all that, could he, if he didn't even manage it more than once or twice a year? Not to mention the fact that Delilah had left him in Chester without warning and without involving him in her plans, whatever they were. She couldn't love him that much, could she, to have left him with a note and an empty bed?

Alex did, however, have a six-bedroom house in his favour, plus acres of land, horses, cars and enough cash to send Delilah off shopping first-class all over the world whenever she felt like it.

But Dig took this as a sign – this was another facet of his major revelation – it was time to step his career plans up a gear. He was thirty years old – he was supposed to be the millionaire owner of his own record label by now. He was supposed to be driving a big fuck-off Mercedes and spending half the year abroad in his tax haven in Monaco. He should be up there with Alan McGee in the *Times* 1000 Richest supplement. He wasn't ever supposed to have ended up in a poky flat on Camden Road driving a clapped-out old Honda Civic and feeling pleased to be earning £27,000 a year.

Somewhere between his A levels and his thirtieth birthday, Dig realized, he'd lost his fire. Somewhere along the line he'd become complacent and *laissez-faire*, happy to get by with the bare minimum. When he'd first started work at Electrogram Records music had been his life. He used to pinch himself in disbelief that he was *being paid* to go to gigs. He felt *privileged* to be working in the music industry. What had happened to his ambition, his overpowering need to be a success, leave his mark, make something of himself? Contentment was a dangerous thing.

There were guys out there, guys still in their twenties,

making twice, three times, *ten* times what he was making. There were guys out there who'd done it, made it, got there, achieved – *and they were younger than him*.

He thought about Nick Jeffries – twenty-four, hyperactive, restless and always on the move, always sniffing around, asking questions, pushing, pushing, pushing. He was a pain in the arse but you could bet your bottom dollar that in a year or two he'd be gone from Johnny-Boy Records, gone and on to the next salary increment, the next rung of the ladder. He'd be running his own company by the time he was twenty-eight and rolling in it two years later.

Nick Jeffries would *not* be driving a G reg Honda Civic when he was thirty years old.

This was what Dig had missed most about being in love. This was the effect that being in love had on Dig. It lit a fire in his belly. And now he could feel it returning, like the blood rushing back to an anaemic complexion.

£27,000 a year *wasn't enough*.

A Honda Civic *wasn't enough*.

Seventeen-year-old students *weren't enough*.

Signing up only one big band in his career *wasn't enough*.

Delilah expected more, and he wanted more.

He pulled the vacuum nozzle out of its holder and began ferreting around the fluff-laden nooks and crannies of his car, sucking out years' worth of dust and fag-ash and tiny ribbons of Cellophane unfurled from cigarette packets.

Pretty phallic places, petrol stations, Dig thought, looking around him. Nozzles, pumps, cars, dipsticks and all those things that were designed to fit into holes and spew forth petrol, air, water and oil. Even this innocent-looking vacuum was behaving like a lascivious old pervert, groping around frantically inside his car's underwear.

The first weapon in Dig's anti-Alex arsenal was his 'groovy' London lifestyle. Alex might have cash and assets and a business but he couldn't excite Delilah the way Dig could, with nights out schmoozing with celebrities, first viewings of hot new bands and cab rides all around London Town with that air that 'smells of life' rushing up her nostrils.

The second weapon was his libido. He had one. Alex didn't. Full stop.

And the third weapon was his culinary skills. Dig was very proud of his attention to detail and his eye for aesthetics. Nothing pleased him more than the simplest of high-quality ingredients, plainly cooked and beautifully presented, and it had always saddened him slightly that he had no one special to regale with his lovingly prepared plates of food. It wasn't the sort of food you would cook for just anyone, for your mates, or your mum, or some girl who you weren't all that serious about.

Delilah was giving him the perfect opportunity to show off.

So – it was all sorted.

Dig and Delilah's Big Night Out.

A gig at the Forum – an all-girl band called Pesky Kids who Dig, personally, couldn't stand but who Delilah would love, because they were fresh and trendy and poppy and all those things that seemed to appeal to her so much.

Then on to the after-show party – lots of celebs for Delilah to get her rocks off over. A couple of drinks, a bit of a mingle and then back home, where Dig was going to surprise her with a slap-up midnight feast.

He'd been to the fishmonger in his lunch hour and bought a pound of absolutely enormous prawns – complete bruisers – plus a great thick wedge of Loch Fyne smoked salmon and a small pot of caviar. He'd bought a packet of blinis and a large pot of smetana from the organic supermarket on Parkway, and he was going to boil up some dinky miniature new potatoes and serve them crushed with melted butter and rock salt. Nice and simple. The sort of stuff he could just whisk out of the fridge at the last minute and have ready with the minimum of preparation and fuss. And very, very classy.

And during dinner, over the candle-light, he would talk to her, *really* talk to her, about her plans, her trip to London, about that letter from her shrink, and her mission to 'uncover the past'. After all, he couldn't help her if he didn't know what her secret was.

Dig sneered a bit as he unpeeled half a Harvest Crunch bar from the floor of his car. This was somewhat confusing, as he'd never in his entire life eaten a Harvest Crunch bar and could only imagine that someone else, someone he'd been kind enough to offer a lift to, had left it there. It was one thing chucking litter about in your own car, but in somebody else's? Fucking cheek . . .

Dig gave his dashboard a last going over with a cloth and clambered from his car to appraise his handiwork. Not bad, not bad at all.

'What d'you think of that then, you little gremlin?' he said, bending to address Digby, who was now shivering on the forecourt, looking like an abandoned orphan. 'Pretty good, huh?' It looked almost like it belonged to someone who actually *liked* their car.

263

He opened the passenger door for Digby and patted the seat. 'In you get, titch. We're going home now.'

Digby sat motionless.

'Come on, mate. Get in.'

The dog eyed Dig fearfully, and then the passenger seat, and began to quake even more.

'Oh Jesus, what kind of a dog are you? You're descended from the *wolf*, for God's sake. Do you realize that? Come on – show some balls.'

Digby emitted a small whimper and looked at Dig imploringly.

'You can look at me all you like, and you can make your pathetic little noises, but I'm not going to put you in the car. We're going to stay here until you get in on your own.'

Digby whimpered a bit louder.

'Listen, you raggedy little excuse for a dog, I am not going to help you, OK? You might be used to the life of Riley where you come from – you've probably got your very own personal valet, or something, but you're in Dig country now and you're going to have to learn to fend for yourself. So get in.'

He patted the seat once more, and this time Digby seemed to have a change of attitude. He girded his loins and readied himself, an expression of determination on his face, and suddenly launched himself, with a tremendous effort, towards the passenger seat. He looked like he was just about to make it – his little legs gripped for dear life on to the edge of the seat, his eyes bulged with strenuous effort, his claws dug into the beige upholstery, his back legs scrabbled to keep him aloft – and then he fell off, rolling on to his back on the forecourt.

Dig couldn't help it. He burst out laughing. The dog threw him an injured look.

'If at first, mate, if at first. Try again.'

Digby did try again, and again he fell. He tried twice more in fact before finding enough impetus to finally land on the chair.

'Yeah!' cheered Dig, patting the distinctly triumphant-looking dog on the head. 'What a geezer! What a dude!' He picked up Digby's paw and shook his hand. 'See – wasn't so bad, was it?'

Dig gently closed the door, walked around the car and got into the driver's seat. He turned to look at the dog, and the dog turned to look at him, and Dig could have sworn he smiled at him.

'OK, boy. Let's go home and show your mum how much we've both changed, eh?'

He switched on his ignition and pulled out of the garage.

CHAPTER TWENTY-SEVEN

Nadine stopped off at her local corner shop on the way home that Friday evening and bought a fresh loaf of bread and a packet of bacon. She was going to eat lots of bacon sandwiches. She couldn't remember the last time she'd let herself eat a bacon sandwich, and then a courier had walked into her studio eating one a couple of hours ago and she hadn't been able to get the smell out of her nostrils or the thought out of her mind since. And besides, she deserved a big fat bacon sandwich after her hugely strenuous work-out with Delilah at the gym this morning – she must have burned off at least twice as many calories as she usually did, when she was on her own.

She'd spent most of that day and the last thinking about what Delilah had said to her that morning at the gym. It had been a revelation. Delilah had been jealous of *her* at school. It all made sense now and threw a different complexion on two of the worst years of her life. She felt stupid for all the angst she'd put herself through and she respected Delilah hugely for her honesty. Of course Delilah wasn't interested in Dig. Why would she want Dig, with his skinny legs and his poky flat when she had a mansion and a handsome husband waiting for her at home? For the first time since she was fourteen years old, Nadine could feel her resentment towards Delilah fading away.

She'd also been thinking a lot about what had happened between her and Phil on Wednesday night, and shuddering a lot – how could she? how could she? *how could she?* – but it had been nearly forty-eight hours now and there'd been no word from him, so maybe, just maybe, *please God*, he was just going to disappear down whatever dark, dank hole he'd emerged from, and she'd never have to see him again.

She dropped a thick stack of paperwork on the table in her hallway, hung up her coat and kicked off her shoes. She dropped the plug into the bath-tub, flicked on the hot tap, bunged in a huge dollop of marshmallow and rosehip bubbles and padded into her living room.

As she passed the telephone she noticed the answerphone flashing and did a double take. It was telling her that she had eighteen new messages!

The display must have malfunctioned. Either that or something bad had happened. Oh God. Maybe her mother. Or . . . or . . . maybe it was Dig, trying to make things up with her, maybe he wanted to see her that night. Nadine's heart began racing as she pressed the Play button.

'Er – hi,' began the first message, 'Nadine. It's me. Phil.' Nadine's burgeoning excitement deflated like a punctured tyre. 'It's . . . erm . . . it's eight fifteen. On Friday morning. I must have just missed you. Just phoning to say hi and that I hope you have a great time in Barcelona, and I can't wait till you get back.'

So much for her theory that he'd forgotten about her, thought Nadine. She tapped her fingers impatiently against the plastic covering of the machine while she waited for the next message, hoping for the sound of Dig's voice.

'Hi. It's me again. It's ... eight thirty now. I know you're not there, but I was just thinking about you. So ... I'll call back. Bye.'

Oh for God's sake. Nadine didn't have time to listen to this crap. She had bacon sandwiches to eat, packing to do, Channel Four comedy shows to watch. A beep heralded the next message.

'Me again. It's nine thirty now. I was thinking – maybe I could see you off at the airport tomorrow. Maybe. If you like. I just really, really need to see you, Deen. Soon. So give me a call. OK?'

Oh God. Oh God. Nadine fast-forwarded to the next message.

'Nadine Kite. It's me again. At ... er ... ten o'clock. Thinking about you still, about Wednesday night. I'm still just ... blown away, by you, by what happened between us.'

She fast-forwarded again.

'It's ten thirty. I've been thinking about Wednesday night again. I can't wait to see you, Nadine Kite. I don't think I can wait till next week, y'know? I think we should meet sooner ... I'd really like to see you before you go ... Anyway – give me a call.

'Hi. Me again. Ten forty-five. Yeah. Definitely meet up before you go to Barcelona, I think. Let's talk later.

'Hi. It's ten fifty. I've got to go out now. I'll ... er ... I'll call you later.

'Nadine Kite. I'm back. It's amazing, everything feels so different. You've changed everything. Everything felt so black and so fragile and now I feel like I'm alive again.'

Oh Jesus. Oh no. Oh no. Nadine began fast-forwarding through the messages faster and faster.

268

'Hi – it's me again . . .

'Nadine – it's me . . .

'It's three fifteen, still thinking about you . . .

'It's me. What time do you get home? Shit – I wish I had your work number. I need to talk to you . . .

'Hi – it's Phil again . . .

'It's five twenty . . .

'It's me. It's five forty-five . . .

Nadine heavy-heartedly wound the tape on to the last message.

'You'll be home any minute. How many messages have I left? Yeah. Too many, probably. Look, I have to see you. Tonight. OK? I'll call you again. Please, Nadine Kite. I have to see you. Bye.'

Beep, said the machine, *you have no more messages*.

A chill went up and down Nadine's spine. Oh God.

She felt herself beginning to panic. The flat felt suddenly oppressive and horribly, horribly empty. The phone sat ominously in its cradle, frighteningly silent but pregnant with the prospect of the next ringing tone and the inevitable sound of Phil's voice invading her home and her freedom.

She sat like that for a few minutes, listening to the sound of her own heartbeat in her ears, trying to assimilate the fact that what she'd done on Wednesday night wasn't over, and was in fact just beginning, until she heard the bath water change its pitch as it reached the top. She got up slowly and shuffled towards the bathroom. As she approached the door the phone finally rang, making her jump in spite of her expectation.

She turned and watched as the answerphone clicked on.

'Oh. Hi. Thought you'd be back by now. It's . . . er . . .

269

six forty-five. Where are you? Maybe you got stuck at work? I'll phone you later. Bye.'

Nadine sighed and turned off the bath taps.

Oh God, she thought, I can't handle this.

I've got to get out of here.

I have got to get out of here.

She picked up her handbag, threw on her coat and left her flat, the door slamming loudly behind her.

She was going to the place in the world where she felt safest. She was going to Dig's and she was going to apologize for her hideous behaviour, and by the time she left, everything was going to be back to normal.

CHAPTER TWENTY-EIGHT

Dig's prawns tasted like unwashed towelling socks.

His smoked salmon tasted like damp kitchen roll, and the blinis had all the flavour and consistency of old cardboard.

'Mmmmmm,' he murmured, through a mouthful of mush, 'these prawns are excellent, aren't they?'

Delilah nodded sadly, and sighed.

She had slipped into a pair of pyjamas, and her hair was hanging limply around her face. Dig had seen her looking better. She hadn't said a word since they'd sat down to eat a quarter of an hour ago, just nodded and sighed and made the odd grunting noise in response to his questions.

This evening was not turning out how he'd planned.

Delilah had claimed to be feeling unwell when she'd finally returned from wherever it was she'd been all day at eight thirty that evening. The Pesky Kids were due on stage at eight so they'd blown that one, and she didn't want to go out anyway, so she said, fancied a 'quiet night in'.

Funny, Dig had thought, how people in bad moods always take precedence over people in good moods.

Dig had been trying so hard to get her to open up, but it seemed he'd chosen the wrong night. All his questions hit a dead end and were ricocheted back at him. Delilah was quite patently *not* in the mood for talking. Dig's heartfelt concern from earlier in the day had dissipated, and now he was just plain irritated.

He didn't know what to do. He knew what he *wanted* to do. He wanted to slam his cutlery down on the table and shout at the top of voice, *'Delilah Lillie, what the fucking hell is the matter with you?!'* But he couldn't, because this was Delilah, and Delilah didn't give answers; you weren't allowed to ask her questions – that was against the rules. So he just had to swallow it and pretend that her deathly silence wasn't happening, compensating for her cerebral absence from the table by being ludicrously jolly and gratingly convivial.

But he'd run out of mindless prattle now, spent the last dollar in his jolly-bank. He wanted to walk over to the stereo, turn it off and switch on the telly instead. That would take the pressure off. But he couldn't, because that would be an acknowledgement of the fact that something was wrong, that they weren't talking. It would make a mockery of the candles and the lollo rosso fronds and the shiny cutlery.

Delilah was pushing a tiny, ant-like ball of caviar around her plate with the tine of her fork, and Dig could feel her long bare feet tap-tap-tapping against the table leg. This latest silence had lasted about two minutes, so far. The longest yet. What was it, thought Dig, what was it that was so painfully unbearable about silences between people? It was like a failure. A silence in the midst of a lively conversation could negate in a second everything that had come before, as if the rest of the evening's seamless chatter had been just a fluke and it had always been only a matter of time before the truth emerged – that nobody *really* had anything to say to each other. Why couldn't people just sit together in silence without feeling inadequate, boring and distanced from their companions? Silence also seemed to act as a laxative for bullshit, desperation to fill the hole in the conversation leading to ever more frantic and tedious commentary.

'So,' began Dig, admitting defeat, breaking the silence, splitting open a prawn, belly-up, 'what are you up to tomorrow?' He felt like an emotionally withdrawn father trying to make conversation with a recalcitrant teenage daughter.

Delilah gently rested her fork on the side of her plate and sighed again.

'I've . . . er . . . I've got a lot to do tomorrow . . .' She trailed off.

Dig sensed an opening. Finally. He took a deep breath. 'Anything I can help with?'

Delilah shrugged and picked up her fork again. 'No,' she said, eventually, 'no – I'll be fine. But thanks.' She looked up briefly through heavy eyes and then down again.

Dig sighed with frustration.

'What are *you* doing?'

'What?' replied Dig, slightly shocked by Delilah's first opening gambit of the evening.

'Tomorrow. What are you doing tomorrow?'

'Oh. Right. I don't know.' That was a point, thought Dig. It was Saturday tomorrow, and for as long as he could remember, Saturday had been Nadine day. A fry-up either round the corner from her, or round the corner from him, and then, depending on the weather, a walk in the park, flying the kites, or just sitting in and watching some sport on the telly before getting ready to go out. That was what he did on Saturdays. Well, that was what he *used* to do on Saturdays, before he and Nadine had fallen out with each other. He wasn't quite sure what he would do now that they weren't talking to each other.

The thought made him feel single. Which struck him as odd, because he'd been single, pretty much, for the last ten years. But, with Nadine in his life, he'd never actually *felt* single. He'd never had to contemplate huge, empty weekends with no one to share the minutiae. Even when Nadine was going out with someone, she usually spent her Saturdays with him, grateful to have whichever hugely unsuitable man she currently had in her life out of her hair for a few hours.

Dig felt his stomach swill with unexpected anxiety. What would life be like, without Nadine? It was impossible to imagine. Horrible, probably, absolutely horrible. That settled it. He would definitely, definitely make things up with her, tomorrow. He would phone her first thing and they would go out for breakfast and everything would be back to normal.

He smiled and looked up. Delilah was still pushing the bead of caviar around her plate and appeared to be having trouble controlling her breathing. Her chest was rising and falling like billows and her mouth was slightly puckered.

'Are you all right?'

As he watched her, he saw a slick of sweat appear on her upper lip and the colour drain entirely from her face.

'Are you OK? Delilah?'

She dropped her fork noisily on to her plate, scraped back her chair, cupped her hands to her mouth and ran towards the bathroom, her napkin falling from her lap as she went.

A moment later Dig heard his prawns, his caviar, his

blinis and his smoked salmon hitting the toilet bowl in a dramatic stampede from Delilah's stomach.

He sighed and began clearing away the food. He heard the shower being operated and the lock going on the bathroom door. Well, that was that, then. It looked as if Delilah's problems and her secret mission to uncover the past were to remain a mystery for at least another night.

Dig was just about to blow out the candles, when he heard the doorbell ring.

Dig's disembodied voice on the entry phone sounded surprised to hear her – 'Oh, Nadine. Hi' – almost like he'd been expecting someone else.

She took the linoleum-clad steps two at a time, oblivious to her already tender, post-gym leg muscles screaming at her to stop. She hadn't yet thought about how she was going to tell Dig that she'd had E'd-up sex with Philip Rich within hours of meeting up with him again and how he was now turning out to be a bit of a psycho, plaguing her with phone calls and scaring her half to death. She hadn't thought about any of that. None of that mattered any more. All she wanted to do was make up and be friends again.

She rounded the corner at the top of the last flight of stairs and stood nervously outside Dig's front door. He was standing in his hallway, looking tired and uncomfortable, wearing his best shirt, his new jeans and a pair of oatmeal socks.

'Hi,' she said, squeezing out a smile. She felt suddenly and inexplicably tearful.

'Er – hi.' Dig scratched his head and looked distinctly unthrilled to see her.

'Sorry to – er – turn up like this.'

'That's OK.'

'Are you going to invite me in then, or what?' She grinned, attempting to bring a little levity to the tense atmosphere.

Dig didn't smile, didn't say anything, just scratched his head again and moved out of her way.

'So – how've you been?' she asked.

'Oh – fine. Fine. You?'

'Yeah. Fine.'

There was a silence. It was awkward.

She dropped her bag and coat where she always left them and made her way into the living room – which was when she became slowly aware of the seductive surroundings, of the veritable *come-on* spread out all over the table, and candles, and the music – it sounded like – sounded like – *Robbie Williams*? Couldn't be, couldn't possibly be. Dig wouldn't be listening to Robbie Williams. And the lights were very low, and what was that *thing*, that furry little thing on the sofa? It looked like one of those Russian hats, except smaller and hairier. Nadine jumped in her skin when the Russian hat thing wriggled and then she screamed when it jumped off the sofa and started walking towards her.

'Oh God!' she exclaimed, clutching at her heart. 'What the fuck is that?'

As it approached it revealed itself to be a very, very small dog.

'It's a dog,' said Dig, helpfully.

'Yes. I can see it's a dog. But what's it doing here?' She crouched down to pet the trembling little creature, who immediately flopped on to his back and offered up his stomach.

'It's – er – he's Digby.'

It took a second for Nadine to twig. She thought it was a feeble joke at first, and then it dawned on her. Digby. Delilah's dog. This was Delilah's dog. What the hell was Delilah's dog doing in Dig's flat? Nadine was starting to think that she'd stumbled into some parallel universe; empty prawn shells, jars of caviar, Robbie Williams, small dogs – she fully expected a wife and kids to appear from nowhere at any second.

And then her thought processes began to clarify.

Sexy food – low lighting – Delilah's dog.

Oh God.

Oh God.

Oh no.

At the very second that Nadine worked out what was going on she heard a click and there was a sudden blast of light and steam from the bathroom door. And there she stood, emerging from the steam like a rock star coming on stage through a cloud of dry ice, her hair tied up in a towelling turban and her body wrapped in a minute towel that barely covered the tops of her thighs. She smiled widely when she saw Nadine standing there.

'Deen,' she said, 'what are you doing here? We weren't expecting you.'

Oh God. Oh God. Nadine's chest constricted and her breath came fast and furious.

She looked at Delilah, towelled and scrubbed and steaming.

She looked at Dig, shirted and combed and blushing.

She looked at the table, laden and clothed and sparkling.

277

Nadine had never felt less like she belonged somewhere before, in her life. The flat stank of Delilah. She'd scented it, like a cat. She saw Dig and Delilah exchange a look. There was single moment of dreadful silence.

'You two-faced, conniving, lying *BITCH*!'

The words came from nowhere. Nadine's anger was uncontrollable.

She stood rooted to the spot for a while, staring at Delilah through teary eyes. Delilah was staring back at her in horror.

'No . . . no,' she began, 'you don't understand, honestly, it's fine, Nadine.' She put a hand out towards Nadine.

Nadine shook it off, picked up her coat and bag and pushed Dig out of the way. At the door she turned around. 'You haven't changed, have you, Delilah, you haven't changed at all.' She slammed the door closed behind her and ran down the stairs. Behind her she heard Dig's door opening and his voice echoing down the stairs: 'Deen, where the fuck are you going?' She heard his footsteps, faster than hers, catching up with her, and she increased her pace.

She spun herself around the twists and turns of the narrow stairwell, her hand gripping the rail, her feet moving faster than Michael Flatley's. She snagged her tights on the pedal of a bicycle crammed into the entrance hall and threw open the front door, clattering down the stone steps leading to the pavement.

Dig caught up with her on the street.

'Nadine! What the fuck is going on?'

'Nothing – I'm going home.'

'But what's the matter with you? What was all that about?'

'I don't want to talk about it. Just go back inside. Go

and look after your precious, *beautiful* Delilah! Poor helpless innocent little Delilah. Go and wrap yourself back around her little finger. Go on!'

'Nadine!' Dig grabbed her arm. She shook his hand off her.

'*Leave me alone!*'

Dig stood back and eyed Nadine with surprise. 'All right then,' he sniffed, 'all right. Fuck off then, go on – fuck off.'

For a moment they stood and stared at one another, both breathing heavily and both wearing expressions of disbelief that something this horrible could be happening to their perfect friendship.

Nadine opened her mouth to say something, then turned and ran away. A gap in the four lanes of traffic on Camden Road prevented her from killing herself as she sped across the road towards her car, flinging open the door and grinding her gears before screeching away.

The last thing she saw before she took off was Dig, standing in his socked feet in the middle of Camden Road, rain pouring down his face, staring after her with his jaw hanging open and his hands outstretched in front of him in a gesture of pure bewilderment.

CHAPTER TWENTY-NINE

Nadine started talking to herself as she threw her little white car around corners, across roundabouts and over traffic lights, muttering, under her breath, like a mad woman.

What had she done? What was happening to her? What had happened to all those years she'd spent being cool and together and happy and well adjusted? Had she actually been but a whisker's width away from this insanity all along, without ever realizing?

In the space of less than a week Nadine had dumped a perfectly lovely man because she didn't like his choice of mugs, had spent an entire evening phoning Dig when she knew he was going to be out, had actually driven round to his bloody flat in the middle of the night in her Bart Simpson slippers, for Christ's sake, to spy on him, had impulsively telephoned her horribly beautiful ex-boyfriend of ten years ago only to find that he was just horribly horrible now, had ignored this, and the fact that he was completely fucked up, and slept with him anyway, in someone's garage, on a cocktail of drugs and alcohol, she had broken her kitchen window while in the throes of a ridiculous Delilah-induced panic and now she'd done that. That thing just now, in Dig's flat. That hideously embarrassing, Scarlett O'Hara-style exit, all flouncing and tripping and hands-held-to-throat drama-queen.

'Oh my God,' she muttered, 'oh my God, I'm a fucking psycho. Maybe I deserve Phil. Maybe we were made for each other. We could *stalk* each other and send each other sick letters and video tapes.' Tears sprang to her eyes. 'I'm mad,' she sniffed, 'I'm barking mad. I used to be sane but that part of my life is over now . . . oh God!' The tears were now splashing down her cheeks as she contemplated a life of unwashed hair, episodes of uncontrolled eccentricity and stretches of residential care wearing paper clothes.

Dig had told her to fuck off. Her stomach lurched and wriggled and rucked. She felt nauseous. She scratched at her tears distractedly and tried to ignore the little voice inside her head telling her something that she'd known all along, really, ever since Delilah had first reappeared six days ago, the little voice that was telling her that the reason she was so jealous was that she wanted Dig for herself, that she loved Dig – that she was *still in love with Dig.*

'*Ridiculous!*' she exclaimed, slamming the heels of her hands against the steering-wheel, '*completely, totally and utterly ridiculous!*'

A woman in a Fiat Uno and a bobble hat shot her an alarmed glance and Nadine cleared her throat and collected herself. 'Ridiculous,' she muttered again, this time barely moving her lips, and caressing her steering-wheel apologetically.

How could she possibly still be in love with Dig? She'd always loved him, of course she had, but this was a completely different story. She'd never felt jealous of him before. She'd sat next to him at parties and night-clubs while he was chewing young, flat-stomached girls' faces off. She'd listened with relish to every last detail of every last encounter he'd ever had with nubile, perky-breasted little imps. They'd even shared a bedroom together once, at some cottage in the country, him with a girlfriend, her with a boyfriend, and they'd giggled at each other's half-hearted attempts to keep their respective noises down. All without even the smallest sign of the green-eyed monster.

'"*You two need each other*"' – she mimicked Delilah's husky voice – '"*you two were made for each other. You two should be together.*"' Pah!' she exclaimed, under her breath. 'Pah! Two-faced, sneaky, conniving, secretive, lying BITCH!

'He's *my* Dig, Delilah Lillie,' she moaned, as she drove past her house for the fourth time, frantically looking out for a parking space, '*he's my Dig, not your Dig. Go and get your own Dig, you bitch. Leave mine alone. He's my Dig, my Dig, my Dig, my Dig . . .*'

But it was too late, she knew that now, too late for her and Dig. She was never going to see Dig again, ever. It was over . . .

At this thought, yet more tears sprung from her churning stomach and erupted like a geyser all over her face. Rain cascaded down her windscreen and tears ran down her cheeks, and she couldn't see a bloody thing. The world was a blur of orange and white saucers, splintered discs of light that grew and danced and converged together.

She indicated left to make one final attempt at parking somewhere within walking distance of her home and swung her car violently around the corner. 'Why do I live in this *fucking* city?' she muttered. 'Can't even park outside your own *fucking* home, bloody palaver, every single *fucking* time . . .' Her eyes swivelled this way and that, looking desperately through tear-soaked lashes for a space, or a gap, or a person getting into a car, or anything, anything a-fucking-t'all . . .

And then she saw it – there it was, definitely – a car, about to pull out of a space, literally twenty feet from her own front door. She felt a moment of elation, slammed her indicator to the right and brought her car to a screeching halt parallel to the car behind it, so full of determination and defensive territorialism, so paranoid that another car would appear from nowhere and claim the space before her, her eyes so clouded with tears and her vision so obstructed by the sheets of rain bouncing frantically off her windscreen that she didn't see the thin, bowed-over figure in front of her, she didn't notice that he'd stepped out into the street, without warning, from between two parked cars, and the first she knew of his existence was the sound of his knees crunching against her bumper.

'Oh Jesus!' screamed Nadine, her hands jumping off the steering-wheel to cover her mouth. 'Oh no, oh *Jesus*!' She pulled on her handbrake till it almost came off in her hand and started desperately trying to get out of her car, her hands shaking, the old handle clunking and creaking but refusing to budge. 'Jesus Jesus Jesus, oh Jesus, let me out of *this car*!' She suddenly remembered that she'd locked it from the inside, force of habit, to stop car-jackers, and finally threw the car door open. A passing car swerved out of the way and let loose a loud and frightening blast of its horn. Nadine's handbag fell from her lap and everything in it fell on to the wet, black Tarmac. She skipped over the pile of her belongings and ran to the front of her car. 'Oh God, oh God, oh God!'

There was a small, raggedy bunch of bones lying at

the foot of her bonnet, not moving, its limbs arranged at strange angles.

'Oh no oh no oh no,' she thought to herself, whimpering slightly, 'I've killed someone, I've only gone and killed someone.'

She crouched down next to the crumpled figure and leaned in towards his face.

'Hello,' she ventured tentatively, gently prodding his shoulder, 'hello. Can you hear me? Are you all right? Oh Jesus oh Jesus . . . hello . . . hello . . . hello.' The figure remained still. Nadine started thinking *ER*, thinking recovery position, thinking mouth-to-mouth resuscitation, thinking 'mustn't move him, mustn't move him,' thinking '*Defib! Clear!*', thinking 'oh my God will someone please call an ambulance?' The rain cascaded down her damp curls and all over her face. She was paralysed with fear and indecision.

She turned feebly to face the empty street and shouted at the top of her voice, '*Will someone help me – please!*'

And then the man moved, moved just a few inches, and groaned. Nadine spun round and stared at him. He groaned again.

'Oh God – you're alive! Oh thank God!' Tears of relief began to flow down Nadine's face.

The thin, wet figure turned slightly from where he lay on his stomach, on to his side, and began moaning under his breath, 'Oh my leg, my fucking leg.'

Nadine stopped in her tracks – she recognized that voice.

'You dopey cow, you dopey fucking cow – what 'ave you done to me?'

He was beginning to sit up now, his back to her, clutching his knee and rocking back and forth. Nadine definitely recognized that voice. And, now she came to think of it, that hair was pretty familiar, too. And those jeans. And that raggedy old jumper.

'What the fuck were you playing at?' The man turned to face Nadine with this last question, and his jaw dropped when he looked at her.

'Nadine!'

Oh God, thought Nadine, her eyebrows dancing in disbelief, this can't be happening, this just *can't be happening*.

'Phil!' she reciprocated painfully, staring in horror at her worst nightmare. 'Christ – are you OK?'

CHAPTER THIRTY

Nadine peeled down Phil's sodden and grimy jeans while he perched on the edge of her bath, wincing and clenching his teeth. He was, she noticed, wearing lemon underpants. She hoped they weren't the same pair he'd had on on Wednesday night.

As his jeans unfurled she sucked in her breath.

'Oh Jesus,' she said. His lower thigh was blooming into huge, misshapen roses of black and purple and grey. There was a small trickle of blood seeping from a deep graze where the corner of her number plate had embedded itself into his skin. His knee was swollen up to twice its normal size. 'Oh Jesus,' she said again. 'I'm taking you to the hospital.'

'No,' stated Phil, too firmly.

'Yes,' retaliated Nadine, disbelievingly, 'come on.' She got to her feet and held her hand out to him.

'No. No hospitals. It's only a bruise. I just need to rest it.'

'Phil – you're bleeding. And look at the size of your knee, for fuck's sake. Now will you please let me take you to the hospital – you should have this X-rayed.'

'No,' he stated again, 'I'm not going to the hospital. If it hasn't gone down by tomorrow, then I'll go.'

Nadine took a deep breath. 'OK. Fine,' she said, 'so let me take you home.'

Phil winced again and doubled over in agony. 'Aaaah,'

286

he moaned under his breath, 'aaah. Have you got any painkillers?'

Nadine passed him a couple of Advils from her bathroom cabinet and headed towards the kitchen to get him a glass of water. As she stood over the sink, staring through the broken and taped-over window into the wet blackness outside, she started feeling a little uncomfortable. She still hadn't asked Phil what exactly he'd been doing hanging around in the rain outside her house at half past nine on a Friday evening and she wasn't sure that she wanted to.

She turned off the tap and headed back to the bathroom. Phil wasn't there. Her heart missed a beat. Maybe he'd gone. Gone away. Stumbled back out into the darkness. A selfish and worried voice deep inside her said, 'I hope so.'

She stuck her head around the living-room door – no sign of him. Neither was he in the toilet nor in the entrance hall. She pulled back the 1950s *Homemaker* print curtains in her living room and surveyed the street outside. It was empty.

And then she wandered into her bedroom, not expecting at all to find him sprawled all over the Bollywood duvet cover on her bed in nothing but his lemon briefs and a pair of black ribbed socks, smoking a cigarette and with the remote control for her TV in his hand.

'Oh,' she said, when what she'd really wanted to say was 'Get the fuck off my bed and take your horrid lemon pants with you!'

'Had to lie down,' he said, sucking on his Rothman and wincing a bit theatrically. 'Don't suppose you've got a TV guide, have you?' He blew out a stream of smoke and regarded Nadine defiantly through faded-denim-blue eyes. He was challenging her, daring her to make him leave, to get off her bed and out of her flat.

Nadine flinched a little in the face of his audacity. She didn't want him on her bed. She didn't want him in her flat. She didn't, in fact, want him anywhere within a five-mile radius of her. But what could she do? She'd nearly run him over out there. That was her fault. Bad driving, lack of concentration. And just look at the state of his leg – there was no way he'd be able to walk on that unaided, and she couldn't *force* him into her car, she couldn't force him to do anything.

She approached her bedside table stealthily and placed the glass of water on a mother-of-pearl coaster embedded with tiny little mirrors.

'There you go,' she said, in her best jolly voice. 'I'll – er – just get you a TV guide, then. Won't be a sec.'

'Cheers.' He was staring ahead at the TV, not even looking at her.

She glanced at him as she left the room, at the rock-star pallor, the twelve-year-old-girl legs, the white skin sprouting incongruous black hairs in places, the thin arms and the yellow briefs. An involuntary shudder worked its way up her body.

But the minute she walked into her living room she started feeling bad. Oh God, she thought. Poor Phil. Poor poor Phil. He's got no one. He's all alone in this world. His parents are dead. His fiancée's dead. His house is burned down. And now I've run him over. None of this is *his* fault. None of it.

And it was me – *me* – who invited him back into my life. It was me who phoned him out of the blue and me who sat in a pub with him, ghoulishly pushing him for more and more details about the tragedy that was his life. He didn't ask to get involved with me again. He didn't force me to take an E. He didn't force me to have sex with him.

She remembered what Murdo, the Scots landlord, had said to her in the pub on Wednesday night, about looking out for Phil. He was right. Phil was her responsibility now – she'd taken on that responsibility when she'd agreed to go back to his flat. Murdo had warned her and she hadn't listened and now she was paying the price. She sighed and began pulling animal-print cushions from her sofa as she searched for last week's Culture section from the *Sunday Times*. It was only one night, she told herself. Just one night. She would let him stay in her bed – she would sleep on the sofa – and then she'd drop him home tomorrow on her way to the airport.

It was the least she could do.

CHAPTER THIRTY-ONE

The front door slammed, staccato heels clattered down the front steps and Digby bounced joyfully on to Dig's bed.

'OK,' thought Dig, chucking him under the chin, 'I'm awake now.' It was eight forty-five. Dig couldn't remember the last time he'd been awake before eleven on a Saturday morning. And not just awake, but unhungover and somewhat refreshed. He'd been in bed by ten thirty the previous night – because Delilah had wanted to turn in early – and pretty much stone-cold sober.

He stepped out of bed into a little rectangle of sunshine that was warming up his seagrass and strolled towards the window. As he pulled his curtains apart he saw Delilah on the street below. She was standing on the corner of Hilldrop Crescent and Camden Road looking around distractedly for a cab. She was wearing her sheepskin over a very smart suit and high heels, and her hair was held back from her face with sunglasses. In one hand she held her incredibly expensive-looking little Hermès doeskin attaché case and in the other a huge Hamleys carrier bag, poking from one corner of which was the tip of what looked like a large rabbit's ear. Dig scratched his head and wondered where the Hamleys bag had come from, what the rabbit was doing in it and how come he hadn't noticed it when he'd cleared the living room for dinner last night. Delilah must have hidden it somewhere. Why?

He watched as Delilah impatiently paced the corner, back and forth, back and forth, swivelling her head constantly as she listened for the rumble of a cab. She glanced at her watch a couple of times. Dig untwisted the security lock on his sash window and lifted it up a couple of inches, letting in a blast of fresh autumn air and the roar of early morning traffic.

A cab appeared on the horizon and Delilah lifted the attaché-attached hand to hail it. Dig pushed his head further through the gap in the window, stretching his legs backwards into the seagrass to flatten himself out and straining to hear Delilah's voice above four lanes of traffic.

He was sick of this. Sick of tiptoeing around Delilah and avoiding the truth. Sick of not being able to discuss anything of any importance with her, sick of doing everything in his power to make her life comfortable and easy while she rewarded his efforts with nothing more than evasion, avoidance, bad moods and the dubious honour of looking after her dog and putting her bed away every fucking morning.

Yesterday night had been the last straw. He had, officially, run out of patience.

It was clear to Dig that the only way he stood a chance of getting close to Delilah now was to know all her secrets, to know everything that Dr Rosemary Bentall knew. And if she thought that he was too immature and unprepared to deal with them, then he was going to uncover them for himself.

He poked his head a little further through the window

and, as if by magic, just as Delilah grabbed hold of the cab door-handle and twisted her head towards the driver to tell him where she wanted to go, a hush fell across Camden Road. The traffic stopped and the wind died and Delilah's words were carried from her lips on a puff of fresh air and deposited on Dig's window-sill.

'Waterloo Station, please.'

Dig cracked his head off the window, withdrawing too quickly in his panic to reach his jeans and top and get out of the flat.

'Ow fuck . . .' He rubbed his head.

Within two minutes he had dressed, knocked back half a mug of cold coffee left by Delilah in the kitchen, thrown on his leather coat, scooped Digby up in his arms and was pacing up and down Camden Road looking for a cab.

He briefly wondered at this strange, alien world, this early-morning-Saturday world peopled by the kind of men and women who didn't spend every Friday night down the pub, who didn't go to bed at two in the morning and who didn't have to spend their entire Saturdays stumbling from one attempt at curing their hangovers to another. There was something appealing about that, something refreshing. A whole new array of possibilities. His thoughts returned once more to the golden world of Nadine's imagination – the one with the kids and everything. It was becoming more alluring by the minute.

Dig flapped his free hand up and down like an over-excited schoolboy who knows the right answer when he saw a little amber lozenge glowing mutely in the distance.

The cab pulled up next to him.

'Do you mind taking a dog?' Dig asked pleasantly,

as the bleary-eyed driver looked disapprovingly at the quivering furball in his arms.

'Trained, is 'e?'

Dig nodded frantically. 'Better trained than me,' he joked feebly.

'OK – get in. Any mess though, an' you'll 'ave to clear it up.'

Dig nodded again and placed Digby on the ribbed plastic floor.

'Where you going?' asked the driver brusquely.

'Waterloo station, please – and I'm in a real hurry.'

'No problem,' said the driver, his face relaxing at the prospect of a breakneck drive around the near-empty streets of London. 'No problem at all.'

CHAPTER THIRTY-TWO

It was five thirty a.m. and Nadine was doing one of her five-minute, condensed, early-morning preparations. It was possible, if in a big enough rush, to do everything one normally squeezed into forty-five minutes in only five. She'd packed the night before, laid out her travelling outfit, put coffee, milk and sugar in a mug, and had a good long soak in the bath just before she had gone to bed so she wouldn't have to shower.

The only thing she had to do this morning that she didn't normally have to fit into her five-minute regime was to make sure that Phil was up and ready to go. She'd spent the night on her sofa, and when her alarm went off, the first thing she'd done was throw open the bedroom door and switch on the overhead light. It was cruel, but she didn't care – this was a military-style operation.

'How's your leg?' she'd said, when she popped her head around the door thirty seconds later, her toothbrush protruding from between frothy lips.

'Uuuuuppphhhh,' Phil had said, throwing his arm over his face.

'Come on,' she'd said, all brisk efficiency, 'all you have to do is put your clothes on – here.' She lobbed them on the bed. 'I left them on the radiator overnight so they'll be nice and dry and snug. You've got' – she looked at her watch – 'two and a half minutes. Chop-chop.'

Thirty seconds later and Phil did not appear to have moved a muscle, let alone a limb.

'Phil! Will you please move it!'

'Fucking hell, Deen,' he mumbled, squinting at her from beneath his own elbow, 'you've turned into a right little sergeant-major.'

'Yes – well – lots of things about me have changed,' she said. 'Let me have a look at your leg.' She strode around to his side of the bed and flung the duvet back mercilessly.

Phil watched her carnivorously, a smug smile twitching the corners of his mouth. 'Ooh yes,' he drawled, 'I like you much more like this. All stern and Miss Whiplashy. Are you going to spank me?' He said this last in a flesh-crawlingly horrible little-boy voice.

Nadine blanched and her face dropped in horror. Jesus. Who was this repulsive person?

'Hey,' he said, attempting to sit up a little, 'this is like *Misery*, isn't it? You could just leave me tied up on your bed all weekend and then come back next week, tie my ankles together and hobble me!' He laughed, too loud, and searched Nadine's face for a trace of amusement. He raised his eyebrows in a 'suit yourself' sort of way when he failed to find one and lay back against the pillows.

She tutted and turned her attention to his leg, which resembled an overcooked chipolata sausage, all gnarled and blackened and knobbly. 'Jesus,' she said, 'you really are going to have to do something about that leg, you know. Do you want me to drop you at the hospital now, or can you make your own way there from home?'

Phil looked at Nadine with bemusement. 'I don't think I'm going anywhere, to be honest.'

Nadine let the duvet drop back over Phil's legs and regarded him with growing horror. 'What do you mean?'

'I mean – this leg ain't going to get me anywhere beyond the bedroom door, not for a while, anyway.'

'What? But it was fine yesterday – you walked all the way from the road to here and then you made it on your own from the bathroom to the bedroom and . . .'

Phil nodded sagely. 'Yeah – that was *yesterday*. It's sort of seized up overnight.' He wiggled his chipolata leg and winced. 'You know, it's gone all stiff. I can hardly move it. I reckon I'm gonna need a wheelchair to get me out of here.'

Nadine gulped. Her five-minute plan was unravelling – this was a nightmare. Wheelchairs, cripples, lascivious comments, men in her bed – at five thirty in the morning. Part of her thought Phil was lying about his leg – the swelling, as far as she could see, appeared to have gone down, and Phil was in mighty high spirits for someone who was supposed to be a cripple. But what could she do? She could hardly accuse him of lying, could she? She couldn't say, 'Oh yeah, pull the other one, it's got bruises on,' and yank him out of bed and into her car. The only thing she could do was believe him. And if she was going to believe him, then she was going to have to get the situation sorted. She couldn't leave him in her flat – alone – without her. It was unthinkable. She looked at her watch again. She had a bit more time now that she didn't have to drop Phil off at Finsbury Park, time to organize things.

Think – think – think . . . But the only thing that Nadine could think was that it was five thirty in the morning and there was no one – not even her father – who she would feel comfortable phoning at this time of day to help her remove an immobile ex-boyfriend from her flat.

She reached for the phone book.

'What are you doing?' asked Phil, suddenly alarmed.

'I'm going to call the hospital, see if they'll send someone round for you with a wheelchair.'

'No!' snarled Phil, grabbing her wrist, 'I told you – no hospitals.'

Nadine loosened his grip on her arm and eyed him uncomfortably. 'OK.' She placed the phonebook carefully on the floor. 'Why not?'

'Because,' he said, 'because it's . . . er . . . I've got some stuff in my bloodstream that shouldn't be there – *comprende*? And the last thing I need right now is a bunch of fucking hassle off a load of junior doctors – all right?'

'OK – OK. I won't call the hospital. But I've got to call someone. Is there anyone I can call?' she asked hopefully. 'A friend or something – maybe that Jo girl – who could come and collect you, or sort out a wheelchair for you?' She bit her lip, hoping that her sense of selfish desperation hadn't come through too loudly in her words.

Phil winced again and shook his head. 'Not at this time of the morning,' he breathed, 'no way. Jo's probably still out clubbing and, as you know' – he eyed her poignantly – 'there's no one else . . .' He lowered his eyes and let his shoulders slump forwards.

Nadine was harpooned, once again, by guilt. Oh God. She kept forgetting. Every time she started feeling antipathetic towards Phil, he would say something or do something to remind her how mean-hearted and self-centred she was, she who had everything, a family, friends, a future, a beautiful home – legs that worked.

She sighed and gave in to the guilt. It couldn't hurt, could it? To leave Phil here in her flat. I mean – what could he *actually* do, when you thought about it?

Make a mess? Big deal.

Snoop through her things? He wouldn't find anything very interesting.

Eat all her food? He was welcome to it, it was only going to go off otherwise.

Invite his young student friends over? Where was the harm in that?

Still be here when she got back? She shuddered. No – that wasn't going to happen. No way.

Oh God, she wailed silently, why is this happening? *Why is this happening?*

'OK,' she said, firmly, 'you can stay. But promise you'll get some help. Promise you'll call Jo a bit later. Yes?'

Phil did that awful little-boy thing again, pouting ever so slightly and nodding chastely. 'I pwomise,' he said, and Nadine had to fight back a burst of nausea.

'Right,' she said, backing uncertainly out of the room, 'I'm just going to load up the car. I'll be back in a second.'

She felt vaguely sick as she lugged boxes and boxes of aluminium-clad photographic equipment down her front steps and out to her Spider. It was still dark outside, and invisible birds chattered happily from shrouded tree tops. Jesus, she thought, am I mad? I'm leaving my flat, my beautiful flat, my refuge from the world, in the hands of Philip Rich, a man I was hoping just yesterday that I would never, ever see again as long as I lived. He's lying in my bed, in his foul underpants, on my lovely Indian-cotton sheets, under my Bollywood duvet cover *that I made with my own hands*, and I don't want him to be there, but there's nothing I can do about it because my flight to Barcelona leaves in two and a half hours and there's a whole team of models, hairdressers and stylists expecting to meet me in an hour, and if I'm not there I'll get sacked, and it's five thirty in the morning and I don't want him to be there, I just really, really don't want him to be there.

She threw her coat over the boxes in the boot to stop them being bounced about, slammed down the door and locked it, taking a deep breath to try to calm her nerves.

Back indoors, she performed a last-minute check of the flat, making sure she hadn't forgotten anything. In the kitchen she stopped for a second, noticing the yellow plastic bucket sitting by the back door, and picked it up. Well – it wouldn't hurt, would it – you never know – he might be telling the truth. And then she opened the door to her bedroom, warily and heavily.

'Right,' she said, over-brightly, a spare set of keys clutched in one hand, the plastic bucket in the other and her bag slung over her shoulder, 'I'm off.' She walked briskly towards the bedside table and dropped the keys. 'Spare set of keys for you,' she said, twirling a strand of hair behind her ear. 'Just drop them back through the letter box when you go. I've . . . er . . . left tea and coffee stuff out for you but I don't suppose you'll be able to get to it, will you?'

He looked at her and shrugged sadly, as if he was growing used to the idea of life as a helpless cripple.

'Make any phone calls you need and – um' – she glanced down at the bucket and put it down next to the bed – 'I thought you'd probably need this. You know, seeing as you can't get to the toilet.'

He smiled at her warmly.

'So, good luck. Hope everything works out with the leg. And, Phil . . . I'm so sorry. So, so sorry for what happened last night. I hope you can forgive me.' She forced a smile and Phil picked her hand up from where it hung at her side. She looked at him awkwardly and he smiled at her gratefully. Very slowly and very measuredly he brought her hand to his mouth and kissed the back of it, deeply, passionately and intensely, breathing the scent of her skin into the depths of his lungs and letting his lips moisten her skin. She looked down at him, willing him to stop, resisting the urge to pull her hand away from his mouth. She attempted a smile and failed.

'Nadine Kite,' he drawled, letting her hand drop from his lips but not letting go of it, 'you're the best. The best girl ever. Look at you – bringing me buckets, worrying about me, looking after me. I could so easily fall in love with you all over again, you know. In fact' – he smiled and squeezed her hand – 'I think I might already have done.'

Nadine managed to extricate her hand from his without seeming rude and began backing away from him. Her face was flaming red, which was annoying, because Phil was arrogant enough to presume that she was blushing with desire and pleasure rather than the all-consuming revulsion and horror she was feeling.

'I really have got to go now, Phil,' she said, looking at her watch, 'I'll try calling later, from the airport, or something. Good luck.'

Phil stuck one hand in the air and smiled again. 'Farewell, lovely lady,' he said, in a pretend Shakespearean tone, and then performed a ridiculous little twiddle of his hand and the mock-bow of a courtesan.

Nadine smiled stiffly, found the door handle and left the room.

She felt horribly sad as she closed the door on her lovely little flat, like a mother forced to leave her beautiful daughter alone with a lecherous baby-sitter.

'Sorry,' she mouthed to her front door as she made her way towards the car. 'I'm sorry.'

She flopped down into the driving seat and locked the door. Her heart was heavy and full of dread as she switched on the ignition and began the drive out west to Heathrow.

CHAPTER THIRTY-THREE

Who was that? Up ahead?

Dig slunk down in the back seat as he recognized the shape of Delilah's head in the cab in front, leaving just his eyebrow visible above the partition. His driver had certainly made up time, flying through the streets of north London, and now Dig's cab was sitting directly behind Delilah's at the traffic lights on the Strand, about to turn left on to Waterloo Bridge.

Dig glanced at his watch. It was twenty past nine. The lights changed and Dig grabbed the armrest as the cab took the corner a little too fast. He wanted to tell the driver that he could slow down now, but realized how silly that would sound. He just hoped that they wouldn't overtake Delilah's cab.

Dig stared in disbelief at the top deck of a tourist bus, which had pulled over in the bus lane on the bridge and was packed full of cagouled tourists listening raptly to a man in a blue-nylon blazer with a microphone. It was nearly December, for Christ's sake, and it wasn't even ten o'clock yet. If Dig was a tourist in London, he would be making his second visit to the breakfast buffet bar right now, buttering his croissant, slicing the top off his hard-boiled egg and hatching gentle plans for a trip to the Royal Academy or Fortnum and Mason's later in the day, maybe. He would *not* be sitting on an open-topped bus, on the windiest bridge in London, in a day-glo cagoule with some bloke from Kidderminster shouting in his ear.

'*Which entrance do you want*?' came the tinny, disembodied voice of the driver as they approached the Imax cinema on Waterloo roundabout.

Dig sat up straight and tried to look like he knew where he was going. 'Oh,' he said, 'the main one, please.' He realized instantly that this was the wrong answer when he heard the driver sighing wearily through the intercom.

'*Eurostar? Mainline? The Underground? Which one, mate?*'

Oh God. He was going to have to say it, wasn't he? Ten years ago he'd have been excited at the prospect, but now – well, it was a bit embarrassing, really.

'Can you just, um' – he cleared his throat – 'would you mind just following that cab?' He cringed a little as he heard the words leave his lips and saw the driver's eyebrows arch sceptically.

'*Bet you've wanted to say that all your life,*' he chuckled happily.

Delilah's cab pulled up in front of the creamy stone steps leading towards the main concourse of the station and Dig watched her extricating herself from the vehicle – one long, trousered, heeled leg followed by another, and then the Hamley's bag with the rabbit in it.

His cab squeaked to a halt behind hers and the driver eyed Dig as he attempted to pay the fare from an almost entirely prone position in the back seat, sliding a ten-pound note through the crack in the window and crouching down to open the door only once he was sure that Delilah had fully disembarked and was half-way up the steps.

As Dig picked his way carefully up the magnificent stairway, Digby started quivering with excitement in his arms, his little suede nose exploring the air. He could smell her – Delilah. He let out an excited, high-pitched groan and tried to wriggle his way out of Dig's arms, towards his mistress. 'Shhhh,' said Dig, clamping his hand over the dog's tiny, damp snout. 'Shhhh.'

On the concourse Dig hid behind a row of phone booths to watch Delilah's movements. She was striding towards the ticket office, her heels clicking against the marble flooring, the rabbit ear flopping up and down as she walked.

Dig waited until Delilah was firmly ensconced in a queue and then dashed furtively to a leaflet stand offering colourful information about day trips to Hampton Court and Loseley Park. He dropped his head and pretended to study the leaflets, scooting quickly to the other side of the stand as Delilah picked up her change and turned to leave the ticket office.

He had no idea where she was going. According to the clattering arrival boards set high above the platform entrances, she could be going anywhere from Basingstoke to Bagshot, from Exeter to Epsom. She could be going to Hook, Fleet, Liss or Wool, not to mention Surbiton, Staines or Sunningdale.

Dig's heart was starting to race now. This really was primeval, bringing out deeply buried instincts and emotions, stalking his prey, hiding in the undergrowth, using the pillars and phone booths of Waterloo station as trees and bushes.

Delilah was walking slowly now, heading back towards the far end of the station, past platform nine, eight, seven, six – stopping at the Accessorize shop,

feeling up some fur wraps, leather gloves, fake pash-
minas, beaded handbags, before wandering past platform five, four, three, popping into Knickerbox, fingering
bits of silk and satin, lime-green G-strings, gingham bras
and tiny jersey vest tops printed with rosebuds. Did
women have any idea how absolutely devastating they
looked browsing in lingerie shops?

As she emerged she glanced up at the arrival board
above platform one. Dig followed her gaze from where
he stood in the doorway of a closed pub, on the other
side of the concourse. He squinted to make out the
words.

9.52 to GUILDFORD via CLAPHAM JUNCTION

OK, he thought, Guildford here I come.

Dig moved stealthily down the platform, following Delilah's swaying hips and floppy bunny ear. Digby was still
frantically trying to liberate himself from Dig's arms,
squeaking every time he saw Delilah's form in the distance, and Dig was starting to wish he'd brought a lead
or a harness to restrain the creature. The mutt was
jeopardizing the whole operation.

When Delilah stopped midway down the platform and
mounted the train, Dig increased his pace. He got into
the carriage one down from her, so that he could keep
an eye on her through the adjoining windows. There she
was, sitting with her back to his carriage, thankfully,
and flipping through a sheaf of paper. Yet another
blessed sheaf of paper. What was it with all that paper?
Maybe she was practising to be a newsreader . . .

Between stations, Dig cupped his chin in his hand and
stared through the window, watching the grey, grimy

backside of inner London morph into the shampoo and set of suburbia.

He watched as the tiny, rust-filled, overgrown gardens of Battersea, Clapham and Streatham gave way to the conservatories and aluminium-framed windows of Wimbledon, Kingston and New Malden, where the gardens sprouted bright plastic swings and slides, shiny barbecues and pristine sheds, and where Dig felt entirely alien. Suburbia, he considered, might well be a hotbed of creativity and inspiration, its very blandness acting as an inducement to escape and achieve, but he hated it. It made him feel trapped and suffocated, as if he were entering a big, green plastic bag that someone was about to tie a knot in.

As the train slunk through Surbiton – the fatherland, Dig had always thought, of suburbia – Dig threw a furtive glance towards the next carriage. Delilah had stopped flicking through papers now and was staring out of the window, nervously nibbling at the skin around her fingernails. God, thought Dig, as inappropriately as ever, she really is so shockingly beautiful.

Nondescript office building followed nondescript shopping parade followed nondescript garden; anonymous station after anonymous station zipped by in little flashes of red, white and blue Network Southeast insignia, and within twenty minutes Dig found himself being deposited somewhere called Walton-on-Thames.

Delilah dismounted and turned left, leaving Dig in a perfect position to follow her unseen. His heart, which had slowed down while sitting on the train, resumed its frenetic tattoo as he pulled his sunglasses from his coat pocket and slipped them on. Not, he hastened to reassure himself, in a sad attempt at subterfuge but because the sun was quite blindingly bright.

He held back as he made his way down the platform – only a handful of people had dismounted the train and he was highly visible – and then had hurriedly to throw himself behind a pillar when an increasingly anxious Digby spotted Delilah in the distance and emitted a high-pitched yap. Dig saw Delilah slow down like a suspicious cat when she heard the yap, and his breathing stopped momentarily as he held his hand over Digby's muzzle and waited for her to continue on her way.

This rat was a fucking liability. Dig should have left him at home and, besides, he thought with a growing sense of horror, he probably looked like a sad homo-sexual walking around with this ugly thing under his arm like an Alexander McQueen clutch-bag. Why, he wondered, not for the first time, had Delilah chosen this dog from among the packs of puppies she would have had access to, the spaniels and the collies, the sheepdogs and the retrievers? What was it about this greasy, quivering little bag of bones that had appealed to her? It was a mystery to him, a complete mystery.

Delilah disappeared into the ticket hall up ahead, and Dig quickened his pace, narrowing the gap between them. He rounded the corner into the ticket hall and leaped ahead when he saw Delilah crossing the road outside the station, striding purposefully away from him.

He headed briskly through the chilly hall and nearly jumped out of his skin when a man with a big scar on his cheek, a broken nose and a cauliflower ear suddenly bellowed into his face, '*Can I see your ticket please, sir?*'

Oh fuck. Dig glanced at the man and then at the road opposite, where he could see Delilah shrinking to doll-sized proportions. Oh bloody hell. He stepped from foot to foot as he desperately tried to think of what to do next. He could stay here and waste five minutes trying to sweet-talk this unfortunate-looking fellow into letting him off with a fine or a telling-off or he could just make a run for it.

'*Sir, I need to see your ticket.*'

Oh sod it. He clutched Digby tightly to him, threw the man a deeply apologetic look which he hoped conveyed within it every nuance of the story that had brought him to Walton-on-Thames without a ticket, and legged it. It was a risk – the guy looked like an ex-bare-knuckle fighter, but he might be a bit slow now in his middle age. The risk paid off. The mashed-up ticket collector sighed deeply and returned to his newspaper, tired beyond words, apparently, of breathless homosexuals with greasy terriers arriving at his barrier without the required piece of cardboard.

Dig stood impatiently at the edge of the road, waiting for a bus to complete its U-turn before dashing across the road towards the now empty street he'd last seen Delilah disappearing up. He looked around very quickly and was startled to notice that he was in the middle of nowhere – literally – but not in the good sense of the phrase, not in the way of endless meadows and wide horizons and featureless panoramas, not in the way that suggested solitude and space and mind-expansion, just . . . nowhere . . . nowhere at all. Apart from the station, all that existed in this silent and eerily uninhabited junction of two slumbering roads was an estate agents' office and a bus stop.

The heaving, creaking bus disappeared up the road in a miasma of grey smoke, leaving the area feeling even more abandoned, Dig's T-shirt was sticking to his back with the layer of viscous sweat that had broken out all over his body. He was operating on more than just conscious thought, his body was producing all sorts of reactions, effluents and chemicals as he hunted his prey. He was feeling curiously stimulated.

Dig breathed in sharply and slowed down when he heard Delilah's heels echoing around the next corner – thank God, he'd been worried that she might have disappeared into one of the overgrown Wendy houses that lined this meandering avenue and that he would be left stranded in Walton-on-Thames for the rest of his life.

Finally, the interminable road gave way to a fork, and signs of civilization and human life began to appear: a school, a church, a low-level office block, people. Within a few seconds a busy high street emerged, and Dig found himself jostling for space on the pavement with large, meaty-armed families, with nervously shuffling pensioners and pushchairs, prams and double buggies. Delilah kept striding.

Robert Dyas, Dorothy Perkins, Boots, Fads, Smiths and Marks.

Dig mopped his brow.

He ducked into a doorway when Delilah stopped in her tracks ahead of him. What must he look like, he wondered to himself, all sweaty and unkempt, with uncombed hair and a weird dog, dashing around furtively and hiding in doorways? If he could see himself in the street today, he would be able to reach only one conclusion: Care in the Community.

Delilah was consulting one of her bits of paper, turning it round and viewing it from all angles in a manner that suggested she was looking at a map. Dig looked at his watch: 10.51 a.m. They'd been walking for bloody ages. He hoped they were nearly there – wherever the hell 'there' was. He didn't think he could stand the suspense for much longer.

Delilah slid the piece of paper back into her doeskin attaché and continued on her way, her heels beginning to echo again as the pedestrian population thinned out once more.

Outside a pink pub, she turned right, and Dig followed her down a steep footpath, his heartbeat increasing with every loose pebble his trainered feet dislodged. At the bottom of the footpath Dig stopped and caught his breath and had his first reality check of the day. What the *fuck* was he doing? I mean – what the *fuck*? Where was he? Where was he going? Why was he here? He didn't do things like this, people in films did things like this, not him.

He looked down with disgust when he noticed that Digby was greedily licking the salty sweat off the palm of his hand with a hot little pink tongue, sneered and wiped his hand down the leg of his jeans. And then he felt guilty again when he realized that the poor creature was probably parched, not to mention starving, and possibly, probably, almost definitely, in need of voiding some part or parts of his body. Dig looked at Digby. Digby looked back at him, blinked and gulped. There were tears in his eyes, and he looked desperately unhappy. Dig felt mean beyond belief.

The river lay beyond the fringe of trees in which Dig was hiding. Despite the name of the town, Dig was slightly surprised to find it there, wide and curved and sparkling, small flotillas of rented boats peopled by fam-

310

ilies in overcoats skimming the surface, a large lock to the left, a small reservoir to the right. Behind him sat a fantastic clapboard pub covered in flaking white paint and lichen, a large balustraded balcony on the first floor and several tables outside. What a gem of a place, thought Dig, as he mentally added it to the 'summer' section of his infinite list of nice-looking pubs he'd like to drink in one day.

A panting pack of varied dogs scampered by on the sand-covered towpath, followed by strolling, Barboured owners clutching limp, unclipped leads. Digby twitched in his arms and Dig soothed him by purring into his ear.

Finally, Delilah came off the path and disappeared up a small turning, and Dig breathed a sigh of relief as he realized that they were probably there. They had to be. The sun was beating down on him even harder now and he was boiling. There were big damp patches under his arms and he could feel sweat trickling down his back and collecting in his sternum. He pulled at the collar of his T-shirt with a crooked index finger and blew down his top on to his chest. He just wanted to sit down now. He didn't want to walk any further.

At the top of the turning were three houses, set well back from the road and all backing directly on to the river. These weren't the mini-mansions that Dig had seen on the way from the station, these were the real McCoy. Gravel drives that hadn't just been tipped off the back of a delivery van, tangles of ancient laburnum climbing to the top floors, uncurtained sash windows, old estate cars in the driveways, hexagonal turrets and warped old boot-scrapers embedded into doorsteps. Delilah was walking towards the middle of the three houses, her pace diminishing, the Hamley's bag no longer swinging.

311

Even from fifty feet away, Dig could hear her nervously clearing her throat.

He stationed himself behind a small skiff that was being decorated and had been left upturned and unfinished, painted half white and half green. It was called 'Sun King' and had been pulled on to the verge next to a mulberry bush, where it provided Dig with more than sufficient cover.

Delilah slowed down even more as she approached the large, handsome house. And then she did something really annoying. After all this, after a ten quid cab ride at the crack of dawn, after nearly being done for fare evasion, after walking through some godforsaken bit of Surrey for nearly half an hour, after everything that Dig had been through this peculiar and surreal morning to discover what Delilah was up to, she rewarded him by placing both of her bags side by side on a bench and sitting on it.

Dig grimaced and ground his teeth. What was she doing? For God's sake. What the *hell* was she doing? Sitting down. In Walton-on-Thames. Sitting down – on a bench – for no discernible reason – apropos of nothing at all – just sitting there. In Walton-on-Thames. *Why?*

The bench was situated between the middle and right-hand houses and faced away from the road, directly towards the river. It afforded, it had to be said, a very attractive view of the river and a small eyot accessed by a charming wooden bridge. It was very pretty indeed. Extremely pretty. But, *why*?

Dig took the weight off his toes and sat back on his bottom. The ground underneath was cold and damp, but he didn't care – he was knackered and hot, and now he was also deeply frustrated. He searched his coat pockets

312

for a piece of chewing gum or a packet of mints – his breath tasted like curdled milk – and sighed with ever-increasing frustration when he failed to find either.

Delilah had crossed her legs on the bench and draped one elbow across the back of it. Dig watched her knock her sunglasses from the top of her head to her nose and then do something vaguely peculiar with her hair, arranging it over her face, almost as if she were drawing curtains, and then she turned up the collar of her sheep-skin jacket. She was, Dig realized with a sense of mounting excitement, attempting to disguise herself. This was more like it, he thought gleefully, this was more like it. He was about to witness some kind of illicit rendezvous, some kind of espionage, something a bit . . . *exciting*.

As he sat behind the boat and the bush, clasping a very-keen-to-escape Digby to his chest and keeping an eye on Delilah, Dig's imagination began to run away with itself. His mind filled with images of wartime escap-ades, of James Bond shenanigans, of the trench-coated woman in *Allo Allo* who says, 'Listen very carefully', of excellent bits of electronic surveillance equipment, of false moustaches and video cameras in briefcases. This was starting to look more interesting than he'd imagined. He rubbed his hands gleefully and waited for the excitement to begin.

Nearly an hour later Dig was starting to run out of enthusiasm.

His body had lost every degree of the heat it had built up on the walk here. His hands and nose were freezing and his arse had gone numb. He was starving hungry and bored stiff.

313

Nothing had happened in Eyot Reach for nearly an hour – not a single thing. Someone's dog had strayed from the towpath at one point and come haring towards Dig when it spied the tasty morsel sitting shivering on his lap, but had been quickly recovered by its owner. The weather-vane on top of one of the houses had turned a few times. A car had used the road for a three-point-turn a few minutes ago. And that was it.

Delilah was still sitting on the bench, still wearing her sunglasses and still hiding behind her hair.

Five more minutes, Dig told himself, five more minutes and then I'm going home.

And then he heard something – a click, followed by another click, followed by laughter. Someone was finally coming out of one of the houses. He tucked Digby into his coat and rearranged himself to give himself a better view of the proceedings.

The front door of the middle house was wide open now and Dig could see the silhouetted form of a family as they jostled to leave the house, bickering and squawking and shouting. Delilah, he noticed, had swivelled slightly on the bench and was regarding the open door with interest, her fingertips touching the arm of her sunglasses.

'Maddie, stop it!' he heard a woman's voice shouting, in perfect Surrey tones. 'Leave the dog alone!'

A large Newfoundland bounded through the door and across the gravel, bearing a small child on his back, who was gently whipping the dog's bottom with a plastic ruler. 'Gee up, Monty! Gee up!' squeaked the pretty, dark-haired little girl.

'Get off the dog, Maddie!' A tall woman emerged from the house, carrying a large duvet and a pressure cooker.

314

She was too thin and had obviously been extremely beautiful in her youth. Her hair was jet black and cut into a big tousled wedge which suited her. She was wearing an enormous ex-army greatcoat with a fur collar and green wellingtons.

She was followed by a young boy of about ten, who had his nose stuck in a Harry Potter book while simultaneously dribbling a football across the crackling gravel.

The mother pulled a clunking set of keys from her battered old handbag, selected one with her teeth and thrust it into the keyhole at the back of her silver Mercedes estate. The door sprung open, and the dog, the duvet and the pressure cooker landed in the boot.

Maddie was now pretending to ride a horse, trotting round and round in circles, kicking up the gravel and making neighing and clip-clopping noises.

'Maddie, stop it! Get into the car!'

The dark-haired boy kicked his football towards the garage and slid into the back seat, his eyes still glued to his Harry Potter book, and Maddie continued to ignore her mother, who was getting into the driver's seat, tucking her acres of coat around her.

'Maddie! Get into the car right now or I shall leave you here and you won't get a McDonald's.'

Maddie immediately dropped her ruler and skidded across the gravel towards the car, hopping into the back seat next to her brother and strapping herself into some kind of harness. The Newfoundland in the back snuffled at the top of Maddie's head and she turned towards him and beamed.

Well, thought Dig, this is all very sweet – cute dog,

315

cute girl, wonderful domestic vignette and all that – but what the hell has this got to do with anything? Where's the swarthy stranger in the raincoat, where's the mysterious package, where's the excitement?

The woman sounded her car horn and Dig jumped a mile. *Jesus*, he muttered, clutching his heart, *Jesus*. She wound down her car window and stuck her head through it.

'*Sophie!*' she roared, banging the car horn with the heel of her hand again in exasperation. '*Will you get down here immediately!*'

Dig had the feeling that she was one of those women who made everything in life far more complicated and dramatic than it needed to be.

The front door squeaked open a few seconds later and Dig saw Delilah stiffening on the bench, cupping the side of her face with one hand in a further attempt, he presumed, to disguise herself, as a very tall and slim young girl emerged into the sunshine.

'*Honestly, mother*,' the young girl shouted, turning to look at her while she locked the front door behind her, '*the neighbours must think you're a bloody child-abuser.*' She tutted and tucked her door keys into the pocket of her rucksack. She looked about twelve years old, and was wearing black pedal-pushers, chunky fluorescent trainers and an outsized grey fleece. Her hair was long and parted in the centre and was a warm, shining golden-brown, in stark contrast to that of the other members of her dark-haired family. She was the sort of fresh-faced, lanky and even-featured young girl who Dig could imagine being approached in shopping centres by scouts from modelling agencies. She might have been only twelve, thirteen years old, but she was gorgeous, com-

316

pletely drop-dead, slaveringly, put-a-spring-in-an-old-man's-step gorgeous.

Stop it, you pathetic pervert, he chastised himself, stop it.

As she walked around the car and approached the passenger door, Dig got a better look at her. Full, plump lips, like silken cushions, wide blue eyes with dark lashes, creamy skin and a sulky, resentful attitude. Her mother said something to her as she slid into the passenger seat, and she smiled – a reluctant smile, he noticed, her mouth trying to persuade the rest of her face to join in – and as she smiled she turned towards Dig and, like a brick lobbed through a window, a thought splintered his mind.

Oh my God, he thought, she looks just like Leslie Ash in *Quadrophenia*.

He turned to look at Delilah, who hadn't moved a muscle since the young girl emerged from the house, and then he turned back to the girl, who was strapping herself into her seatbelt. Uncanny, he thought, uncanny the resemblance between the two, the same height, attitude, lips and smile, the same rangy figure, swaying hips and peaches-and-cream complexion. The same . . . exactly the same. Realization coursed through him and he began to experience difficulty breathing. He was back in the playground at the Holy T, cross-legged on the grass, perusing his new timetable and experiencing the character-forming shock of seeing Delilah for the very first time. Jesus, he thought, this is eerie. That girl, he thought, that girl is the spitting bloody image of Delilah.

He turned to look at Delilah again, who was clutching the back of the bench with two white-knuckled hands

317

and staring helplessly at the Mercedes as it reversed out of the driveway and away from her. Her hair had fallen away from her face and her jaw was slack with shock and dismay. As the car straightened itself out on the street, Delilah mindlessly pushed her sunglasses from her nose to her hair, and Dig could see tears shimmering on her cheeks. He felt bad. He felt elated. He felt cheated. He felt horrified. He felt scared. He felt excited.

He looked back at the car and at the girl in the passenger seat, who was now arguing with her brother in the back. Is it possible, he thought to himself, that that girl, that that beautiful, sullen, wonderful girl, is my daughter?

CHAPTER THIRTY-FOUR

Nadine hadn't had time today to think about Dig and Delilah, about Phil in her flat, about anything very much apart from exposure levels, light readings and F-stops. Which was a good thing. But then, after four hours of lugging all her equipment around the streets of Barcelona, sweet-talking policemen and bribing shopkeepers into letting her use locations, not to mention holding back the drooling crowds of men trying to get a look at Fabienne, the eighteen-year-old star of the new Renault advertising campaign, in a gold-sequinned bikini, it had started raining. Absolutely bucketing down. And Nadine had had to abandon the shoot for the day.

She was sitting in her hotel room now, listening to the rain ricocheting off the tiled roof overhead, sorting narrow yellow canisters of film into piles and trying desperately to resist the temptation to phone home. It would do her no good at all to hear the sound of Phil's voice echoing down the line from hundreds of miles away. It would only upset her. Better not to know. But the second she managed to tear her thoughts away from Philip Rich, lying in all his underpanted splendour on her bed, in her flat, her mind filled instead with the equally alarming image of Delilah in Dig's flat, all scrubbed and shining and ready to have sex with Dig. Urgh. She shuddered at the thought.

Jesus, thought Nadine, last night was just *horrible*.

She looked at her watch. It was only three o'clock, but the dark, low cloud that hung over Barcelona, inches, it seemed, from the roof-tops, made it feel more like early evening. She yawned, stretched out on her lovely, firm, quilty hotel bed and closed her eyes. A little snooze would be nice – just a few moments of luxurious, foreign hotel-room shut-eye. After all, she had been up since five thirty.

The sounds from outside her window soothed her. Angry cabs, impatient trucks, the doorman at the front entrance whistling for taxis, rain beating in treble off the roof and in bass off the canvas awning stretched over the front door, like long fingernails tapping a drum. Every few seconds muffled foreign voices would drift past her door, reminding her that it was the middle of the day and other people were busy doing things, didn't have time to lie around.

She pulled up the bedcover and wrapped it over her cold bare feet and naked arms. Her thoughts drifted as she warmed up and snuggled down. Ideas for tomorrow's shoot, plans for dinner tonight, a reminder to herself to get some more Polaroid from the camera shop downstairs because she hadn't packed enough . . . just . . . stuff . . . nice, normal, boring . . . stuff.

And then – *wallop* – there it was. Bang – right there, in the midst of all that lovely driftiness. Delilah. In her fucking towel. In Dig's fucking flat. About to have fucking sex with fucking Dig. And *bang* – there she is again, silhouetted in the back of a black cab at two in the morning, with her arms around Dig's neck and her lips against his mouth. *Crack* – Delilah in the playground at the Holy T, sitting on Dig's lap, throwing Nadine ice-blue daggers, making Nadine feel small and fat and ugly, insufficient, inconsequential and inadequate.

Nadine threw the quilted cover off her and leaped to her feet. Delilah was even robbing her of her sleep. She wanted to scream at the injustice of it all.

Delilah, Delilah, Delilah.

She threw open the door of the mini-bar and eyed it furiously, challenging it to offer her *a real drink*, something that could even *begin* to take the edge off her wretchedness and misery, and sheer, belly-rotting jealousy. Come on you pathetic excuse for a fridge, what have you got, eh? What have you got?

She eyed a quarter-bottle of Louis Roederer and a dinky little bottle of José Cuervo. There was something horribly sad about the idea of doing tequila slammers alone, in the middle of the afternoon but, in her current frame of mind, it appealed to her. To fuck with it. The rain outside was even heavier, the sky was growing darker, she was in a foreign country and she was in a foul mood. If there had ever been a moment to pay a visit to Alcy-land, this was it.

She pulled a tooth mug off her bedside table, poured in the little bottle of tequila, filled it to the top with lovely, cold, frothing champagne, covered it with her hand, slammed it down hard on the table-top and necked it in one.

The bubbles and the taste made her shudder. Disgusting. She burped loudly and licked the champagne off the palm of her hand.

The alcohol reacted immediately, lending a lovely soft focus to the room, the view from her window and her mood. Now she wanted a cigarette. Not just wanted

321

but *craved* a cigarette. Her room was non-smoking. Her window was fixed closed.

She poured the remainder of the champagne into the mug, gulped it down, put on her shoes and a cardigan, picked up her door key and made her way downstairs to the hotel bar.

Hotels, especially extremely *posh* hotels like this one, were like another world, for Nadine. She could quite happily spend the rest of her life in a hotel, absolve herself of all responsibility for the minutiae of life like housework and cooking and plumbers and paying bills and calling mini-cabs and remembering to buy Corn-flakes and ironing things and polishing your own shoes and deciding where to eat and buying stamps and ordering newspapers.

But the best thing about smart hotels was that they were the same the world over. From continent to continent, from First World to Third World you could always depend upon the availability of a boiled egg or a decent bottle of champagne, a safety-deposit box or a mini-bar. Wherever you were, the moment you stepped into a smart hotel you were in another country, entirely unconnected to the land in which it happened to have been constructed. You were in *Hotel-land*, one of the nicest countries in the world as far as Nadine was concerned.

And look at all these lovely twiddly bits you get with everything. Look at this little paper coaster she's been given with her champagne cocktail, with the pretty scalloped edges, and look at all those newspapers over there, hanging off polished mahogany poles. This carpet's great – it's got the hotel insignia all over it. Nadine wants some personalized carpet in *her* flat, with 'NK' woven into it and swirls and curlicues all over the place.

Nadine was hidden in a cosy little corner of the bar, nestled on to a tiny, squishy sofa but within easy eye-contactable distance of the barman. Her head swam pleasantly and the lines of Spanish current affairs she was attempting to translate, using her school Spanish, in the newspaper in front of her were starting to lose their clarity. It was five thirty and it was still raining outside. Nadine was drunk.

'God – there you are! Thank God!' A small pixie-faced girl with cropped black hair and a bindi on her forehead collapsed next to Nadine on the sofa. 'We've been looking everywhere for you.' It was Pia. 'Fabienne's doing all the shops in the lobby and Sarah's doing a corridor-by-corridor trawl for your butchered body. We've been phoning your room all afternoon. I was about to call the fucking police.' Her tiny little nose wrinkled up and down with the drama of it all and she slapped Nadine on the arm with annoyance at so much expended worry.

'God, I'm sorry,' said Nadine, suddenly very conscious of her lips not working in harmony with her tongue, of the fact that if she didn't watch out she could very easily start slurring. 'I didn't think. I'm sorry. Hit me again.'

Pia grimaced and slapped her arm again. 'Bad photographer,' she scolded, teasingly. 'What are you?'

'I'm a bad photographer,' said Nadine, dropping her head into her chest.

'You're also a *pissed* photographer, aren't you? Breathe on me,' Pia ordered, pointing her minute nostrils towards Nadine's mouth. Nadine let out a small puff of air. 'You are! You're drunk! Blimey, Deen. It's not even six o'clock yet, and you're off your trolley! Well,' she said, getting to her platformed feet, 'there's only one thing for it. I'm going to find Sarah and Fab and get them down here. I expect a full round of whatever that is you're drinking, on the table by the time I get back. OK?'

'OK.'

Nadine watched Pia striding across the insignia-ed carpeting towards the twinkling lobby outside, her tiny little hips twitching from side to side in skintight black pedal-pushers, her ankles looking like they might snap with the weight of the platform shoes that were strapped onto them. Every man in the room turned to watch her as she went.

She was back within minutes with Sarah, the Sloaney, blonde, pencil-thin make-up artist with the dirty laugh, and Fabienne, the voluptuous and ripe-fleshed Renault-ad girl with the vertiginous cleavage. Nadine supposed that in company like this she was probably the dumpy red-head with the stupid clothes on. Nadine smiled to herself. She didn't care. She *loved* drinking with beautiful women. It was so much fun, the night-time equivalent of going to the park with a cute dog. You got loads of attention and everyone talked to you.

'You dirty old lush,' said Sarah, peeling off a cashmere cardigan and revealing elegant arms and shoulders in a tiny pink vest-top, 'how much have you had to drink?'

Nadine giggled, shrugged and hiccuped. The three girls laughed. 'Say no more,' said Sarah.

The bartender arrived at their table and off-loaded four more champagne cocktails, each with its own little scalloped coaster, and a tiny bowl of pistachios. Brave now, in the company of other women, Nadine threw him her best smile and said *gracias* with all the Spanishness she could muster. He smiled back at her and she blushed, and the girls all nudged each other and teased her and Nadine settled down to enjoy what was obviously going to be a top girly night.

By eight o'clock the previously sedate bar had exploded into Saturday-night mayhem, and the quartet of lary English girls drinking champagne cocktails in the corner were no longer drawing quite so much attention to themselves. Pia had been entertaining them, as ever, with hilarious accounts of the men in her life, peppering her stories with well-chosen swear-words and physical demonstrations of various events using her tiny little stick-drawing body to great comic effect. Nadine was so drunk by now that she was hugely appreciative of Pia's diverting behaviour, meaning as it did that she could just sit there grinning like a fool and not have to make any kind of intelligent conversation.

Her bladder was telling her that a trip to the *Señoritas* was imminent, but her head was telling her that she was too pissed and too red in the face and her heels were too high and she didn't know where they were and she'd have to wander around for ages, gormlessly trying to locate them, and that when she did there'd probably be some poor anaemic Spanish woman in there whose job it was to sit in a toilet all day, and there'd be three pesetas in her little saucer and Nadine would feel really guilty about not leaving her anything and it was all far, far too much trouble, so she should just cross her legs and not drink anything for a while because that would just make her need to go even more, and she was half-way through this desperate mental monologue when she suddenly realized that Sarah was asking her a question.

'Sorry,' she muttered, pulling herself back into the proceedings.

'I said, are you still going out with that really cute-looking bloke I met last time I saw you?' said Sarah.

Nadine racked her mind. The last time she'd seen Sarah socially was about six months ago when she was going out with? . . . with? . . . Jimmy, of course, the thirty-nine-year-old chiropodist whose hair, spookily enough, was exactly the same shade of red as hers. Everyone had taken them for brother and sister in the couple of months they'd been together, which Nadine had found deeply insulting given the age difference and the fact that he was – well, not *bad*-looking as such, but certainly not what you would describe as a 'really cute-looking bloke'. Sarah couldn't possibly mean Jimmy.

'You know,' said Sarah, noticing Nadine's confusion, 'the guy with all the hair and the big eyebrows – he had some kind of weird name. The A&R guy.'

Nadine choked on her cocktail. 'What!' she exclaimed, wiping her chin with the back of her hand and laughing, unnaturally loudly. 'You mean Dig?'

'That's it,' cried Sarah, 'Dig! I knew he had a silly name. Yeah, Dig. What happened to him – are you still seeing him?'

Nadine laughed over-loudly again and shook her head. 'Dig and I are just friends,' she said, 'we're not going out together.'

'God, you're joking,' said Sarah, 'could have sworn the two of you were as together as Posh and Becks.'

Nadine laughed again.

'No, really,' continued Sarah, her eyes glittering with the excitement of intimate revelation, 'what is it with the two of you? There was a real chemistry there. I remember it really well – he had his arm around your shoulders.'

'Yeah, well,' said Nadine, 'we've known each other for a long time. We're very affectionate with each other.'

Sarah was shaking her head. 'No,' she said, 'no. There's more to it than that. I told Neil about you two when I got home that night. I said to him that I'd never been able to understand why you never went out with decent men, but that it looked like you'd finally found one. I was full of it, how happy I was for you and how lovely he seemed and how well matched and all that. Have you ever met him?' She turned towards Pia.

Pia nodded, effusively. 'He's *gorgeous*,' she drawled and Nadine wondered, not for the first time, at Pia's ability to tailor her opinions to fit the moment. She'd always agreed with Nadine, before, that he was too skinny and too short and had too much hair.

'Honestly,' said Sarah, addressing Fabienne, 'he's really cute-looking and sweet and polite, and you should see the way he looks at Nadine – Neil never bloody looks at me like that and he's asked me to marry him!'

Nadine laughed again. This wasn't the first time someone had told her what a lovely couple she and Dig made – many other people had made that mistake over the years – but tonight, with her heart broken and her head full of Delilah and all the stuff that had happened over the last week, it was hugely reassuring to hear. Her stomach did a strange floppy thing that made her feel all weak.

'What do you mean,' she asked, 'the way he looks at me?'

'I dunno,' said Sarah, 'he just seemed – so *proud* of you. It was like he was showing you off. The way he had his arm around your shoulder and the way he laughed at your jokes. I honestly thought that he was some new boyfriend who was completely besotted with you.'

'Hm,' smiled Nadine, 'well. He's not. He's my mate.' Nadine was feigning nonchalance. She wanted to hear more – more about how Dig looked at her and more about how good they looked together and more about what a great couple they made. She needed to hear it.

'So why haven't you two ever got it together?' asked Sarah. 'Is he gay?'

Nadine snorted and slapped her thighs. 'Dig? God, you're joking. He's deeply heterosexual. *Too* heterosexual, if anything.'

'So why not? Oh – don't tell me. He's trapped in some long-term relationship with the wrong woman?'

'No! He's a serial monogamist, like me – except his relationships are even shorter than mine.'

'So, the two of you are unattached, you're affectionate with each other, you're best friends and you've known each other half your lives?'

Nadine nodded.

'Why the hell aren't you going out together? That's more than most supposed couples have going for them, y'know?'

Nadine nodded again and felt a little hysteria building in her stomach.

'Don't you fancy him, even a little bit?' asked Pia, nudging her playfully in the ribs.

Nadine was about to give her usual knee-jerk response to this question, asked of her in the past, many times. 'Oh no,' she was about to sneer, 'he's too small for me.' That's what she always said – he's too short. And then she'd make some joke at his expense about his lack of stature and his skinny legs and his big eyebrow and his sticky-uppy hair, and everyone would laugh and the subject would get dropped immediately. But tonight – tonight she was going to be honest. She needed to get it off her chest, off-load on to someone else the frightening realization that she was in love with her best friend. And Dig was gorgeous. Of course he was. Anyone could see that. His eyes twinkled and his lips curled when he smiled. He was small, but he was taller than her. He had great eyelashes and wonderful buttocks. He was sexy as hell. As sexy as he'd always been.

Nadine looked at Pia and grinned mischievously. 'We–ell,' she grinned, and all three girls began screeching with pleasure, 'he is kind of cute.' Blood rushed to Nadine's head as the words left her lips. She felt strangely excited and unburdened. She joined in the excited laughter of her companions and then had to stop herself sharply when she realized that she'd almost peed herself – almost, but not quite – a very close thing. 'Ooh,' she said, covering her mouth with a hand, 'excuse me, girls. Nature is shouting very loudly.'

'Oh no!' sighed Pia, in dismay. 'Not now. You can't go now. You've just admitted to fancying your best friend, for God's sake!'

She stood up stiffly, every muscle in the lower half of her body clenched tightly. 'Gotta go, girls, really, really gotta go.' She shuffled from foot to foot while she waited for Pia to get out of her way and then made as incon-spicuous a dash for it as she possibly could, across the insignias and towards the large marble lobby.

Nadine felt a bit wobbly on her feet as she negotiated the small gaps between tables and chairs in the crowded bar. She was much more drunk than she'd thought. She

329

felt heavy and ungainly. Her shoes felt like breezeblocks and the cool, high-ceilinged lobby felt as vast as a skating rink as she tapped her way across it towards the toilets. She was sure everyone – all these business types with their smart little suitcases and their unsmiling, not-on-holiday faces – was staring at her, staring at the red-faced, slightly panic-stricken girl with the ginger hair and the strange dress walking uncertainly across the marble floor. It was like another world out here – Nadine had that odd walking-out-of-a-cinema-into-bright-sun-shine feeling.

She pushed open the toilet door with her shoulder and was pleased to find the large, plush, mirrored and wallpapered room empty. Not an anaemic Spanish woman clutching a paper napkin in sight. She threw open the door of the first cubicle, lifted the hem of her dress and then began fumbling with the tops of her knickers, which just didn't seem to be where they usually were. She started panicking as she felt her bladder weakening and threatening to explode before she'd sat down. She finally located the tops of her knickers, yanked them down and then landed somewhat heavily on the seat, sighing with unspeakable pleasure as she released her tensed muscles and let it all out. 'Aaaaah,' she smiled to herself. 'Aaaah.'

Afterwards, she confronted her reflection in the mirror and started giggling. She wasn't quite sure why: it was a combination of how awful she looked (flushed and wild-eyed) and how pissed she was feeling (it was always a sure-fire sign that you were really drunk, when you started laughing at your reflection in the toilets).

But it was also a slightly nervous reaction to what had happened just now, in the bar. That comment about

330

Dig. That sudden rush of feelings. Admitting to a bunch of girls she hardly knew that she thought Dig was 'cute', when she hadn't even admitted it to herself since she was eighteen years old.

'So – do you? Do you fancy Dig?' she asked her reflection, trying to pull a serious face and dissolving into laughter yet again. 'Do you? Do you want him? Do you want to see him naked? Do you want to see his *willy*?' She slapped her hands down on the marble surface and laughed out loud. 'How do you feel about Dig's willy, Nadine? Do you want to hold it in your hand? Do you want to kiss it, kiss its little shiny head?' She nearly overbalanced as her laughter increased and had to grip on to the marble to keep herself upright.

'Do you *want* him? . . . Do you want him to kiss you? Would you like it if Dig held your face in his hands and kissed you on the lips?'

Nadine eyed her blurred reflection, her blotchy, disproportional features, her messy hair, her diametrically opposed eyes – the woman in the mirror who looked like an older, fatter and sartorially less refined sister.

'I *vont* you, Dig' – she experimented with a Garbo approach – 'I *vont* you.' She laughed at her reflection again and then let her head fall into her chest. She sighed heavily. 'Oh God,' she moaned to herself, 'oh God. Dig. I do. I want you. Oh, bollocks.' Her head felt too small, far too small, to accommodate all the stuff that was going on in there.

Her mind started sending her picture postcards from the past. There was one postmarked 12 September 1987, a shot of Dig wandering down Bartholomew Road in the dark, jumping up on that wall when he didn't know she was looking and punching the air. There were the doodles she'd drawn all over her old diary when she was a teenager. *Nadine Ryan Nadine Ryan Nadine Ryan*. And there was Dig's old kite, the one he'd given her the day they went to Primrose Hill. *Dig 'n' Deen, 13 September 1987, for ever* ♥.

More pictures flashed through her mind. Flying kites on Southend beach with Dig and his dad. Waiting for buses in the rain on Saturday mornings with Dig to go down to the Notting Hill Record and Tape Exchange. Queuing up outside the Electric Ballroom on Saturday nights, hair thick with backcombing and Elnett. Saying goodbye in the setting sun on the last day of school, the burning car outside Caledonian Park that was now inextricably linked with her memories of that night – broken hearts and burnt-out cars.

She pictured Dig's flat, his anally arranged knick-knacks and ornaments, his spotless little kitchen, his plumped-up cushions and fluffed-out duvet. She saw him launching himself from the sofa, suddenly, in the middle of a film, as he often did, to pick a bit of lint off his floor. She remembered his endearing excitement at finally leaving home at the age of twenty-seven and buying his flat, all those nightmarish weekend trips to Ikea in Brent Park and hours spent discussing the relative merits of seagrass carpeting versus wooden floors, and then trawling around Allied Carpets for two, three hours at a time to find exactly the right shade of beige.

She imagined the two of them, sitting side by side on his blue-cord sofa drinking big bottles of Bud, watching the telly, smoking and snuggling up to each other, the warmth where their thighs pressed together, the weight of his head on her shoulder, the smell of his sweet, beery breath when he turned to share a joke with her. All that stuff she'd taken for granted for ten years, all that lovely, warm, easy, intimate Diggy stuff.

All that lovely stuff that Delilah was currently getting her perfectly manicured mitts all over.

As these thoughts surged through her mind, Nadine became filled with a sense of resolve and strength. She couldn't let Delilah win, not again, not this time.

Nadine squinted to focus and glanced at her watch. Quarter past eight. Quarter past seven in London. She felt her pocket for her door key, pushed open the toilet door and strode purposefully towards the lifts. She didn't feel self-conscious now as her heels clattered against the hard marble. A smile twitched at the corners of her mouth while she waited for the smoothly humming lift to slink its way down to the foyer and collect her.

She wove a bit as she made her way down corridor after corridor on the fourth floor, her heels sinking into the soft carpeting, one stiff flower arrangement blurring into another, brass-plated light fittings with pleated shades guiding her on her way. Nadine liked being drunk and alone in a hotel. She wanted to break into a run and start careering around the place like a kid. She wanted to shout and scream and play hide-and-seek.

She wanted to speak to Dig. Right now. This instant.

She was going to tell Dig that she was in love with him. Why should she let Delilah win again?

In her room, Nadine threw off her shoes and landed with a bounce on her freshly made bed. She found the bit of laminated plastic that gave instructions on how to make an international call and began dialling.

Her heart raced as she waited for the call to connect. 'Come on,' she muttered to herself, 'come on, Diggy-boy, pick it up.' The phone rang, five times, six times, seven times, and Nadine was about to hang up when there was a click, a second's silence and the muffled sound of someone's skin rubbing against the mouthpiece. Nadine caught her breath.

'*Hello?*' came a woman's breathless voice.

Nadine dropped the receiver and it landed with a crash on to the cradle. Delilah. Delilah Lillie. Answering Dig's phone. In Dig's flat on a Saturday night. The slightly insane smile that had been etched on to Nadine's face for the last quarter of an hour disappeared. Stinging, salty tears sprung to her eyes, taking its place.

Nadine pulled a handful of Kleenex from the box on her bedside table and rubbed her damp face into them. Her hysterical happiness turned to hysterical misery, and the more she wiped away her tears, the more she produced. She didn't have a place on Dig's corduroy sofa any more, she didn't belong in his flat. She'd lost again – lost to Delilah Lillie. She'd had ten years to love Dig, to have Dig, to be Dig's – *ten years*. And she'd left it a week too late.

She didn't laugh now as she looked at herself in the mirror opposite her bed. There was nothing funny about the blotchy-faced girl staring back at her; there was nothing funny about being in love with her best mate; there was nothing funny about Dig being in love with Delilah. None of it was even vaguely amusing.

She slowly lifted two fingers to her head, made them horizontal, pressed them into her temple and pulled the trigger with her thumb.

'Bang,' she said, sadly, letting her hand drop to her side.

CHAPTER THIRTY-FIVE

Dig had sat numbly for a moment after the family disappeared in their Mercedes estate, unable to absorb what had just taken place. He looked over at Delilah, who had turned to face the water and was staring pensively across the river, her hands clasped together tightly in her lap and, for a moment, he desperately, desperately wanted to rush over to her and take her in his arms and share her trauma. He had to bite his tongue and hold himself down.

Instead he waited for a while and watched her. After a few minutes she stood up and shuffled down the grass towards the towpath. She stopped a man with a red setter and he nodded and pulled something out of his inside pocket. As she walked back up the hill, Dig saw what he'd given her. She was smoking a cigarette. She took a couple of puffs, looked down at it between her fingers, scowled and threw it out towards the river.

She stood at the top of the grassy hill, nibbling at her fingernails. And then, finally, she picked up her two bags and strode towards the middle house. She stopped at the front door, pulled the gigantic bunny from inside the Hamley's bag and perched it on the doorstep.

It was a grey and white rabbit, with a large bow round its neck, and was carrying in its paws a red-felt heart with the words 'Birthday Girl' printed on it.

Jesus Christ, Dig thought, this is so fucking heavy.

And then he started doing some pretty basic maths. Today was 21 November. He counted nine months backwards on his fingers: 21 February. Delilah's eighteenth birthday. The last time they'd had sex. The last time they'd been happy together. Just before everything had gone sour and Delilah had disappeared. There was still the possibility that the girl was younger than twelve, had been born long beyond the end of his relationship with Delilah, but it was looking increasingly unlikely. She couldn't have been younger than twelve – she looked sixteen as it was.

And then another thought occurred to him. Maybe she *was* older than twelve. Maybe Delilah had had her and given her away before she'd moved to north London, before he'd ever even met her. But then . . . but then . . . no – he would have known. She would have told him. She used to say that young girls who got themselves pregnant were pathetic. She said that she would never let that happen to her. She said that she never wanted children. She said . . . oh God. Dig dropped his forehead on to his fist with frustration and confusion. This was so heavy, so unbelievably heavy.

Delilah was crouched down on the front doorstep of the middle house. She was fussing with the rabbit, arranging it, trying to balance it. She leaned in towards it, and Dig was rooted to the spot with sadness and tenderness when he saw her suddenly grab it in her arms and squeeze it tightly, her face buried against its cheek and tears rolling down her face.

Enough, he thought to himself, I've seen enough.

He got to his feet and very quickly, before she turned around, scampered down towards the towpath and ran, through the crowds, along the river, down the high street and back to the station.

He was home a couple of hours later.

His thought processes were dizzying as he went from train to Tube, from Tube to bus and from bus to front door. Absolutely breathtaking. His head felt like it was strapped into a terrifying fairground ride. He was frightened, exhilarated and nauseated, all at the same time.

Most days the most important thing Dig had to think about was his car breaking down or having a row with Nadine or forgetting to send his mum a Mother's Day card. Today he was being forced to reconsider his entire existence, his history, his identity.

He felt bigger, physically larger, as he paced his flat back and forth that afternoon, waiting for Delilah to get back. His feet felt wider, his arms felt thicker, his legs felt chunkier. He felt older, too, like all those grown-up people he'd seen out and about at quarter to nine this morning.

His initial instinct was to say nothing to Delilah when she returned. He might have been reeling from the shock of it all, but Delilah would be feeling worse. He'd spied on one of the most intensely private moments of her life. He'd seen her crying into the rabbit's fur when she'd thought nobody was looking. He'd been somewhere he had no place to be. He felt guilty. The last thing Delilah would need on her return from such a traumatic event was Dig sticking his nose in, asking questions, turning the whole shocking situation into his own drama.

But as afternoon turned to evening and the sky darkened and his head became so inflated with questions it felt like it would explode, his mood changed. He became angry. Delilah was in the wrong. No matter whether that beautiful girl was her daughter or not and whether he was the father or not, no matter what the truth of the situation, Delilah should have involved him. She should have told him why she was in London. She'd treated him like a child with no capacity for dealing with adult realities. Which was, he supposed, true on many levels. But still, she'd found other uses for him, hadn't she? He was grown-up enough to own the flat she was staying in, to have paid cash for the sofabed she was sleeping on, and he was responsible enough, apparently, to look after her precious dog every day.

As his frustration and impatience had grown during the course of the afternoon he'd tried phoning Nadine. Over and over. He'd never before needed to speak to Nadine so badly, never needed to hear her voice, the voice of normality and routine, of light-heartedness and easiness, the voice of his best friend in the world. He didn't care about all that awfulness the previous evening. He just wanted to see her. But where was Nadine when he needed her? Not at home, that was for sure. Nadine's absence in his hour of need had served only to compound his sheer, throbbing panic, and by the time he heard the key in the lock and lifted himself from the sofa to confront Delilah at the front door, he'd lost all sense of reason. He no longer cared whether or not Delilah was emotionally ready to discuss the blonde girl in Surrey, and he was no longer ashamed of his act of deception and craftiness in following her there this morning. All Dig cared about now was getting answers to questions.

And, it had to be said, that of all the possible opening gambits to such a monumental conversation, he'd probably chosen the most bizarre and unsuitable.

'So,' began Dig, 'what happened to the rabbit?'

Delilah jumped and clutched her heart. 'Oh God, Dig,' she said, 'you nearly gave me a heart attack.' She hooked her sheepskin on to the coatstand and clicked the front door shut behind her. Digby bounced off the sofa and went hurtling towards her. Dig leaned against the living-room doorpost and folded his arms.

'What did you do with the rabbit?'

Delilah glanced at him curiously and then with concern. 'What rabbit?' she asked, slipping her sunglasses off her head and dropping them on to a table.

'Oh, you know, the big one' – he extended his arms to describe the height – 'the big one, with the floppy ears.'

She looked at him quizzically. 'Sorry, Dig. You've lost me.' She moved towards the kitchen and Dig followed her.

'You had him when you left the house this morning.'

Delilah stopped in her tracks for a moment and then spun round towards Dig. 'Ah!' she said, brightly, '*that* rabbit.'

'Yes,' said Dig, '*that* rabbit.'

'Oh he was a – er – gift. For a little girl I know. In Surrey. It was her – um – birthday.' She pulled open the fridge and removed a large jar of pickled onions, twisted off the lid nervously and forced an onion the size of a satsuma into her mouth. 'Mmmm,' she mumbled through the sphere, 'yummy.'

Dig looked at her with disbelief.

'Anyway,' she frowned, 'why do you ask?' A dribble of vinegar ran down her chin and she wiped it away with the back of her hand. Dig was surprised to notice that this failed to ignite in him even the slightest flicker of desire. In fact, it almost disgusted him.

339

'Did she like it?'

'Hmm?'

'The little girl. In Surrey. Did she like the rabbit?'

Delilah shrugged and crunched. 'Yes. I think so.'

'It was a nice rabbit.'

'Yes,' said Delilah, looking at Dig worriedly, 'it was.'

She popped another onion in her mouth, picked up the jar and walked out of the kitchen.

Dig leaned back against the work surface and put his face in his hands. Great, he thought, bloody great. I really am a *smooth* operator, aren't I? I really handled that so well. 'It was a nice rabbit.' Jesus. What an arse.

But then what, exactly, was the right way to handle a situation like this? Dig was fairly sure that no rules applied to how to conduct yourself on discovering that you have unknowingly fathered a child in your youth and that the mother of that child has kept you in blissful ignorance of the situation while taking full advantage of your flat, your facilities and your good nature.

He'd thought that by mentioning the rabbit he would immediately confer upon Delilah a full realization of the day's events, that she would instantly understand that he'd followed her to Surrey and watched her crying into the rabbit's fur and that a luminously enlightening conversation would immediately follow. Instead, she probably thought he was mad.

It was time to start this all over again.

'Delilah,' he said sternly, striding into the living room, 'I know about Sophie.'

His heart bounced into his throat as the words left his mouth, and his voice caught on the last syllable. It was the most dramatic thing he'd ever said in his life. He suddenly felt like an actor playing a part in a silly soap

340

opera. He didn't know quite what to do with his arms while he waited for her to respond.

Delilah looked up at him. She'd been unzipping her black-suede boots. She kicked one off mindlessly and continued to stare at Dig.

'What?'

'Sophie. I know about Sophie.' His arms felt like strange, long things over which he had no control. He folded them across his chest to get them out of the way.

'Sophie who?'

Oh God, this was starting to sound like the rabbit conversation. Dig walked over to the sofa and sat down next to Delilah. He turned towards her, looked into her red eyes and felt himself relax. He stopped feeling like a soap actor.

'I followed you today, Delilah. I followed you to Surrey and to the river. I watched you. I saw everything.'

Delilah froze momentarily, one boot suspended from her hand.

'I saw the girl. I saw Sophie. She's beautiful . . .'

Delilah placed the boot carefully on the floor and rested her hands on her kneecaps. She stared into space for a moment and then turned towards Dig. 'Why did you do that, Dig?' she sighed, and Dig suddenly felt ten years old again.

'I don't know,' he shrugged. 'I didn't give it too much thought really. Just saw you outside, waiting for a cab this morning, and something snapped. I didn't plan it, or anything . . .' He tailed off.

There was a moment's silence. Dig contemplated the dirt under his thumbnail while he waited for Delilah to say something. The silence continued, leaving Dig more than enough time to ponder again his lack of emotional

341

finesse. He wanted, as ever, someone else to take responsibility for the situation. He wanted Delilah to take over now – he'd done his bit. But he realized that that wasn't going to happen. He'd started this, therefore it was his responsibility. There were a million questions he could ask her right now, but only one truly definitive one. He took a deep breath and opened his mouth.

'Is she – Sophie – is she mine?'

Delilah spun round and stared at him. Dig held his breath. This was it. This was, potentially, the biggest moment of his life.

Delilah's eyebrows knitted together and she frowned. And then she grimaced. 'No,' she stated, 'of course not.'

Dig exhaled, felt his heart start beating again, a little too fast. He licked his dry lips and nodded distractedly. 'Ah,' he murmured, feeling curiously deflated, 'of course not.'

Dig had never known his flat so quiet before, as if the entire building had been wrapped in cotton wool. He heard the pilot light flick on in the kitchen, signalling the arrival of central heating. It was the only sound.

This wasn't what he'd expected. He'd expected floodgates to open at the mere mention of the girl in Surrey, he'd expected Delilah to abandon her reticence of the last few days and open up to him. Instead she was still keeping it all locked away inside, even now she didn't have to. Dig took a deep breath and forced himself to keep pushing. He hadn't come this far to let it all slip away again.

'But she is yours – right?'

Delilah was silent again. She let out a huge sigh and turned towards Dig. 'I can't believe you followed me,

Dig. I really can't.' There was a trace of disappointment in the tone of her voice which cut right through him like a switchblade.

He looked at her then and felt suddenly and icily detached from her. Who was she? Who the hell was this girl, Delilah 'Biggins', who he thought had left him twelve years ago because she was scared of commitment but who'd actually gone off and had someone else's baby, who lived some fairy-princess existence in the countryside that he couldn't even come close to relating to, who had a horrible dog and terrible taste in music, who veered constantly between onerous silence and bubblegum chatter, who was incapable of hanging up a wet towel or cleaning a cup?

He had absolutely no idea.

The Delilah of his dreams and memories was a girl; this person eyeing him with disappointment and disdain was a woman, a real woman, a woman who'd given birth and had to give her child away, a woman who had moved on in her life and had left her past behind her. Including him.

He'd been a fool to imagine that there was a future for him and Delilah. He felt faintly ridiculous to have ever considered such a notion.

Dig suddenly felt a burst of intense anger.

'Jesus, Delilah,' he shouted, 'what the hell was I supposed to do? You turn up here at my flat without warning, you – you kiss me in the back of a cab, you dump your dog on me, you make – you make – you make a . . . a . . . fucking *mess*, you tell me *nothing* about what you're doing here. You treat me like a mug. You haven't made me a casserole. I clean up after you all the time. And then I ask you a perfectly *normal* question and you don't even give me the decency of a straight answer. I'm sorry, Delilah, if I stuck a toe into your private areas, but I didn't know what else to do.'

Dig gulped when he realized he'd just said 'stuck a toe into your private areas'. What a ludicrous thing to say . . .

'I just want some answers, Delilah,' he sighed, before getting up off the sofa and walking meaningfully towards the kitchen.

He pulled open the fridge door and enjoyed the blast of cold air against his flushed skin. He picked up the last of his big Buds and made a pig's ear of trying to get the lid off on the corner of the work surface before giving up and taking it off with a bottle-opener. Had he ever, he wondered, been less cool?

He stomped back into the living room and sat next to Delilah again.

She turned towards him and placed a cool hand over his hot one. Her face had softened. 'Dig. I'm sorry. You're right. I've been unfair. I hadn't really thought about any of this from your point of view. I've been so preoccupied, trying to track the family down, trying to avoid . . . trying not to see other people, and you've been so patient and so sweet. You've kept out of my way and I don't know what I'd have done without you.'

Dig pulled his hand away. 'There you go again,' he said, 'you're doing it again, treating me like a pet, or something, treating me like Digby here.' He pointed at the dog. 'Well, you might have named him after me but I am *not* a Yorkshire Terrier, Delilah, I am not your pet,' he finished indignantly, his features set with pride, his thoughts in shock at the sheer idiocy of some of the things he was coming out with this evening.

344

Quote of the Night: 'I am not a Yorkshire Terrier', closely followed by 'you haven't made me a casserole' and 'it was a nice rabbit'. It wasn't like this on the television.

'Look, Delilah. I'm not very good at this sort of thing, as you've probably noticed. But I'm confused. I appreciate what you must have gone through for the last week – well, the last twelve years, I imagine. I appreciate how hard this must all have been for you, how emotional and tough. And I understand why you kept it all from me, I really do. But I haven't had a moment's peace since you kissed me in the back of the cab on Tuesday. You sent me down the wrong turning when you did that. Made me think you were here because of me. Made me think that what we had when we were kids still existed. You being here has made me re-evaluate my entire life, you know. I was *happy* before you turned up. And then you kissed me. And then you moved into my flat. And then I thought we'd had a bloody kid. I've fallen out with my best mate over you. And now – and now, I'm just in a right old two and eight.'

Nice finish, he thought, really stylish closing line.

'Please include me in your life, Delilah,' he said, 'please tell me everything. What happened twelve years ago?'

Delilah pinched the bridge of her nose between two fingers. 'God, I've made a real mess of this, haven't I?' she sighed. 'It wasn't supposed to be like this. I was just supposed to come to London, find Isab– find Sophie, have a look at her, make sure she was all right and then decide what to do about . . .' She cast her gaze downwards, cryptically, towards her crotch. Dig eyed her with confusion but she ignored him and carried on. 'I had no idea

345

I was going to bump into you and Nadine and how that was going to make me feel.'

'How d'you mean?'

'Look – I saw you first, on Saturday, in the park. I saw you before you saw me and I actually sped up, you know, to avoid you.'

'Why?'

'It just wasn't part of the plan. The plan was all so clean and simple. But then you saw me and you caught up with me and I found myself feeling nostalgic. And I thought, why not? Why not have a bit of fun while I'm in London. You know, I'm the same age as you and Nadine, but the life I live and the life I've *lived*, I feel like a middle-aged woman most of the time. Which is fine. But when I sat there in that coffee-shop with you and Nadine I suddenly felt so old and you seemed so young, with your wacky clothes and your free-and-easy lifestyles, and I was so envious of you both.

'So I went back to Marina's and started thinking about the old days, about going to gigs with you and wearing outrageous clothes and behaving like a rebel, drinking and smoking, sneering and pouting and being obnoxious, and I suddenly really missed that person. I missed that person who didn't give a toss what anyone thought, who was streetwise and rude and true to herself. So I met up with you. I wanted a holiday from being Delilah Biggins, Chester Wife, I wanted a night out as Delilah Lillie, Kentish Town Rebel, and there was no one I enjoyed being Delilah Lillie with more than you, Dig.

'It was only going to be the one night. That's why I kissed you, I suppose. I didn't think I'd ever see you again, and I was so full of adrenalin and so excited to be

346

out with you, away from Alex, away from the country and back, very briefly, in my youth, that I just got carried away. And I kissed you. I shouldn't have. I know you, Dig. I know how sensitive you are. I should have realized how seriously you would have taken that kiss. It was stupid and self-indulgent of me. Please forgive me . . . I didn't mean to lead you on.'

Dig nodded sagely, wondering at the irony of a beautiful woman asking his forgiveness for kissing him on the lips.

'I didn't think twice about turning up here and asking you for a bed. You've always been one of the kindest-hearted men I knew, Dig. It didn't occur to me that you still had any feelings towards me – I felt like a charity case, not a woman, when I turned up on your doorstep. I was so desperate, I didn't think about your feelings. I'm sorry. And I'm sorry about the mess. I'm terrible, I know that. I always mean to be tidier – I always intend to put things away – but then I get distracted and I completely forget. And as for the casserole,' she smiled, 'let me take you out for one. Tonight. Please! I'll take you anywhere you like, for any kind of casserole you like.'

'How about a curry-flavoured one?' teased Dig.

'Absolutely,' smiled Delilah, 'a curry-flavoured casserole it is.'

'God, Delilah. I'm sorry to have lost my temper with you like that. It was out of order and it was selfish. It's just been so frustrating, and then I've spent all day thinking I was a dad.' He laughed wryly. 'I shouldn't have got on your case – not after the day you've had. You must be feeling shitty.'

Delilah shook her head and smiled again. 'D'you know

what?' she said. 'I'm really not. I thought I would be, but I'm not. Because she's fine, isn't she? Sophie's just fine. The woman who adopted her – her mother – seems a bit of a panicker, but then, maybe if my mother had been a bit more like her . . . She's just fine. Lovely house, brother and sister, she's got everything. The thing I was most scared of was that she'd look like her father – that I'd see him in her. But he's not there – not at all. She's all me. She's fine.'

'Delilah,' said Dig, seriously, 'promise me, over dinner, promise me you'll tell me everything. About Alex and Sophie and who her father is and what happened? Yes?'

'Yes,' nodded Delilah, 'I promise.'

'Bengal Lancer?'

'Bengal Lancer sounds great.'

Dig slugged back the end of his beer and got to his feet. 'I'm sorry I followed you – it was sneaky and low.'

Delilah shook her head. 'No,' she said, 'don't be sorry. I'm glad you followed me. It's good to be able to talk to someone about things. And' – she paused for a moment – 'I'm going to need your advice, too. There's something else I haven't told you – haven't told *anyone*. We can talk about that, too. OK?'

'OK.'

Dig held his hand out to Delilah. As she stood up she leaned into Dig's chest and wrapped her arms around him. 'You really are the loveliest bloke in the world, Dig Ryan,' she said, and Dig squeezed her back, and was delighted to note that there was no sexual response anywhere in his body to the proximity of her warm, fragrant body.

Well – only a tiny bit.

He grabbed his coat and passed Delilah her sheepskin,

348

and just as they were about to leave the house, the phone rang.

'Leave it,' he shouted out to Delilah, 'let the answerphone pick it up.'

'No,' she said, 'I'll get it.'

She was frowning when she wandered back into the hall a few seconds later.

'Who was it?' asked Dig.

She shrugged. 'God knows,' she said, 'they hung up when I answered. I did 1471 but it was "*from a network which doesn't transmit numbers.*"'

Dig shrugged, too, and held the front door open for Delilah.

He felt curiously light-hearted as he pushed his front door closed behind them and locked it. He was going out for a curry on a Saturday night with a beautiful woman, who, he suddenly and overwhelmingly realized, he wasn't in love with.

For the first time in over a week, a sense of normality began to return to him, a sense that things might just be getting better.

CHAPTER THIRTY-SIX

Delilah was in one of her effervescent moods as they walked down Camden Road towards Kentish Town Road, bubbling enthusiastically about a deli she'd found in Great Portland Street earlier in the week that had made her the best salt-beef sandwich she'd ever had in her entire life, even better than the ones she'd had in New York on her shopping trips there, and really, really good coffee – but then London was finally getting to grips with the whole coffee thing, wasn't it, what with Seattles and Aromas and Coffee Republics all over the place, and it was about time, too, because how could London ever hope to be taken seriously as a sophisticated city if you couldn't even get a decent cup of coffee, for God's sake?

Crossing over Torriano Avenue she babbled on, about how awful the suburbs were and how she'd never realized because she'd gone straight from inner London to the deepest depths of the countryside, and it really was very depressing to see how the vast majority of the population actually lived, in terracotta-coloured houses with funny little porches and their two allocated parking spaces among the garden-centre rockeries, with their characterless high streets full of Nexts and Robert Dyases and lacklustre branches of Marks and Spencer which didn't sell any of the top-of-the-range lines they sold in town, and how she'd actually rather live in an unheated squat in Mile End than live her life in suburban mediocrity with borders on her walls and all over her garden.

As they trotted briskly down Caversham Road, Delilah regaled him with her thoughts on Gwyneth Paltrow's love life, and how it looked like she was turning into another Julia Roberts, constantly falling in and out of love with the wrong men, trying to find something real inside all that Hollywood bullshit while labouring under the weight of self-doubt and feelings of insecurity, and how if she wasn't careful she could end up single and lonely.

Unsurprisingly, Dig found himself zoning out, and his eye was caught by a couple walking the other way down the road.

The man was average-looking with a bad haircut and a damp raincoat and the woman was small and more than a little overweight. There was a sense of completeness to them and when the woman reached up on to her tiptoes and put her lips to the back of his neck, softly, slowly and unselfconsciously, Dig felt an overwhelming sense of sadness. The gesture suddenly struck him as the most intimate thing one person could do to another, more intimate than sex. The back of the neck, he thought, is where it's at, where all of human intimacy can be found.

Dig couldn't remember the last time he'd been intimate enough with someone to want to kiss the back of their neck.

In fact, the last person he'd felt that way about was Nadine, and that had been twelve years ago. Twelve years! The hairs on Dig's arms stood on end as the enormity of this realization hit home. He was thirty years old, and he had no intimacy in his life whatsoever.

He remembered the conversation he'd had with Nadine in the café, what felt like months ago now, about their disastrous love lives, and how they'd made a joke out of it and made that stupid bet. It had seemed funny then, the fact that none of his relationships lasted longer than a couple of weeks, the fact that his taste in women was veering towards the jailable-offence end of things, the fact that ever since he'd had his heart broken twice in his eighteenth year, he'd been able to relate to women only on either a purely sexual or platonic basis. It had seemed funny then, but now, walking down Caversham Road with Delilah and watching love's slightly over-weight dream walking the other way, oblivious to anyone else on the street, Dig felt suddenly and desperately overcome with disappointment.

He looked at Delilah and analysed his responses to her now that he knew for a fact that he wasn't in love with her. Well, there was the obvious and most imme-diate response, that of the unblemished desire to undo all her buttons and clips and zips and watch her clothes fall effortlessly to the floor leaving her luminously white-underweared and ready to party, but then, that was Dig's obvious and most immediate response to looking at any beautiful woman. There was nothing that Dig could do about this constituent of his character – he was *always* going to want to undress beautiful woman. It was just the way he was made.

But did he feel intimacy for Delilah? Did he feel close to her, part of her, *connected* to her? Did he want to kiss the back of her neck on the street? It was an interesting question.

As he followed Delilah's still talking figure through the streets of Kentish Town, he looked at her narrow back and swaying hips and shiny golden hair, and he realized that they were strangers, complete and utter strangers, and that he most certainly did not want to kiss the back of her neck.

Delilah was still going on, about some film that he'd never heard of that had just come out in London and had been number one in the States for the last eight weeks, which was amazing apparently because it had been directed by a twenty-two-year-old woman, and Dig felt that no intelligent response to this conversation was required on his part and he could therefore safely drift back into his thoughts without fear of being asked to comment.

As they walked, Dig found himself staring at other couples, watching the ways they interacted together, deciphering their body language, judging the attractiveness differential between the two parts of each couple and then wondering what other people might make of the Dig and Delilah pairing. Well, they'd probably think that she was very tall and he was very . . . not so tall. But would other people assume that they were an established couple, nothing out of the ordinary, been together for a couple of years – or maybe they looked like they were on a first date? Would anyone be able to guess just by looking at them that they were ex-teenage-sweethearts reunited coincidentally after twelve years and currently sharing a tiny one-bedroom flat together with a ratty dog that she'd named after him? Would anyone guess that he looked at Delilah now and wondered who the hell she was, that he'd once been completely bonded to this person who was now so thick with secrets that talking to her about anything of any importance was like wading through molasses?

353

Dig had had a strange week, a week of change and metamorphosis. For the first time since he was twenty years old Dig was thinking seriously about the future. His ill-judged and unsuccessful attempt at romance last night had been just the tip of the iceberg, because, as he looked at the top of Delilah's golden head, he realized with a mind-cleansing start that even if he wasn't *in love* with Delilah, he wanted to be *in love* with somebody. Anybody. He was on for it. Totally.

CHAPTER THIRTY-SEVEN

At the Bengal Lancer, Archad greeted Dig warmly and with surprise.

'You are very early this evening,' he joked, looking at his watch, and Dig thought, Yes, I am – I have never, in fact been here before eleven o'clock, I have never been here sober and I've never said a word to you that wasn't pliant with alcohol.

Dig was surprised to find the restaurant heaving. It alarmed him to see his favourite restaurant full of so many smart, sober and quiet people – like finding out that your best mate sings folk songs in his spare time.

Archad seated them in a booth at the back of the restaurant and handed them a pair of menus, smiling with excitement at Delilah as he backed away. As Dig looked at Delilah across the table he had a sudden *déjà vu* – the two of them, in Exmouth Market, on Tuesday night – God, had it really been only five days ago? – when he'd been so entranced by her, so thrilled to be sitting in a restaurant with *Delilah Lillie*, the Love of his Life, praying that she'd stay in London, hoping that . . . hoping that – What had he been hoping? Hoping that something would happen, he supposed, that someone would let him fall in love with them, *hoping that something would change.*

And there was no denying that things had changed, although not in any of the ways he might have imagined.

355

It had been a week of firsts. He'd cleaned his car, he'd woken up before nine on a Saturday and arrived at the Lancer before eleven. He'd taken a woman out to dinner, he'd been seen in public with a Yorkshire Terrier, he'd been to Walton-on-Thames and his towel rota was now so royally fucked that he no longer cared whether he was using Tuesday's towel or Thursday's, let alone whether it was black, green, red, dry, damp or dirty.

But most importantly, he felt unblocked. He felt free and alive. Delilah had changed everything. He was ready for love.

He looked up from his menu and scanned the busy restaurant, looking for potential lovees. There were plenty of attractive women in there, that was for sure. *Women* being the operative word. But they were all sitting at little tables for two, smiling at the large, smug men sitting opposite them, men who'd worked it out before Dig, worked out the whole love thing and got there first. The world, he reminded himself, was full to the brim with couples. Everyone knew that. That was what he and Nadine always joked about together. The 'ands', they called all their friends these days. Tim *and* Cat. Si *and* Angela. Robbie *and* Rachel.

Alex *and* Delilah.

Couples. Everywhere. No wonder Dig went out with young girls – they might not be on his wavelength, they might have different interests and priorities, but at least they were available. You know – at least after you'd gone to all the trouble of approaching them and talking to them and getting to know them, they didn't turn round and say, 'Sorry, you're a lovely bloke and everything, but I'm in a long-term committed relationship with that large, smug guy over there.' Or, 'Sorry, but I'm married

356

to a handsome restaurateur who buys me horses and sends me on shopping trips to New York and I only kissed you for a laugh and I'm really only here to track down my long-lost daughter and . . .'

'Dig?'

Dig shook the thoughts from his head and looked up at Delilah. 'Sorry,' he smiled, 'miles away.'

'Are you ready to order?'

'Yeah,' he said, closing his menu, 'yeah.' He didn't have to look at the menu to know what he was going to order. 'So, what are you going to do now?'

'What do you mean?'

'Well – now that you've found Sophie. What are your plans?'

He tensed his body as he waited for her to answer. Please say you're going home, he thought to himself, please say you'll be tidying all your shit away and packing those enormous suitcases and going back to Chester with your weird dog and your pickled onions and your crystals. Please.

'Are you trying to get rid of me?' teased Delilah, grinning at Dig.

'No!' he almost shouted. 'No! Of course not. I just wondered . . .'

'Well. I guess I'll be going back home. To Alex.'

'Is that what you want?'

She nodded. 'More than anything. I've missed him so much.'

'I don't get it,' said Dig, 'if Alex means so much to you, why didn't you tell him you were coming to London? Why did you leave him? You must have really hurt him.'

Delilah nodded again, stiffly, and Dig was alarmed to notice her eyes glaze over with tears. Oh shit – now he'd made her cry. Dig couldn't bear it when girls cried, especially when it was his fault.

'I'm sorry,' he said, grasping her hand across the table, 'I didn't mean to . . .'

She shook her head. 'It's all right,' she said, 'it's fine. It's just that – you're right. I should have told him what I was doing but I was in such a state, it was all so unexpected, I couldn't think about anything else for two weeks and then I just took off. I just never thought it would happen to us, it didn't seem possible, and I never wanted it, I really never wanted it and . . .'

'Delilah!' barked Dig. 'Slow down, for God's sake. I've got no idea what you're talking about.'

'Oh God – I'm pregnant, Dig! I'm pregnant for fuck's sake. Can you believe it? We had sex three times last year *and* we used a diaphragm and I still managed to get pregnant!'

Dig clicked his hanging jaw closed. 'A-ha,' he said. That explains all that puking, he thought.

'And I never wanted a baby. Never. What would I know about being a mother? Look at the example I had.' She raised her eyebrows indignantly. 'I've already given one away and I don't want to do that again. But I can't have a baby, Dig, I just can't! I don't want one and Alex would be so angry. He complained enough when I got the dog.'

Dig was panicking. More heavy stuff. Oh God. 'Can't you – you know,' he stammered, 'can't you?'

'Get rid of it? Oh God – I've thought about it. That was one of the reasons why I came down to London. I couldn't have an – an – a termination at home. It would have been round Chester in seconds, and it's no one's business, is it?' She eyed him angrily. 'And ever since I found out I was pregnant I haven't been able to stop

358

thinking about Isab– about Sophie. She's been haunting me. I suddenly felt like I couldn't make any decisions about this' – she looked at her groin again and Dig realized what she'd been trying to say earlier on when she'd eyed her crotch so cryptically – 'until I'd put a full-stop on the Sophie chapter. The agency told me she'd gone to a good family, a nice family, but at the time I didn't care. I just wanted her away from me – gone. I couldn't bear to look at her or touch her. I didn't care whether she went to live with the Queen or the fucking Yorkshire Ripper, just so long as I never had to see her again. Because, you see, she looks like me now, but when she was born she looked just like him – she really did.'

'The father?'

She nodded, and her face hardened, and Dig sensed that they were approaching the crux of the matter.

He leaned back into the red velvet of the banquette and waited for Delilah to start talking.

silver toenails

The sun was shining the day after Delilah's eighteenth birthday. She'd spent the previous night at Dig's, as she did nearly every night. He'd taken her out for a birthday treat to a wine bar off Oxford Street and they'd shared a bottle of Mateus Rosé and felt like grown-ups. Her mother's house was empty when Delilah let herself in at nine thirty. She'd left a birthday card outside her bedroom door. It was the first time her mother had remembered her birthday in ten years, and Delilah felt a curious surge of warmth rising in her chest.

In her bedroom, Delilah ripped open the envelope and pulled out an embossed and gilded card with a picture of a young girl riding a pony on the front.

> *Daughter Dearest,* said the printed message inside the card,
> *Once you were a tiny thing, with toes and thumbs so small*
> *And now you are a woman, strong and proud and tall*
> *I've fed you and I've loved you, I've nurtured you through strife*
> *But now it's time to let you go and learn to live your life*
> *I'm so proud of you, daughter dearest*
> *Happy 18th Birthday*

She'd signed it 'All love, Mum' and she'd even scribbled a couple of kisses underneath her name. Delilah felt choked with strange emotions. Despite the fact that a stranger had worded the message inside the card, it was her mother who had chosen it, who'd picked it up in a shop and paid for it, put a Biro to it, licked the envelope and left it outside Delilah's room. It was the kindest, least selfish thing her mother had ever done. Delilah felt a wondrous sense of her life opening up: she and Dig were going to get engaged, he was going to get them a place to live, she could sign on at last and stop working at that shitty chemist, and now this – an unprecedented gesture of maternal love. The future looked brighter than it had ever done before.

She had a bath, washed her hair, slipped into her dressing-gown and enjoyed the rare peace and quiet in her usually chaotic home. On her bed, she stretched out a long, white leg, picked up a bottle of silver nail polish and began to paint her toenails.

Downstairs, the front door slammed shut, loudly enough to make Delilah jump. The brush slipped in her hand and left a smear of polish down the side of her toe.

'Fuck.'

She got to her feet and peered down the stairwell, towards the front door ahead.

It was Michael, her stepfather.

He was leaning heavily against the door, his clothing awry, his face caked in dirt and bloody scabs.

'What the fuck happened to you?' she said, climbing down the stairs. Michael looked at her sheepishly. 'Jesus Christ, look at your face.'

Delilah had known Michael since she was five years old. He was a quiet, repressed, almost terminally shy

man who rarely spoke. Delilah suspected he had
learning difficulties. He'd been teetotal when he'd met
Delilah's mother, just after her father died of cirrhosis,
but thirteen years and five children later was a consummate drinker, his life punctuated by pub opening times
and visits to the off-licence. He lived on beef-and-onion
crisps, which he ate six packs at a time, and he had about
him a permanent aroma of stale smoke and Monster
Munch.

Michael let Delilah manoeuvre him into the front
room and on to the threadbare sofa. He stank. She peeled
his leather jacket from his obese frame and threw it over
the arm of the sofa.

'Where've you been, Michael? What's happened?'
Delilah often found herself talking to Michael as though
he were a child.

Michael shook his head distractedly.

'Did someone hit you?'

He opened his mouth to speak and Delilah was almost
knocked sideways by his vaporous breath. 'Oh Jesus,
Michael, you're pissed. It's bloody ten o'clock in the
morning and you're pissed.'

'Your mother,' he said, shaking his head slowly, 'your
mother.'

'What did she do?'

'She kicked me out, didn't she? Kicked me out last
night. Your mother. Hadn't even finished eating my tea.
And it was sausages and all.'

'Why did she kick you out, Michael?'

He shrugged. 'Hadn't even finished my tea. Your
fucking mother . . .'

Delilah raised her eyebrows. She wasn't going to get
any sense out of him, that much was obvious. 'Here,' she

said, 'I'll go and put the kettle on, make us both a coffee, eh?'

'Yes please, D'lilah – that would be nice.'

Delilah had always felt sorry for Michael. He'd gone straight from the home of his overbearing and abusive mother into the home of another overbearing and abusive woman, taken on her four children and given her another five. Despite the indubitable quality of his sperm, there was no respect in this household for Michael, and now that Delilah was escaping, could see a future beyond these four oppressive walls, she almost wanted to help him. He was more a victim of the Lillie curse than her, in a lot of ways. He was never going to escape. He dug himself further into this open grave with every pint he drank.

She walked back into the front room holding the two mugs of coffee. Michael looked pathetic – fat, unkempt, drunk and pointless.

'There you go,' she said, guiding the mug into his dirty fingers, making sure he'd got a firm grip on it, 'that should make you feel a bit better.'

She stood over him while he took a first tentative sip. He looked up at her, over the rim of the mug, his eyes brown and nicotine-stained, full of disappointment. As he pulled the mug away from his lips, Delilah could see he was smiling.

'Thank you, D'lilah,' he said, 'thank you.'

And for a moment Delilah felt warm and good.

'Delightful . . . de-lovely . . . delicious . . . Delilah,' said Michael. He laughed to himself under his breath. 'Delightful . . . de-lovely . . . delicious . . . Delilah . . . delightful . . . de-lovely . . . delicious . . . Delilah.' He was laughing loudly now and rocking back and forth as he

363

repeated his strange mantra. Delilah began to back away – he was weirding her out – but suddenly the smile fell from his face and he began to cry. He stretched his vast arms upwards and grasped Delilah by the waist. He buried his face into her stomach and began muttering into the cotton of her dressing-gown. 'Thank you, D'lilah, thank you, D'lilah.'

Delilah didn't know what to do. His hair was greasy and smelled bad. His breath was hot against her flesh, his arms suffocating around her waist. She tried to peel his fingers apart and extricate herself from the foul embrace, but the more she tried to get away from him, the harder he held her. Beautiful Delilah, he kept saying, such a beautiful girl, such a nice girl . . . such a nice girl.

She could feel a damp patch on her stomach where his snot and tears were seeping through the cotton. Her heart began to race as a feeling of being trapped over-came her. And then suddenly she was on her back. Suddenly Michael had her by the wrists and was pinning her to the sofa. But you're not a girl, he was saying, his face inches from hers, you're not a girl, not any more, you're a woman now, aren't you, you're eighteen, and you're a woman, and you can do whatever you like, and I can do whatever I like because we're both adults, isn't that right, isn't it, and his breath, his breath smelt like raw meat, and his tongue, when it forced its way through her clenched lips, tasted of stale vomit.

Delilah heard a song in her head while it was happening. It was a song she'd heard on the radio at Dig's that morning. It played over and over in her head in rhythm with Michael's laboured thrusting. As she listened to the song in her head, she stared at her feet, her eyes

364

focusing on the smudge of silver nail polish left on her toe, a reminder of the last thing she'd done before this had happened, the last thing she'd done while she was still happy. Because, even as it was happening, Delilah knew for sure that she was never going to be happy again.

He lay on top of her afterwards, breathing heavily and sweating on to her skin. Delilah felt her breath escaping her as his bulk crushed her diaphragm. And then the front door went. Delilah heard her brothers shouting and careering around, and her mother's harsh Golden Virginia voice telling them to shut up. Thank God, she thought, thank God, Mum's home, she'll look after me.

'*Mum*,' she wheezed, trying to lever Michael's frame off hers, '*Mum. In here.*'

She should have known better. All those years of disinterest and she'd let herself be sucked in by one flimsy birthday card, let herself believe that her mother cared.

'You filthy little fucking slapper!' Delilah felt herself being dragged from the sofa by her elbow and thrown to the floor. 'You *whore!*' She felt the toe of her mother's shoe connecting with her stomach. 'You disgusting *whore*!

'Can't you get your own man, is that it?' she said. 'What's wrong with that eyebrow-on-legs you're always hanging around with? Isn't he giving you enough?'

And then she slapped Delilah around the face, there, in the living room, her husband with his stinking knob still hanging out of his trousers, her daughter with her husband's cum running down the insides of her legs, and her children clinging to her legs, watching everything.

365

She didn't give Delilah a chance to wash herself, or pack more than a few essentials. 'Get out of my house and never come back! As far as I am concerned, I don't have a daughter any more.'

She'd slammed the door behind her, opening it again two seconds later to throw Delilah's jacket out after her, on to the pathway.

Delilah picked it up, dusted it off and began to walk. As she walked, she turned briefly to look behind her at a house where she'd known no joy, and she knew for a fact that she would never see it again.

CHAPTER THIRTY-EIGHT

Dig gulped. 'Why didn't you come to me, Delilah? That day. Why didn't you come to me?'

Delilah had been looking at the ceiling, but now she dropped her head, and the tears that had been suspended in her eyes tumbled down her cheeks. She rubbed her face with her pink napkin and looked into Dig's eyes for the first time since she'd started talking. She looked so vulnerable and so young and Dig wanted to absorb her slight frame into his own.

'I didn't want to be with *anyone*, Dig. I was ruined. Michael ruined me that day. You have to understand that. You were good and pure and kind. You were love to me, Dig, and after that day, for a long, long time, I was a tiny shrivelled-up lump of dog-shit. I couldn't even think about being anywhere near you and your lovely mum and your neat little house and your clean, clean lives. And when you found me that day, at the DSS, I just wanted to disappear. I was standing there with you in the rain and you were so concerned about where I'd been, there was so much love in your eyes – and all I wanted was for the rain to turn to acid and dissolve me, there and then, dissolve me into a pile of mush and wash me away down a drain.

'I tried to make it work with you, for your sake, not for mine. But every time I touched something in your house, every time I got into bed with you I felt like I was contaminating things, dirtying your bedsheets. Every time you touched me I wanted to tell you not to, almost like you'd tell a child not to put their finger in an electric socket. Your mum would bring me a cup of tea in every morning and I used to wash the mug in the bathroom sink before I gave it back to her. I was totally fucked up, Dig, the most fucked up I've ever been, and when my period was late I just lost it. Packed up my stuff and went back to Marina's.

'Of course, it was the last place I should have gone. Once it was confirmed that I was pregnant there was never any question of an abortion, it didn't even come into the equation. Marina's such a devout Catholic. It was unthinkable. And I was too much of a vegetable to do anything about it. I just sat in my room, staring at the walls, feeling this thing growing inside me, day by day totally resigned to my fate, totally resigned to bringing this thing into the world, to giving it life. I felt like a vessel, not a human being. I wasn't Delilah Lillie any more. I didn't wear make-up any more, stopped dying my hair, didn't watch telly, listen to music, anything.

'But that was when I met Alex – he was studying on Primrose Hill. I was nine months pregnant and I tripped and fell. He took me to the hospital and they had to induce the baby because I was bleeding internally and there was a chance that it might have gone into trauma from the fall. So Alex was there when Sophie was born. I told him everything, about Michael. He was so acceptant – he didn't even flinch. He made me feel so calm. Clean, almost. I don't suppose there are many twenty-two-year-old men who would have had the maturity to deal with a situation like that, are there? I knew he was special.

'He kept in touch after that day, took me out every now and then. And then – well – you already know the rest, don't you? Alex always understood, about the sex thing, about me not wanting it. He didn't have a problem with it. I've been seeing someone about it – a shrink – trying to get better, trying to be a sexual person again. It's a very slow process. Every now and then I burst over with love for Alex and I want to give him something. He never asks me for it. I offer it, when I feel strong, when I feel clean. And, if I'm really honest, when I get scared that he's going to find it somewhere else. And I offered it to him six weeks ago and now I'm pregnant, and I thought that coming back to London, finding Sophie, would help me decide what to do. And it just hasn't, Dig. It hasn't at all.'

She started crying then, not loud sobbing, but silent tears. 'What do you think, Dig? Do you think I should have it? Do you think I'd make a good mother? I wouldn't be like my mother, would I? Do you think?' Her expression changed abruptly. 'Sorry. Sorry. That's not fair. I shouldn't have asked you that. You haven't asked for any of this. Oh God. Oh God. Just when you're starting to think that maybe life's quite simple really, it turns around and asks you to divide a hundred and twenty-eight by nineteen.' She smiled, unexpectedly. 'That's something Alex always says,' she said. She put her elbows on the table and ran her fingers through her hair.

Jesus, thought Dig. We might be the same age, but Delilah Lillie is centuries older than I'll ever be. Thirty, to me, just means being a slightly-older-than-I'd-like-to-be teenager. Thirty to Delilah means a lifetime of growing and surviving and really living. I'm just a child, he thought, compared to Delilah, an overgrown child.

I've done nothing. I'm still living in Kentish Town, still in the same job, hanging out with the same people in the same places – I'm even wearing the same jeans. My parents adore me and everything I do. They adore each other. Nothing bad's ever happened to me. I've never known what it's like to be broke. I've never had to make sacrifices or life-and-death decisions. I've never had to keep secrets or face the truth. I've never even been mugged. I've had it *so easy*, he thought, so fucking easy.

'So,' Delilah was saying, 'that's the story. That's Sophie's heritage. She'd be *so* proud, I'm sure, to know where she came from.'

'Fuck, Delilah,' sighed Dig, eloquently, 'what a fucking nightmare.' He shook his head slowly and exhaled loudly and hated himself for being so ill-equipped to deal with this sort of situation, especially as it was him who'd been so desperate for Delilah to open up and talk about things in the first place. He exhaled again and felt his brain scrambling with the effort of finding something, *anything* substantial or helpful to say.

And then, through the fug of thoughts, it came to him, the one thing he could say that he knew was true, that he meant wholeheartedly and that might actually help Delilah.

He took hold of her hands and looked her in the eye. 'You'll be a wonderful mother,' he said, 'I know you will. You shouldn't worry about that.'

Her face softened and she sniffed loudly. 'Do you think so?' she said, and Dig thought to himself that tonight was the first time in a week that he'd seen the old Delilah, the tender, vulnerable, scared girl he'd fallen in love with all those years ago, the Delilah who'd leaned on

370

him so heavily and needed him so much, and made him feel like a man even though he'd been only eighteen years old.

He felt strong suddenly and gripped Delilah's hands even harder. 'You want this baby, don't you?' he said. 'You really want it?'

She nodded, snottily.

'And you're scared, aren't you, scared that you won't be able to love it, like you couldn't love Sophie?'

She nodded again.

'And like your mother couldn't love you?'

'Mmm.' She blew her nose into her napkin.

'Delilah – you're not your mother. I sometimes find it hard to believe that you're from the same gene pool as your mother. You are so full of love. You loved me, I know you did, and look how much you love Alex. You love your horses. You love your dog. You love your little brothers. And I think that deep down somewhere, you did love Sophie. I saw your tears today on her doorstep, I saw the way you looked at her. You love, Delilah, and you will be a great, great mother. Really.'

Delilah looked at Dig with watery eyes and he was moved to see the warmth inside them. 'Thank you, Dig,' she sniffed, 'thank you. That means a lot. It really does. It means – it means – you know – Alex – he'd be such a wonderful dad.' She started to brighten. 'He doesn't think he would. But he would be, I know it. And his parents have got this big treasure chest full of fancy-dress things and there's china dolls and old teddy bears and so much land. We've got ponies and dogs and ducks and trees to climb and secret gardens to explore. Any child would be happy there, don't you think? Even with an old bag like me for a mother!' And then she

371

laughed and Dig laughed, and he noticed that she'd picked up her cutlery and was spooning cubes of chicken tikka on to her plate, and he supposed that must mean that the crisis was over. But there was still something he wanted to ask her.

'Don't you ever want, you know – revenge? Don't you ever want to kill him?'

Delilah stopped, her spoon suspended over her plate. 'Who? Michael?'

Dig nodded.

'No,' she said, thoughtfully, 'no. He's going to spend the rest of his life with my mother. In that house. That's punishment enough. That's a life sentence.' She cleared her throat and deposited some rice on to her plate.

'I would have,' said Dig, decisively, 'I would have killed him. If you'd come to see me that night and told me what he'd done I would have gone straight round there and killed him. With my bare hands. Honestly.' Dig stopped when he realized that Delilah was smiling at him. 'What?'

'Oh, Dig. You're so lovely, aren't you? So good.' She patted his hand, which he'd unconsciously furled into a fist, and Dig blushed. 'Why the hell haven't you got a girlfriend? What are you doing wasting your time with all these young things when you could be making someone so happy? Someone real?'

Dig averted his gaze from hers and busied himself piling curry on to his plate, barely aware of what he was doing. His face was burning crimson. He wasn't used to people telling him how lovely he was.

'I mean,' continued Delilah, 'you're hardly the archetypal playboy, are you? It's not you. It doesn't suit you. Don't you ever want – more?'

372

Dig laid down his cutlery and rested his head in his hands, as much an attempt to cover his blazing face as to compose himself. Still feeling rather pleased with himself for the way he'd handled the whole drama-in-the-Lancer scenario just then, for having been able to dispense useful, helpful advice to a friend in distress, he now felt capable of doing the mature thing and opening up to Delilah.

'Never even thought about it till you turned up,' he said, frankly. He told her about the girl he'd slept with on his thirtieth birthday and the conversation he and Nadine had had over breakfast, which neither of them had taken at all seriously. He told her about his reaction to bumping into her in the park, how excited he'd been about their dinner date, how spellbound he'd been by her that night and blown away by their unexpected kiss in the back of the cab. He described the feelings of growth and change that her presence instilled in him, his sudden need to extend himself and expect more from life – more money, more success, more respect, more ambition and, most importantly, more love.

'This morning, when I left the flat to follow you, I was looking at all those people out and about, doing their thing, with their kids and their jobs and their responsibilities, and for the first time ever I found myself thinking, Yeah, I could do that, I could be like those people. You know, a nice woman, a kid, a dog – a nice, *big* dog – a proper flat instead of a shoebox, holidays twice a year, in-laws, anniversaries, early nights, all that. But then I realized something. It's too late, isn't it? I've left it too late. Basically, the foundation for all that stuff is the right woman – yeah? None of that is going to happen without the woman, that's where it all starts.

But all the women I know are in couples. Everywhere I look – couples. There aren't any decent single women around. I thought you were single and look how wrong I was. All the good ones are taken.'

Delilah smiled and nodded. 'You're just saying what women of my age have been saying for years. But I don't think it's true, actually. This is about the age when a lot of relationships that started at school or college or whatever start showing the strain, start breaking down. There's a whole seam of newly single men and women looking for someone, but the *right* person this time, someone they can spend the rest of their lives with, have children with.'

'Desperate women, you mean. I'm not interested in desperate, last-chance-saloon women who are looking for sperm and – and – ' he puffed a bit as he ran out of steam and held his hands up in defeat.

'What are you looking for, Dig? Who's your ideal woman? Describe her to me.'

'Well – she'd be you, I suppose, but without the husband and the baby and the dog.'

Delilah raised her eyebrows. 'Seriously.'

'Hmm. Well, seriously, she'd be beautiful, of course, and slim, definitely. Blonde would be good and nice perky tits. Sorry' – he shrugged – 'I'm shallow about that sort of thing – I live in London, I can't help it. And – well – she'd be the same sort of age as me – or she could be a very mature twenty-two, I suppose.

'She'd have to be intelligent, but not intellectual. Intellectual people scare the life out of me and you could never go to the cinema to see crap films or watch *EastEnders*. She'd have to have a healthy appetite, you

374

know, really enjoy her food. Especially curry. And it would be great if she could cook.

'She'd like pubs, have similar taste in music to me, be sociable, but sensible, too, if we're going to have babies. She couldn't be too much of a party animal. I'd want her to be someone who I could rely on, who'd be where she said she was going to be, not too flighty.

'And . . . and' – he tapped his fingernails off his teeth as he considered – 'money would be good.' He nodded. 'I wouldn't object to a woman with a nice healthy bank balance. A family girl would suit me, too – someone who's as close to her parents as I am, who understands the little apron-strings I can't quite cut off. And' – he clicked his fingers at the arrival of a new thought – '*tidy*. She would absolutely have to be reasonably tidy. I mean, I wouldn't expect her to be quite as over-the-top as me, obviously. But reasonably tidy would be good.'

'So, you're not too fussy, then?' smiled Delilah, teasingly.

Dig smiled and leaned back in the banquette. 'I guess,' he said, 'the most important thing is a girl who I can look at in bed when I wake up on a Saturday morning and just think – great, it's the weekend and I'm with my girl, and whatever we do today it's going to be great because she's my best friend and I love being with her.'

Delilah was nodding and smiling. 'Well, congratulations,' she said, offering him her hand to shake, 'that was the correct answer. You are, officially, mature enough to handle a grown-up relationship. But hmm . . . let me think . . . there's only one problem, isn't there?' She was camping it up, rubbing her chin with her fingertips and feigning confusion. Dig wondered what the hell she was doing.

'What's that?' he said.

'Well, where *on earth* are you going to find a woman to fit those criteria. I mean, they don't exist, do they?'

'Exactly!' said Dig. 'Exactly.'

'There's just no such thing as a beautiful, intelligent, single woman who likes curry and pubs, who's tidy and sensible and family-minded and who you could consider to be your best friend, is there?' She slapped her forehead with the palm of her hand in mock-exasperation. Dig was thoroughly confused by her strange carrying-on.

'Not in my experience, no,' he said, conclusively.

'Oh, but wait! Silly me! I know just the girl. I can't believe I didn't think of her before. She's perfect for you. You'll love her.' She leaned down to pick up her handbag and started ferreting around in it. 'I'll give you her number.'

Dig was suddenly all ears. 'Oh yeah,' he said, 'who is she? What's she like?'

'She's like your perfect woman, Dig. She's thirty, she's beautiful, she's successful, she's sweet and she's kind, and you'll absolutely love her.'

'Yeah but – will she like me? If she's that great won't she just think I'm a bit of a wanker?'

'No,' said Delilah, scribbling on a piece of Filofax paper, 'no. She'll think you're perfect. You're just her type, I promise you.' She clicked the lid back on to her pen and slid the piece of paper across the table towards Dig. 'Ring her,' she said, sternly, 'ring her right now.'

Dig picked up the sliver of paper and held it in front of his nose:

020 7485 2121

His face creased in confusion. 'But – but – I don't get it. This is *Nadine's* number.'

Delilah smiled at him.

'Why have you given me Nadine's number?'

Delilah frowned. 'Blimey, Dig,' she said, 'no wonder intellectuals scare you. You're not exactly bright spark of the month, are you?'

'Oh,' said Dig, smiling grimly, 'oh, *I see*. You're back on one of these matchmaking crusades. *I* get it.' He shook his head and handed the piece of paper back to Delilah. 'You just don't get it, do you? This isn't going to happen. Nadine and I are never going to be like that. If it was going to happen, it would have happened by now.'

'*Why?*' exclaimed Delilah. 'I don't understand. What the hell is the matter with you two? Why hasn't it happened?'

Dig sighed and rubbed his face with the palms of his hands. 'I dunno,' he sighed, 'it just wasn't meant to be, I guess. I tried and she wasn't interested and she's never shown even the slightest sign of . . . you know?'

Delilah slapped her hand down on the table-top and made Dig jump. 'So you have! I knew it! I knew that there must be something more than just this supposed platonic friendship bullshit. Tell me what happened. Tell me everything.'

Dig was starting to regret his candour – it was taking him places he had no interest in being. He took a breath and composed himself to tell Delilah the story of September 1987.

'So,' he said, afterwards, 'Nadine didn't want me, OK? She told me: "I don't want you." You don't get the truth much plainer than that. She wanted more than me.

She wanted a Man. She wanted sports cars and trendy clothes and life experience and brooding good looks. Not spotty little Dig Ryan with his Honda Civic and his crappy job and his skinny legs. And it took me a while to get used to the idea, you know. For months I found it hard to be around her without wanting to – you know – but it's good now. She's my mate. She's a huge part of my life and I'm grateful for that. Life without Nadine would be empty and meaningless. But, Delilah – I know you mean well and everything, but forget it, OK. Because it just isn't going to happen.'

Delilah was shaking her head. 'God, Dig. I wish you could sit where I'm sitting just for a few moments, see what I see, what *anyone* can see when they look at you and Nadine. I wish you could see it, get over some stupid, childish shit that happened ten years ago and see it objectively.' She sighed deeply and passed the piece of paper back to Dig. 'Keep this,' she said, folding it into his palm, 'keep this bit of paper. Maybe one day you'll find it in your wallet and you'll remember this conversation and you'll do the right thing. Yes?' she said, beetling her eyebrows and squeezing his clamped hand.

'Yeah,' sighed Dig, 'whatever.'

He slid the piece of paper into his coat pocket and set about trying to consume some of the food that was congealing on his plate.

What a day, he thought to himself as he masticated on a flavourless piece of lamb – why did food always taste so awful when he was with Delilah? – what a fucking unbelievable day. He suddenly felt exhausted beyond words. He wasn't hungry, he wasn't thirsty, and there was no way he could revert to smalltalk with Delilah now.

378

But the funniest thing of all was that in spite of the painful conversation they'd just had and everything that had happened in the past week, as he sat there contemplating his cold curry and absorbing the strange atmosphere, Dig suddenly realized that all he wanted in the whole world was to see Nadine.

CHAPTER THIRTY-NINE

Bang Bang Bang

'Uuurgghh.'

Bang Bang Bang

'Neuuughhh.'

'*Nadine!*'

'Oh. Jesus.' Nadine peeled open one eye and then the other. The blurred images of textiles, bits of furniture and the watercolours on the wall that were forming on her retinas meant nothing to her.

She attempted to stand up. 'Oh, Jesus!' She started to panic. She couldn't move her legs. She didn't *have* any legs. She was crippled. She was paralysed. She was . . . oh . . . she was all twisted up in the bedcovers.

'*Nadine! Are you in there? Are you all right? Let me in.*' *Bang Bang Bang.*

It was Pia. It was . . . she was . . . oh, God. Nadine's head was like a . . . like a . . . a horrible thing, just a horrible, horrible, *horrible* thing. Where was she? Where the hell was she? What was this place?

She opened her mouth to try to shout something through the door, but nothing left her lips but foul, sticky breath. Uuugghh. She was going to have to get to the door somehow. It was dark, the only light coming from a tangerine streetlight just outside her open curtains. Barcelona, she suddenly remembered – she was in Barcelona. But what day was it?

She finally managed to extricate herself from the bed-clothes and crawled across the carpet towards the door. 'Coming,' she managed to croak, as she dragged herself along on hands and knees, 'I'm coming.'

She hauled the door open and blinked into the bright light. Looming above her was Pia and, on either side of her, two enormous Spanish men wearing black jackets and concerned expressions.

'Christ, Deen,' squeaked Pia, crouching down and putting her skinny little arm around her shoulders, 'are you OK?'

'Mmmm,' grunted Nadine, shielding her eyes from the light and the gaze of the two huge men above her, 'my head. My head. What day is it? How long have I been asleep?'

'It's still Saturday night, Deen,' said Pia, stroking some hair out of Nadine's face. 'It's nearly half ten. You've been gone two hours.' She turned to smile at the two men behind her, one of whom, Nadine could now see, was carrying a large bunch of keys.

'Looks like it's OK,' she grinned at them, 'sorry to have dragged you all the way up here. *Muchos gracias* and everything.'

'The señorita is well?' asked the man with the keys.

'The señorita's going to be just fine,' she soothed.

'We get room service maybe, to bring up some coffee?'

'That,' grinned Pia, 'would be absolutely smashing. Make it two. *Multo gracias!*'

Pia clicked the door closed behind them and lay down on the floor next to Nadine's prone figure. They lay and contemplated the ceiling for a moment.

'You know your phone's off the hook, don't you?' said

Pia, turning towards Nadine, who had covered her face with her elbow and was groaning under her breath.

'Shit,' she moaned, 'fuck.'

'When you didn't come back from the toilet, we tried to phone you, and when it was engaged we just assumed you must have run up here to phone Dig. After two hours we started thinking that even *you* couldn't spend that long on the phone. So, did you? Did you call Dig? Were we right? Were we right?!' She rolled over on to her stomach and faced Nadine, holding her chin on her hand.

Nadine nodded. 'Mmmm,' she mumbled.

'Yes!' exclaimed Pia triumphantly. 'I knew it. Jesus – that Sarah really opened a can of worms, didn't she, coming out with all that stuff about you and Dig? You should have seen your face, Deen – it was priceless! So – what did you say to him? What happened? Did you declare undying love, or what?!'

Nadine rolled on to her side. 'Got to hang the phone up, Pia, it might still be – you know – what's the word? Attached. No . . . no . . . that other word – you know? Urrgghh.'

Pia leaped to her feet and strode towards the telephone. She put the misplaced receiver to her ear and listened. 'No,' she said, replacing it, 'it's all right. You're not connected.' She perched on the edge of the bed. 'So. Tell me. What happened?'

Nadine pulled herself to a sitting position. It was all coming back to her now. Oh yes – it most certainly was. Oh bloody hell. Oh bloody bloody hell. Blood rushed to her head with the shame of it and her face creased up with mortification. 'Oh no,' she muttered, 'oh Pia. I can't believe what I did. It's too awful. I can't tell you.'

382

Pia's face blossomed with excitement. 'What?' she screeched. 'What have you done?'

'Oh no. Oh no. I'm never going to be able to face him again. Oh fucking hell.' She cradled her head on her knees and began rocking back and forth as she remembered every last detail.

'What happened – will you just tell me – please. I can't bear it!'

'I left a message on his answerphone.'

'Oh no!' Pia clasped her hands over her mouth. 'You mean like Rachel did in that episode of *Friends*.'

Nadine threw her a bemused look.

'You know! When she went on a date with that bloke and got really drunk and phoned Ross and said "this is closure" to his answerphone and then' – she picked up on Nadine's lack of comprehension and trailed off – 'no? Never mind. Anyway' – she brightened – 'what did you say?'

Nadine shuddered and caught the cigarette that Pia had just thrown her. 'Well – first time I phoned him, *Delilah* answered.'

'Delilah? Who the fuck is Delilah?' Pia lit her cigarette and threw the lighter to Nadine.

Nadine sighed. 'Delilah,' she said, 'remember? I told you about her last week. The Love of Dig's Life. They were teenage sweethearts.'

'Oh, yes,' nodded Pia, although Nadine knew full well she had no recollection whatsoever of the conversation.

'She and Dig split up when they were eighteen and they lost touch. And now she's back, for some unknown reason. And ever since she's been here she's been attached to Dig like a fucking leech. I don't *exist* any more as far as Dig's concerned. We haven't even been

383

talking to each other for the past week.' She hauled herself off the floor and joined Pia on the bed, to share the empty champagne bottle she was using as an ashtray. 'And then last night I went round there because of Phil . . .'

Pia rolled her eyes dramatically. 'Who is Phil?'

'Don't ask. No one. Nothing. Anyway, I turned up there and there was this flash meal laid out on the table – candles, music, the works. And this disgusting little dog who turns out to be – guess who? – *Delilah's* dog. And then *she* appears, just got out of the shower, all skinny, wearing a towel this big.' She indicated half a centimetre between finger and thumb. 'I just lost it, you know? I suppose it was pretty immature of me but I couldn't help it. It just really, really upset me. I ran off, got into the car, went home – all very drama-queen. But it was just – it was just – *Delilah*, you know? Delilah-fucking-Lillie. All over again. She gets to me, she's under my skin, even after all these years, she's there and I've tried so hard to put it all in the past, start afresh with her, but I just can't do it. She has this effect on me. And she has this other effect on Dig. He can't see sense while she's around. He turns into a total spaz.'

Pia nodded empathetically.

'So when I heard her voice just now on the phone, in Dig's flat, like she fucking *owned* the place, I went a bit mad. I burst into tears first – snot and everything – and then afterwards I calmed down a bit. And then . . . and then – oh God' – she ran her fingers through her mussed-up hair – 'I managed to convince myself that I needed to be a grown-up about all of this. I decided that the best thing to do would be to confront Delilah, talk to her, find out what her intentions were, kind of thing.

So I called back – but this time there was no answer. I hung up. I was *furious*, convinced that they were both there, deliberately not picking up the phone. I got myself really wound up, imagining them there, looking at the phone, laughing at poor, mad Nadine.'

'*Room service.*'

Pia stubbed out her cigarette and grinned widely at the embarrassed young waiter who'd arrived with their coffee. 'Gracias,' she beamed at him as he backed nervously out of the oestrogen-rich room.

As she lowered herself back on to the bed, her smiling, flirting face automatically rearranged itself back into its former picture of sympathetic attentiveness. 'Go on,' she said.

'Yeah. So. I got myself more and more wound up, and before I knew it I'd picked up the phone again and – and – when the answerphone clicked on I just let rip.'

'Oh God – what? What did you say?' Pia passed her a cup of coffee.

Nadine slurped on it gratefully. 'I said something along the lines of' – she cleared her throat – '"I give up. He's yours. Have him."'

Pia winced.

'Oh but it gets worse,' warned Nadine, ruefully, reddening as her words echoed in her ears, 'it gets much worse.'

She'd thought she was being so calm, so mature, so *wise*.

'Have him,' she'd said, trembling, a hastily lit and illicit cigarette shaking between her fingers. 'He's yours. I've had ten years to do something about it and I didn't, so I guess it's fair enough. I'm not going to let you get

385

to me any more – oh no – I'm moving on, Delilah and you're welcome to him. Have him, wind him round your finger for a while and then dump him again. See if I care. Break his little heart again. It's not my problem any more. I'm done. I'm through. Goodbye.'

She'd put the phone down then, her heart thumping loudly under her viscose dress and before she'd even had a chance to think about what she'd just done, she'd had another thought and was picking up the phone again and dialling.

She'd stubbed her cigarette out viciously as she waited for Dig's bloody stupid James Bond message to finish. She was on a roll now and couldn't stomach delays and time-wasting.

'And,' she'd said, hysterically, after the beep, 'another thing. This is a message for you, Dig. *I lied*!' she'd cried, adrenalin almost leaking from her ears, 'I lied when I said I didn't want you. OK? L-I-E-D. Because I did. I did want you, actually. And I always have and I still do. And – and – I'm drunk. I'm very, very, *very* drunk. I'm plastered. And I've been thinking about things and thinking about *your* things, you know, your willy, mainly, and your flat and your sofa and Ikea and bits of lint on the carpet and I miss them all and I miss you and I lied. Just so long as you know that I lied. Have a good life. Bye. I'll always love you. Bye.'

And then she'd hung up – and then again and then again as the blessed phone refused to sit in its cradle. She remembered feeling quite pleased at the time, quite pleased with the way it had gone. 'That's that sorted, then,' she'd thought to herself, her mouth set hard and her hands still shaking. She'd lit another cigarette, opened her mini-bar, made some kind of hellish cocktail from brandy, gin and San Miguel, knocked it back, been to the bathroom, thrown it up and then collapsed on the bed into a stuporous and immediate sleep.

'Oh shitting hell, Deen,' tutted Pia, shaking her head from side to side, her eyes like saucers. 'Shitting bloody hell. You've really done it now, haven't you?'

Nadine nodded heavily and collapsed backwards on to the bed. 'This is – awful. This is the most awful, awful thing. Just awful . . .'

'Did you mean all that, then? All that stuff about wanting him?'

Nadine nodded. And then shook her head. And then nodded again. 'Oh God. I don't know. This is all too much. I can't deal with it. My head hurts.'

'You know something, Deen. If all that was true, then it's good, you know? It's good that you said it. Life's too short and you're not getting any younger and at least this way you'll know. You'll know one way or the other. And I wouldn't get too worked up about this Delilah chick. It's like . . . it's like – ' her face lit up suddenly – 'it's like *Dawson's Creek*! You know – Joey not realizing how she really felt about Dawson until glam Jen came along with all her New York sophistication. But Dawson wasn't really into Jen, not really. She was just a fantasy. But she was also the catalyst for both of them to wake up and see that they really wanted each other. Except they split up – but then, they are only sixteen, I suppose. Even though you wouldn't think it, the way they talk to each other . . .'

Nadine eyed Pia with disbelief. 'You watch *way* too much television,' she sighed disparagingly, 'and besides. This isn't television. This is real life. *My* life. And I've just fucked it up.'

387

Pia shook her head sagely. 'Television *is* life. And life *is* television.'

'Well, your life is, obviously,' snorted Nadine, wondering at the shallowness of the youth of today.

'No. Everyone's lives. And I'll bet you that by the time we get back to London, Delilah will be gone and you'll see Dig and you'll kiss, and it'll be Ross and Rachel and Joey and Dawson and Harry and Sally all rolled into one. I mean – *Delilah* – honestly. There is *no way* Dig could end up with someone called Delilah. It just wouldn't happen. It's not real life.'

Nadine wanted Pia to go now. The conversation was getting unbelievably silly, and her head hurt, and she just wanted to lie there for a while on her own, torturing herself with word-perfect recollections of the messages she'd left on Dig's answerphone. She clutched her face as she remembered what she'd said about his willy.

Oh God.

How could she have said that? How could she have mentioned Dig's willy? Nadine had never even *seen* Dig's willy. It threw the entire dynamic of their friendship, their relationship, inside out. It changed everything. She could have covered up everything else she'd said, made out she was just being drunkenly overemotional. She could have got away with all the other stuff – but not that. Not the willy thing.

It was all over now. Things were never going to be the same again.

CHAPTER FORTY

A sense of madness descended upon Dig as he drove towards Nadine's.

That message. It can't have been real. It just can't have. Must have been some kind of joke. There was just no way – no way.

'Did you put her up to this?' he'd asked Delilah after the stunned silence that had followed the end of the second message. Delilah had just shaken her head, numbly.

'Do you promise?' he'd asked desperately.

'Of course I didn't,' she'd snapped. 'Don't be so ridiculous. I've had slightly more important things to worry about the last few days than constructing some kind of elaborate practical joke. I told you. It's what I've been telling you all along. That's all. It's the truth and now you're actually going to have to do something about it. I'll put the kettle on,' she'd sighed, stroking his arm, 'you'd better give her a ring.' She'd looked horribly tired and Dig had felt guilty, inadvertently dragging her through yet another emotional quagmire after the day she'd had.

He'd phoned Nadine after he'd recovered from the initial shock and had been more than a little surprised to find that she was having a party. He couldn't believe that she hadn't invited him. Some girl whose voice he didn't recognize had answered the phone, and there'd been loud music in the background. He'd said, 'Is Nadine there?', and she'd said, 'I dunno, I dunno. Hold on.' She'd sounded very drunk, and when he was still holding on nearly three minutes later he'd hung up and attempted to watch the telly, instead, intending to deal with it in the morning. No point discussing it with her now, he'd thought, she'll be too pissed. Better to wait until tomorrow, until we've both had a chance to think about this, much better to wait. But waiting had, of course, been impossible. This had to be talked about now. It was too weird and too scary. It was *madness*.

She couldn't really have said that thing, could she? That thing about his willy. He must have misheard it.

It was a clear night for once as Dig drove in a daze towards Gordon House Road. A Saturday night, he reminded himself, the night when he and Nadine would usually be in a pub somewhere, either locally or in town, either with friends or just the two of them, either single or with current partners. They would be getting their last round in about now, a curry would be imminent. The world would be a simple place, full of warm friend-ship and deep affection and unspoken feelings of love and togetherness all wrapped up in a lovely, lagery blur. Nadine would be wearing some outrageous dress or other that she'd picked up earlier in the week from a second-hand shop, and wherever they were, her loud laughter and loud clothes, her vociferousness and her humour would light the place up, even the dingiest corner of the dingiest pub. There'd usually be some bloke sitting next to her, some sad idiot, shell-shocked by his extraordinary companion, amazed that someone like her had ever agreed to go out with someone like him, his face inert with nervous delight.

Could that incredible, bright, flamboyant and utterly unattainable woman, that self-contained, self-assured, and infuriatingly independent woman really be the same one who'd left that hysterical message on his answer-phone, the same one who claimed to have been thinking about his willy? Nadine? Thinking about his willy? Maybe she was on drugs. Maybe someone at this party of hers had slipped her a little something. Yes, he decided, turning left into her road, that was the only explanation. Nadine was on drugs.

He could hear the music pounding from her flat even before he'd got out of his car – which was another worrying thing. Nadine had never had a party at her flat before. She'd had parties, but she'd always hired rooms and studios and restaurants because she couldn't bear the thought of her lovely, mad, overstuffed, piled-up, spilling-over, bright and colourful flat being trashed by a load of drunken friends who she'd feel too guilty to shout at. Dig felt a little uneasy concern rising in his chest.

It took a few minutes for someone to come to the door. Dig watched the smudged blur of a human form making its way to the internal front door through the thick opaque glass. Looked like a bloke. Dig cleared his throat and breathed in deeply, trying to quieten his thumping heart. He felt suddenly and overwhelmingly awkward. What was he going to say once he was face to face with Nadine? What the hell was he going to say? He'd been in such a rush to get round here that he'd hardly given a thought to what would happen once he *was* here.

'*Yeah – who is it?*' rumbled a hoarse male voice on the entry phone.

'It's Dig,' he shouted back, 'who's that?'

'*Eh?*'

'It's Dig,' he yelled, this time through the letter-box.

'*Dig! Little Dig! Cool. Fucking excellent!*' He could hear various locks and chains being undone and then the door slowly opened. A very thin, gaunt man with a mop of dirty hair and a threadbare lambswool sweater on shuffled out into the hallway. He was barefoot against the mosaic terracotta tiling in the communal hall and was holding in one hand a can of Kestrel and half a mangy-looking spliff. He was grinning so much that Dig could see his gums. He had terrible teeth. And he was limping.

As he opened the front door he placed his hands on Dig's shoulders and grinned at him even more. 'Looking good, Dig, looking really good. Fuck, man, it's great to see you.'

He enveloped Dig in a minor hug then, and Dig was almost knocked out by the smell of fags and booze and unwashed hair. Jesus Christ, who *was* this person? It was only as the man released him from the hug and pulled back to appraise him that Dig realized who it was. He hadn't recognized him because he'd been smiling, and he'd never seen him smiling so genuinely before.

'Phil?' he said, uncertainly.

'Come in, man, come in. I tell you – it's fucking blinding in there.' He began limping across the tiled flooring again, towards the door.

Dig followed him, suspiciously. Phil? What was Phil doing here? And what the hell had happened to him in the last ten years? He looked terrible – ravaged, ill and half destroyed. There was nothing left to remind Dig of that shiny, pretentious, leather-trousered tosser he'd first encountered all those years ago, except maybe the shape of his jaw and the line of his nose. But these once-defining features were lost now in a network of sharp angles and deep crevasses that looked like they'd been carved into his face by a psychopath.

As they entered Nadine's pink-foil-wrapped hallway Dig stopped in his tracks. This wasn't right. Something wasn't right. These weren't Nadine's friends. They were all far too young. There was a girl sitting on Nadine's art deco cabinet, the one she'd picked up off a skip in Highgate one night after a party and had made Dig help her carry all the way home. It had taken them two and a half hours and they'd had to keep stopping every minute or so to put it down because it weighed a ton and was cutting into their hands. Dig had resented every minute of it and complained the whole way, but he'd had a soft spot for it since, feeling that although it was Nadine's cabinet it was for ever a part of him. And now there was a girl he didn't know sitting on it, sitting on a pile of Nadine's precious magazines, swinging her fat-trainered feet back and forth and hitting the shiny walnut of the cabinet clunk clunk clunk. She had several facial piercings and was drinking Ernest & Julio Chardonnay from the bottle. She threw Dig a disinterested look as he walked past her and knocked back another mouthful. There was a bloke sitting at her feet on the floor, also multi-pierced and flicking through a copy of *Red* magazine. He was tapping his feet manically, to the beat of some kind of unidentifiable dance music emanating very loudly from Nadine's living room.

Dig followed Phil's skinny, limping figure towards the living room, stepping over the man on the floor, and began scanning the flat for any sign of Nadine. He saw a nugget of ash drop from the end of Phil's spliff, and rubbed it into the dark-green carpet with the sole of his foot as he passed over it, tutting under his breath at Phil's lack of respect for other people's carpets. He was starting to make a little sense of the situation now. These were obviously *Phil's* friends. Nadine had thrown a party and invited Phil and he'd invited some of his mates, and it explained entirely why Nadine hadn't invited him – quite apart from the fact that they weren't on speaking terms: because she knew he didn't like Phil.

Poor Nadine he thought to himself. She must be hating this. I bet she's wishing she'd never even suggested the idea now. And I bet she's wishing she'd never got in touch with Phil again, out of the blue – he's not exactly heart-throb material any more. And all this weirdness here might go some way to explaining her bizarre telephone messages.

Dig tapped Phil on the shoulder and shouted into his ear. 'Just going to get myself a drink,' he said, indicating the kitchen at the top of the hallway. He suddenly realized that there was no way he'd be able to face Nadine without at least a glass of wine.

'Yeah,' said Phil, effusively, 'yeah. Of course, man. Get yourself a drink and I'll see you in there. We can have a chat – I want to find out what you've been up to. Yeah?'

'Yeah,' said Dig, straining to hear him over the thump of the music.

As he approached the kitchen, Dig noticed that someone had spilt a bottle of red wine on to the green carpet, leaving a large brown stain roughly the same shape as South America seeping into the pile. The bottle was still on its side, next to the stain. Dig leaned down to pick it up and tutted again. He couldn't *believe* that Nadine was letting her flat get trashed like this. There were about ten people in the kitchen. Most of them were sitting around her table, making spliffs and flicking mindlessly through yet more of her beloved magazines. Some of the glossy publications were being used as table mats and had buckled with spilt liquid. A copy of *Wallpaper* lay on the floor and had been walked all over a few times by the look of it. It was smeared with muddy brown footprints, and pages from it had been dislodged and dragged across what Dig could now see was a sodden, booze-soaked linoleum.

There was a page at his feet. '*Pouffes*,' ran the now-grubby headline, '*the last bastion of bad taste.*'

A girl with scarlet hair was in the middle of telling the rest of the room what was, she seemed to think, a very interesting story about her mother's new boyfriend. 'He's a fuck-in' wanker,' she said in a soft Cardiff accent. 'He calls me Tania – I keep tellin' him it's pronounced Tar-nia, but 'e's so thick. It's always Tan-ia. And I wouldn't be at all surprised if he was a fuck-in' *paedo*-phile, you know? The way he looks at my little sister . . .' She shuddered and a few people mumbled in response. It was quite obvious from the reaction that nobody was very interested in what Tarn-ia thought of anything.

A couple of people looked up as Dig walked in and then looked down again. He walked towards the fridge and nearly gasped out loud when he saw the state of the kitchen work surfaces. There was a veritable *Withnail and I*-style arrangement of festering washing-up piled up in the sink, which made no sense, as Nadine had a dishwasher. There were empty soup cans just left, their lids only semi-removed and sticking up like snapping jaws, and there was some kind of multicoloured, uniden-tifiable goo slavered all down the white plastic sides of the swing bin. The pools of liquid all over the oak surfaces had attracted particulated detritus – ash, sugar, crumbs and tobacco clung to the work surfaces, hardened and dried. Packets of cereal sat around, open-mouthed, and a crumb-embedded tub of Olivio had developed a rancid yellow coating.

Jesus, thought Dig, this is disgusting. And look – how the hell had that happened? – one of the panes in the window that looked out over Nadine's neighbour's garden had been smashed, and there was a Dorothy Perkins carrier bag taped over it.

This was all wrong. The image confronting him was at complete odds with everything he knew about Nadine's kitchen, with every memory of it. Nadine's kitchen was one of the best places in the world. He lost count of the hours he'd spent sitting at her faux-gingham, Formica-topped table (donated by the Italian owner of their previously favourite greasy spoon when it had closed down three years ago) watching her knocking together a quick pasta or a moussaka or – it made him drool just thinking about it – one of her home-made pizzas with chorizo and chilli. She always had some kind of music playing, it had been Belle and Sebastian last time, he recalled.

Her smart little CD-player was festooned now with destitute CDs, the neat pile that usually rested against it up-ended, disordered and pilfered.

On summer evenings, the sun set directly into Nadine's kitchen, it sometimes seemed. She'd have the windows wide open, and as the sun sank the walls of the room would turn a warm, toasty peach, and the birds outside would turn up the volume and Nadine would twitch her floral-clad bottom from side to side in time to the music, and the smell of garlic would hit the air, and at moments like that Dig would feel a happiness that emanated almost entirely from his belly, a happiness that had a short shelf-life but was unspeakably wonderful nonetheless.

How was he supposed to reconcile that with this, with this dark, stinking, dirty, soulless room full of strangers and their mess? Finding no wine, he plucked a beer from the fridge and strode towards the living room. He was now thoroughly unsettled. He had to see Nadine. This couldn't be right, it just couldn't. The vibe was all wrong, totally negative. Nadine's flat felt like it was being squatted. There was no one, he decided, in this room, who he could even vaguely imagine liking, even if they all tried their hardest.

He pulled his cigarettes from his coat pocket and lit one from a dripping red candle before picking his way back over the shredded magazine pages stuck to the floor. He was now so unsure of his place in this once-familiar environment that he wouldn't have been at all surprised to find Nadine stripped-naked and cross-legged in the middle of the floor having rashers of raw bacon stapled to her body by a team of gimps in head-to-toe leather.

The living room was almost pitch black and, at first, appeared to be empty, but as Dig's eyes grew accustomed to the dark he could see that it was, in fact, heaving. The beat pulsated gently through the floorboards, fizzing into the soles of his feet and making him want to dance, despite himself. The Homemaker curtains at the other side of the room had been left open and the window on to the road let in wafts of cool, fresh air which did nothing to alleviate the intense, syrupy body heat that suffused the room.

397

There was, he could now see, a proper DJ set up at the far side of the room, and as he walked towards the centre of the room the bpm. tripled and the room exploded into dazzling strobe lighting. At least thirty people seemed to jump in the air at the same time, their eyes wide and staring.

Jesus, thought Dig, Nadine's having a bloody rave in her flat.

He scanned the room nervously for Nadine, his brain throbbing in time with the flashing lights. All her furniture had been cleared out of the room – her leather deco sofa, her mirrored cocktail cabinet, her bookshelves and bucket chairs, her fluffy leopardskin cushions and purple suede pouffe. Every picture and mirror on the wall had been knocked to a dishevelled angle and – oh no – her favourite mirror of all, the oval bevelled one with the chrome frame, had been smashed cleanly in half.

There were fag-ends on the carpet.

Unable to spy Nadine anywhere, Dig began walking towards Phil, who was sitting on the window-ledge with his bad leg resting on an upturned plastic crate in front of him. The tip of his tongue was just protruding from his lips as he licked the corner of a Rizla, and his face broke open into another gummy smile when he saw Dig approach.

'Dig. Mate. Sit down.' He slid along the window-seat and patted the space.

Dig didn't want to sit next to Phil. 'Erm – actually – I wouldn't mind just going to say hello to Nadine first. I haven't seen her yet. D'you know where she is? Is she in here?'

Phil burst into uproarious laughter. 'Come on,' he

said, 'sit down. *Sit down.*' He patted the seat next to him again. He stuck a roach into the end of the spliff he was constructing, adjusted it, lit it and passed it to Dig. 'Yeah,' he said, immediately starting to make another one, 'Nadine told me you two had fallen out. Over a girl, yeah?' He was pinching pale-green grass from the most enormous bag of grass that Dig had ever seen.

'Yeah,' Dig said, inhaling, 'sort of. It's all really complicated.'

'Isn't it always, mate, isn't it always?'

'Look – I really need to speak to her. Where is she?'

Phil exploded into another peal of blood-curdling laughter. 'I couldn't say, precisely, Digby. No – not precisely. You'd have a long search on your hands, let's put it that way.' He guffawed happily to himself and then looked up at a young man with a mop of peroxide hair who'd just whispered something in his ear. He whispered something back to him and patted his arm. ''Scuse me a minute, Dig. I'll be back in a tick.' He heaved his bad leg off the crate and hobbled towards the corner of the room with the young man.

Dig frowned. What was that supposed to mean, 'I couldn't say, precisely'? That sounded ... ominous. Deeply, deeply ominous. Dig began to feel the slightly nauseous sensation of butterflies in his stomach.

What had Phil done to her? He stood up abruptly and strode from the room. He checked the kitchen again. Tarn-ia was still talking. He stepped over the *Red*-reading bloke in the hallway and threw open Nadine's bedroom door. He backed out immediately when he saw the haphazard piles of Nadine's furniture, *thrown*, seemingly, from a distance into the room. The sofa was sitting on her bed, on top of her Bollywood duvet cover, and everything else was just lying where it had landed. There was certainly no one in the room.

The bathroom door was locked. He banged on it hard with his fists.

'*Busy,*' came a gruff, male voice.

'Is Nadine in there?' Dig shouted.

'*Who?*'

'Nadine. I'm looking for Nadine.'

'*Come back later. We're busy.*'

Oh Jesus. Oh Jesus. Dig ran his fingers through his hair despairingly. He was half-tempted to kick the bathroom door down. Oh Jesus. Nadine. What the hell had happened to Nadine?

He strode back to the living room and towards Phil, who was just tucking a banknote of some description into his jeans pocket.

'What the fuck have you done with her?' he demanded, his face inches from Phil's.

'Whoa,' grinned Phil, 'calm down, man. Calm down.' He rested one hand gently on Dig's arm. Dig shrugged it off.

'Where is she? Where the fuck is Nadine?'

'What are you trying to say, Digby?' Phil was frowning, confused.

'I'm saying, what's happened to Nadine? Where is Nadine?'

'I told you, man. I don't know for sure . . .'

'What do you mean, you don't know? This is her flat, for fuck's sake. Now where is she?' A fleck of spit flew off the end of Dig's tongue and landed on Phil's cheek. He didn't notice.

'Shit. I dunno,' he shrugged, 'Spain, somewhere. Take it easy, for fuck's sake.'

'Eh?' Dig grimaced. Spain? That was the last thing he'd been expecting Phil to say.

'Yeah. Spain. She's on a business trip, taking pictures of tits and arses.' He laughed again and lowered himself back on to the window-seat.

Dig's head began to swim. Spain? Actually, that did sound kind of familiar now he came to think about it. She might have mentioned something about a Spanish trip a while back. But that explained nothing. It didn't explain her desperate visit to his flat last night. It didn't explain the messages on his answerphone and it certainly didn't even *begin* to explain this nightmare of a party currently taking place in her lovely flat. Dig rubbed his face with the palms of his hands and sat down heavily next to Phil on the window-seat.

'When did she go?' he sighed.

'This morning. Really fucking early this morning. Woke me up and all,' he laughed, 'expected me to get up, cheeky bint!'

'You were here this morning?'

Phil nodded.

Dig digested this unsavoury little fact with a dry gulp. Phil was here, this morning. Which meant, of course, that Phil had been here last night. Dig shuddered.

'So,' he managed to squeak, 'what's the story, then?' He attempted to imbue his voice with a blokish camaraderie but couldn't quite veil the creeping nausea rising in his gut. Surely not. *Surely not.*

'The story, man? What story?'

'You. And Nadine. What's happening?'

He could hardly bear to hear Phil's answer.

'Not too sure myself, mate,' he grinned. 'Nadine just phoned me, out of the blue. We went out for a drink,

401

went back to mine, and suddenly she was all over me, like nothing had ever changed, you know. That girl is something else, isn't she? That girl is – *hot*.' He nudged Dig and Dig had to stop himself punching him in the face.

'So, it's all on again. Me and Nadine. I've got the front-door key, mate.' He winked and Dig felt sick.

'So,' he said, taking a deep breath, 'where are you living now, Phil?'

Phil shrugged and indicated the room with his eyes. 'Wherever I lay my hat, Digby, wherever I lay my hat.'

'And have you – have you laid your hat here?'

'It certainly looks that way. I could do much worse than Nadine, couldn't I? She's an angel, that girl, a true angel. She's got a lovely little place here and a nice bit of money coming in. You seen her motor?' He made on 'O' of his mouth.

'So Nadine's asked you to move in?' Dig's eyes were starting to bulge with the improbability of it all.

'That's right, mate. That's right. Bit of a result, *non*?'

'But – but – but – '

'That's taken you a bit by surprise, hasn't it?'

Dig nodded.

'Look,' said Phil, draping one arm around Dig's shoulders, 'you've got to understand a woman like Nadine. She's got everything, right. She's got the looks and the job and the flat and the car. But she hasn't got a man. Not a real man. So she's flailing around for ten years, making do, compromising, and then she turns thirty – the old biological clock clicks in and it gets her thinking – about the old days – about what we had together. She phones me – her lost love. Who can blame her? I was a bit surprised, to be honest, by how fast everything happened, especially the sex – you know – on the first night. But it was blinding, Digby, blinding. Some of the best sex I've ever had.'

Dig felt bile rising in the back of his throat. He swallowed it.

'So I give her a load of what I know she wants – sweet talk, messages on the answerphone, declarations of undying love – and the next night, I'm in. Foot in the door, hat on the old metaphorical bed. In – like – Flynn.' He nodded smugly and inhaled deeply on a spliff. 'It's a shame she had to go away, really. She would have loved this.' He indicated the party.

'Does she know?' muttered Dig. 'Does she know about this party? Does she know you're having a party?'

'Nah. Nah. But she won't mind. You know what she's like. Sweet. Laid back. Make yourself at home, she said, help yourself to anything, this is your flat now, treat it like your own.'

Two small girls with spiky pony-tails wandered towards Phil. 'Yes, sweethearts,' he smiled. One of them leaned down to his ear. He nodded and leaned into hers and then the three of them disappeared into the corner of the room, Phil turning to wink at Dig before he went.

Dig's eyes were wide open and his mouth was shut tight. This was all surreal. He must be dreaming all of this. Nadine was in Spain. Phil was in Nadine's flat. Nadine had had sex with this mop-haired skeleton. She'd invited him to live with her. All this at the same time as phoning *him* and leaving bizarre messages on *his* answerphone about *his* willy. No no no. The entire universe had gone stark staring raving mad.

He felt suddenly and horribly claustrophobic. There were too many people in here, not enough air, too much

403

noise, and this terrible strobing light was sending him just about over the edge. He had to get out of here, absolutely had to get out, fresh air, clear his head . . .

As he left the room he saw the two girls walking away from Phil and examining something in their hands. Phil tucked yet another banknote into his jeans pocket and started chatting to a bald bloke who was dancing.

Right, thought Dig, OK. Phil's a dealer. Phil's a dealer.

He put the realization into a mental To-Do list for digesting later, when he was out of here, away from here, gone.

As he passed the bathroom, the door opened and in the brief second before it snapped closed again, Dig had a fleeting vignette. Toilet bowl: broken. Bath: full of people. Sink: full of sick. Cistern: busy heads bowed down over it. Floor: covered in wet toilet paper. He backed away. He couldn't bear it. Not for another second. He found the front door handle and forced it open, stumbling into the relative tranquillity of the tiled hallway. He stood statue-still for a split second. His head was spinning. He pushed open the main door and felt a sense of release when he heard it slam loudly behind him.

His feet sounded like giant's feet as he clambered clumsily down the front steps. A fat tabby cat perched on the bottom step eyed him up. Where had he parked his car? Where? Shit. Yes. Over there. That's right. He ran down the pavement, unlocked the front door, slipped into the driver's seat, locked the door, leaned into the beige upholstery, breathed out – big, long, deep, out. Jesus – Jesus. Pulled on his seatbelt, switched on his ignition, reverse, forward, reverse, out of here, gone.

The world seemed to get brighter as Dig left Gordon

House Road. Brighter and lighter. His racing heart slowed down, his strobe-blinded eyes regained clarity, the tape playing in his car stereo was melodic and clean. A group of fresh-faced, friendly-looking people were gathered on the corner of Chetwynd Road, waiting for a cab. They looked like nice people. It was only eleven thirty.

Slowly, yard by yard, Dig's head cleared. He turned left into Highgate Road and tried to focus his thoughts. He should be doing something, that was what he was aware of above all – he should definitely be doing something. What? What should he be doing? Nadine had invited that man into her flat. She'd slept with him. She'd given him a front-door key. She had no one to blame but herself. But parties – drugs, students, broken toilets and trashed carpets – she hadn't asked for any of that.

Dig pulled up at the traffic lights at the top of Highgate Road and rested his head on his steering-wheel. This had been the weirdest fucking twenty-four hours of his life.

As he lifted his head to check the lights, another light caught his eye. A light on Kentish Town Road to his right. A deep-blue, trapezium-shaped light. It said 'Police'. Of course, he thought, of course. Absolve himself. Let someone else deal with it. Clean it up. Sort it out. That's what they were there for, after all. That's what we paid them for. Let them take the strain.

The car behind him hooted as he dithered in front of the now-green light. He slipped into first, flicked his indicator to the right and pulled up in front of the police station.

CHAPTER FORTY-ONE

Dig returned to Nadine's flat, with DCs Farley, Stringer, Short and McFaddyen. He rang on the doorbell, asked for Phil, waited until both doors were opened and then stood back and allowed the officers to go about their business.

He'd never seen anything like it. Within seconds, hordes of people began spilling from the house like insects, hurriedly pulling on jackets and shoes and hats as they went. A second later the music died, leaving the entire street with a strange, dead, ringing sound. And then a couple of minutes later Dig watched with a morbid fascination from his hiding-place across the street as Phil himself was marched firmly towards the waiting police car and lowered into it.

He was still smiling.

Dig remembered what Phil had said at the party: 'Wherever I lay my hat, Digby, wherever I lay my hat.' Of course. It made perfect sense to Dig. He probably thought of prison as just another place to lay his hat and, no doubt, when he got out, he'd find somewhere new to 'lay his hat', some other poor woman's lovely flat.

He didn't believe a word Phil had said earlier on. There was no way, *just no way*, that a wrinkly old git like Philip Rich with his dead eyes and his dirty hair and his bad teeth could possibly have got Nadine to drop her drawers, to invite him to move into her flat. It made him feel sick just thinking about it.

There must have been some other explanation for it. There must be more to Philip Rich than met the eye. Dig had always had his suspicions about him, never trusted him. He would get to the bottom of this peculiar state of affairs. But first he needed to speak to Nadine.

For the first time ever Dig felt protective and tender towards Nadine, Nadine who needed no one, least of all Dig Ryan. He'd protected her property. He'd looked after her. The thought left him feeling curiously warm inside.

He watched the blue-and-white car pull away from Gordon House Road and then walked sadly towards Nadine's house. The front door was open. He moved into the hallway and towards Nadine's flat.

Inside he wandered around desolately. The mass stampede from the flat had created even more damage. Nadine's weird pink-foil wallpaper had been shredded by the hordes of people all rushing to the front door at the same time. The pile of magazines on the deco cabinet had been thrown to the floor and mashed underfoot. Wine bottles and lager cans littered the carpet.

Dig's head filled up with images of happier times, thoughts of all the evenings he'd spent here with Nadine in her eccentric little castle, listening to music, getting stoned, getting ready to go out, discussing their disastrous love lives. He'd been with her when she'd first been to see the flat. She'd fallen madly in love with it and he'd tried to persuade her it wasn't right for her. It's characterless, he'd told her, it's got no soul and it's overpriced. But she hadn't listened to him. She'd bought it for the asking price and he'd shaken his head and said, 'You're making a huge mistake – you're going to be desperate to move in six months' time, and then you'll be imprisoned in here by negative equity and you'll start hating it. Take my word.'

Nadine had, of course, proved him entirely wrong, compensating for the beige Anaglypta, dark-stained-oak and magnolia walls of her childhood with flights of fancy and bright colours, turning the dull, echoing flat she'd bought into a mad, welcoming, warm and cosy refuge from the world. Dig loved it in Nadine's flat.

Imagine, he thought with a sudden sense of dread, if something happened and I was never allowed to come back here again. Imagine if something happened to Nadine and I never saw *her* again. What would be the point, he wondered, of going on? Would he have any desire to get up in the mornings or to go out at the weekends if there was no Nadine?

Imagine if she died. Imagine if she got run over by a bus and someone phoned him and said, 'It's Nadine, something's happened.' He couldn't, he just couldn't countenance it – he'd never smile again . . .

Dig was surprised and just a little horrified to find that his eyes were filling up with tears as he explored this morbid train of thought. He gulped to force them back and wiped away an escapee as it slid down the side of his nose. How ridiculous. He must be over-tired. That was the only explanation. Over-tired and over-emotional and – and – Jesus, what a day.

. . . and imagine, his mind forced him to keep thinking, imagine if something happened to Nadine and you never got a chance to apologise for not phoning her last night when she was so upset, never got the chance to explain to her about Delilah, to assure her that nothing had happened between you, to ask her about that message

408

on the answerphone, to find out why she lied to you all those years ago about how she felt about you.

There was so much that needed talking about, and where was Nadine? In Spain, that's where, in bloody Spain, while his head pounded and his heart ached and his life twisted itself in and out and all around like a fucking Möbius strip.

Dig sighed heavily and lowered himself on to his haunches. He picked up one of Nadine's poor, destroyed magazines and held it to his chest.

Please come home, Nadine, he breathed to himself, please come home.

CHAPTER FORTY-TWO

Nadine piled all her cases and aluminium-clad boxes on to the pavement and eyed her front door with suspicion.

London was still soggy and unhappy, and the crisply sunny days of her weekend in Barcelona suddenly seemed like a distant memory. Her neighbour's cat leapt up onto the wall to greet her and Nadine gently scooped the bedraggled creature into her arms, let herself into the house and deposited him in the terracotta-tiled hallway, where he could dry out while he waited for his owners to get home from work.

She felt for her key in her pocket and breathed in deeply as she brought it towards the keyhole. She'd managed to work herself up into a complete paranoid frenzy over the course of the weekend about what might have happened to her flat while she was gone. She had images in her mind of spilt wine, broken glass, wild parties and police raids. Ridiculous, of course, she knew she was being ridiculous. Pia and Sarah had spent most of the last three days persuading her how silly she was being. 'Don't be daft,' they kept saying, 'don't be so over-dramatic. The flat's going to be just fine. Phil will be home by now, back in Finsbury Park,' they soothed. 'The worst thing that could happen is that you might be minus a few cornflakes or he might have finished the bog roll. Take it easy.'

Instead they encouraged her to discuss the whole

'Phoning Dig' fiasco. That was *much* more interesting as far as they were concerned – a real-life soap opera for Pia, unfolding in front of her very eyes. They were all convinced she'd done the right thing, especially Sarah, of course, who'd started the whole bloody thing in the first place and was already planning what she going to wear to the wedding. They'd been on her case all weekend to phone him again.

'No way,' she'd insisted, 'don't even waste your time thinking about it. I am never phoning Dig again. Ever, OK?' She had a plan anyway. A plan to work her way out of the awful nightmare she'd landed herself in. If Dig *did* ever phone her again, for whatever bizarre reason, then she'd just tell him that she'd been playing Truth or Dare with the girls and that phoning him and telling him she'd been thinking about his willy was the punishment they'd concocted for her.

OK. So it was a crap excuse. But at least it was an excuse. And actually, she supposed, men were generally so bemused by the carryings-on of drunken women *en masse* that he'd probably just shrug and accept it as gospel. Of course, he'd think, 'Women – they're weird, we all know that.'

But that was just on the very slim off chance that he did ever phone her again. There was no reason why he should. She'd dissed his new girlfriend, she'd been pissed and belligerent and slightly insane – she'd been deeply unattractive.

'Ah yes,' she could hear Dig sighing in years to come, 'Nadine. She was a great girl. We were so close. But I had to let her go when she became unstable. Poor Nadine. It's all rather tragic.' And then he'd squeeze Delilah's hand and throw her a slightly sad but very relieved look

411

and they'd both silently thank God for the day that they excised Mad Nadine from their perfect, pure, *impeccable* fucking lives.

Hmph. She clenched her jaw and stabbed the front-door key into its hole.

It was going to be fine, she told herself. Everything was going to be just fine. Her flat would be fine. Her life would be fine. It was all going to be perfectly – fine. She took a few deep breaths to psych herself into believing that everything really was going to be fine before slowly twisting the key in the lock and pushing the door open.

She flicked the hall light on and clamped her hand over her mouth.

A strange, strangulated little yelp slipped through her fingers.

A million thoughts landed in her mind at once as she absorbed the physical reality of her trashed hall, the most insistent of which was that this wasn't, *couldn't possibly be*, physical reality at all, was, in fact, some kind of dream or psychological trick precipitated by the preceding three days of irrational concern. Like a mirage. Yes – that's right – a mirage.

This comforting thought lasted less than a micro-second before reality hit with a vengeance. Her flat was destroyed. She'd been burgled. Her hand still clamped to her mouth, she slumped her shoulders and fell to her knees, bags and cases slipping from her shoulders and hands, her keys clanging to the ground. Oh God. Look at this place. Look at it. Look at her walnut cabinet. Look at all her magazines everywhere. Look at the pink-foil wallpaper, all scuffed and ripped.

She hobbled on her knees down the hallway. Spilt wine, fag-ends, ripped pages from magazines, huge, dirty footprints – everywhere. There was a lump the size of an egg in her throat. She breathed deeply to prevent useless tears escaping and got to her feet using the bathroom doorframe to pull herself up. She pushed open the bathroom door and waited helplessly while it creaked open.

'Oh God,' she moaned, when she saw what was within, 'oh no. Oh no.' Tears began spilling, despite her attempts to control them. 'Oh no,' she sniffed.

She began moving more quickly then, from room to room, from kitchen to living room, and everything she saw increased the knot in her stomach and the sadness in her heart. Her flat. Her lovely, lovely flat. The flat she'd created with her bare hands, from skips and second-hand shops, from clearance sales and her parents' generosity, month by month, year after year, piece by piece. All ruined. All dirty. All broken and shitty and fucking fucking *horrible*.

Anger started to erupt inside her as she stepped over empty wine bottles, and she felt a primal scream building in her chest. Her fists clenched themselves tightly and then she let it go. She opened her mouth, closed her eyes and screamed, not a scream of fear but a deep, sonorous scream of pure rage.

'*FUCKING BASTARDS!*'

She began half-heartedly to collect bits and pieces together – empty beer cans, half-full beer cans afloat with stinking, swollen fag-butts and spliff-ends. There were articles of discarded clothing lying around the place – *other people's* discarded clothing. She picked up a rancid-looking flannel shirt gingerly, between two fingernails. A soft-top packet of Camels fell from the pocket. She let the shirt drop to the floor. She hadn't been burgled – that was obvious now. There was nothing

413

actually missing. Just lots of grim stuff added, things moved around and other things broken. She hadn't been burgled – she'd been partied.

Phil.

Fucking Phil.

She'd known this was going to happen, from the minute she'd closed her front door behind her on Saturday morning to the minute she'd opened it again just now. Her instincts had been spot on. She felt sick. She found it impossible now to rustle up even the smallest shred of sympathy for Philip Rich. She was *glad* in fact, glad his parents had died, glad his girlfriend had topped herself, glad his house had burned down. He deserved it. All of it. He deserved worse. He deserved more. Much more.

Her head filled with thoughts of retribution, most of which revolved around the general theme of cutting off various bits of his horrible pasty body and making him eat them.

'*You fucking bastard,*' she shouted out loud, '*you fucking bastard.*' She kicked the doorframe, collapsed to her knees and began to howl. She wailed and thrashed and sobbed and shouted. And then had rapidly to pull herself together when she heard the doorbell ring.

'Oh Jesus,' she muttered to herself, pushing tear-sodden tendrils of hair from her cheeks and wiping her eyes. She got heavily to her feet and stumbled towards the front door. As she crossed the hallway towards the main door she saw a sight she knew would stay with her for ever, a vision that brought goosebumps to her flesh and a lump to her throat, that turned her stomach to liquid and her knees to jelly, the sweetest, most beautiful thing she'd ever seen in her life. Everything that

414

had occurred in the past week and a half, from sleeping with Phil to running him over, from having her flat trashed to leaving appalling messages on answerphones, every bad moment of every bad day, every feeling of insanity and misery and unhappiness just dissolved when she pulled open her front door and saw Dig standing there.

He was wearing a frilly apron, a cap and a daft smile.

In one hand was his precious purple Dyson, in the other a dustpan and brush and at his feet sat a tiny, quivering Yorkshire Terrier.

'I've come about the cleaning position,' he grinned. 'I've got excellent credentials and references. I've been voted the cleanest person in NW5.'

Nadine melted then and dissolved into fresh tears. 'Oh Dig,' she snuffled into his shoulder, 'oh Dig. Thank God you're here. Thank God.'

Dig squeezed her back, hard as anything, tighter than he'd ever hugged her before.

'God, I've missed you,' he said, smiling at her.

Nadine smiled back at him and looked into his soft, dark eyes, pain just falling away from her as she did so. 'It feels like ages,' she sniffed. She looked down at the trembling dog. 'Is that the feather duster?'

Dig laughed and leaned down to pick him up. 'No,' he said, 'this is the world's smallest and most unappealing dog and this small and unappealing dog is getting the early train back to Chester tomorrow morning. Aren't you, mate?' The dog looked at him fearfully, as if he'd just suggested the knacker's yard.

'What?' said Nadine. 'On his own?'

Dig threw her a pitying look.

'Oh,' she said, breathlessly, 'you mean Delilah's going home?'

'Yes,' smiled Dig, 'Delilah's going home. Back to her husband. Back to have a baby.' He smiled.

'But – but – but . . .'

'Nothing ever happened between me and Delilah, you know. Nothing. We had one kiss. I've done a lot of thinking since you went away and there's a lot of stuff you need to know, Nadine. About Delilah. You need to hear about Delilah. You've got her so wrong. She's a good person. She's a very good person who's had a very hard time. And we need to talk about Phil. About why he let this happen to your flat. He *isn't* a good person. But,' he said, seriously, 'most importantly, we really, *really* need to talk about us.'

'What do you mean – about us?' Her stomach fizzed at the very concept, at the fact that Dig had even mentioned it.

'Look,' he said, ushering her into the hallway, 'get your rubber gloves on and get into the kitchen. We'll talk as we clean.'

CHAPTER FORTY-THREE

There was a lot of talking that rainy Tuesday afternoon and a lot of explaining. Dig had spent twenty minutes on the phone the previous day to a DI Wittering, who had been more than expansive on the subject of Philip Rich, a character who the Metropolitan Police had been familiar with since his ex-wife had first reported him twelve years earlier for the theft of her black MG and the contents of her savings account.

They'd come into contact with him again seven years later when his suicide was reported to them by a distraught woman called Mandy Taylor, claiming to be his fiancée. She'd watched in horror as he threw himself off Putney Bridge two weeks before they were due to be married. He had, apparently, taken the precaution of emptying their joint bank account before taking his life and when Mandy Taylor bumped into him coming out of a pub off Tottenham Court Road six months later she'd been too shocked to press charges.

His parents – who were alive and well and had attended his funeral – refused to have anything to do with him after their first reunion and these days he was a squatter dabbling in a bit of small-time drug-dealing.

'You . . . you mean, he made all that up – all that stuff about his parents and his girlfriend and everything?'

Dig nodded. 'He's a con artist, Nadine. He's been a con artist from the day you met him.'

417

After a tip-off from Phil's elderly father, Haringey council had evicted him and eight students from a flat in Finsbury Park on Friday morning, and it seemed he'd decided that Nadine and her flat would make a much better alternative to finding a new building to squat.

'Of course,' sighed Nadine, 'of course. That flat. It didn't seem right. All those students and that strange furniture. And . . . and' – she was growing quite animated as so many of the events of the last few days began to make sense – 'and – of course! The old man. And the portable telly. That was his father! And that's why he left me all those messages. That's why he was hanging around outside my flat. That's why he wouldn't leave. He had nowhere else to go. I thought he was desperate to see me, but he was just desperate for a roof over his head. Oh my God. To think . . . I just . . . oh God, Dig, I'm such an *idiot*. I can't believe I fell for all that . . .'

Her face fell even further after Dig had related the story of Delilah's visit to London, of Sophie and Michael and her unplanned pregnancy.

'Oh Jesus,' she said, 'I feel so bad. All that time I spent bitching about her and hating her and she was going through so much. And I had no idea. None at all. I just thought she was here to make trouble, to take you away from me. Oh God, Dig, I feel like such a fucking bitch . . .'

It was getting dark by the time they'd finished cleaning the kitchen and discussing the events of the past week and they still hadn't even brushed on the subject of the answerphone messages.

Both of them were aware that it was next on the agenda but both of them industriously spun out the other subjects until finally, at five o'clock, they ran out

418

of things to say. The atmosphere in the kitchen was plump with the prospect of their next conversation.

'Well,' said Dig, getting off his knees and looking around the kitchen, 'I think we've done in here. Pretty much spotless, I'd say.'

'Mmm,' murmured Nadine, looking around her and feeling awkward with Dig for the first time in years. 'Do you want to get started on the other rooms now? Or we could have a cup of tea? Or you can go if you like? You don't have to stay. I'll be all right. I'll make you dinner, though, obviously, if you do stay. So . . .' She trailed off and turned abruptly towards the sink, stowing a jumbo-sized bottle of Domestos into a cupboard and feeling her cheeks flush to a warm pink.

Dig smiled at her back. Of course he was going to stay. This was the only place in the world he could think of that he wanted to be right now. It was where he'd wanted to be since Saturday night. Here, in Nadine's kitchen, with Nadine looking fantastically cute in threadbare old grey jogging bottoms, a crappy old Paul Weller T-shirt that he'd given her years ago and a lime-green pinny with Miffy the Rabbit patch pockets. Her thick copper hair was all over the place, her toenails were bubblegum pink and she had a smudge of something grey across her upper lip that made her look like she had a tache. She looked like a madwoman. She *was* a madwoman. A gorgeous, lovable, sexy, red-haired, suc-cessful, together, strong-minded and about-to-be fabu-lously wealthy madwoman. He smiled again. What a combination.

Dig opened his mouth to say something. He wasn't sure what. A compliment, maybe, or a joke. Nothing came out. He closed his mouth again.

419

Nadine spun around. 'I just thought of something,' she said, 'we should do it now – in case we don't get round to it later – all that furniture on my bed – I'm going to need a hand getting it off. Do you mind?'

Digby had made a little nest for himself on the corner of Nadine's duvet that was still showing, and Dig gently scooped the sleepy creature off the bed with the palm of one hand and laid him on his jacket in the hallway.

'Aw,' smiled Nadine, watching him tenderly, 'cute. You're quite fond of him, aren't you?'

Dig started. 'No,' he said. Then more softly, 'Well, he's all right, I suppose. He's sort of grown on me the last few days. But he's just not my kind of dog. Well, he's not *any* kind of dog, really, is he? I mean, look at him.'

They both cast their eyes downwards at the slumbering little ball of greasy whiskers and bulging eyes. He sighed deeply in his sleep and emitted a little whistle.

'He's knackered,' said Nadine.

'Well,' said Dig, 'it's not surprising, really. He's had a tough few days.'

'Yeah,' said Nadine, moving back towards the bedroom, 'haven't we all.'

'It's been a very strange week,' agreed Dig.

'Mmm,' murmured Nadine, turning pink again, 'to put it mildly.'

'But good, I think – a good week.'

'Do you?'

'What?'

'Think it's been a good week?'

'Yes. In a funny way.'

'In spite of everything?'

They were on either side of Nadine's bed now, each holding an arm of her leather sofa.

Dig nodded.

'Why?'

Not just yet, thought Dig. In a minute.

'Here,' he said, 'let's get this sofa into the living room.'

Nadine nodded stiffly, and on the count of three they heaved the ancient sofa off the bed and lumbered around with it for a while until they'd manoeuvred it through the bedroom door and into the living room. Exhausted, they both collapsed on to the sofa and gasped in unison.

'D'you remember getting this thing in here, when you moved in?' asked Dig, turning to smile at Nadine.

'Yeah. Of course I do. This was the first thing I bought for the flat. From that old house-clearance place that used to be up on Agar Grove. £38.50. I always wondered what the 50p was for.'

'I thought you were mad. Why would anyone want to buy some rancid, stinky sofa with horsehair falling out of the bottom and cracks all over the place? I kept trying to get you to go to Habitat but you just weren't interested in anything new – or clean – or' – he cast Nadine a cheeky look – '*nice*. "Oh no, I don't want something that hasn't been used by at least twelve people before me – oh no, that's *far too clean* – you mean, it came in a box? How common."'

Dig flinched and laughed as Nadine picked up a cushion and hit him over the head with it. 'You bastard! You're just jealous because you've got no imagination. "Ooh, I *just* don't know – shall I go for the mid-beige or the light beige? Or maybe I'll be *really* daring and go for the deep beige. Or do you think that'll clash with the navy blue . . .?"'

Dig picked up a cushion now and boffed Nadine with

421

it, harder than he'd intended, accidentally clipping her on the temple with his knuckle.

'Ow!' she yelled, rubbing the side of her face. 'That really hurt!'

'Oh God,' said Dig, immediately dropping the cushion and sliding along the cracked leather towards Nadine, 'oh God. I'm sorry.' He cupped the side of Nadine's face with his hand and stroked his thumb across her temple. 'I'm really sorry, Deen.' Her skin was smooth and flushed under his and her eyes were still slightly red around the rims. She looked so young and vulnerable. He brought his thumb down to her upper lip and wiped away the grey smudge.

As he touched her and looked into her green eyes Dig could feel something stirring deep down inside him, something almost magnetic forcing his body and his face closer and closer to hers. She eyed him with a mixture of fear and excitement.

Dig could tell she'd stopped breathing.

So had he.

'Oh, Deen,' he said finally, pushing a messy copper curl away from her face, tucking it behind her ear, 'we're such a pair of idiots, aren't we?'

Nadine nodded, and Dig knew then that they were on the same wavelength, knew that he wouldn't have to do too much explaining.

And for once Dig wasn't stuck for words. For once he was going to open his mouth and all the right words were going to come out of it. Because, for once, Dig had it all planned.

He took a deep breath and started talking.

'We've been a couple for the last ten years, do you realize that? We go shopping together. We go on holiday

422

together. We spend our weekends together. We even spend alternate Christmases with our parents. We bicker. We hug. We help move each other's furniture around. You know all my colleagues, I know all yours. The only thing we *don't* do is sleep together and wake up together. And I used to think that that was because you'd rather die than even contemplate the idea of being – *intimate* with me.'

Nadine opened her mouth to say something and Dig put a finger up to hush her. 'Shhh,' he said, 'listen to me.

'Remember that weekend – in Manchester, when I came to stay?'

Nadine nodded again.

'I didn't show it at the time because I didn't want to make you feel bad, but I didn't know that you were living with Phil until I got there – I still thought I was in with a chance. And that weekend – it was the worst weekend of my life, Deen. Pretending I didn't care was the hardest bit of acting I've ever done. I had to listen to you and him – having sex – and I thought my heart was going to break, I really did.

'It wasn't Delilah who broke my heart, Nadine, it was you. And I never got over it. I really didn't. And now I know what I've been doing for the last ten years. With all these young girls. Now I know why I haven't had a decent, proper girlfriend in all this time. It's because I didn't *need* one. *You've* been my girlfriend, Nadine, and I've subconsciously chosen women who were no threat whatsoever to what I have with you. And all this time I've thought that I could be happy living this compromise for the rest of my life, happy loving you and having sex with other women because I thought that friendship was all I'd ever get from you. But then you left that message on my answerphone and now everything's changed. Did you mean it? Did you mean what you said? About lying – about wanting me?' He stared into her unblinking eyes.

Nadine stared back into his in wonder. She felt almost faint with excitement. 'Yes,' she said, 'I meant it.'

'So why?' said Dig. 'Why did you tell me you didn't want me? Why did you reject me? Why did you go off to Manchester and fall in love with someone else?'

Nadine sighed. 'Because of Delilah,' she said.

'Delilah? What did Delilah have to do with it?'

'You were my best friend – my world. Delilah broke my heart when she took you away from me. It wasn't just *you* that she wanted at the Holy T, it was what you and I had – that intimacy, that exclusivity, that complicity. She wanted to take my place. Dig 'n' Deen. Dig and Delilah. I knew it, and I hated her. I didn't know who I was without you. My last two years at school were miserable and lonely.

'And then I went to St Julian's and I felt strong again. I became someone in my own right, and when we met up and spent that weekend together and you started making all these plans for the future, I just got scared. I couldn't bear to lose you all over again, not when I'd only just found myself. So I rejected you. It made me feel strong. I wasn't expecting to meet Phil, to fall in love so quickly, and I really thought, that weekend when you came up, that you'd got to grips with the idea that we were never going to be together. And, you know, I've done it too, what you've done. The reason I've been out with so many unsuitable people is because I had the most suitable person right here, all along. I haven't been looking for love because I haven't needed to. Because I love you and

I don't want to love anyone else and I really don't think I *can* love anyone else . . .'

'No! That's exactly it. Neither can I. I thought I could love Delilah, because I'd loved her before. I thought it would be different. But it wasn't. I tried to love her, but I couldn't . . .'

'And I thought I could love Phil again! But . . . bleughhh.' She grimaced and she laughed, and Dig laughed, and for the first time in ten years Nadine could feel herself getting a grip on one of those happiness seeds. She could feel her hand tightening over the little seed, she could feel it nestling against the palm of her hand, and this time she was not going to let go of it.

'It's always been you, Nadine. You and me. Dig 'n' Deen. Nobody else stood a chance, did they?'

Nadine shook her head and smiled widely. 'I used to think that you and I would get married when we left school. I used to think . . . here – wait.' She ran from the room, into her bedroom, ferreted around inside her wardrobe for a minute and then came back clutching something in her hands. 'Look,' she said, handing it to Dig, 'look at this.'

It was a diary. It was old and musty. On the front was a sticker of Steve Strange wearing a silver hat and black Cupid's-bow lipstick. Funny the way that schoolgirls couldn't resist a blatantly gay man, thought Dig. He turned it over. And there it was, written over and over again in selfconscious adolescent handwriting.

Nadine Ryan. Nadine Ryan. Nadine Ryan.

'And look,' said Nadine, turning the pages, 'look at this.' She pointed at a section at the back entitled 'Mrs Nadine Ryan'. 'Read that bit,' she said.

Dig threw her an amused look and started reading.

He chuckled as he read. 'Oh yes, I like this bit – powder-blue E-type,' he smirked.

'*Four children!*' he cried at one point.

'Gloucester Crescent. Yes. I could live in Gloucester Crescent. So,' he said, closing the book and turning to face Nadine, 'when shall we start?'

'Start what?'

'House-hunting, of course.'

Nadine searched for the hint of sarcasm in his voice, but it wasn't there.

'Jesus, Nadine. We've wasted so much time, haven't we? Ten years. Let's not waste any more. Eh?'

And then he put the book down, took Nadine's hands in his, and he kissed her. On the lips. And even though he'd thought it might feel strange, kissing Nadine, it didn't. It felt the opposite of strange. It felt so unbelievably right.

And Nadine gripped Dig's hands in hers and felt his lips moving against hers, and she couldn't believe they'd waited so long to do this because this was what her lips were designed for. For kissing Dig Ryan.

They fell backwards together into the leather of Nadine's deco sofa and smiled at each other, and then they kissed again.

It grew dark while they kissed and soon the only light in the room came from the cactus fairy lights over the fireplace, and in that cool, green glow, in the debris of her flat, on a rainy November evening, Dig and Nadine finally got it together.

EPILOGUE

Dig looked out through the tangles of ice-blue clematis and snowflake jasmine that framed his study window. The sky outside was turquoise and smudged with white. The air was warm and full of pollen. It had taken its time but, finally, in the second week of July, summer had come to London.

Dig's study was a minimal refuge in the chaos of their new home. He'd acceded to Nadine's taste in interior décor and let her run amok with her strange wallpapers and bits of bohemian junk in the rest of the flat. It was funny how easy he found it to live with Nadine's mess – it was so much a part of her that he almost loved it. He could *breathe* amongst her clutter. But in here was all white walls and modern furniture, angle-poise lamps and linen filing boxes from Muji. His old corduroy sofa sat against the wall.

This tiny, neat, well-organized room was now home to Dig-It Records, the smallest independent label in the world. Only two weeks old and only one band to its name but – they were *the* greatest guitar band since Oasis. Absolutely. Dig could feel it in his gut, his heart and his soul. He just had to persuade the rest of the world now.

This new life still felt a little like playing at grown-ups. He and Nadine kept expecting someone to come to the front door in a uniform and ask them what the hell they thought they were doing living in this adult's house in this adult's road, to march them out, throw them into the back of a van and deposit them in a bedsit in Tufnell Park.

Dig gulped back the dregs of his tea and looked at the clock. Six thirty. Nadine should be back any minute. He smiled at the thought. It was her turn to cook tonight. His stomach growled appreciatively in anticipation.

The doorbell rang and Dig made his way wearily down the hallway but he snapped out of his long-day-in-the-office reverie when he opened the door and saw a stunningly beautiful woman with golden hair and skin standing on the doorstep.

'Delilah!'

Delilah's face burst open into an enormous smile and she threw her arms around Dig and squeezed him hard.

'Oh Dig,' she said, 'it's so great to see you!'

'What are you doing here?'

'God. I'm *so sorry*. I was determined not to turn up unannounced again, not after last time. I kept trying to call you and there was no answer so I wrote to you. Two weeks ago. We've been shopping all day and then we turned up at your flat this afternoon and there was no one there, so we drove round to your mum's and she told me you'd moved . . .'

Stunning, thought Dig, eyeing Delilah with amazement, you are absolutely stunning.

'She told me you'd moved up in the world and she wasn't wrong – I mean, *look at this place*!'

She poked her head into the hallway and began looking around. She was wearing a pure white crêpe viscose dress, short and flirty with shoestring straps. On her feet were pale-blue strappy sandals. Her hair was twisted up and clipped back with some kind of plastic

428

claw affair. Dig could see her knickers through the semi-opaque viscose. She was wearing a G-string. He gulped. Jesus bloody Christ.

The sound of a car door slamming drew Dig's attention away from Delilah's underwear and towards the road. There was a large four-wheel-drive jeep parked opposite, and a tall man was unloading stuff from it – funny bags made from quilted fabric, and plastic boxes. He was about six foot four with coal-black hair and an imposing physique. He was wearing jeans in the same effortless way that Delilah wore hers, with a grey V-neck T-shirt. He was very brown and, when he turned around, quite guttingly handsome. He threw Dig a smile and Dig worked it out.

Alex.

Alex reached further into the jeep and brought out something very carefully with both arms – a Ming vase, maybe, thought Dig, or a particularly large Fabergé egg. No – it was another plastic contraption with a large handle, and nestled within it was a small pink thing wearing a stripy all-in-one.

Alex picked up all his quilted things and plastic things and headed towards them. Delilah beamed. 'Dig,' she said, 'let me introduce you to the two most gorgeous men in the world. Dig – this is Alex – Alex, *this is Dig.*' Dig was touched to notice a trace of pride in Delilah's voice when she said his name. He went to shake Alex's hand and laughed because his hands were all being used up for other things. Alex laughed, too, and Dig was nearly blinded by the fabulous whiteness of his teeth and shaken again by the uncanny resemblance to Pierce Brosnan.

'And,' continued Delilah, taking the contraption with

the pink thing in it from Alex and thrusting it towards Dig, 'this is the fantastic Oliver – isn't he *beautiful*?'

Dig looked down into the contraption, at the funny little sausage of pinky-white flesh and into the cloudy blue of the sausage's eyes and tried to think of something to say. 'Lovely,' he managed, eventually, 'he's lovely.'

They went indoors then, and Dig felt inordinately proud as he showed this perfect family his elegant and classy new home, with its high ceilings and original features, this airy two-bedroom flat that spoke of hitherto alien concepts such as *being settled* and having *made it*.

He made tea and sat his guests down in the garden, on dark-green wrought-iron furniture. The garden looked spectacular – tiny but mature, all brambly rose bowers and ivy-clad walls. The air was heavy with heat and fragrant with jasmine. The sound of a violin being played somewhere further down the street wafted into the garden.

Delilah fiddled with a plastic bottle and slipped it into the sausage's mouth. 'Dig,' she said, looking around her, 'this is incredible. Gloucester Crescent. Did you win the lottery or something?'

Dig laughed. 'No,' he said, 'I wish. No. This is a childhood dream of Nadine's. A *very expensive* childhood dream. I have never been poorer in my entire life. I had more money was I was eighteen, earning £6,000 a year. But we sat down together and worked out that we could afford it, even with me giving up my job. Just. We both made quite a lot on our old flats and Deen's doing so fucking well and – oops.' He covered his mouth and glanced apologetically at the sausage.

Delilah laughed. 'His language skills aren't quite up

to picking up swearwords just yet. He's only four weeks old. Don't worry.'

'Anyway, Nadine's career has really taken off, since the Ruckham's calendar – she's earning a mint. The mortgage repayments are crippling, we can't afford to go out or buy clothes or go on holiday or anything but' – he looked around him – 'it's worth it, you know. I could die here, do you know what I mean?'

They both murmured affirmatively and for a second or two it was silent. Delilah fed her baby. Alex appraised the back of the house. Dig stared at Alex and imagined him wearing a tux, leaping from a moving BMW Z3 and shooting at Chinese men with a ballpoint pen. The small patch of baby vomit on the sleeve of his T-shirt somewhat spoiled the image.

Delilah and Alex glanced at each other and exchanged a look.

'Shall I tell him?' said Delilah.

Alex nodded happily.

Delilah turned to face Dig, anticipation pulling at her face. 'Dig,' she said, 'we've got something we'd like to ask you. Well – two things, actually.'

Dig felt his face muscles tense up. Delilah asking him favours was, in his experience, a very worrying thing.

'Ye–es,' he said, smiling stiffly, trying to sound excited.

'The first thing is – and I know, you're not religious or anything, but neither are we so it doesn't matter – but I'd – *we'd* – be so honoured if you would be Oliver's godfather.' She beamed at him and Dig was surprised to notice a little flush of pleasure in his stomach area. He looked down at the suckling sausage and felt a burst of warmth. He looked at Alex and Delilah, who were both staring desperately at him as if they'd just proposed marriage, and he smiled. 'Shit,' he said, 'yeah. Definitely. I mean – yeah!' And everyone just sat there and beamed for a while.

'That's fantastic,' said Delilah grabbing the back of Dig's neck and kissing him on the cheek. Alex gave him a large hand to shake, and Dig couldn't believe how happy he was to be asked to stand in a church and tell lies with a stupid suit on, all for the sake of a dimply sausage who couldn't have cared less either way.

'So,' he said, happily, 'what was the other favour?' He was on a favour roll now – he could handle favours like this.

'Well,' said Delilah, her face becoming serious, 'it's – er – actually, hold on, just a sec. Alex – can I have the car keys?'

She plopped the sausage down into Dig's arms, took the keys from Alex and disappeared back into the house.

Dig sat for a while, holding the sausage as if it were an unpinned hand-grenade.

'Here,' said Alex, smiling, 'let me take him. You don't look very comfortable there. It takes a bit of getting used to, this baby lark.' He grinned warmly at Dig and gently scooped the pink thing from his arms.

Dig felt awkward for a second, now that Delilah was gone, not sure what he and Alex were going to have to talk about, but Alex saved him from himself.

'Dig,' he said, and Dig nearly jumped out of his skin because his voice was so deep – he sounded like he should be doing trailers for Hollywood movies. 'Dig. I wanted to thank you.'

Dig threw him a not-sure look.

432

'For what you did for Delilah last year.' He was *very* posh.

'What do you mean?' said Dig, thinking about his complete lack of doing anything for Delilah last year, except for following her around and sprinkling her with dog pee and ogling her in her underwear.

Alex put the sausage back in its contraption and tucked a blanket round its legs. 'For looking out for her. For having her to stay. For talking her out of not having this little chap. She told me what you said to her, about being a great mother, about her ability to love. You were very wise and you were right. I dread to think what would have happened if you hadn't talked her round.'

They both turned to survey the pink thing and Dig felt himself blushing. 'Well,' he said, 'God. You know. It was nothing. It was . . .' And then, just in the nick of time, just before Alex would have reached the conclusion that he was an illiterate buffoon, the proper grown-up bit of Dig came to the rescue and he realized there was something important he wanted to say. 'It was the least I could do,' he said, breathing easy, 'after all, Delilah did the same for me.'

'Oh yes?' said Alex, crossing his legs and looking at Dig with interest.

'Yes. She set me on the path to true happiness.'

'Really. How?'

Dig looked at Alex and tried to gauge how honest he could be. His eyes were brown and gentle. He looked like he could take a bit of romance. 'She stopped me being blind. I'd been in love with someone for ten years and was too much of a coward to risk rejection so I just made do with being her friend. Delilah showed me that I could have more. That this girl loved me, too. I thought she

433

was interfering at the time. But she was right. And now I've got the girl of my dreams.'

Alex smiled. 'And you're happy?'

Dig lit a fag, inhaled and nodded. 'I have never been happier in my life. This is it' – he indicated their surroundings – 'this is my castle and Nadine's my queen.'

And Alex and he exchanged a long, deep look, and Dig knew that Alex knew exactly how he felt and that they were both lucky, lucky men. Dig decided he liked Alex.

'What are you boys talking about?' said Delilah, striding back into the garden. Dig was about to make a joke of some description when he noticed what Delilah was holding in her arms.

'No way,' said Dig immediately, crossing his hands in front of his chest.

'You don't know what I'm going to ask you yet.'

'I don't need to. I don't care. There's just no way . . .'

In Delilah's arms, shivering even in this balmy heat, was Digby. He wagged his tail when he saw Dig and tried to escape from Delilah's arms.

'See,' whined Delilah, 'see how much he loves you. He's never forgotten you, you know. He's had this empty look about him since I took him home last year.'

'What do you want? Do you want me to look after him? OK. One night only, though. One night and that's it.'

Delilah shook her head slowly from side to side and deposited the dog on Dig's lap. 'It's a bit more than that,' she said, nervously, 'you see, you wouldn't think it to look at him but he can be quite aggressive, and the thing is, is that – and there's no way we could have known this in advance – but he hates babies. Hates them. And he

434

hates Oliver. Snarls at him. It's awful. And I couldn't bear to give him away to a stranger. And I just keep remembering how well the two of you got on together. And . . .'

'He hates babies?' asked Dig.

'Mmm,' Delilah nodded, sadly.

'All babies?'

'Well. Yes. At first we thought it was just Oliver, but now we've noticed it's all babies.'

A large, smug smile spread across Dig's face, and he shook his head. 'Sorry,' he said.

'Can't you just give it a go? You could have a trial run?'

Dig shook his head and looked up when he saw someone walk into the garden. A stunning redhead in a blue crushed-silk dress wearing red 1950s plastic sunglasses and butterflies in her hair.

She stopped in her tracks when she saw the group in the garden and looked quizzically at Dig. And then she smiled widely when she recognized Delilah and stooped to hug her. Delilah introduced her to Alex and Oliver.

'Nadine,' said Dig, tucking his arm around her waist and drawing her hips towards his shoulders, 'Delilah's just asked us a favour. She needs a new home for little Digby and she thought maybe we'd like to have him.'

Nadine smiled at little Digby. 'Oh,' she said, 'well . . . we *could*, I suppose.'

'There's only one thing, though. He hates babies.'

'Hates babies?'

'Uh-huh.'

'Oh dear.'

'Oh dear indeed.'

Delilah looked at them questioningly and they smiled

at each other and then at her, and Dig spun Nadine round so that she was sideways on. Nadine pulled at her dress so that it clung tightly to her body and there, silhouetted by the white-gold sun and barely perceptible, was a tiny, hard, perfect little bump.

Delilah screamed, leaped to her feet and cupped the bump with the palm of her hand, asking a million questions all at once about due dates and scans.

Alex smiled warmly and shook their hands.

Digby ran around barking in an attempt to draw attention to himself.

And Dig and Nadine just beamed at each other because although it was scary as hell, although it was entirely unplanned, although they felt far too young and far too immature to bring another life into the world, and although they had no idea how they were going to afford it, none of that mattered because that little bump was the best thing that had ever happened to them.